"Happy?"

"No"—he tucked her hair behind her ear—"not until I get a real smile. I want to see your adorable dimple." He touched her cheek and smiled. "There it is."

"Stop it," she said, fighting a laugh, her earlier anger and hurt subsiding.

He smiled down at her. "So are we okay?"

"Yeah, we're good."

"How good?" He stepped into her, wrapping his arms around her. "Last night good?"

"I don't know. I liked Harry, and you're not him anymore."

"Harry was an idiot. But just for curiosity's sake, how much did you like him?"

"A lot."

"Good. You'll like me even more."

"You're—" She went to say "cocky," but he stole the word by slanting his firm, warm lips over hers. And this kiss was even hotter than the last. So hot that she thought he might be right and poor Harry didn't stand a chance against Grayson Alexander.

Praise for
Debbie Mason and
Snowbound at Christmas

"Christmas, Colorado, will get you in the spirit for love all year long."
—Jill Shalvis, *New York Times* bestselling author

"Come celebrate a Christmas you won't forget."
—Roxanne St. Claire, *New York Times* bestselling author

"A laugh-out-loud treat. Readers will chortle over the Christmastime antics of the spoiled sister, overprotective mother, meddling grandmother, loyal friends, and jealous castmates." —*Publishers Weekly*

"*Snowbound at Christmas* is filled with mystery, family drama, quirky characters, and romance."
—Harlequin Junkie

"Mason's brisk pacing and inventive plot define this first-rate entry in her Christmas, Colorado series."
—*RT Book Reviews*

Snowbound
at Christmas

Snowbound at Christmas

Debbie Mason

FOREVER

NEW YORK   BOSTON

Copyright © 2015 by Debbie Mazzuca

Cover illustration and design by Elizabeth Turner Stokes.
Cover copyright © 2019 by Hachette Book Group, Inc.

Hachette Book Group supports the right to free expression and the value of copyright. The purpose of copyright is to encourage writers and artists to produce the creative works that enrich our culture.

The scanning, uploading, and distribution of this book without permission is a theft of the author's intellectual property. If you would like permission to use material from the book (other than for review purposes), please contact permissions@hbgusa.com. Thank you for your support of the author's rights.

Forever
Hachette Book Group
1290 Avenue of the Americas, New York, NY 10104
read-forever.com
twitter.com/readforeverpub

Originally published in September 2015
Reissued November 2019

Forever is an imprint of Grand Central Publishing. The Forever name and logo are trademarks of Hachette Book Group, Inc.

The publisher is not responsible for websites (or their content) that are not owned by the publisher.

The Hachette Speakers Bureau provides a wide range of authors for speaking events. To find out more, go to www.hachettespeakersbureau.com or call (866) 376-6591.

ISBNs: 978-1-5387-5020-9 (mass market), 978-1-4555-8802-2 (ebook)

Printed in the United States of America

OPM

10 9 8 7 6 5 4 3 2 1

This book is dedicated to the memory of my father, Norm LeClair. Not a day goes by that I don't think of you. You are my hero, and always will be.

Snowbound
at Christmas

Chapter One

Cat O'Connor sat in a white club chair in a bubblegum-pink dressing room, dreaming of her sister's demise. Not her actual sister, of course, but the character her sister played in the daytime drama *As the Sun Sets*. The soap's sliding numbers could use a boost, and what better way to boost them than by killing off leading lady Tessa Hart. At least in Cat's mind it was the perfect solution. With her sister out of work, Cat would have the excuse she needed to move back to Colorado.

Wishful thinking on her part, she knew, and went back to adding up the numbers of the job-satisfaction quiz she'd just taken. It wasn't like she needed a quiz to tell her that she was dissatisfied. But other than dreaming of Tessa Hart's demise, she didn't have anything else to occupy her time. Whoever thought the entertainment industry was exciting had never spent fourteen hours on the set of a daytime soap opera. Mind. Crushingly. Boring.

Okay, so sitting in an unmarked car on a stakeout had been kind of boring, too. But at least there'd been the potential for excitement. Nothing beat the thrill of taking some lowlife off the street. Of taking…She closed her eyes. She couldn't go there. Couldn't think of the hell the FBI had put her through and what she'd been forced to give up.

Refocusing on the magazine, she read the level that corresponded to her score. "Danger Zone! You are burned-out. Leave your job immediately before you destroy your mental and physical well-being."

Cat tossed the magazine onto the glass table. It was true. She couldn't wait for fate to intervene. Working for Chloe was sucking the life out of her. She felt like she was fifty instead of thirty-one. She pinched her stomach through the *I Love Tessa Hart* T-shirt that Chloe insisted Cat wear to work and jiggled the quarter inch of fat between her fingers. Her identical twin wasn't driving Cat to drink—she was driving her to eat donuts. Cat had consumed more donuts in the year that she'd worked for Chloe than in her five years with the Denver PD.

She stood up and bounced on the balls of her feet, shaking out her hands. She'd do it today. As soon as Chloe returned from blocking out her scene, Cat would tell her. She'd been protecting Chloe since they came out of the womb five minutes apart. Something her sister would no doubt deny, but it was true. Pudgy with an overbite and a lazy eye, her nose always buried in a book, her head in the clouds, Chloe had needed Cat's protection from grade school to high school. She didn't need it now.

Cat tensed when the door opened and her sister swept into the dressing room wearing a ruffled peach dress and matching high heels, her long, wavy dark hair flowing down her back. Sinking gracefully onto the chair Cat had just vacated, Chloe brought the back of her hand to her forehead with a dramatic sigh.

Cat rehearsed her speech in her head, gave her hands another quick shake, then opened her mouth.

"Kit Kat, I need my pills. Get me my pills, please," Chloe said before Cat got out a single syllable.

What Chloe needed was a good, swift kick in the derriere. But instead of acting on the thought, Cat retrieved the prescription bottle from her sister's makeup table. Calm Chloe was easier to deal with than Dramatic Chloe. Her sister had no idea they were sugar pills. Their sister-in-law, Skye, had come up with the idea as a way to deal with Chloe's attacks. Or as Cat privately referred to them, her Scarlett O'Hara act. Most of the time they worked.

Cat opened the bottle and shook two pills into her sister's waiting palm. Chloe raised a perfectly plucked brow. "I need something to wash them down. Did you get my tea?"

Oh, she got her tea, all right. She'd scoured the streets of LA looking for her Anglophile sister's special British brew. Battling gridlock traffic, it took Cat three hours to get back to the studio in Burbank.

She stifled a sarcastic retort and poured the freshly steeped tea, timed as always to be ready for Chloe's return, into the Royal Doulton teacup.

Her pinkie raised oh-so-daintily in the air, Chloe took a sip, then pulled a face. "Kit Kat, this is not the brand I asked for."

Silently counting to ten as she retrieved the yellow box from the shelf, Cat held it up. *This* is what you told me to buy."

And this was why she had to quit. Not only was she

bored, Chloe was driving her insane. At times Cat wanted to strangle her. She wouldn't, of course, but their relationship had suffered. Cat loved her sister, but lately she didn't like her very much.

"Well, it's not the one I want." Chloe pursed her peach-glossed lips, then waved her hand. "Don't worry about it. I have an hour before I have to be on the set. You have time to get me—"

"I'm not buying you more tea." Cat rubbed her sweaty palms on her jeans. It was now or never. "I have something important to talk to you about."

"Me too." Chloe popped the pills in her mouth, then took a sip of tea.

"I quit."

Chloe choked, motioning for Cat to pat her back. Gritting her teeth, Cat leaned over and did as her sister directed. Chloe's rapid blinking caused her bottom and top false eyelashes to stick together. While tugging her lid from her eyeball, she squinted at Cat. "You're quitting? But you love working for me."

It wasn't an act. Chloe saw what she wanted to see. And at the genuine confusion on her sister's face, guilt wormed its way into Cat's heart. Which Chloe erased with the next words out of her mouth. "Is it because I get all the attention?" She gave Cat a sympathetic smile. "Believe me, I remember what it's like to feel invisible. But honestly, Kit Kat, where else would you make the kind of money I'm paying you for doing, well, nothing?"

There was so much Cat could say to that, but it wouldn't do her any good. Better to leave with their relationship somewhat intact. "Since I don't do *anything*, you shouldn't need two weeks' notice." She headed for the door before her sister could insert her foot in her mouth again and Cat said something she'd regret.

"You're leaving now?" Chloe asked, a hint of panic in her voice.

"I thought I'd go home and start packing. Book my flight. Don't worry, I'll be back in time to pick you up." Just one more of her duties. Cat was Chloe's chauffeur, as well as her bodyguard, manager, and gopher. A smile played on her lips as warm, giddy relief flooded her body. Not anymore she wasn't. She'd bask in the freedom for a few days before facing the reality of looking for a job.

Chloe flapped both hands in front of her face. "Kit Kat, I don't think the pills worked. I feel faint."

Cat walked over and shoved her sister's head between her legs. "Just breathe," she said. "Not like that," she added when Chloe started braying like a donkey. Dammit, she was not letting her suck her back in. Chloe was a hypochondriac. There was nothing wrong with her. Cat removed her hand from her sister's head and crossed to the makeup table, opening a drawer to retrieve a brown paper bag. As soon as Chloe put it over her mouth and nose, her breathing evened out.

Lowering the bag, Chloe lifted beseeching green eyes. "Kit Kat, I know you have much more important things to take care of, but…" She swallowed convulsively and rubbed her chest. "I have a physical scene this afternoon. And after my spell, I worry about my heart. I'd hate to think how guilty you'd feel if I dropped dead, when you so easily could take my place."

As Cat opened her mouth to say no, Chloe continued. "I don't like to bring it up, but…" She brought it up all the time. Her sister was a delicate flower with the mind of a Venus flytrap. "... if you hadn't been so greedy in the womb and sucked up all the oxygen, I wouldn't have been born with a hole in my heart. So the least you can do is this one small favor for me."

Chloe wasn't exaggerating. Much. She had been born with a hole in her heart and spent the first months of her life in a NIC unit. Up until age four, she'd been in and out of the hospital before the hole closed on its own. When they were growing up, their parents had overprotected Chloe, treating her like an invalid. In Cat's opinion, that had been more damaging than the hole had ever been.

Though she supposed she shouldn't cast stones. Like her parents, Cat enabled her sister, too. And while intellectually she knew she was making matters worse, emotionally she couldn't seem to help herself. Which is the reason why, an hour later, she awkwardly lowered herself into the stylist chair wearing a tight black pencil skirt and black bustier.

"Wipe the smirk off your face, Ty," Cat said, adjusting the satin top.

"Moi, smirk? I think not, my darling Pussy." Ty, in his uniform of skinny black pants and tight T-shirt, grinned at her in the mirror. "If you're going to keep doing this, you should consider extensions." He tugged on Cat's wig, and it slipped to the side. In her senior year of high school, Cat had lopped off her long locks after another episode of trading places with her sister had gone horribly wrong.

Tutting, Ty reached across her for the bobby pins.

If any other man called her Pussy, Cat would probably slug them, but Ty meant it as an endearment. And she kind of liked that the nickname horrified her proper sister. Besides that, the hairstylist was one of Cat's favorite people on the set of the daytime drama. She'd miss him when she left. But he was about the only thing she'd miss. She didn't like Hollywood. Or Hollyweird, as she thought of it. "This is the last time."

"That's what you said two weeks ago."

"I quit, Ty. I'm heading home on Monday." She winced when he jabbed her scalp with a bobby pin.

"I nearly lost my lunch." He patted her head. "Don't scare me like that ever again."

"I'm serious. I'm leaving." Pressing his palms together, Ty rested his chin on the tips of his manicured fingers and looked at her mournfully through large, square, red-framed glasses. She sighed. She loved him, but he was as much a drama queen as her sister. "I'm going to miss you, too. But I'll see you when you come to Christmas."

A few months back, Chloe heard that the production team was looking for a location in the mountains to film their holiday segments and suggested their hometown. She put them in contact with Madison McBride, the town's mayor, who offered free room and board to sweeten the pot. It didn't take much sweetening once the production team got a look at Christmas.

Nestled in a valley at the foot of the Rocky Mountains, the small town was a nature lover's dream. But it was the recently completed Santa's Village that had sealed the deal.

Ty swept the back of his hand dramatically across his cheek. "Who is going to vet my dates and make sure I'm safe? And who is going to let me cry on their shoulder when I get my heart broken?" He wrapped his arms around her neck, meeting her eyes in the mirror. "You can't leave me."

Sam, one of the crew, walked by with George, the classically handsome man who played Chloe's on-screen husband Byron Hart. Given that the two men were caught up in an animated conversation, Cat doubted they'd overheard her and Ty, but she had to be careful. "Chloe, remember?" she whispered, because no one could know she was taking her sister's place. Cat wasn't a member of the Screen Actors Guild. And no matter how ticked she was at her sister, she wouldn't do anything to mess with her career.

Ty straightened, fluffing her hair. "You're leaving because Chloe is such a biatch, aren't you?"

She checked to be sure Sam and George were out of earshot before answering. "No, it's time for me…" The set manager called Chloe's name. "We'll go out this weekend. I'll bring Chloe along. If you give her a chance, I think you two could be friends."

He flipped up his hand. "Just because I'm a fairy doesn't mean I have a magic wand that will turn your sister into *you*."

Cat sighed and pushed to her feet.

"Hang on." Ty grabbed her arm and shoved two more bobby pins in her hair. "Be careful. Brunhilda attacks you in this scene, and after your sister pushed for the change that cut down her on-air time, she won't hold back," he said, referring to the redheaded actress Molly. She'd auditioned for the part of Tessa Hart and ended up with the lesser role of Tessa's backstabbing sister, Paula.

Cat thanked him for the warning and headed for the set. Walking without tripping in the mile-high shoes was one thing, walking with the elegant grace of her sister another. Ten minutes at most, Cat reminded herself, and she'd be out of here for good. The thought lightened her step as she walked onto what served as the foyer of the Hart mansion.

Her heel shot out from under her on the polished black-and-white faux marble. Smothering a gasp, she clamped a hand on her head to keep her wig in place. Once she regained her balance, Cat made a show of checking her shoe.

"Tessa darling, are you all right?" the silver-haired Byron called down from the top of an ornate wooden staircase.

Cat frowned. *Tessa darling?* She shrugged. What did she know? Maybe he liked to get into character before taping. She acknowledged his concern with a small wave and took her mark, mentally going over the scene she'd practiced with Chloe earlier.

All she had to do was keep Molly from pulling off her wig. Piece of cake. Cat had a black belt and had aced her defensive-tactics training. But when the doorbell chimed and she opened the mansion's door to the redhead, Cat had an aw-hell moment. She'd never fought in heels on a slippery floor. She contemplated kicking them off when Molly launched herself at her, which wasn't supposed to happen until later in the scene. Ducking, Cat raised her arm to block the woman's bloodred nails. Molly kept coming, pushing Cat off her mark. Why today of all days did the actress decide to improvise? They were supposed to have their come-to-Jesus moment at the front door, not in the middle of the foyer.

Lines, Cat reminded herself. *Just say Chloe's lines.* "Paula, what's wrong? What..." She trailed off, following the redhead's gaze to the large crystal chandelier swaying drunkenly over Cat's head.

Grabbing Molly by the arms, she spun them out of the way. A gust of air brushed against Cat's back and the chandelier crashed to the floor.

Shouts went up from the cast and crew as they converged on them. The director in his yellow Hawaiian shirt pushed through the crowd. "Chloe, are you all right?"

"I'm good," Cat assured him.

"So am I, Phil." Molly glared at Cat before storming off the set.

The director's gaze followed the other actress before he returned his attention to Cat. "Quick thinking, Chloe. Well done." He patted her shoulder, then moved from her side, waving over the set and crew managers. "Would someone like to explain to me how the hell this happened?"

Exactly what Cat wanted to know. Glass crunched underfoot as she moved to crouch beside the chandelier. She examined the brushed silver chain links; the wire had been cut. *Careful what you wish for*, Cat thought, looking up at the beam. Her plan to leave her sister's employ was now on hold.

*   *   *

Special Agent Grayson Alexander couldn't remember the last time he'd taken a vacation. To his way of thinking, the bad guys didn't take one, so why should he? But his last case had changed his mind. He was skirting the edge of burnout. It was the only explanation he could come up with for his epic screwup. He'd put not only the operation on the line, but his life.

Valeria Ramos had played him, and he hadn't uncovered her deception until it was almost too late. A gorgeous brunette with a killer bod, she'd passed herself off as a victim, when in truth she'd been the head of the human trafficking ring. The memory of how badly his instincts had failed him grated. They'd never failed him in the past. Forget that he was damn good at his job; for a guy who'd grown up around actresses, he should have made Valeria from day one. So yeah, he needed a couple of weeks off to decompress and get his head back in the game.

He propped his bag and skis by the door of his Beachwood Canyon home, anxious to get out of the smog-filled city. The mountains were calling his name. He'd get his thrills and chills on the black diamond slopes instead of on the job. Whatever tension remained at the end of the day, he'd burn off with a ski bunny or two or three. It wasn't as if he had someone to come home to. He'd learned the hard way that his job wasn't conducive to long-term relationships. Or maybe it was just him.

As he opened the panel to activate the alarm, his cell rang. He thought about not answering until he saw who it was.

"Mr. Alexander, Linda Hanson from Shady Palms. Your grandmother has gone missing again."

And he knew exactly where she'd turn up. He should have moved. He pressed a button, angling his security camera at the street. Sure enough, a yellow cab was pulling into his driveway. "She's here, Linda. I'll have her back to the home within the hour." If he had to tie her up to get her there. He wondered what her story would be this time. Last month, she was sure the nurses were drugging her.

The woman on the other end of the line cleared her throat. "Mr. Alexander, I'm afraid that won't be possible. The previous administrator was more willing than I am to look the other way. Dame Alexander is a disruptive influence. You'll have to find another facility—"

Yeah right. Shady Palms was just one of many retirement homes his grandmother had terrorized in the past five years. And he should know, since the duty of taking care of GG fell on him. Not on his cousins or his father or his aunt and uncle—him. In a voice infused with as much charm and warmth as he could manage given his frustration, he said, "Linda, we'll discuss this when I get there. I'm sure we can come to—"

"No we won't, Mr. Alexander. Your charm and good looks are wasted on me. I'm too old to be swayed by a handsome face."

He was wondering if his badge and an imaginary infraction might do the trick when a five-foot-nothing, immaculately groomed older woman with a white Angora cat tucked under her arm scowled up at the security camera.

"Grayson, I know you're there. Let me in," Dame Estelle Alexander demanded in an upper-crust British accent, lifting her cane to knock on the door.

"Linda, I'll..." He blew out a noisy breath. She'd hung up. At the insistent rapping, he shoved the phone in the pocket of his black leather jacket and jerked open the door before Estelle bashed it in. "GG, you promised you weren't going to run away again."

She batted him out of the way with her cane, lifted her aristocratic nose, and sniffed. "I didn't run away. I escaped. They're trying to kill me."

He wouldn't be surprised if some of the staff at Shady Palms *wanted* to kill her. He'd felt the same on occasion, as he imagined her last four husbands did. His grandmother was a drama queen and a royal pain in the ass.

alty, Grayson was playing the part of Lord Harry Halstead, a wealthy aristocrat who dabbled in acting. Other than the executive producer and the agent, the director was the only one who knew Grayson's true identity.

"We should keep this car," his grandmother said as he parked the black Jaguar XJL in the studio's lot. "I prefer it to your truck. James Bond drove one just like this in *Skyfall*. Did I tell you the director's an old flame of mine?"

"Yes, GG, you did." *Four times*. "And no, *we* aren't keeping the car." Though it would serve Jamie right if he did. His cousin had reluctantly lent Grayson his pride and joy, conceding it was a better fit for the part of a British aristocrat than Grayson's truck. "I can't afford—" Grayson sneezed. "...a Jag."

"You could if you'd let me call my director friend. Did I tell you we had an affair five— No, maybe it was ten years ago. He'd give you a screen test if I asked. You'd make a much better James Bond than Daniel Craig. And with your role in *As the Sun Sets*, you'll have something on your resume besides undercover work for the FBI. Which is good, mind you, but it's your time in front of the camera he'll want to see." She dug around in her purse and pulled out a lace-trimmed hankie. "Stop sneezing. Your eyes are red and puffy. It's not the least bit attractive."

He wiped his nose, stuffing the hankie in his breast pocket. "If you'd left Fluffy at home like I asked, I wouldn't be sneezing." She ignored him, turning up the air conditioner instead of the radio to drown him out.

The overpowering smell of cologne filled the car. Maybe it wasn't the cat making him sneeze after all. It was probably the half bottle of aftershave GG had slapped on his face. As soon as he'd put one foot in the hall this morning, she'd been waiting for him in full makeup, wearing a winter-white pantsuit. She must have turned up her hearing aids when she went to bed. In the end, he decided not to argue with her and use her as a lookout. He planned to check out the set and Chloe O'Connor's dressing room before the cast and crew arrived.

As the urge to sneeze once again overtook him, Grayson turned off the air conditioner. Strands of cat hair floated around the interior to land on his black suit. With a muttered curse, he brushed them off his shoulder and thigh.

"If you must use foul language, say *bloody hell*. Did you not pay any attention to me last night?" His grandmother tapped his temple with an arthritic finger. It was about the only thing she hadn't had Botoxed. "Get in character. From this moment on, you are Lord Harry Halstead, ninety-eighth in line to the British throne."

His grandmother had taken to her role as a female Henry Higgins with a vengeance. Jamie had called her on the sly and asked her to prep Grayson for the part. He'd spent the entire night before being taught to walk and talk like a proper British lord while devising ways to make his cousin pay. He might keep the Jag after all.

Ignoring his grandmother's comment, Grayson unfolded his six-foot-three frame from the XJL. He wasn't worried about fooling Chloe O'Connor. He made a living pretending to be someone else.

He rounded the car and opened the passenger-side door. As he waited for GG to alight, he tugged the cuffs of his white shirt a precise inch below the black suit's sleeves and scanned the lot.

His grandmother rummaged through her purse. "I can't find my pills, Grayson. I must have forgotten—"

"Harry," he said in a clipped British accent. "You didn't forget your pills, Estelle. I gave them to you at breakfast." He didn't eat the morning meal as a rule, but with his grandmother there, he had no choice but to feed her.

She glanced at him, covering the flustered look on her face with a brisk nod. "Your accent is quite believable, my boy. Well done."

"Thanks. Now come on. There's the director." Grayson lifted his chin at the short, rotund man with gray hair and a goatee. Offering his grandmother his arm, Grayson studied her as he did so. With all the work she'd had done, she looked two decades younger than her actual age. But she was seventy-six, and he wondered if he should be taking her moments of forgetfulness more seriously. They'd been happening more frequently, as he'd noticed on his weekly visits to Shady Palms. And obviously she was aware enough to be concerned. He'd mention it to Jamie. Have him... Grayson's shoulders rose and fell on a heavy, inward sigh. No, as he'd learned in the past, when it came to GG, there was only one person he could depend on: himself.

The director extended his hand as he met them at the door. "Good to meet you in person, Grayson." They'd spoken the night before.

He shook Grayson's hand, then took his grandmother's, lifting it to his lips. "An honor to meet you, Dame Alexander. I'm a big fan. I'd love you to do a walk-on if you're interested."

Estelle's eyebrows rose, and her nostrils flared. Obviously, she felt the role was beneath her. Grayson was thankful good manners prevented her from saying so. "Quite impossible, Phillip. I have a job to do. I will be my grandson's eyes and ears on the set. We're partners, you know."

Sweet mother of God. He never should have agreed to bring her with him. She continued before Grayson had a chance to correct her. "I'm playing his manager. As me, of course. I'm too recognizable to pass myself off as someone else."

If you were of a certain age and a fan of Broadway, Grayson conceded she had a point.

"I can't say I'm not disappointed, but I understand. We want this wrapped up as soon as possible," Phil said as he opened the door and handed Grayson a script. "Sorry to put you on the spot. But we need you to start today. You'll be playing Rand Livingstone, an ex-lover of Tessa Hart."

"Not a problem." Grayson had a photographic memory, so that was the least of his concerns. But he worried that springing him on the cast today would raise suspicions. "Was this a story line the cast has been expecting?"

"Yes. Though another actor was hired to play the role. Unfortunately for him, but lucky for us, yesterday he caused a furor on social media with some inappropriate pictures, and we've been scrambling to find a replacement."

His cousin's work, no doubt. Grayson wasn't the only one who was good at his job. Once they'd done a walkthrough of the set, which took longer than it should, thanks to his grandmother lobbying for Grayson's role to be expanded while suggesting how to capture his best side, Phil gave Grayson a key to Chloe O'Connor's dressing room. "I'll leave you to it. Chloe arrives around eight, so you have a good hour."

As Phil walked away, Grayson said, "Estelle, stand at the end of the hall. If you see anyone coming this way, tap your cane twice. I'll leave the door— What do you think you're doing?" he asked as she pushed past him into the dressing room.

She handed him the cat. "I have to go to the loo."

"No, there's no…" He trailed off when she closed the bathroom door. "Bloody hell," he muttered, placing Fluffy on the white club chair. At least her hair would blend in.

Grayson scanned the dressing room. The three drawers in the makeup table were the most likely place to find what he was looking for. If he didn't solve the case in the next twenty-four hours, he'd break in to Chloe's Redondo Beach house. He needed something Cat O'Connor had written to compare to the threatening letter. Although the note was comprised of words cut and pasted from a magazine, he could check it for phrases she commonly used.

Cat O'Connor remained his primary suspect. She had the motive and opportunity. She hadn't been on the set at the time of Chloe's "accidents." An unusual occurrence according to Phil. Cat was always close at hand during filming in case her sister needed her. Which, invariably, she did, Phil confirmed. Grayson didn't share his suspicions with the director because, if he wasn't mistaken, Phil had a crush on Cat. From the file Grayson had already gathered on her, he understood why.

Like her sister, Cat O'Connor was gorgeous. Not surprising, since they were identical twins. But Cat's natural beauty appealed more to Grayson. Her chin-length dark hair framed intelligent green eyes and high, sculpted cheekbones. Combined with her lean, athletically built frame, she came across as a strong woman, one who could take care of herself. The only thing soft about her was her lips. Full, pouty lips Grayson had fixated on while studying her photo.

A women's magazine open facedown on the glass table caught his eye. There's no way as a former detective she'd leave evidence lying around in plain sight. Then again, she'd been involved with a guy running a Ponzi scheme. Maybe she was unraveling. Her relationship with Michael Upton was another reason she'd ended up on the top of Grayson's suspect list. She'd been engaged to the guy, living with him, and she expected people to believe she had no idea what he was up to? Grayson didn't buy it, and neither did the special agent in charge in Denver.

As far as SAC Turner was concerned, the file on Cat O'Connor was still open. And the fact that she'd cleaned out her bank account last month, anonymously giving it to the victims of the fraud, only made her look more guilty in Grayson's and Turner's eyes.

Grayson retrieved the women's magazine from the glass table and leafed through the pages, checking for missing words. He didn't find any, but what he did find caused his mouth to lift at the corner. He was on the right track. Because unless Chloe had taken the job-satisfaction quiz, which he highly doubted, Cat O'Connor hated working for her sister. Now the question was, did she hate only her job or did she hate her sister as well? It had to be difficult living in Chloe O'Connor's shadow. The money notwithstanding, would it be enough for her to commit cold-blooded sororicide? If Cat had also confided her involvement in the Ponzi scheme to Chloe, he imagined it would. Her sister was a loose end that needed to be taken care of.

*   *   *

Chloe had been gloating ever since Cat informed her that the job she'd lined up had fallen through and she wasn't leaving. She'd held off telling her until late the night before. Cat didn't want Chloe to connect her change of plans to the incident with the chandelier. But with the crew blaming a piece of steel on the overhead beam for the cut wire, there should be no reason for her sister to be suspicious.

Even though Cat didn't buy the explanation, it worked to her advantage. The last thing she needed was for Chloe to think she was in danger. The exhausting reality of dealing with a hysterical Chloe aside, Cat wanted to find whoever was responsible, not send them to ground. She didn't want her sister spending the rest of her life looking over her shoulder. And Cat didn't want to spend the rest of hers protecting her sister from an unknown enemy.

Chloe, looking far from her glamorous self in a pink velour tracksuit, shot her a disgruntled glance as Cat parked the SUV. "There's no one here. I told you the clocks were wrong. There must have been a power outage last night."

"Guess so." There wasn't. Cat wanted to come in early and check the set without raising her sister's suspicions. It was just Cat's luck that Phil had decided to arrive early today, too. She didn't recognize the black Jag and wondered who else was here.

As she got out of the Range Rover and scanned the lot,

Cat skimmed her hand over the back of her brown leather jacket to be sure it hadn't ridden up to reveal her gun. The late November morning was cool enough that she could get away with wearing the jacket for now. She'd probably have to change by midday.

Chloe yawned as she met her at the stage door. "I could have used the extra hour to get ready, you know." She touched her disheveled hair and pursed her naked lips.

"Hair and makeup just redoes it anyway. I don't know why you bother. Seems like a waste of time to me."

"Of course it does. Because all you do is wash your face and finger-comb your hair. But unlike you, I have an image to uphold. I can't come to work looking like a hot mess."

Cat put a defensive hand to her head. It wasn't like she fussed over her appearance...but a hot mess, really? She looked down at her ripped jeans and scuffed boots and reluctantly conceded Chloe might have a point. Before Michael had turned Cat's world upside down and she got stuck in a soul-sucking job, she'd put more effort into her appearance. But she didn't know why she let her sister's comment get to her. It wasn't like she wanted to attract attention. The lower she flew under the radar the better. Besides, she'd sworn off men for the foreseeable future.

"Good thing no one's around to see you, then," Cat said as she opened the door, making a mental note that it needed to be kept locked until the guard was on duty. Security was usually here by the time they arrived.

From somewhere on the set, she heard Phil's gruff voice. If she had the slightest suspicion he was involved with the attempt on her sister's life, she'd stop and listen to his conversation. She continued walking.

Chloe might be a pain in Phil's derriere on occasion, but only because she strived for perfection. Her sister expected everyone to work as hard as she did to make the daytime drama a success. Cat had to give credit where it was due, Chloe was a good actress. She admired her sister's passion and work ethic. She had no doubt that one day Chloe would make her dream of winning an Oscar come true. *As the Sun Sets* was just a stepping stone for her. And there was no way Phil would endanger his star. After all, as the latest issue of *People* proclaimed, Chloe was America's sweetheart.

"What are you doing? You're freaking me out."

Cat glanced over her shoulder, looking up to meet her sister's eyes. They were both five foot five, until Chloe put on her four-inch heels. Which she wore every day, even when they were at home. She said heels made her legs look long and lean. Chloe was all about looking good. Cat was all about comfort. And right now the look in her sister's eyes was making her uncomfortable. "What are you talking about?"

"You're acting like a cop. All tense, looking around as if someone's going to leap out at us at any moment."

That was the thing about Chloe. She acted like an airhead, but she wasn't. She was smart. She read body language almost as well as Cat. "I told you to stop watching *Criminal Minds* before you go to bed. It makes you jumpy the next day."

Cat focused on relaxing the muscles in her neck and shoulders as she rounded the corner to . . . Chloe's dressing room door was ajar.

"I'm not jumpy . . . What are—"

"Quiet," Cat whispered, her forearm across Chloe's

chest as she gently shoved her against the wall. "Stay here." She went to reach for her gun, then decided to check out the situation first. If she could avoid drawing her weapon, so much the better. She didn't have a permit to carry concealed in California, and Chloe would wonder why she was armed.

Cat crept toward her sister's dressing room and slowly inched the door open. A tall man, his dark wavy hair curling at the collar of his expensive black suit, stood beside the coffee table with his back to her.

Chapter Three

"Take one more step toward me, Cat, and I'll shoot you," the dark-haired man said in a smooth baritone.

When he moved his arm as though to reach for something in his jacket, Cat launched herself across the room and took him down. His well-developed muscles rippled beneath her fingers as she pushed her hands into the wide expanse of his back.

He fell forward, his forehead bouncing off the arm of the club chair at the same time a cat, its white hair standing on end, hissed and flew at her. Startled, Cat jerked back, raising an arm to push the animal away. The thought that the man might have been threatening the cat, and not her, crossed her mind. But it didn't explain why he'd broken into her sister's dressing room.

Straddling him, Cat grabbed his arm to twist it behind his back. She felt the tension in his body as he shifted, and suspected he meant to throw her off. "I wouldn't if I were

you. Stay..." she began to advise him when an outraged
cry cut her off. She twisted to see an older woman come
charging out of the bathroom with her cane raised.

The man beneath Cat took advantage of her brief
moment of inattention and effortlessly broke her grip on his
arm. Before she could react, he flipped over in one smooth
movement so that she now straddled his stomach. Along
with her disbelief that he'd gotten the best of her was the
thought that he reeked of cologne. It was worse than walking through the perfume aisle at a department store.

"Est..." He removed his hand from Cat's hip, a hand
she hadn't realized had been there until now, and sneezed
into his arm. "...elle, put down the cane." He directed his
command at the older woman.

As the woman did as he asked, his ice-blue gaze
returned to Cat. She blinked as much from the disdain
she saw in his eyes as to his traffic-stopping beauty. Thick
hair the color of dark chocolate was slicked back from his
chiseled features, a strong masculine nose, square jaw,
and full lips on a wide mouth. Only the dent on his forehead and a white scar bisecting his left eyebrow marred
his perfection. Well, that and his puffy, bloodshot eyes.

"Kit Kat, what did you do? This poor cat ran terrified
from my dressing—" her sister began from behind her
before the older woman cut her off.

"Fluffy, my poor baby. Come to Mommy."

Cat swiveled to see the woman trying to extricate the
purring animal from her sister's arms. Chloe, attempting
to remove Fluffy's nails from her velour hoodie, stared
at Cat with an appalled expression on her face. "Why are
you sitting on that man?"

"I..." Cat looked from her sister to the man in question. She *was* still sitting on him. On his rock-hard abs. Why hadn't she moved? Because everything happened too fast. It was the only acceptable explanation. It had nothing to do with being stunned stupid by his movie-star good looks.

He raised an eyebrow. What was with the sardonic look? Oh, no, he was not putting her on the defensive. He'd broken into her sister's dressing room. Cat attempted to get off him without any further rubbing of her body on his, which wasn't easy. She gave up and awkwardly scrambled to her feet.

"About bloody time," she thought he muttered, but couldn't be sure because she was back to being stunned stupid when he flashed her a smile. A smile so gorgeous it belonged in a toothpaste commercial.

Pathetic. Cat was so off her game, it wasn't even funny. Here she was thinking about his full, seductive lips and his perfect white teeth when her sister's life was on the line. Cat fisted her hands on her hips, put on her cop face, and went to glare down at the man. Only, he rose to his feet with leonine grace, tugging the sleeves of his white shirt below his suit sleeves. She had to look up and took one step back, then another.

Behind her, Chloe sucked in a breath. Cat knew what that sucking sound meant, and it wasn't good. Her sister had gotten her first good look at the man. "Chloe, wait for me in the hall. I need to question—"

Her sister practically threw the animal at the older woman, shoving Cat out of the way with her hand extended. And there it was again, his smile. Only, this one seemed friendlier, more genuine, and just as flipping gorgeous. She waited for her sister to react. She didn't disappoint.

Right on cue, Chloe fluffed her hair, did a flirty head
tilt, and went to bat her eyes. Without her fake lashes
beating against her cheeks, Chloe remembered she was
makeup-less, which earned Cat a you'll-pay-for-this look.
She had no doubt Chloe would make good on her wordless threat for having to meet this man at less than her
best. But Cat didn't have time to worry in what form that
payback would come.

"Ms. O'Connor, your photos don't do you justice. I apologize for intruding on your privacy. My manager"—he
nodded at the older woman, who was too busy examining
her cat for injury to take part in the conversation—"needed
to use the loo." He held up a key. "Phil didn't think you'd
mind."

Cat pinched the bridge of her nose. How did she miss
that he was a Brit? On top of everything else, he had to
have one of those obnoxiously sexy accents. Add the
smooth baritone in which it was delivered, and she was
surprised Chloe hadn't melted into a puddle of quivering
ecstasy. Cat chanced a glance at her sister, who gaped at
the man while vigorously pumping his hand. Then her
other hand joined in on the action, clasping his large,
masculine hand between hers.

"No, no. My goodness, it's my sister who should apologize for attacking you." Chloe widened her eyes at Cat,
nudging her head in the stranger's direction.

As if. She didn't believe one word coming out of tall,
dark, and too-charming-to-be-real's mouth. "Who are
you, and why would Phil give you a key to my sister's
dressing room?"

"Halstead. Harry Halstead." His pale blue eyes briefly
locked with Cat's before he directed his answer to Chloe.

"My dressing room wasn't ready yet, and as I said, Phil didn't think it would be a problem. I'll be—"

"Lord Harry Halstead, ninety-eighth in line for the throne, to be precise," the older woman said in a snotty British accent, rubbing her cheek against the cat's head. "I advised my client against taking the role, but it seems he's a fan of yours, Ms. O'Connor."

Cat thought she groaned inwardly, but from the raised eyebrows Lord Harry and his manager directed at her, she hadn't. It didn't matter. All she cared about was her sister's reaction to the news. Chloe pressed a hand to her chest and released a breathy "Oh my."

Which would have been comical if it wasn't also worrisome. This guy checked every box on her sister's to-marry-a-Brit list. Five months ago, a man who'd done the same failed to tell Chloe he was married. His wife, who caught them in flagrante delicto, had threatened to kill her sister. Cat had been in Christmas looking after her mother at the time.

If Lord Darby and his wife hadn't kissed and made up and weren't safely ensconced in their London flat, her ladyship would be on Cat's suspect list. Cat closed her eyes. She didn't need the added complication of protecting her sister from another smarmy British lord while trying to figure out who wanted Chloe dead.

Cat opened her eyes to see his lordship bent over her sister's hand. While Chloe fanned herself, the man lifted his head, hurriedly reaching in his breast pocket to retrieve a...hankie. He sneezed. Cat stared at the lacy starched-white fabric, then took in his long, broad manicured fingers. And as the smell of his cologne filled her sister's dressing room, laughter bubbled up in her throat. She bit the inside of her bottom lip, then managed to smile at the man now looking at her over her sister's head. Cat had been worrying for nothing. Chloe could flirt with Lord Harry Halstead to her heart's desire, and the man wouldn't end up in her sister's bed. He was gay.

*   *   *

Cat O'Connor's beautiful, wide smile hit him with the same force as her lithe body had only moments ago. He couldn't explain why. Maybe it was the way her long-lashed green eyes lit with amusement or the cute dimple that flashed to the left of her lush lips. Wait a minute, why had her earlier suspicion suddenly turned to amusement? He followed her gaze to the lace-trimmed hankie in his hand, his manicured nails—courtesy of GG—and had a flash of insight. She thought he was gay.

If he'd gone with his natural instinct—the one that had taken some effort to control—and flipped her onto her back, his response to her would have wiped that conclusion from her brain. His reaction had surprised and pissed him off. Sure she was hot, and having a hot woman straddle him, her heat warming his skin through his silk shirt, was hotter still. But he knew it wasn't her face or body that had drawn the response—it was the holstered gun his fingers had brushed against under her leather jacket. Seems he'd developed a thing for dangerous women. Following so close on the heels of his screwup with Valeria Ramos, this was not a happy realization.

He worked to keep his mouth from flattening and refocused on her sister. At the covetous look in those identical green eyes, he decided gay was good. Until he remembered the whole point of him playing a British lord was to get close to Chloe. It would make it easier to protect her.

"Oh my gosh, you're playing Rand Livingstone, aren't you? This is so perfect. You're perfect. Isn't he perfect, Kit Kat?"

Her sister smirked. "Oh yeah, he's perfect, all right."

Obviously Chloe didn't pick up on her sister's sarcasm because she continued to stare at him while smoothing her hands down the lapels of his jacket. "I couldn't have picked better myself. You're everything I want in a lover. The boy they'd hired to—"

"Everything *Tessa* wants, isn't that what you meant to say, Chloe?"

Chloe frowned at her sister. "That's what I said, isn't it?"

Before her sister could respond, his grandmother said, "Harry, perhaps you should ask Phillip if your dressing room is ready. I'd like to sit and have my morning tea while we read through the script."

Grayson inwardly cursed; he should have known building his acting resume would outweigh GG's interest in the investigation. She'd been trying to get him to become an actor since the day he'd moved in with her at the age of eight.

"Where are my manners? Please have a seat. You too, your lordship. My sister will make us some tea." Chloe gently took his grandmother's arm and steered her to one of the club chairs.

"Chloe, I don't have time to make tea. I have—" Cat pinched the bridge of her straight and narrow nose as her sister talked over her. Grayson lowered himself in the other chair, watching the sisters' interaction with interest.

"I'm sorry, I didn't get your name," Chloe said to his grandmother.

Settling in the chair with Fluffy on her lap, GG lifted her chin. "Dame Estelle Alexander."

Chloe's expressive eyes widened, her mouth opening and closing before she said in a high-pitched voice, "Dame Estelle Alexander. You're *the* Dame Estelle Alexander? What am I saying, of course you are. I should have recognized you. I can't believe you're sitting in my dressing room." She flapped a hand in her sister's direction. "Kit Kat, I feel faint."

Cat's shoulders rose on a sigh as she walked to the makeup table, returning with a chair and a container of pills. Grayson leaned forward, trying to get a better look at the prescription bottle in her hand. Her eyes slid his way, and she arched an eyebrow. He forced a smile, sat back in the chair, and tugged on his shirtsleeves. With a slight shake of her head, she placed two pills in Chloe's waiting palm. He needed to get his hands on that prescription bottle. An overdose or a pill laced with cyanide would be a convenient way for her to eliminate her sister.

"I'm sorry, I don't know what's gotten into me today. I'm so scattered." Chloe sank gracefully onto the chair Cat had brought to her. "Tea, Kit Kat. I need to wash them down." Her sister opened her mouth, then closed it, stalking to a narrow counter on the opposite wall.

"Don't mind her. She's always cranky in the morning," Chloe stage-whispered at the rattle of teacups and the slamming of an electric kettle. "We were late and had to rush out this morning, as you can see from the state of me." She did an embarrassed sweep of her hand from her hair to her waist.

Grayson figured it was time to lay on the charm. "I have never seen a woman as stunning at seven in the morning." His grandmother stroked Fluffy, the considering look she sent from Grayson to Chloe putting him on edge. He needed to remind her that any flirtation on his part was an act. He'd married the last actress she set him up with and that relationship had crashed and burned. He still had the scars.

"Thank...seven?" Chloe sent an exasperated look in her sister's direction. "Honestly, Kit Kat, when are you going to listen to me?" Cat grunted in response and slammed something else. "I told her there must have been a power outage."

Interesting. "Were your cell phones affected as well?" That earned him a glare from Cat. He smiled. Her eyes narrowed. He'd have to be more careful.

"I don't know. I couldn't find mine. Kit Kat, what time is it on your phone?"

"What does it matter? We're here now," she muttered, unplugging the whistling kettle.

It mattered quite a bit actually. Because if Cat had come in early to tamper with the set, he'd need to keep a closer eye on her. After yesterday's "accident," he'd assumed she'd wait a couple of days before trying again.

"I suppose it is a good thing that we arrived earlier than usual. Now we have more time to get better acquainted," Chloe said with a winsome smile. "I can give you some background on the story line if you think it would helpful. I don't want to mess with your process though."

"I'm sure he doesn't need you to fill him in. Estelle said he's a big fan. Isn't that right, Harry?" Cat handed him a cup of tea with a suspicious look in her green eyes.

"Bang on. Never miss an episode. I'm a card-carrying member of the Tessa Hart fan club." He crossed his legs, raising his pinkie as he brought the cup to his mouth.

He didn't quite catch it, but he thought Cat said *stalker* before turning to give his grandmother her cup. Okay, maybe he'd gone a little overboard.

Chloe pressed a hand to her chest. "I apologize for my sister's lack of propriety. Kit Kat, it's Lord Harry and Dame Alexander. You must use their titles when you address them."

"Why? We're not in the UK. I'm sure they don't expect—"

His grandmother's penciled eyebrows rose to her hairline. "We most certainly do."

"Really? Because I seem to remember Harry calling you Estelle."

"We're family. It's—"

She crossed her arms. "You're family?"

He needed to have his head read for bringing GG along. "We're *like* family. Estelle's been my manager for years. And let's not concern ourselves with propriety. You may address us in any manner you wish, Kit Kat."

Her lips flattened. "Thank you, Your Highness."

He held back a grin. If he wasn't investigating her for attempted murder, he might just like this woman. He had a feeling they had a lot in common. Pain-in-the-ass actresses, for one.

As she lifted the teacup to her lips, his grandmother's narrowed eyes moved from him to Cat. She knew him too damn well. He was relieved when she didn't say anything, instead taking a sip of tea. She jerked back and stared at the cup. "This is the worst cup of tea I have ever tasted."

Chloe took a sip and made a face. "You're right, it is. Kit Kat, I think it needs to steep longer."

"You'll have to make it yourself. I have things to do. Why don't you take a crack at it, Estelle? You must be an expert." Cat headed for the door, and before Grayson could come up with a reason for her to stay, she was gone.

Grayson stood up. "I'll take care of the tea." He needed an excuse to leave the dressing room and follow Cat. With his back to Chloe and Estelle, he slid the tea bags into the inner pocket of his jacket. He turned and started for the door. "You appear to be out of tea bags. I'll just—"

Chloe cut him off. "I don't know what to say. I'm so embarrassed. My sister hasn't been herself lately."

That stopped him in his tracks. "Why's that?"

She grimaced, fiddling with the zipper on her hoodie. "She hates LA. She'd rather be back in Colorado, but no one will hire her because..." She lifted a shoulder. "I don't know what else I can do."

He felt bad for Chloe. She seemed to care a lot about her sister. He didn't like to think how she'd feel once she learned the truth about Cat.

"She's jealous of you. I saw it straightaway," his grandmother said.

"You did?" Chloe bit her bottom lip, then nodded. "I've suspected it myself, but I didn't realize it was so obvious."

"Sibling rivalry is a dangerous thing. Look at Goneril and Regan in *King Lear*."

Sweet mother of God. What was she thinking? "Estelle, I—" Grayson began.

Chloe twisted the neckline of her hoodie. *"What Ever Happened to Baby Jane?"*

He frowned. "Who's Baby Jane?"

"Bette Davis," his grandmother said, then, at what he imagined was his blank look, she set her tea on the coffee table, put Fluffy on the floor, and stood. Placing one hand over her heart, she threw out the other one. " 'Sister, sister, oh so fair, why is...' "

" '...there blood all over your hair,' " Chloe whispered.

Chapter Four

Cat couldn't put a finger on what it was about Lord Harry Halstead that sent her bullshit meter to the red zone. But she'd spent enough time interrogating cons to know that his lordship wasn't who he said he was. She'd caught the wordless exchanges between him and his manager, the way his pale blue eyes focused intently on her and Chloe. And not in a way that suggested he was thinking of a threesome. Although he could just be curious about the identical twin thing. A lot of people were. All the questions had been annoying growing up. Mr. Manners would be too polite to ask them. Because he was polite—freakishly so.

She gave her head a mental shake. She'd worry about his agenda later. Everyone in Hollywood had one. But for now, Cat felt confident her sister was safe with Lord Harry and his manager while she got down to the business of identifying Chloe's attacker before it was too late. She'd just hit the set when she heard voices. Several members of the cast and crew started to trickle in. With little time to spare, she headed for the dressing room of her primary suspect.

Last night Cat had gone over Molly's actions before the chandelier fell, and her reaction afterward. They didn't add up. It was as if the actress had known the chandelier was going to fall. Then again, unlike Cat, Molly had a clear view. But it was when Cat tried to recall the number of times the actress had gone off script and improvised during a scene that her suspicions grew. As far as she remembered, yesterday was a first. And everyone knew the actress hated Chloe, except maybe Chloe. Cat knocked on Molly's dressing room door.

When no one responded, she pulled the bump key from her pocket. She kept an eye on the long hallway as she jiggled the key in the lock. If her former partner at the Denver PD could see her now, he'd have a good laugh. He'd nicknamed her Detective Straight and Narrow. Drove him nuts that she had to do everything by the book. No, he wouldn't laugh, she reminded herself. Those days had ended when everything came out about Michael.

Just like the FBI, her partner thought she'd been in on the fraud. That had cut deep. More than a year later, the wound had yet to heal. She didn't know if it ever would. Her family had been angry she'd quit the force instead of fighting to clear her name. Especially her brother Ethan, who was a district attorney.

They didn't get it. She may not have been in on Michael's Ponzi scheme, but indirectly it was her fault he'd been able to bilk so many victims of their savings. The stories of what people had lost broke her heart. She should have clued in to what was going on right under her nose. She was a good cop, but she'd been blinded by love. It's why she'd anonymously given all her savings, the money her father had left her, to the victims of the fraud. It hadn't been enough. It would never be enough.

She rubbed her face in frustration. She couldn't do this now. Ignoring the familiar weight of shame and guilt lying heavy on her heart, she refocused on the lock. She applied pressure to the key and heard the snick of the tumblers. With one last look down the hall, she opened the door and stepped inside. Quietly closing the door behind her, she did a quick visual search of the room.

It was smaller than Chloe's and messier. The furniture and walls were monochromatic. The only splash of color came from the bright piles of clothing littering the floor, a fuchsia bra hanging from the chair in front of the makeup table. Cat walked to the coffee table and riffled through a stack of papers. Nothing of interest; just some old scripts and newspaper and magazine clippings. She didn't really expect Molly to leave anything incriminating lying out in the open. But if Cat didn't do a thorough search of the room, she'd always wonder if she missed something.

Given the timeline, Molly couldn't have cut the wires on her own. She had a partner, either one of the cast or crew. Now Cat had to figure out who. Hoping to find even a small clue, she walked to the makeup table and opened a drawer. Jam-packed with cleansers and moisturizers, it was a bust, just like her foray onto Molly's social media accounts last night. Cat needed access to the actress's phone and computer.

As Cat closed the bottom drawer, she heard something in the hall. She glanced over her shoulder. The doorknob turned. Sucking in a panicked breath, she ran on her tip-toes to the closet. She'd just closed the louvered door when someone entered the room. Carefully sliding the shoes out of the way, then the hangers of clothing, she pushed to the back of the closet before looking through the slats.

Her eyes widened. It wasn't Molly, as she'd first suspected—it was Harry. Her immediate reaction was to open the closet door and ask his lordship what he was doing in the actress's dressing room. Since she didn't want to alert him or anyone else to what she was up to, she stifled the urge and watched him instead. He crouched by the coffee table. She leaned forward, pressing her eye to the slat to get a better view. His head swiveled in her direction. Holding her breath, she slowly eased back.

He came to his feet with that same contained grace she'd noticed earlier, holding what appeared to be a maga-zine clipping in his hand. For an anxiety-filled moment she thought he'd seen or heard her, but just as she was reassuring herself it was impossible, Molly's voice filtered into the room from the hall.

Before Cat could blink, Harry opened the closet door and slipped inside, crowding her against the wall. He didn't seem surprised to see her. She didn't have long to contemplate this because he banged his head on the upper shelf and cursed. Cat inwardly did the same, covering his mouth with her hand. The idiot was going to get her caught. He raised an eyebrow, his words muffled in her palm.

"Be quiet," she whispered, doing her best to ignore the ticklish sensation working its way up her arm, the feel of his warm lips on her skin.

From her earlier up close encounter with the man, she

knew he was ridiculously tall, broad shouldered, and leanly muscled, but she wasn't prepared for just how big he actually was. The confined space was too small for the two of them and decidedly uncomfortable with her sandwiched between him and the wall. Her discomfort intensified when he removed her hand and brought his mouth to her ear, the ticklish sensation morphing into a full-out body shiver. Which, from the glint in his eyes as he looked into hers, he hadn't missed.

Wonderful, just wonderful. How was she supposed to explain her reaction? She could tell him the truth—he was the first man she'd rubbed against in over a year. Right, as if she'd tell him that.

"Fancy meeting you here, love." His mouth quirked.

His sexy accent and grin ignited a warm tingle in a place that hadn't tingled in a very long time. Oh good grief, she was as bad as her sister. But seeing as how she'd been in a spell as dry as the Mojave Desert, she couldn't blame her girl parts for their undiscriminating taste.

She scowled at him, shoving lightly on his chest in hopes the slight distance would cool her off. It didn't, but the sound of Molly and a man talking in the hall did. Cat inched her way around him, her back to his chest, and pressed her eye to the door.

"What are you doing?" he whispered in her ear.

"Shush," she murmured, straining to make out what the couple were saying, or at the very least, discover to whom the male voice belonged. Youngish and pleading was all she got. She regretted her decision to search Molly's dressing room, and not only because she was enveloped by Harry's muscles and his overpowering cologne. If she'd hung out in the hall, she'd have her other suspect and wouldn't have to explain what she'd been doing in Molly's dressing room to his lordship. After she found out what he was doing here.

As the door started to open, Harry wrapped his arms around her, drawing her away from the louvers. He must have heard her huff a ticked-off breath as once again he lowered his mouth to her ear. "She'll see you. I did."

Cat wasn't able to respond. Molly stepped into her dressing room, disappointingly alone. The redhead flipped on the light, then tossed an oversized bag on the floor beside the coffee table before walking across the room— thankfully in the opposite direction. Cat remembered seeing Harry pick up a clipping and reached behind her. His fingers closed around her wrist before she dipped hers in his pocket. Her body reacted to the strength and size of his hand with another annoying zing. She tipped her head to arch a questioning eyebrow at the same time he lowered his. She bumped the back of her skull on his chin. He stifled her unintentional *ouch* behind his hand. She froze as Molly turned and scanned the room. Cat pressed deeper into Harry's embrace, afraid he was right and Molly would see her.

She sagged against him when the redhead returned her attention to the makeup table, withdrew something from the drawer, and headed for the bathroom. Cat prayed she'd shut the door so they could sneak out, but she didn't. Molly turned on the water and began singing the theme song to *As the Sun Sets*. Cat had to come up with a plan. She couldn't remain in the cramped closet with his lordship until the actress was called to block out today's scene.

Removing Harry's hand from her mouth, she pulled her sister's confiscated cell phone from her pocket. Molly was making enough noise to muffle the sound of Cat texting, but to be on the safe side, she shuffled around until she faced Harry's wide chest. She bit her bottom lip at the feel of a particular part of his male anatomy pressed snug against her. Obviously, she hadn't thought this through. Her brain wasn't firing on all cylinders today.

Then she reminded herself he was gay, and it wouldn't faze him. Which was good, 'cause it was kind of fazing her. Ignoring the telling clench in her stomach, she accessed her sister's e-mail account and sent Molly a message from Chloe. An invite to meet the new cast member. Molly's cell beeped... in the bag on the floor beside the coffee table. Cat glanced up to see Harry smiling down at her.

Jolly good try, he mouthed.

She rolled her eyes and called Molly instead, blocking the number. At the ringing of the actress's cell, the water shut off. Harry gave her a thumbs-up along with one of his tingle-inducing smiles. Just as Molly reached her bag, Cat disconnected and prayed the actress would read her sister's e-mail. Which she did; only Molly didn't immediately race from the room as Cat had hoped. She muttered, "Yeah right, bitch."

Cat should have included a picture of Harry or a video clip of him talking. Since she hadn't, and couldn't, she quickly sent another e-mail. This one guaranteed to get a reaction from Molly. *I know what you've done. You won't get away with it*, she typed.

It was a risky move, but if Molly assumed Chloe was talking about the incident with the chandelier, as Cat hoped she would, maybe the actress would do or say something to implicate herself. Cat looked over her shoulder. With Molly's back to the closet, she couldn't gauge her reaction. Then the actress grabbed her bag, shoved the phone into it, and stalked from the room, slamming the door behind her.

Cat and his lordship did an awkward little dance as they both tried to get out of the closet at the same time. Apparently he was as anxious as her to end their forced confinement. She shoved him. "Go, go."

"That was close," he said as he exited the closet, straightening his jacket. "Whatever did you say to her?"

"It doesn't matter. What were you doing here?"

He scratched the back of his neck, a splash of color deepening the tanned skin at his cheeks. "I thought it was my dressing room. Phil pointed me in this direction."

"Molly's name is on the door."

"Which was unlocked, as Phil informed me it would be. So I assumed—"

"If it was an honest mistake, why didn't you say as much to Molly instead of hiding in the closet?"

"You mean the closet you were occupying at the time?"

Annoyed by the way her stomach fluttered in reaction to that deep, accented voice, Cat headed for the door. "Not that it's any of your business, but I was looking for Chloe's favorite pair of Louboutins. She thinks Molly stole them."

"Ah, well, I can understand the need for skulking about, then. Did you find them?"

Opening the door, she peeked into the hall to make sure no one was around. "No, I didn't. What about you? Did you find what you were looking for?" she asked casually, hoping to trip him up.

"As I was in the wrong dressing room, no, I did not. Perhaps you could direct me. I'd prefer not to bother Phil again." He joined her in the hall, his hands in his pockets.

"Sorry, no idea. But you might want to return whatever you stole from Molly's dressing room." She nodded through the open door at the coffee table.

"Kit Kat, you wound me. I'm not a thief."

She closed the door. "Not buying it, your lordship. I saw you put something in your pocket."

He removed his hands and raised his arms. "Check for yourself." There was a challenge in his eyes, one that was at odds with his relaxed demeanor.

So she took him up on it and searched the pockets of his jacket. When she found nothing but a piece of lint, she patted him down. Fighting an urge to kick herself as her hands skimmed over his hard-muscled torso.

"You're very good at this. One would almost think you were an officer of the law."

"Been patted down before, your lordship?"

"Well, there was this delicious—"

"Sharing's overrated. You can keep that little tidbit to yourself." She held up the tea bags she discovered in the inner pocket of his jacket. They weren't exactly incriminating, but still...

"I'm a tea aficionado, love. I don't go anywhere without my favorite brand. Nothing but the best for me. Now, we should probably get back to your adorable sister. I've left her in my manager's company long enough, don't you think?"

*   *   *

"I'm in love." Ty sighed, standing on the sidelines with Cat as they watched the last of Harry and Chloe's reunion scene. "Did I tell you how divine his hair is? A gorgeous, thick mane of mocha magnificence."

Only about twenty times. She was getting sick of hearing how perfect Lord Harry was. Everyone loved him, including her sister. "He probably dyes it and has plugs."

"Sheathe your claws, Pussy. You're still my favorite." Ty grinned and slung his arm around her shoulders. He gave her an exuberant squeeze. "It's so good to have you here. I don't know what I would have done without you. I'm glad that little incident with the chandelier changed your mind."

She leaned back to look at him. "Why do you think that's the reason I changed my mind?" Was she wrong about Molly? Could Ty have been the one who set it up so she'd stay?

"Give me some credit. I know how protective you are of Chloe. Though I have no idea why. That little barracuda is perfectly capable of looking out for herself."

"It's not why I stayed, Ty. My job offer fell through. And it's not like there's anything to protect Chloe from. It was an accident."

He chuckled quietly. "Other than Miss Molly. What set her off today? I bumped into her coming from your sister's dressing room breathing fire."

Cat had missed all the action and her chance to catch Molly's reaction to the e-mail. Since her sister didn't know anything about the message, she'd been baffled. And mortified that Dame Alexander had witnessed such an embarrassing scene. Honestly, Cat didn't know how much longer she could put up with his lordship and ladyship— or her sister, who insisted he was *the one*. Chloe hadn't been amused when Cat asked *one what?*

"Molly's probably ticked that Chloe met Harry first," Cat responded to Ty, catching a glimpse of George, who stood a few feet down from them watching his "wife" flirt with another man. His arms were crossed, his jaw tight. "Uh, Ty, what's up with George?"

Ty lifted a shoulder. "Probably nervous they're going to replace him with Tall, Dark, and Gorgeous. I wouldn't be surprised if they did. Georgie hasn't been himself since his wife left him last year, and it's coming through on the camera." Ty nodded at the couple dancing at the "gala." Harry in a tux and Chloe in a red formfitting gown moved around the ballroom in perfect time to the music. Her sister beamed up at the man holding her in his arms with a mesmerized look on her face. After being held in those arms, Cat understood Chloe's fascination all too well.

"The way your sister is eating up Harry with her eyes, I wouldn't put it past her to suggest that they do. And we all know they'll do anything to keep America's sweetheart happy."

Cat glanced from the beautiful, young couple to the haggard-looking George. The older man was an institution. He'd been on *As the Sun Sets* since its inception. If Chloe did what Ty thought she might, there would be one more person gunning for her sister. Cat had to make sure that didn't happen. "George is a better actor. They wouldn't replace him with Harry."

"Are you kidding? Harry's a fabulous actor. You can't pick up even a hint of his British accent. But it has nothing to do with who's the better actor. It's all about the ratings. And my bet's on the numbers going through the roof when the female viewers get a load of Harry."

"Phil won't get rid of George. They're best friends."

"In this business, friendship means nothing. Dame Alexander has been buttering Phil up all day. Look at them."

She glanced to her left. The older woman sat beside the director, petting her cat while talking to Phil, who appeared to be hanging on to her every word.

No, no, no! Cat couldn't deal with the two of them on the set every day. Everywhere she'd turned today, they were there. And they were winding her sister up. There had to be some way to get rid of them... "If word got out that Harry was gay, the female viewers wouldn't be so hot and heavy for Rand Livingstone and those ratings would fall."

"Pussy," Ty said in a strangled voice.

"You know what I mean. I'm not saying *As the Sun Sets* fans are homophobic. I'm just saying that it's hard for women to fantasize about a man when they know he's fantasizing about another man."

Ty bowed his head, pressing his hand to his mouth. She shook his arm. "Ty, I didn't mean to your hurt feelings. I don't care if you or anyone else is gay or straight..."

He looked up. He was laughing. She swatted his arm. "It's not funny. I thought I'd upset you."

Once he got his laughter under control, he put his hands on her shoulders. "Lord Harry is about as gay as I am straight."

Chapter Five

Grayson had never wanted to wrap up a case as badly as he did this one. After spending ten hours, forty-five minutes, and seven point five seconds in the company of Chloe O'Connor, he wanted to off her himself. Once she hit the set, Chloe transformed from the sweet woman he'd met this morning into a controlling, neurotic diva. He didn't know how her sister put up with her constant demands. She was cold and needed a sweater, she was hot and needed to be fanned, she was thirsty, she was... a royal pain in the ass. And until he had evidence against Cat, he was stuck shadowing her.

Because, despite sympathizing with Cat, she remained his primary suspect. Sadly for his sanity and the clock ticking down on his vacation time, the woman wouldn't make it easy for him. As he'd discovered while trapped in the closet with her, she was sharp; nothing got past her. Which he found as hot as the gun she was packing. If he was honest, he'd admit there wasn't much about the sexy ex-cop that he didn't find attractive. Including her smart mouth.

But as a special agent with ten years' experience, even though all signs pointed to Cat, he'd added four more people to his suspect list. Molly currently held second place on that list. The actress made no attempt to hide her feelings for Chloe, and the magazine clipping he'd found in Molly's dressing room had been missing several words.

Something Cat would have discovered if he hadn't slid the article up his sleeve before she patted him down. Odds were Cat had planted the evidence, but if she hadn't, she wouldn't have thought anything of it. Other than to question his reason for pocketing the article.

Chloe's agent and the daytime drama's executive producer had decided to keep the threatening letter from Cat as well as Chloe. They'd been afraid that in an effort to protect her sister, she'd shut down production. More than one person today had commented about her being protective of her sister. Unlike Chloe, Cat appeared to be well liked and respected by the cast and crew. It was the reason he'd widened his investigation.

He hadn't had an opportunity to compare the missing words in the clipping to the letter yet, but he planned to as soon as he left the studio. They'd just wrapped up filming for the day, and once he'd seen Chloe safely off the lot, he was off duty. Because of the clause in her life insurance policy that doubled the payout should she die in a work-related accident, chances were good that Chloe would be safe once she left the studio. A killer typically didn't change their MO at this stage of the game. And Cat wouldn't want to risk becoming a suspect if the accident happened at the beach house they shared without witnesses present. No, the lady was too smart for that.

As they walked off the set, Chloe looped her arm through his. "See what a little coaching can do? You did so much better the fifth time around."

"Indeed," he clipped en Brit. She'd called cut so many times that he was surprised Phil didn't toss her pretty little ass off the set.

"There's just one more teensy suggestion I'd like to make," she said with an ingratiating smile. One he was unfortunately becoming familiar with.

"Go ahead, my dear. You are the star after all." Her smile widened. So it wasn't just her sister's sarcasm she was oblivious to.

"You need to smolder more."

He cocked his head. "Smolder?"

"Yes, you want me in your bed. You need to make the audience feel your heat, your passion, your desire for me." Her pupils dilating, her red-glossed lips parting, she looked like she was having an orgasm.

Grayson held back a grimace, patting her arm as he disengaged her fingers from his sleeve. "You can be sure I'll work on that this evening. I'll practice my smoldering in front of the mirror."

Sensing someone watching him, he looked up. Cat's eyes bored into him, giving new meaning to the word *smoldering*. He wondered what he'd done to annoy her. Whatever it was, Ty, the gossip-loving hairstylist, stood behind her, appearing highly amused. In Grayson's twenty minutes in the stylist's chair, he'd learned more about what was going on behind the scenes at the daytime drama than he would have in twenty-four hours of digging on his own. It had been thanks to Ty that he'd nailed down his four other suspects.

The hairstylist would probably be surprised to learn he was included on that list. He'd given himself away when Grayson asked about yesterday's incident. Animated prior to Grayson mentioning Chloe's close call, Ty's expression had gone suspiciously blank. Grayson imagined he himself had worn a similar expression when, a few moments later, he learned that Cat had planned to leave her sister's employ that very same day. Probably, he surmised, because she assumed her employer would be dead.

But Ty had been "over the moon" that the "accident" had changed his darling Pussy's plans. And it was that reaction that had landed him on Grayson's suspect list. In an attempt to keep his best friend from leaving, it was possible Ty had ensured she stay around to protect her sister. A sister for whom Ty made no attempt to hide his contempt.

"Here comes Dame Alexander." Chloe nibbled on her bottom lip as she once again clutched his sleeve. "I'm so nervous, my legs are shaking. Do you think she'll critique my performance? I don't know what I'll do if she didn't like it." She waved her hand in front of her face. "I feel awfully warm. I need my sister."

He had to calm her down before she sent Cat to look for her pills. They currently resided in his dressing room. He lifted her delicate hand to his lips. Deepening his voice and accent, he said, "You were brilliant. If anything, Estelle will tell you your talent is wasted on a daytime drama. You belong on the big screen, my dear." He stroked his thumb along the inside of her wrist in an effort to relax her.

She looked up at him with a hopeful expression on her face. "Do you really think so?"

"Trust me, I've been in this business long enough to recognize true talent. And you are a natural." She was. And while for the better part of the day she'd also been a spoiled, demanding diva, he found her current insecurity oddly endearing.

He released her hand when her pulse slowed, relieved to see the color returning to her cheeks. She rested her head against his shoulder. "Has anyone ever told you that you have the most calming voice, Harry? It's truly miraculous how easily you banished my nerves."

"Happy to be of service." He concentrated on keeping his own nervousness from showing. Not only because he seemed to have become the object of Chloe's affection, but because his grandmother walked toward them with a smile that reached her eyes. An unusual occurrence, and one that had him girding his loins. She was up to something. He was sure of it.

"You, my boy, are going to be a star." GG tapped his shin with her cane. "Phillip saw it straightaway. There's just a few minor issues to deal with before he offers you a three-year contract." She rubbed her cheek on Fluffy's head. "I feel ten years younger. The lights, the cameras, the action—"

Was she out of her bloody mind? "Impossible, Estelle. As you well know, I have another commitment." He'd go home, toss back half a bottle of Johnnie Walker, and pray today had all been a bad dream. If it wasn't, he was calling his cousin first thing in the morning.

"Pfft, you can—"

He had to cut her off before she blew his cover. Slipping his arm around Chloe's shoulders, he drew her close. "If it weren't for Chloe's coaching, I would have embarrassed you. She's not only gorgeous and a brilliant actress, she's generous with her talent and advice."

Chloe put a hand on her chest and gazed up at him adoringly. "Oh, Harry, that's the sweetest thing anyone I have ever worked with has said to me."

He imagined it was. His grandmother's calculating gaze moved from him to Chloe. "You're right, Harry. I'm thinking too small. With the chemistry you two have, you should be on the big screen. You'll be the next Bogart and Bacall."

"Burton and Taylor," Chloe chimed in, sliding out from under his arm to loop hers through his grandmother's.

GG patted Chloe's hand. "Yes, I can see it now. You'll just have to learn to emote, my boy."

"That's exactly what I said, Dame Alexander. And did you think perhaps he needs to be more aggressive, commanding? He seemed a little effeminate."

Grayson had been looking at the concrete floor, wondering how the conversation had gone so quickly from bad to worse, when he clued in to what Chloe said. His head jerked up. *What the bloody hell did she mean by that?*

"Yes, exactly." *Effeminate . . . him?* "You have a good eye, my dear. A very good eye," his grandmother said as the two of them walked away with their heads together, leaving him staring after them.

"Lord Harry." Molly sauntered toward him wearing a short clingy black dress that showed off her voluptuous curves. "We haven't been formally introduced."

"Not formally, but I think our near-kiss in the men's room qualifies as an introduction." That had been an interesting scene.

"Yes, damn that Tessa for interrupting us." She laughed,

then winked. "Tomorrow I may do some improvising to make sure we're not interrupted again."

"Jolly good." *Jolly good?* Why did he keep saying that? He sounded like an idiot. "Call me if you need help hiding the body."

She snorted, her scarlet-painted lips turning up. "I think I like you, Lord Halstead."

"Harry."

"Harry it is. You know, I'm available anytime you want to go over your lines."

"Thanks for the offer. I may take you up on it."

"I hope you do." Her eyes did a slow tour of his body. "And I mean that."

He shoved his hands in his pants pockets, watching her walk away with a subtle sway of her hips. Might not be a bad idea to hang out with Molly. Befriending a suspect had worked well for him in the past. It was a good way to break down their defenses. And thinking about built-up defenses had him glancing to where he'd last seen Ty and Cat. *More like impenetrable*, he thought as he headed in their direction. He liked a good challenge.

* * *

"I don't know what you're upset about. All I did was ask Harry for dinner. It's not like I expect you to stick around, you know," her sister said as Cat pulled up to the beach house.

All she'd wanted to do after the day from hell was go for a run and clear her head before looking over her notes from today. But no, Chloe had to open her big mouth and invite his lordship home for dinner. Tall, Dark, and Annoying. Who was not gay. She hadn't believed Ty until

she'd checked out Harry's social media accounts. There
were so many pictures of Harry and his harem of beauty
queens on Instagram that Hugh Hefner would be jealous.
The entire male population of California would be jealous. The guy was a total player.

So would she leave him alone with her sister? Not on
your life.

"Once you tidy the house and get dinner on, you can go
for a run. Maybe to Santa Monica?"

Unbelievable. With a snap of her wrist, Cat shut off
the engine. "Pizza or Thai, take your pick. And I cleaned
the house last night." Until two in the morning while she
tried to figure out who was out to hurt Chloe and how to
protect her.

"How uncouth can you be? You do not offer a member
of the British aristocracy takeout, Kit Kat." Chloe opened
the passenger-side door. "It's only seven. That gourmet
market on Hawthorne should still be open. Maybe a lobster
bisque with a cheese brochette and a mixed green salad."
Her sister gave a decisive nod. "Yes, that will be perfect."

"I can buy all that there?" What was she saying? She
got out of the SUV. "I'm tired, Chloe. It's been a long day.
If you can find a gourmet place that will deliver, go for it.
Otherwise, it's pizza."

Her sister stood by the front of the Range Rover, tapping
her foot with an annoyed expression on her face. "Honestly,
Kit Kat, I can't believe how ungrateful you are. Since you
have free room and board, the least you can do, when I ask,
which I very rarely do, is accede to my wishes without an
argument."

That stung. Cat had her pride, and it wasn't like Chloe
was paying her a crapload of money. She was making half

of what she did with the Denver PD. But she hadn't taken the job because of the money. She'd needed to get away from Colorado and lick her wounds. Spending time with her sister had been an added bonus. Or so she'd thought at the time.

"You take room and board out of my salary, Chloe. I also look after the grounds, clean the house, do your laundry, and cook the meals. So don't make it sound as if I'm mooching off you, because I'm not." She stabbed the lock button on the key fob and opened the back gate.

"Don't be so dramatic. You make it sound as if you're Cinderella and I'm the evil stepsister."

Clearly Cat was not Cinderella material, but lately her sister was the poster child for evil stepsister. Chloe must have caught Cat's if-the-shoe-fits expression because she continued. "If I had all the time you do, I'd cook and clean, too. But I don't. You know how busy I am."

Sure, her sister had public appearances, and her campaign for her new perfume, Chloe, kept her busy. But really... "Right, and I don't have a life. That's what you're implying, isn't it?"

"Well, it's true. You don't..." Chloe sighed as she followed Cat up the flagstone path. "I'm sorry. I'm just nervous Harry is coming over. I want to make a good impression. I...I think I might be in love with him."

Cat looked up at the stars blinking in the night sky. "You've known him for less than twenty-four hours, Chloe." Opening the door to the bungalow, she stepped inside and turned to the wall, punching in the code on the panel. As Chloe came up behind her, Cat did a quick scan of the living room, dining room, and kitchen in the open-concept space. Anyone with a modicum of skill could bypass the alarm.

"It was love at first sight. He's everything I want in a man. And you know how I knew?"

"No, Chloe, how did you know?" Cat asked, only half listening as she moved through the house and eyed the deck leading down to the beach and ocean through the sliding doors. Everything seemed to be as it should.

"Why are you doing that? You're acting weird again."

"I'm not acting weird. And if you don't mind, I want to grab a shower and get changed." Once she searched the bedrooms. She was hot and sweaty from keeping her jacket on all day. Tomorrow, she'd wear a leg holster.

"Oh, okay. If you have a white shirt and black pants, that would work."

She turned to the living room. Chloe had her back to her, plumping the petal-pink cushions on the white sectional. "Work for what?"

Chloe glanced over her shoulder. "Don't throw a hissy fit, but I need you to serve dinner. Then you can do whatever you want."

"Serve you?"

"Yes, serve us. It wouldn't be proper for me to. Harry's a lord. He's used to being waited on by servants, and I want him to be comfortable."

She couldn't be serious. "How about I wear that maid's costume you wore to Phil's Halloween party?"

Chloe blew her a kiss. "You're the best. I knew you'd understand. Thanks, Kit Kat."

*   *   *

Cat's wardrobe choice of black leggings, black oversized T-shirt, and fuzzy black cat slippers—a gift from her sister six months earlier, when they'd been speaking, which they currently weren't—hadn't gone over well with Chloe. Nor had Cat's explanation of what constituted sarcasm. Hence the no-speaking thing. Which Cat had to admit she welcomed.

Chloe, banging around in the kitchen, didn't hear the doorbell chime. "His Highness has arrived," Cat called from where she sat cross-legged on the sectional looking over her notes on her iPad.

Either her sister was ignoring her or indulging in her favorite pastime; listening to an audiobook. Cat sighed and placed her iPad on the white pine coffee table. Crossing the ten feet to the door, she opened it. Her jaw dropped at the sight that greeted her, and she fought the urge to press a hand to her chest and utter an *oh, my*. While a man wearing an expensive, well-tailored suit did it for Chloe, the man standing on the front stoop in a black leather jacket, white button-down shirt, and well-worn jeans did it for Cat.

The porch light shone down on his dark, wind-tousled hair, illuminating the smile on his handsome face. A smile that reminded her of the one he'd given her sister this morning and had Cat glancing over her shoulder to see if Chloe was behind her. She wasn't.

Harry arched an eyebrow when she turned back to him. "Hello—"

Interrupting him before he could ruin the moment by calling her Kit Kat or Pussy, she said, "Cat." She wanted to drink him in without her temper spoiling the view. At least for a couple more seconds. No doubt they'd return to their adversarial relationship soon enough. Which she began to think might be a good thing, since she'd sworn off men for the next couple of years. Or at least until she trusted her judgment again.

He drew a bouquet of tiger lilies from behind his back and handed them to her. "We seem to have gotten off on the wrong foot, Cat. I was hoping we could start over."

She stared at the extravagant arrangement, then looked up at him. "For me?"

He gave her a toe-curling smile. "For you."

"I—I don't know what to say. They're beautiful. Thank you." She meant it. Her ex hadn't been a hearts-and-flowers kind of guy. The last man who'd given her flowers had been her father. They'd arrived the day she made detective. Three weeks later he died.

"My goodness, would you let him in?" her sister said, coming up behind Cat. "Sorry, you'll have to excuse my sister's... Oh, Harry, they're exquisite. Thank you." Chloe went to take the bouquet from Cat.

She clutched the flowers possessively to her chest. "They're mine." She felt like a seven-year-old being asked to share her favorite toy.

Chloe gave a shocked laugh, obviously as surprised by Cat's reaction as she was. "Kit Kat, don't be ridiculous. You're embarrassing your..." She tugged on the flowers and Cat tugged back.

Harry neatly inserted himself between them, ending their silent tug-of-war. With a gallant bow, he handed her sister a single pink sweetheart rose. "For you, Chloe. A perfect flower for a perfect woman."

"Oh, I see. Thank you, Harry. It's... lovely. Please, come in. I didn't hear the doorbell." She shot Cat an accusatory stare. "I was busy getting our dinner ready."

"I can see that. You have a touch of"—Harry leaned in, wiping away the strategically placed white powder—"flour on your cheek. I hope you didn't go to too much trouble on my account."

Her sister was too much, Cat thought with a mental eye roll. Chloe wore a black apron—with a pink sparkly crown above the word *Diva* (fitting)—over a flirty pink dress.

She gave Cat a zip-it look as Harry toed off his loafers. Probably worried Cat would spill her secret that the gourmet shop did indeed do takeout. She wouldn't, of course. Though, admittedly, she was tempted to.

Chloe led Harry to the glass dining room table decorated with a fall-themed table setting that was left over from last week's Thanksgiving dinner. It had been depressing with just the two of them to celebrate the holiday. Cat had cheered herself up with the knowledge she'd at least be home for Christmas this year.

Gesturing for Harry to take a seat, Chloe said, "No trouble at all. I love to cook. I made my favorite, lobster bisque."

Harry glanced from the two place settings to Cat. "Aren't you joining us?"

"No, she has work to do." Chloe waved her fingers at Cat. "You can grab a bowl and have it in your room."

"Please join us. I insist."

Because her sister was ticking her off, Cat said, "Sure. Don't mind if I do. I'll just put these in water." She smiled. He smiled back at her and winked. Her heart flip-flopped at the warmth in his eyes. She looked down at her chest as she walked through to the kitchen. Flip-flopping hearts were not a good sign. Maybe she should eat in her room after all.

Her sister followed her. "I don't want you to eat with

us. Harry and I have things to discuss. Make up some excuse," Chloe whispered.

Reaching in a cupboard for a crystal vase, Cat glanced over her shoulder and said, "No."

She didn't know what had gotten into her. Typically, she acquiesced to her sister's every demand, but already today she'd refused her three times. No doubt their relationship would suffer further. Right now, she could barely bring herself to care. But she would, and for that reason, she'd eat, make polite small talk, then get back to work.

"No...no? Really, Kit Kat, I don't know what's gotten into you." Her sister drew back, her eyes widening. "You have a crush on Harry. I should have recognized the signs." Chloe placed her fingers on her mouth, giving a pitying shake of her head. "I'm sorry, Kit Kat. You can hardly expect him to be interested in you when I...He's just being polite, surely you see that."

She knew what Chloe had been about to say. How could he be interested in Cat when he had America's sweetheart throwing herself at his feet? Of course her sister was right. Cat ignored the pinch of what could only be embarrassment. For the space of a heartbeat, when he'd given her the flowers, she'd wondered if he was interested in her. "I'm not interested in Harry or anyone else."

"I'm glad to hear it. I couldn't bear to see you hurt again. Not after what Michael did to you."

Cat chanced a glance at Harry, who appeared more interested in his phone than what was going on in the kitchen. But she couldn't shake the feeling he'd been listening intently to their conversation. Once again, she was struck by the thought there was more to Lord Harry Halstead than met the eye. "Keep it down, Chloe."

"All right. Help me serve the soup."

Twenty minutes into the meal, Cat discovered she was right. There was more to Harry. He was neither as stuffy nor snotty as she'd first suspected. He was interesting and had a wonderful self-deprecating humor that she appreciated. Chloe didn't. She took him to task for making fun of his title and the class system in England.

And if the sullen look on her sister's face was anything to go by, she didn't like the new direction the conversation had taken, either. They'd been talking about downhill skiing for the last five minutes. "Bear Valley's okay, but it can't compete with the slopes in Colorado," Cat said.

Harry leaned back in his chair. "Have you tried heli-skiing?"

"Yes." Cat nodded, wiping her mouth with the napkin. "It's incredible. Nothing like it. Boarding, too." But what was more incredible was what his deep voice and that accent of his were doing to her. She'd happily listen to him read a phone book for hours on end. Why it had had the opposite effect on her this morning, she didn't know.

"Really? I've only tried heli-skiing once. You should—"

Her sister touched his arm, interrupting him. "Harry, I have some wonderful news."

He drew his intent blue gaze from Cat and smiled at Chloe. "Very rude of us for excluding you from the conversation, my dear. Please, tell us your news."

Yes, Harry wasn't what he seemed. She wondered if her sister noticed the hint of sarcasm in his voice. Ah, it appears that she did. Cat's earlier explanation must have sunk in.

Chloe's brow puckered. "I wasn't—" she began, then rubbed her forehead, because God forbid she'd get a line. "I just thought you'd be interested to know that I've contacted the head writer, and he's going to consider killing off George. Isn't that the best news?"

"No," both Cat and Harry said at almost the same time. They looked at each other for a beat, then Harry said to her sister, "Chloe, no matter what Estelle says, I'm not interested in anything more than a short-term role."

"But I thought..."

He patted her sister's hand. "Yes, I know what you thought. But I'm not about to get George tossed on a whim. He doesn't deserve that. He's been with the show from the beginning."

"I assure you, it's not a whim, Harry," her sister said tightly.

Harry's defense of George elevated him further in Cat's estimation. She felt sorry for George. Sure he'd been off his game, but hadn't they all been off their game at one time or another? "Harry's right, Chloe. The writers just have to bump up George's story line."

"Be quiet, Kit Kat. You don't know what you're talking about." Chloe pushed back from the table. "If it's not too much to ask, you can do the cleanup. Harry and I have a scene to go over."

"I'll give you a hand, Cat," Harry said as he picked up his plate and stood.

"Thanks, but I'm good." She reached across the table and took the plate from him, the tips of her fingers brushing his as she did. She wasn't prepared for the electrical charge from that brief touch. She'd touched a heck of a lot more than the tips of his fingers this morning and didn't have the same reaction. Her girl parts objected. Okay, so obviously she'd reacted, but this was different. A worrisome different.

As Cat rinsed off the dishes, she did her best to ignore Harry and Chloe sitting thigh-to-thigh on the sectional across the room. She didn't like the small, telling clench in her stomach. Yes, Harry was incredibly hot, his accent amazing, and he was nice, kind even, but she wasn't attracted to him. Not in that way. She thought guys who made a living pretending to be someone else were sort of weird.

She hummed to drown out their voices as they read the script. A love scene, from the sounds of it. She pushed the lever to increase the water pressure and rinsed the bowl, then turned to put it in the dishwasher. Her gaze was unconsciously drawn to the now-quiet couple. They were locked in a passionate embrace. Cat gasped as the bowl slipped from her fingers. She caught it at the same time she looked up to see Harry's eyes on her.

Chapter Six

Obviously Cat's return visit to his lordship's Instagram account last night had done the trick. She didn't have a single lustful thought or jealous twinge as she watched Harry and Chloe make out in the Harts' richly appointed living room. Well, she hadn't until Harry wrapped Chloe's long hair around his fist to draw her sister's head back.

Cat went up on her tiptoes and leaned to the right. Oh yeah, that was...hot. She caught herself raising a hand to fan herself and cast a furtive glance to her left and right. Okay, she was good; no one was paying any attention to her.

And surely there was no harm in one small, lustful thought. Any woman with eyes in her head and a functioning libido would be thinking the same thing. *Take me, please, Har...Rand. Now, on the floor, on the...* Dammit. She drew her phone from her jeans pocket and once again pulled up Harry's Instagram account. It didn't work. She kept picturing herself in place of the other women.

What she needed was some distance, a breath of fresh air. But just as she was weighing the pros and cons of taking a break—her sister's safety in the cons, her wavering determination to keep her distance from Harry in the pros—she heard a whizzing sound from behind her and glanced back. A heavy equipment boom was headed directly for her. She dropped to the concrete floor and covered her head in case it fell. It didn't.

Oh, God, Chloe. Cat lifted her head, opening her mouth to yell a warning. She was too late, but Harry saw the boom hurtling toward them and dove out of its way with Chloe in his arms. Landing on the oriental carpet, he rolled them toward the cameras, his body lying protectively over her sister's. The boom crashed into the wall and fell. If Harry had chosen the opposite direction, they'd be buried under the heavy piece of equipment.

Cat's arms and legs felt like rubber, and it took a moment for her to get to her feet. With the speed and trajectory of the boom, her sister would have taken a crippling blow to the back of her neck. She could have died, and that was on Cat. She needed to find out who was behind the "accidents," and she needed to find out now.

She scanned the faces of the cast and crew, looking for something, anything that would give them away. George crouched beside Harry, who held her pale and sobbing sister in his arms. Dame Alexander joined them, looking as distraught as Chloe. Cat could hear Harry's deep voice as he comforted her sister. He appeared to be doing a better job at calming Chloe than Cat or her fake pills had ever done. *Good.* Because as long as her sister was safe and in capable hands, Cat could get to work.

She focused once again on George. He got to Chloe too

quickly and from the opposite side. Unless he had a partner, it couldn't have been him. And he appeared visibly shaken, furious when he looked in the direction from which the boom had come. Then again, he was an actor. Continuing to search the faces of the cast and crew now surrounding the couple on the ground, she saw Molly standing outside the circle. As though she sensed Cat's attention, the actress looked back, frowned, then turned away.

Retrieving her cell from where it had fallen on the floor, Cat made a note of Molly's and George's reactions on her phone while she walked toward Sam, the boom operator. The set and crew managers were already there, as was Phil. Sam appeared agitated, spearing his fingers through his shaggy, blond hair. Surfer dude all the way, the guy was usually cool and laid-back. Half the time, he appeared to be in his own world. *Stoned?* Cat wondered. She needed to take a closer look at Sam.

"I'm telling you, I did an equipment check this morning. Everything was good, man," Sam said.

The four men turned to Cat as she approached. She had to be careful not to alert them or anyone else to her suspicions. But she wanted answers. "Any idea what happened?" she asked, paying close attention to their body language, watching for signs of guilt.

Phil rested a hand on her shoulder. "Not yet. But we'll get to the bottom of this, Cat."

"Second-rate equipment is the problem. Half this stuff hasn't been upgraded since the show first aired ten years ago," the set manager said.

"That's what I've been telling you, man. No one's listening to me. I've got two boom mics and two cameras down."

"All right, Sam. We'll wrap up for the day, and I want

every piece of equipment rechecked, with two of you signing off on it," Phil said.

"So we have to miss the party because of this? Geez, how many times do I have to tell you it was an accident." They were celebrating Phil's sixtieth birthday at the Castaway restaurant that night.

But no matter what Sam said, this wasn't an accident. She searched his tanned face, and he avoided meeting her eyes. Something to hide, or did he feel bad the accident had happened on his watch?

Ty rushed to her side. "Are you all right? That thing nearly took off your head."

He'd seen it happen. She shouldn't be surprised. Nothing got past Ty. She needed another pair of eyes and ears on the set. Her gut said she could trust Ty. Deep down she knew he'd never put her in danger. But she'd screwed up so bad with Michael that she hadn't trusted her instincts in a while. And with her sister's life on the line . . . She glanced at Chloe. Cat had to take the risk.

"I'm good, but I could use a glass of water." Taking Ty's hand, she moved to walk away.

Phil snagged her by the arm. "Cat, are you sure you're all right? I didn't realize—"

"I'm fine, Phil. Honest," she added when he gave her a concerned look.

"All right. You're coming to the party tonight, I hope."

Chloe hadn't mentioned that she'd been invited. But with the latest attempt on her sister's life, Cat wasn't leaving her side. "Wouldn't miss it." She nodded at the other men, then led Ty away. Once they were out of earshot, she released his hand and whispered, "Okay, now tell me exactly what you saw?"

"Well, the . . ." His eyes widened behind his red-framed glasses. "You don't think it was an accident. Oh my God!" He pressed his hands to his chest. "Is someone trying to hurt you?"

"Keep your voice down. Not me; Chloe."

"Oh." He shrugged. "As long as it's not you."

She rubbed her forehead with the tips of her fingers. "Ty, I'm serious. I need your help, and you can't breathe a word of this to anyone. Got it?"

"Got it." He drew his thumb and forefinger across his lips, then his eyes lit up. "Oh my God, you want me to help you on a case. A real-life investigation with killers and everything. This is so totally rad. I can't wait to tell—" He rolled his eyes. "Not now, after we solve the case. So who am I, Sherlock or Holmes?"

She was beginning to think she'd made a big mistake. Ty's eyebrows shot up as he looked past her. "Uh-oh, Tall, Dark, and A Hundred Tons of Pure Gorgeousness is not looking happy. And all that smoldering unhappiness is directed at *you*." He sighed. "I wish he'd look at me like that."

"What are you talking . . ." She trailed off when she turned her head and met Harry's penetrating stare.

His long, elegant stride brought him quickly to their side. "Sorry to interrupt your tête-à-tête, but as Chloe only moments ago narrowly avoided being decapitated, I think she could use her sister," he clipped out.

Cat didn't miss the cutting, sarcastic tone or the glint of anger in his ice-blue eyes. But she couldn't tell him the truth. "I hardly think she needs me when she has you, Harry. Thank you, by the way. A little incident like that would typically send my sister into hysterics. You're good for her." It was true. Why that caused her chest to spasm with a small twinge of regret, she didn't want to think about. And she didn't have time to.

"I hardly think a boom nearly taking off your sister's head qualifies as a *little incident*."

Ty puffed out his chest and put his arm around her. "The boom nearly took off Cat's head, and you don't see her crying and making a scene."

"I see." And the way his eyes roamed her face, it was as though he did. "Was that the reason you didn't call out a warning?"

Her eyes narrowed. She didn't like what he seemed to be implying. "I was about to, but you had matters under control by then."

"He so did, didn't he? I've never seen anything like it. Well, other than in a James Bond movie. The way you rolled Chloe out of danger, protecting her with your body." Ty rubbed his chest with his open fingers, staring at Harry as if imagining that tall, muscular frame blanketing him.

She glared at Ty. He'd gotten over his anger at how Harry had spoken to her pretty darn quick. The ho.

She looked beyond Harry to see her sister approaching with the help of two grips while Dame Alexander, who'd been following behind, raised her cane to flag down Phil. Chloe sagged against Harry when she reached his side. "I've been looking all over for you."

He smiled down at her. "I just came to get you a glass of water. How are you holding up?"

"Better now that I'm with you."

Cat stifled a groan at the look of hero worship in her sister's eyes. "Chloe, why don't I take you to your dressing room and make you a cup of tea?" She'd talk to Ty later. Right now, she had to break the spell Harry had cast on Chloe.

"Don't trouble yourself. I'll see to your sister."

Cat's back went up at his tone of voice. "That's not—"

Her sister stared at her, a look of betrayal in her eyes. "Harry was there when I needed him. You weren't. You'd rather be hanging out with your *friend* than protecting me. If that's any indication of how you did your job, no wonder you were fired."

She flinched, feeling as though her sister had slapped her.

Harry looked at Cat. She pressed her lips together, averting her eyes. She felt his momentary hesitation before he led Chloe away.

"What a biatch. I hate her so much. I hope someone does knock her off."

"Ty, don't..." Though she could hardly berate him when, at that moment, on top of the hurt and embarrassment, she felt the same. She sensed someone looking at her. From across the room, Harry's piercing blue eyes held hers, then moved to Ty. He'd heard him.

*   *   *

Pretending to be absorbed in the view, Grayson relaxed in a chair with his legs stretched toward the open fire pit. The restaurant was set in the hills and the night lights of the city twinkling below them were spectacular, but it was the woman sitting on her own on the opposite side of the outdoor patio that held his attention. She was pretty damn spectacular, too.

In the glow from the decorative white lights wrapped around the base of a palm tree behind her, Cat's dark, choppy hair gleamed. The high neck of a black, sleeveless dress framed her stunning face and showed off her toned arms. Just as the knee-high black leather boots she wore accentuated her long legs. He shifted in the chair, dragging his gaze back to her face before he started imagining how those legs would feel wrapped around his waist. She got to him. No matter how much he pretended she didn't, she did. It's why he'd overreacted this afternoon.

The night before, he'd seen another side of Cat, one he wanted to explore further. He'd convinced himself he'd been wrong about her. The more time he spent with Cat, the less he saw her as a suspect. So her behavior after Chloe's accident pissed him off. Made him doubt himself, doubt his ability to do his job. Just like Valeria, he figured Cat had played him.

He'd seen her, standing off to the side watching them film the scene, but he hadn't realized she'd been in the line of the boom until Ty brought it to his attention. A cold, hard knot had tightened in his gut at the thought she could have been hurt, but at the same time, she was back on the top of his suspect list, so he'd been decidedly unsympathetic. With the help of a partner, she could have been behind the accident. And if she had a partner, it would be Ty—which explained why she nearly got knocked off, too.

It was obvious the hairstylist would do anything for Cat. He'd heard what Ty said after Chloe had delivered her cutting remark. Grayson might have given Ty's threat more weight if he hadn't been feeling the same way. A sentiment that had him calling himself all kinds of foolish at the time.

But earlier this evening he'd gotten a call from his cousin with news that caused Grayson both frustration and relief. Cat's prints weren't on the magazine article, and only one of the missing words matched with the threatening letter—not enough to hold up as evidence. Also, the results were back on the contents of Chloe's prescription: they were sugar pills. So while he was relieved to find nothing that directly linked Cat to the case, he was frustrated at how little progress he'd made. He swirled the ice in his glass of scotch as his gaze drifted back to her.

She seemed as relaxed as he pretended to be. But like him, it was an act. He could see the tension in her upper body; she was on full alert, clocking Chloe's every move. Which meant, at the moment, those gorgeous green eyes were focused three tables over, where Chloe and his grandmother huddled with Phil. No doubt pushing for George's untimely demise, since Grayson hadn't been invited to participate in the conversation.

At the thought, he shifted his attention to Molly and the distinguished-looking actor sitting at the table with her. Neither of whom looked happy and were drowning their sorrows in mimosas at the same time shooting apprehensive glances at Phil's table. Grayson lifted the glass to his mouth as he considered his two suspects, then movement by the railing drew his attention. His other two suspects were involved in a spirited conversation. At least Ty was. Sam, on the other hand, appeared to be drinking for two.

Grayson angled his head to get a better look at what Ty was doing. He appeared to be sending hand signals to...Cat. She gave an almost imperceptible shake of her head at the hairstylist, who gave her a thumbs-up. Ah, so definitely partners, but one she perhaps didn't want, he thought as she pinched the bridge of her nose. Something he'd noticed she did when she was frustrated.

He could relate. He had a partner he didn't want, either. Even more so after today. His grandmother had taken it upon herself to share her suspicions about Cat with Phil.

Now the director wanted Cat barred from the set. He'd done his best to reassure Phil, but the man was understandably upset after today. Grayson would have preferred to leave GG at home, but Chloe was making him uncomfortable, so he'd brought her along.

Catching Cat's fleeting glance in his direction, he decided to join the woman who was making him uncomfortable for a very different reason. As he left his table for hers, he assured himself it was for the good of the investigation.

"Cat," he said, pulling out the chair across from her.

"Your Highness." She took a sip from her glass, avoiding eye contact.

Ah, so they were back to that, were they. He couldn't say he blamed her after how he'd treated her this afternoon. "What are you doing sitting over here by yourself?"

"I'm on duty. Soda water and lime," she said in response to his pointed look at her drink.

"I owe you an apology. I didn't realize you had a close call yourself. I wouldn't have been so hard on you had I known."

"Well, you weren't the only who thought I screwed up." She raised her glass and gave him a tight smile.

"I'm sure after you explained to Chloe what happened, she understood and apologized."

"You don't know my sister very well, do you?"

Not as well as Chloe would have him know her, that's for damn sure. One more reason he had to wrap up this case ASAP. "Not as well as you, obviously." He tugged at his shirtsleeves, faking a sheepish smile. "Cat, perhaps you can enlighten me. When we reached your sister's dressing room, she felt faint and asked for her pills. I'm a little embarrassed to admit, after today's accident, I was rather shaken myself and I . . . Well, I took one."

She pressed her lips together, her eyes sparkling with laughter. He had a hard time holding back a smile in response, but he was playing the part of the embarrassed, bumbling lord. Once she had her amusement under control, she said, "You took one of my sister's pills?"

"Um, yes." He scratched the back of his neck. "It was poorly done of me, I know. But I was a bloody nervous wreck." He mentally rolled his eyes. If the guys at the Bureau could see him now . . .

"Really? You didn't look fazed at all. In fact, you responded like a guy who made a living rescuing damsels in distress."

His heart gave an extra thump. He didn't think she'd made him, but he couldn't be sure. "Pfft, you're too kind." And he was an idiot. "But back to the pills." He leaned into her. God, she smelled good, a sultry citrus scent that had him wanting to bury his face in her long, graceful neck.

Her eyebrows raised. "You were saying?"

"Right, yes, the pills." He lowered his voice. "They were very sweet and didn't do a thing for me."

She laughed—a sexy, husky laugh—and leaned into him. "That's because they're sugar pills."

"Really?" They were close. So close that their knees touched under the table, and he could see flecks of yellow in her green eyes. "But Chloe has a heart condition, surely she—"

Cat drew back as if the mere mention of her sister had broken the moment between them. And they had been having a moment, of that he had no doubt. Just as he couldn't deny he wanted more moments with her. Preferably in his bed.

"The only condition my sister has is in her head." She winced, wiping some imaginary crumbs off the white tablecloth. "I shouldn't have said that. Chloe's an actress, she's emotional and high-strung."

Even after her sister treated her like crap, she was still trying to protect her. He wondered if anyone protected Cat. "Aw, the placebo effect. Brilliant."

She gave him a half smile. "My sister-in-law's idea, not mine."

"I'm sure you've had occasion to be happy she came up with it."

"You can't begin to know."

"Oh, I think I can," he was saying when Chloe called his name. He got up from the table. "Why don't you join us? It's warmer by the fire."

"Thanks, but I don't think that's a good idea. Enjoy your night, Harry." Her luscious lips tipped up at the corner, giving him a glimpse of her adorable dimple. "And stay out of my sister's pills."

As a light breeze blew dark, silky strands across her face, he curled his fingers into his palm before he gave in to the urge to brush the wispy bangs from her eyes. Instead he laughed while shrugging out of his black jacket. "I will. And if you won't come sit by the fire, at least take this."

She gave him a startled look. "That's kind of you, but—"

He draped his jacket over her shoulders, giving her a light squeeze through the fabric. "I insist."

*   *   *

Grayson's steak was good, the conversation fine, although a bit insipid and annoying at times, but he kept looking at his watch, counting down the minutes until he could politely make his escape. If he was sitting with Cat, he'd gladly stay all night. It grated seeing her eating alone. He'd mentioned it to Chloe for all the good that did him.

Just as he thought to hell with being polite, he caught movement at the far end of the patio. So did Cat. She was up and out of her chair before he'd processed what warranted the reaction. People stopped eating at the sound of her sharp command. When she pulled a gun from her purse, those same people gasped. Cat ignored everything but the man in her sights and got in position, right arm straight out, left hand holding it steady, feet shoulder-width apart. Grayson had never seen a woman look as hot as Cat O'Connor did at that moment.

Confident and competent, she didn't need his help, but he found himself half rising from his chair anyway. Then, at the possibility of blowing his cover, he sat down.

Chloe gaped at her sister. "What is she doing?"

"I assume she's protecting you. That is her job, is it not?"

His grandmother's eyebrows drew together at his clipped tone. He ignored her as the guy—about six one, 240—made a run for it. Everyone stood up to get a better view while Grayson mentally urged Cat not to shoot. He didn't want to arrest her. She didn't shoot. Instead, she ran and grabbed the guy by the back of his shirt, kicking his feet out from under him. Within seconds she had him flat on his stomach with his hands zip-tied behind his back.

Sweet mother of God, Grayson thought as the blood from his head went south. He grabbed the napkin from the table, draping it over his lap, and reminded himself that while she may not have been involved with the attempts on her sister's life, she had been involved with Michael Upton. And there was nothing Grayson hated more than a dirty cop. A reminder that should have effectively vanquished the image of Cat under him in his bed, but it didn't. Because he was having a hard time convincing himself that the woman he'd come to know and like had been aware of Upton's Ponzi scheme.

"Darren, Darren Smith," the guy on the ground screamed. "I'm the head of Chloe O'Connor's fan club!"

It was too dark to tell for sure, but Cat's cheeks looked flushed. He had no trouble identifying the emotion rolling off the woman sitting across from him. Chloe's eyes flashed with temper, and she opened her mouth. No doubt to eviscerate her sister in front of the cast and crew.

As he watched Cat's shoulders slump in defeat, Grayson knew what he had to do. He didn't care what anyone thought of him. Pitching his voice high, he yelled, "Rat! I saw a rat. There's . . . there's a rat under the table!" And since he already sounded like an idiot, he climbed up on the chair and shrieked, sounding surprisingly like a girl, "Two rats. There's two rats!"

He smiled inwardly when everyone, including Chloe, stampeded for the doors, forgetting all about Cat.

Chapter Seven

Snow-draped pine and ash trees whizzed by the tinted windows of the limo as Cat counted down the miles from the Denver airport to Christmas. She couldn't wait to get home. The heavy weight she'd been carrying around the last few days lifted when they finally reached the road into town.

She smiled at the sight of the familiar pastel-painted shops decorated for the holidays, wreaths hanging from the old-fashioned streetlamps that lined the snow-dusted sidewalks. She glanced at her sister, who sat beside her in the back of the limo, to see if she had a similar reaction. It might give them something to bond over or at least talk about. Their relationship hadn't improved since the accident with the boom. If anything, it had gotten worse.

Cat's cheeks warmed at the memory of running across the patio last week with her gun drawn, taking down the head of her sister's fan club as if he were a gun-toting stalker. She didn't need Chloe to tell her she'd turned into a lunatic. At least her sister had ripped Cat's reputation to shreds in the privacy of the SUV. Not that an audience would have stopped her. Cat was lucky his lordship had an aversion to rats.

Early the next morning while Cat hid cameras on the set, Ty had entertained her with a comical impersonation of Harry's performance. It seemed Harry's "unmanly" display had lowered his hotness quotient in Ty's eyes. It had the opposite effect on Cat. The man she'd come to know and like, and maybe lust after a bit, had being trying to protect her. Or at least that's what she thought. But then everything changed two days ago when there'd been another "accident" on the set.

Harry and Chloe had been blocking out a scene at the top of the stairs when the heel of her sister's shoe snapped. If not for Harry's quick reflexes, Chloe would have hurtled to the bottom of the stairs and broke her neck. The fact that the particular shoe happened to be a Louboutin seemed to have cast Cat in a suspicious light. At least in Harry's eyes, and her interactions with his lordship had been less than cordial the last two days.

But she didn't intend to lose sleep over her up-and-down relationship with him. *Relationship?* More of an acquaintance than anything else, and an annoying one at that. Only he hadn't been annoying when he'd come to the beach house for dinner or at the restaurant last week.

She had to get a grip. She was wasting time and energy thinking about the man. Thankfully, his stint on *As the Sun Sets* would be ending soon. She wouldn't have to put up with him for much longer. He'd be easy enough to avoid in Christmas.

Her sister was another story. She couldn't avoid Chloe. And since she seemed determined to ignore Cat and continue with the silent treatment, she had to fix it. Which was typical. Chloe was way better at holding a grudge and held them often and regularly. But they were almost home, and their mother would be upset if she sensed trouble in sisterland.

"The valley looks magical this time of year, doesn't it?" The ranch, home for five generations of O'Connors, was surrounded by rocky cliffs. They owned six hundred acres of pristine wilderness bordered by the national park.

Focused on her iPad, Chloe gave a noncommittal grunt.

With a clenched-teeth smile, Cat tried a different tactic. "What are you reading?"

"A script." Chloe laid her iPad on her lap and shifted in the seat, her eyes bright with excitement. "It's amazing, Kit Kat. It's a once-in-a-lifetime role, and the director is brilliant. The project has Oscar written all over it."

This was the first time Chloe had called Cat by her nickname in a week. She didn't want to ruin their progress by stating the obvious, but it had to be said. Carefully, of course. "That's wonderful. It's what you've been working toward. As long as they're not casting the part for another year, you should definitely audition for the role."

Her sister chewed on her thumbnail. "No one needs to know."

"Chloe, you have an exclusivity clause in your contract. You can't—"

"I know, I know. And why Helga locked me into a five-year contract without removing the clause is beyond me," she said, referring to her agent. "I'm not getting any younger, you know."

Ever since Dame Alexander had arrived on the scene, Chloe had grown increasingly dissatisfied with her role as Tessa Hart. Some distance from the older woman would be good for Chloe. Cat would be glad to be rid of her, too, at least for a couple of weeks. Dame Alexander had taken an instant dislike to Cat, but there was no doubt she loved Chloe. Probably because they were so much alike.

And it didn't help that Chloe had been angsting about her age since their thirtieth birthday. It was something Cat thought about, too, not that she'd reinforce her sister's concerns with her own. She rubbed Chloe's shoulder. "You're only thirty-one, and you're America's sweetheart. Offers will be pouring in once your contract's up."

"Do you really think so?"

That was the thing about her sister, despite two daytime Emmys and thousands of adoring fans, Chloe didn't see what everyone else did. She still saw herself as the pudgy little girl with the lazy eye and overbite, who no one ever picked to be on their team. Which was probably one of the reasons Cat always forgave her. "I know so."

Chloe smiled. "Are we friends again?"

She bumped her shoulder against her sister's. "Yeah, we are."

As the limo passed through the wrought iron gates and drove up the circular drive, Cat leaned forward. Colored Christmas lights were strung along the roof line and around the windows of the Southwestern-style bungalow. Black iron planters filled with poinsettias lined the flagstone path and steps leading up to the dark Spanish-style doors framed with boughs of evergreen. "Looks like Mom decorated without us."

"Good. It takes forever to put up the lights."

"Hey, I love putting up the lights." Cat had never missed decorating the house for the holidays until she moved to California. Last year, because of a snowstorm, they'd arrived just in time for their brother and Skye's Christmas Eve wedding and their niece's birth.

"Of course you do. You're as Christmas-obsessed as the rest of them."

"Since when did you become a Scrooge?"

Chloe shrugged, her eyes downcast. Before Cat could question her sister's reaction, the limo pulled to a stop, and their mother flew out the front doors. Wearing a pair of low-riding jeans and a plaid flannel shirt with a red vest, her toffee-colored hair pulled back in a ponytail and a wide smile on her pretty face, Liz O'Connor looked a decade younger than her sixty-one years. Paul McBride, her husband of a few short months, stood in the doorway with an indulgent smile on his face. At sixty-five, with only a touch of gray at the temples of his dark hair, the man still turned the heads of women young and old.

The couple looked incredibly happy and in love now, but for a while there, it seemed unlikely they'd ever walk down the aisle. Her mom had been best friends with Paul's late wife, and Paul had been best friends with Cat's dad. But even though their spouses had been gone for years, it had taken time for them to get past their guilt over moving on with each other—time and a little help from the matchmakers in Christmas, namely Dr. McBride's aunt Nell.

Chloe flung open the limo's door, her white fur coat billowing behind her as she raced into their mother's open arms. "Oh, Mommsy, I've missed you."

Cat got out of the car, hanging back to watch the two women she loved most in the world embrace. Her throat tightened as the fear she'd been fighting over the last week swamped her. If something happened to Chloe, her mother would never recover. None of them would.

"Get over here, darling." Liz drew back from Chloe, motioning for Cat to join them. She did, taking comfort from her mother's familiar light floral scent and the strength and warmth of her arms, her sister's smile.

Everything would be okay. It would be easier to protect Chloe in Christmas. Cat wasn't alone here. She had friends she could trust to help her figure out who wanted her sister dead. Whoever was after Chloe was on Cat's turf now.

Paul came down the steps and wrapped his arms around the three of them. "Welcome home, girls. Your mother's spent the last two hours at the front window, waiting for you to arrive." He kissed Cat's and Chloe's foreheads, then gently tweaked their mother's ponytail. "Get in the house. It's freezing out, and I don't want my girls getting sick," he said as he went to help the limo driver with the luggage.

Liz sighed. "We better do as he says. You know what he's like."

Oh yeah, Cat knew exactly what he was like. Dr. McBride had a tendency to be an overprotective worrywart. She thought it was sweet. Her mother, not so much.

The three of them walked arm and arm up the steps. "Were you able to find everything I asked for, Mommsy?"

"Yes, I got every single item on your list. But I have to

tell you, I'm a little nervous about the party. We've never entertained royalty before." Her mother turned to Cat, who'd stopped moving. "Darling, what's wrong?"

Cat stared at her sister. "You never said a word about a party to me, Chloe. It's too much work for Mom. We have to cancel—"

"Don't be silly. The invitations have already gone out. Everyone in town is excited to meet Chloe's boyfriend the duke, and his manager the duchess. I can't cancel now."

Cat covered her mouth with both hands, breathing slowly in and out.

Her sister's tinkling laughter came out on a puff of frosted air. "Mommsy, Harry's a lord, and his manager is a dame."

"Duke, lord, it's all the same. They're royalty." Her mother frowned at Cat. "You have to stop worrying about me. You're getting as bad as Paul." She released the same girlish laugh as Chloe. "The poor man, I've been running him ragged. I made him paint the guest rooms and great room. I want everything perfect for their stay."

"What...what are you talking about? Whose stay?"

"Why, Chloe's boyfriend and his manager, of course. Your sister's invited them to stay at the house. Darling, what's...Paul, hurry, there's something wrong with Cat."

*   *   *

The high beams of the Range Rover Grayson had rented lit up the circular drive as he drove through the wrought iron gates of the O'Connor ranch.

Estelle leaned forward to peer past the wipers clearing the snow from the windshield. She waved her arm, the smell of moth balls wafting from the floor-length sable coat she'd insisted he get out of storage. "You play your cards right, my boy, and this could all be yours."

"GG, this is the last time I'm going to say it. I am not interested in Chloe."

Grayson didn't know why he'd brought her along. Oh, right, he did. No one else would take her while he was away. Somehow he had to convince her to stop with the matchmaking. Living under the same roof with Cat for the next ten days was going to be tough enough. Never mind Chloe. But since he was being paid to protect the actress, he had no choice. Now that they were on location, it's possible the would-be killer's MO would change.

He no longer considered Cat a primary suspect. Yesterday morning, he'd showed up early and caught her skulking around the set. He'd hung back to see what she was up to. She took down spy cameras she'd obviously installed on the individual sets. It was a good idea. One he should have thought of himself. But clearly from her disappointed expression, she wasn't any closer to solving the case than he was. He'd missed his chance to talk to her. She and Chloe left for the airport directly afterward.

Maybe it was a good thing that he did. His immediate reaction had been that they work together. They had a better chance of solving the case that way. But he had to make sure he hadn't misread her intentions. That there wasn't another reason for her to be covertly keeping an eye on the set. He couldn't show his cards just yet.

"You're interested in the other one." His grandmother sat back with a huff. "Well, you mark my words, my boy, you're making a mistake. If you were thinking with your head and not your"—she cleared her throat—"Cat

O'Connor would be at the top of your suspect list, not Molly. But now that you'll be spending more time with them, you'll see that I'm right. Chloe's the perfect woman for you. And she's rich."

He had to distract her. Give her something to keep her busy. "I don't have time to get involved with anyone. Nor do I want to. You're here to help me with the case, GG. I'll expect a daily report, so keep your eyes open and your hearing aids on."

"I'm way ahead of you, my boy," she said as she removed a watch, a pen, and what looked like a tracking device from her purse.

Pulling in behind a red pickup, he turned off the engine. "Where did you get all of this?"

"I ordered it online at Spies Are Us." With a smug smile, she held up the watch. "This is a camera, and the pen is a voice recorder."

He had no idea she even knew how to get online. "How did you pay for it?"

"I used your credit card." At his groan, she added, "Don't worry, I already expensed your cousin. You wouldn't have to worry about money if you set your sights on Chloe. This is all hers, you know."

"I highly doubt that, GG. She has a brother and sister."

"That's what she told me. And unlike her sister, Chloe doesn't lie."

Before he could respond, the doors of the stately bungalow opened and Chloe rushed down the steps, dark hair gleaming, a white fur coat around her shoulders. People started pouring out of the house behind her. An older woman with a red streak in her white hair held one end of a banner while two older men held up the other. The sign read WELCOME, YOUR HIGHNESSES, and in the background he heard "God Save the Queen" playing.

His grandmother beamed. "I think I'm going to like it here."

* * *

The woman with the red streak in her white hair, Nell McBride, hadn't left Grayson's side. "So, your manager, what's her story?" Nell asked, lifting a glass of eggnog at GG who sat holding court in an armchair beside the floor-to-ceiling limestone fireplace. Surrounded by a crowd of people who hung on her every word, she was in her glory. And occupied, which was good. Chloe sat on a stool beside her, which was even better.

"Estelle has many stories. You should join the others. I'm sure you'd enjoy hearing her tales." And he could escape.

Nell pursed her lips. "Tall ones, no doubt."

Obviously not an Estelle fan. Grayson wondered if it had anything to do with the two older men who'd been doing his grandmother's bidding since they'd arrived.

"I can spot a flimflammer from a mile away. You better be careful with that one, Harry." Her brow furrowed when his grandmother and the tall, older man in the green plaid shirt shared a laugh. "You know what, don't worry about it. I'll keep an eye on her for you."

Just want he needed, another seventy-something woman keeping an eye on things for him. And he'd bet his last dollar that Nell McBride could teach his grandmother a thing or two. He'd have to be careful around her.

Nell gave him an up-and-down look. "So, which one are you interested in?"

"Pardon me?"

"Chloe or Cat, which one of our girls does it for you?" He frowned, pretending not to understand what she meant. "Ah, haven't made up your mind yet, have you? Don't worry, I can help you out. I've known them since they were in diapers."

He had to shut her down. He didn't have the patience or energy to deal with another matchmaker. "I'm afraid I don't have time for a relationship, Ms. McBride. I'm busy with my career, honing my craft."

"Chloe," she said with a smirk. "She's the one for you. I thought Cat at first, but you're a bit of a fuddy-duddy, and you're an actor."

Two older women joined them, saving him from a response. One was tiny and heavily lined, the other tall with a white streak in the front of her long, black hair. It took some time for them to rise from their curtsies. Once they did, they extended their blue-veined hands and smiled. "Your Highness."

He didn't think he'd survive ten days of this. He'd been bowed and scraped to all night. "Please, call me Harry. And there's no need to curtsey," he said as he bent to kiss their hands.

"Thank you, your lordship. I mean, Harry." The tall one tittered. "That accent of yours must make all the girls a little giddy."

Nell rolled her eyes, then introduced him to her friends. "Harry, this is Stella Wright and Evelyn Tate. They work with me at the *Christmas Chronicle*. Our town's newspaper."

"Pleased to make your acquaintance, ladies."

"Oh, he's so polite," the tiny one, Evelyn, said, patting her chest. The three of them had on Christmas sweaters. "Did you ask him?"

"It's Chloe."

"Oh, I'd so hoped it was Cat. That horrible man broke her heart. She's such a good girl. She deserves to find a nice young man. Are you sure you won't reconsider?" Estelle asked him hopefully.

"I'm afraid Ms. McBride misunderstood. Cat and Chloe are lovely women, but I'm not interested in either one of them."

"But surely a handsome young man such as yourself—" Stella Wright began, only to be cut off by Dr. McBride who came up from behind Grayson and slung an arm around his shoulders. "Now you ladies leave poor Harry alone. Grace needs a hand."

Grayson was impressed. No sooner had the words left Dr. McBride's mouth than the three older woman toddled off to the kitchen on a mission. "Well done," he said.

Dr. McBride chuckled, reaching for a glass of eggnog from the server's tray. The woman wore a uniform of black pants and a white tuxedo shirt. Cat would have been wearing the same outfit if not for her mother interceding on her behalf. A server had called in sick, and Chloe had tried to guilt her sister into taking their place.

Grayson looked around the room. The elusive Cat was nowhere in sight. She'd barely said more than ten words to him all night. Now that he thought about it, he hadn't seen her since Phil, Molly, and George left to check in at the lodge twenty minutes ago.

"Years of experience dealing with my aunt," Dr. McBride said, handing Grayson the glass. "Who, I imagine, was up to her matchmaking tricks again."

"Yes, as a matter of fact she was. But as I told your aunt, I'm not interested in a relationship at the moment."

Dr. McBride's eyebrows drew together. "I was under the impression you and Chloe were dating."

Now, this was awkward. Chloe had made it clear she wanted a relationship with Grayson, but he'd shut her down. Politely, of course. He wondered what Cat thought when she'd heard of his supposed relationship with her sister. "Cat is . . ." Bloody hell, he needed to get the woman out of his head. "Chloe is a remarkable—"

Dr. McBride pinned him with a stepfather's protective stare, causing Grayson to second-guess his response. Remembering his first impression of Paul and Liz, he cocked his head. "I say, your wife is looking a little peaked, don't you think?"

An anxious expression replaced the protective one, and without another word, Dr. McBride headed for his wife. Grayson set his glass of eggnog on a nearby table and sprinted for the mudroom off the kitchen, then out the side door without stopping for a coat.

He heard Cat's laugh before he saw her. "Let me guess, you got cornered by the matchmakers from Christmas."

Chapter Eight

Grayson turned to where Cat sat under a red wool blanket with her boots propped on an outdoor brick fireplace. "How did you know?"

She tipped her steaming mug in his direction. "No boots, no coat, and a panicked look on your face. Seen it before."

"Mind if I join you?"

She lifted a shoulder. "Suit yourself."

Not exactly an enthusiastic invitation, but he'd take it. "Thanks." He pulled a green Adirondack chair beside her and settled in. Propping his shoes next to her boots on the brick ledge, he smiled and rubbed his arms. "Chilly, isn't it?"

Her long lashes fluttered against her pink cheeks as she briefly closed her eyes, then passed him some of her blanket. It was warm and smelled like Cat and wood smoke. "Thank you." He rubbed his hands together and nodded at her hot chocolate. "I don't suppose you'd be amenable to sharing, would you?"

"I came out here to enjoy some peace and quiet"—she reached beside her chair, handing him a thermos—"so no more talking, okay?"

A woman after his own heart. He made a zip-it motion with his fingers and unscrewed the top of the thermos, taking a sip. He choked.

She sighed, leaning over to pat his back.

He wiped the back of his hand across his mouth. "You could have warned me it was spiked."

Sitting back with a smile on her face, she closed her eyes. He gave his head a slight, amused shake. It wasn't often a woman ignored him. Then again, Cat was an unusual woman. *A stunning woman and difficult to ignore*, he thought as he took the opportunity to study her unobserved.

The crackle and pop of the fire drew his attention to the flames shooting toward the boundless night sky. He tipped his head back, admiring the stars that looked as though they'd been punched into black velvet. Breathing in the crisp, cold mountain air, he felt more relaxed and settled than he had in weeks. If he had to blow his vacation time on a job, at least it would be here instead of LA.

He sensed her looking at him. "Hard to resist its spell, isn't it?" she said when he met her gaze.

"Very." And he wasn't referring to the stars or the quarter moon hanging suspended over the snow-covered pines. "But then, why would one want to?" Because he hadn't figured her out yet. Didn't know if he could completely trust her. It's something he needed to find out. For the case, he reassured himself.

She angled her head. "You surprise me, Harry. I didn't take you for a nature lover, more the guy who hangs out at the après-ski bar."

"Ah, I take it you've lifted your moratorium. I'm allowed to speak?"

"It's a little hard to enjoy the peace and quiet when someone's staring at you. So yes, you can speak."

"I wasn't..." She arched an eyebrow. He should have known she'd sense his attention. He shrugged. "You were watching me, too."

She laughed, lifting her cup to her mouth. "So I was. You're not who you seem, Harry. I'm trying to figure you out."

"Au contraire, love. I'm an open book. Whereas you..."

"Oh, no, you don't. You're not turning this on me."

"All right, you can ask me anything you want. But first you have to answer a question of mine."

"Okay, fine. What do you want to know?"

"Who broke your heart?" He meant to throw her off balance, distract her from asking about him, but as soon as he asked the question, he knew it was more than that.

She gave him a startled look, then covered her reaction with a frown. "I don't know what—"

"Evelyn said you had a broken heart. She thought I might be able to help you with that."

She snorted. "I hope you told her you weren't interested."

He forced himself to nod. "I did. I told the three of them I'm not looking for a relationship." He wasn't sure if the flicker of emotion that crossed her face was disappointment or relief. "I'm a good listener, Cat. It's a small town. You know I'm going to hear about it. I'd rather hear about it from you."

She bowed her head, then lifted it to look across the open field. "You're right, you will. I'm surprised Chloe hasn't already filled you in." She glanced at him, twisting her mouth to the side as though weighing out her words. "I used to be a detective with the Denver Police Department. I met Michael while I was investigating what we suspected at the time was a murder, but later was ruled the suicide of his business partner. And no, I didn't get involved with him until after the case was closed."

He held up a hand. "I didn't say anything." But he planned to say something to Special Agent in Charge Turner. Grayson wanted to know more about Michael Upton's business partner and his alleged suicide.

"I saw the look of disapproval on your face. Anyway, Michael wouldn't take no for an answer. He could be very persuasive and persistent. He was also handsome and charming, and I fell in love with him. I thought he loved me, too, but looking back, I realize he loved himself and money more. He was running a Ponzi scheme out of his office in our home, my home." She gave her head a quick, disgusted shake. "And I didn't have a clue. Me, the youngest female detective in the Denver Police Department, didn't have a clue what was going on right under my nose."

He believed her. Her words were as convincing as the manner in which she delivered them, her posture and tone of voice. But he had to push a little harder if he was going to lay out a case in her defense to Turner. "Surely there were signs the wanker was up to no good."

"Maybe there were, but obviously I missed them." She cupped her mug between her hands. "We were having problems, and I was working a lot."

"What kind of problems?"

"The wedding was a few months away. I wanted a pre-nup, he didn't."

"I see."

"Yeah, too bad I didn't. I lost everything because of him, a job I loved, my home."

"Why did you lose your job? Surely no one believed you were in on the fraud."

"Not everyone, no. My family, my captain, some of the guys on the force gave me their full support. But there were enough of them who didn't, including my partner and the FBI. In the end, I didn't have the energy to fight. The FBI never stopped hounding me. And I'd lost faith in myself, in my judgment."

He understood how that felt and sympathized with her. He took her hand, rubbing his thumb over her knuckles. "I'm sorry, Cat."

She shrugged, but didn't remove her hand from his. "Crap happens to everyone. It could have been worse, I guess."

"It must have blown over by now. You could get your job back."

She released a bitter laugh. "As far as the FBI is concerned, the file is still open on me. Besides, I can't leave Chloe, not... not until she can find someone to replace me."

Ah, so she did realize her sister was in danger. He could work with Cat. They'd make a good team. Though given her history with the FBI, it might not be wise to tell her who he really was, at least not right away. "Cat, there's something I need..." He trailed off at the sound of a door opening.

Nell McBride popped her head around the corner of

the house and yelled, "I found him. He and Cat are canoo-
dling by the fire."

*   *   *

Cat tore her hand from Harry's, sloshing hot chocolate on
the blanket. She jerked her gaze to where Nell stood at the
side of the house, grinning. "You can go back inside, Nell.
We'll be right in. Harry...Harry was...Just go inside,
okay?"

"Are you all right, love? You didn't burn yourself, did
you?" Harry asked, sounding concerned.

Shaking off the blanket as she prayed to God her sister hadn't heard Nell, Cat jumped to her feet. "No, it was
cold." She lowered her voice. "And stop calling me love.
You'll give her the wrong idea."

"You mean *them.* Nell's friends have joined her." He
leaned into Cat, taking the blanket from her hands. "Do
you think perhaps you're overreacting a tad? They're
three harmless old ladies. What—"

She turned, and sure enough, Evelyn and Stella stood
with Nell. Cat latched on to a corner of the blanket, saying, "Harmless? Keep it up, mate, and you'll see how
harmless they are."

His perfect, even white teeth flashed.

"You think it's funny, don't you? Believe me, you won't
if they get it in their heads that"—she motioned between
them—"you and I are a perfect match. They're like heat-
seeking missiles. They won't give up until the job is done."

He lifted a shoulder, his mouth quirked. "I can think of
worse things."

They both looked up when they heard Chloe say,
"What's going on out here?"

Cat briefly closed her eyes. She knew that tone of voice. She was going to pay, and pay big-time, for being caught alone with her sister's supposed beau. She tried to come up with something to put Chloe's jealousy to rest... and got nothing.

Harry handed Cat the blanket and walked to her sister, taking both her hands in his. "Chloe, my dear, your sister was just filling me in on the history of your lovely home. I must say I'm impressed that someone as young as yourself owns such an extensive and storied property."

Cat stared after them as he tucked her sister's arm through his and led her into the house. What was he talking about? Nell, Stella, and Evelyn looked from Chloe and Harry back to Cat. When Nell opened her mouth, Cat raised a finger. "Not a word."

Nell crossed her arms. "I was just going to tell you to be careful with that one."

For once she agreed with Nell. Lord Harry Halstead was dangerous, and not only because he got her to spill her guts. She didn't like the quiet sense of companionship she felt sitting with him under the stars. How the feel of him watching her had sent her heart ricocheting in her chest, or how warmth flooded her body when he took her hand in his.

The warm and fuzzies left Cat as soon as her mother joined the three older woman with a disappointed look on her face.

"Mom, I can—"

"Nell, Stella, and Evelyn, would you mind giving Grace a hand? She's cutting the sugarplum cake."

"Now, don't you be too hard on Cat, Liz. There was no hanky-panky going on. I was just teasing."

"Thank you, Nell. But I'll deal with my daughter as I see fit."

Nell and the two older woman shared a look and headed inside.

Cat wrapped the blanket around her mother's shoulders. "Really, Mom. You're going to *deal* with me?"

"You know what I mean." She waved a distracted hand. "What came over you, Cat? How do you think your sister felt hearing that you were outside in the moonlight with her boyfriend?"

"We..." She released a frustrated sigh. "Mom, Harry isn't interested in Chloe. They're not dating."

A worried frown creased her mother's brow. "Does this have something to do with Easton? I know you were upset with Chloe, but surely you've gotten over it. You were in high school, Cat. That's far too long in the past to be making your sister pay for her little indiscretion now."

"You're kidding, right? You can't honestly believe I'm that petty."

"Well, no, but it's the only thing I can think of to explain your behavior tonight."

"Unbelievable. Did you not hear what I said? Chloe and Harry aren't dating." She held up her hand when her mother opened her mouth, no doubt to argue the point. "If you don't believe me, ask Harry."

"All right, but she obviously has feelings for him even if they're not returned. And I expect you to respect that. You know how easily hurt and emotional she is."

"I live with her. So yeah, I get it." Cat caught her mother's shiver. "Come on, you're cold. Let's go inside."

"Don't be upset with me, darling. I can't help that I'm overprotective of Chloe." She slid an arm around Cat's waist. "We nearly lost her, you know. You're the strong one. You always have been."

"You might be surprised how strong she is, Mom. Maybe it's time to stop coddling her." Cat held the door open for her mother, then followed her inside.

"You sound like Ethan."

She wished her brother and his wife were here. Cat could use the backup. They picked a fine time to go on vacation. She'd been hoping to ask them to help her keep an eye on Chloe. Though at the moment, Cat didn't feel much like protecting her sister.

As they walked through the mudroom, she took the blanket from her mother's shoulders and hung it on a hook. At the sound of Harry's deep laugh and her sister's flirty one in response, Cat remembered what Harry had said. She reached for her mother's arm, stopping her at the entrance to the great room.

Her mother turned. "What is it, darling?"

"It's probably nothing. I'm sure I misunderstood, but you haven't sold off some of the ranch to Chloe, have you?"

Her mother grimaced, her cheeks pinking. "Well no, not exactly."

"What do you mean, not exactly?"

She sighed and put a hand on Cat's shoulder. "Do you remember how emotional Chloe was last Christmas after Ethan's wedding?"

"When is she not emotional, Mom?"

"Don't be like that. She missed your father. His death was a huge blow to her."

"It was a blow to all of us. But Daddy died more than five years ago, so I don't understand—"

"She was talking about how much she loved the ranch. And—"

Cat rolled her eyes. "She hates the ranch. She couldn't wait to leave Christmas."

Her mother glanced over her shoulder. "Keep your voice down. I don't understand where this is coming from, Catalina."

Oh, so she was using her given name now. That never boded well. Her mother had a long fuse, but when she lost her temper... "I love the ranch, and so does Ethan. It's our birthright, too, not just Chloe's."

"Your sister would never deprive you or your brother of your home. If something happened to me, I'm sure she'd allow you full access to the house and grounds."

It took a moment for Cat to recover from her shock. "You left the ranch to Chloe in your will? You cut me and Ethan out completely and left everything to her?" Her legs went weak, and she leaned against the wall for support.

"I didn't leave everything to her. You and Ethan will be amply provided for."

"It's not about the money. It's about our home."

"Ethan's campaign was costly. And you barely make enough to get by. If it wasn't for your sister supporting you..." Her mother grimaced. "The only one who can afford to carry the ranch is Chloe. I did it to protect this place. To protect the O'Connor legacy... Cat, where are you going?"

She skirted several of the guests and headed straight for her sister. "What did you do to get her to leave everything to you? Come on, Chloe, tell me. I really want to know."

Her sister paled, her hand creeping to her neck. "I don't know what you're talking about."

"Oh, yes, you do. Even he knew about it." She jerked her thumb at Harry.

"Cat, I don't think this is the time or place for this." Harry reached for her. "Perhaps—"

She shook Harry's hand from her arm. "How did you know?"

He scratched his cheek. "My manager may have mentioned it."

She looked from her sister, who was chewing on her thumbnail, to Harry, and then, ignoring everyone in the room staring at her, Cat said, "We had a deal. I get one question." He responded with a curt nod, his pale blue eyes laser sharp. "Are you one of those British lords with a title and no money?"

"I am. I work for a living. Do you have a problem with that?"

"Only if you're after my sister for her money."

"Of course I'm not. I...Chloe, are you all—" He lunged for her sister, catching her before she could gracefully crumple onto the slate floor.

Chapter Nine

Cat woke up to the ringing of her cell. It took a moment for her to remember she was in her childhood bedroom with its black-and-white decor. Another moment to recall the events of last night. She was groaning at the memory of the scene that had ensued once her sister recovered from her fake faint when she answered the phone.

"Caught the front page of the *Christmas Chronicle*, did you?" her brother Ethan's smooth, lawyerly voice came over the line.

"Oh God, please tell me you're joking."

"He's not. But don't worry, Cat, it's only online. And I've told Nell to take it down." Vivi Westfield's husky voice came over the line. She was the owner and publisher of the *Christmas Chronicle*.

"Thanks...Wait a minute. What are you doing with my brother?"

"We're all here, sweetie. You're on speaker," her sister-in-law Skye said.

Cat sat up in bed and rubbed her head. "You guys suck. How could you go on vacation when you knew we were coming to town?"

"Chance has sworn us to secrecy. We'd have to kill you if we told you," her brother said.

"O'Connor," a deep male voice growled in the background. It sounded like Chance McBride, Vivi's fiancée.

She heard a muted conversation, then Ethan came back on the line. "Cat, what's going on? The article said 'Cat fight at the O'Connors'. Daughters duking it out over the duke.'"

"He's not a duke, he's a lord, and we weren't fighting over him."

"Whatever he is, he's hot. Like, smoking hot," Skye chimed in.

"Does he have one of those sexy Brit accents, too? Because that would make him off-the-charts hot," Vivi added, laughing when two male voices muttered their disgust.

"Yeah, he is, and he does, and I totally agree, but it doesn't matter because he's not interested." She knocked the back of her head against the white leather headboard a couple of times. "I mean, I'm not interested. And we have a bigger problem than Harry. Someone's trying to kill Chloe."

There was dead silence, and then the four of them started firing questions at her at the same time. Once she managed to get a word in, Cat filled them in on what had been happening on the set.

"You have to tell Chloe, Cat. Shut down production until—" her brother began.

"You can't shut down production. Maddie worked too hard to make it happen," Skye said. "Besides, they'd probably sue the town if you did."

"I hadn't thought of that," her brother, the district attorney, said. "All right, but at least tell Chloe so she can be on her guard."

"You're talking about our sister, Ethan. The one who has a breakdown when she gets a cold," Cat reminded her brother.

"Okay, you're right," Ethan reluctantly agreed. "Does Chloe have anywhere to be today?"

"Yes, there's a casting call scheduled at the town hall this afternoon, and they're holding a meet and greet for the fans at the same time."

"Probably best to come up with an excuse to keep her at home today," Ethan said.

"That might be tough. I doubt she'll speak to me, let alone listen to me." After she'd recovered from her "spell" and Paul had examined her, Chloe tried to kick Cat out of the house, saying that she feared for her life. Then her mother had tried to coerce Cat into staying with them in town. Which she gladly would have done if she didn't have to protect her sister.

And there may have been a small part of her that didn't want to leave Chloe alone with Harry. Cat brushed the thought aside. The twinge in her chest when Harry swept Chloe up in his strong arms, depositing her gently on the couch, holding her hand as he crouched by her side, was due to anger at her sister, not jealousy.

"Cat, who are you looking at for this?" Chance asked.

"So far, I've narrowed it down to three people: George, Molly, and Sam."

"You can count me in when we get back to town. We fly home tomorrow night. Easton's...on a job, but he should be able to give us a hand, too." Chance paused. "On second thought, we'll use him as a last resort. The way he feels about Chloe, we'd probably have to add him to your suspect list."

"Send me whatever you have on them, Cat. And I'll start digging on my end," Vivi said with a touch of excitement in her voice. There was nothing the former investigative-crime reporter liked more than working on a case. Vivi's passion and ambition to get the story drove her overprotective fiancé a little nuts, which probably meant the grumbling Cat heard in the background came from Chance.

Cat relaxed against the pillows. It was good to know she'd soon have her friends and family at her back. "I appreciate it. Thanks, guys."

"We were going to stop off at Disney World for a couple of days, but I think we better come straight home," Ethan said.

"No, I don't want you to do that." Busy with their careers and their daughter, her brother and Skye hadn't had a honeymoon. They deserved a break. And her niece Evie would love Disney World. "We'll be fine until everyone gets here. I'll see you—"

"Hang on a minute, Cat." She heard a door shut, then Skye came back on the line. "Okay, it's just me and Vivi. Give us the scoop on the royal hottie."

She shifted and did a face-plant in the pillow to muffle a groan, then lifted her head. "There's no scoop."

"Uh-uh, friends don't hold out on friends," Vivi said. "You're interested in this guy."

"Vivi's right, Cat. Come on, we're old married women. *Oomph*. Vivi, why did you elbow...Oh, um..."

"No way! Vivi, did you and Chance get married?"

"Keep your voice down. We want to keep it on the down-low for a bit."

"I thought friends didn't hold out on friends?"

"Don't try to distract us, Cat. This is about you. And it's about time you showed some interest in another man," Skye said.

They wouldn't give up unless she gave them something. "Look, he's hot." She thought of his wavy, dark hair brushed back from his traffic-stopping face, those pale blue eyes, and the way he filled out his worn jeans and white button-down shirt. "Like, really hot, and he has a deep voice that makes your toes curl, so when you throw in the accent...I guess it does put him in off-the-charts territory, but he's really nice, kind of sweet actually, and thoughtful, too. The other day he..." When their amused whispers came over the line, she pinched the bridge of her nose. "But he's totally not my type. Come on, the guy's an actor. And he crosses his legs like a girl. Oh, and says, 'Jolly good.'" She mimicked his voice. "Ridiculous, right?"

"You are so into him," Skye said once she stopped laughing.

"You better be careful, Cat," Vivi warned. "Nell will have you and his royal hotness pegged for the hero and heroine of her next book."

"No, she won't. She's already set her beady little matchmaking eyes on Chloe and Harry." She took the phone from her ear and closed her eyes. That came out sharper than she intended.

"Um, Cat, is Chloe interested in him in that way?"

"What do you think, Skye? Of course she is. She took one look at him and you could almost see her heart beating outside of her chest. Then he opened his mouth, and I thought she was going to have a big O right on the spot. You don't want to know what she looked like when she heard he was a lord and ninety-eighth in line for the throne. My sister's had a vision board since she was ten. And right smack in the middle is her, or the her she wanted to be, wearing a tiara. She'd known him for less than twenty-four hours, and she told me he was *the one*."

Dead silence. Cat scrunched up her face, silently tapping the phone on her head. Giving them something, just a little something, would have been fine, but vomiting everything out there for them to dissect . . .

"Is he interested in Chloe?" Skye asked carefully.

"No, he told me, and half the town, he isn't interested in either one of us." Maybe it was wishful thinking on her part, but there were times when Cat thought he might be interested in her. Sheesh, what was she doing? This was so high school. Next she'd be pulling out her Magic 8 Ball.

She threw back the covers and got out of bed. She had to shut this down. She was putting herself in a bad mood. And given last night, she hadn't exactly started the day in a good one.

"I know it sucks, sweetie. But if Chloe thinks he's *the one*, it's probably for the best he's not looking for a relationship right now. You don't want a repeat of the Easton love triangle."

Okay, she should have hung up five minutes ago. "It wasn't a triangle, Skye. We were in high school."

"Would someone fill me in, please? Everyone keeps bringing up you and Easton, and I don't have a clue what they're talking about."

"It was nothing," Cat said. The last thing she needed was Vivi digging up something that was better left buried for all of their sakes. "Just a high school crush."

"That may be how *you* feel, Cat. But I'm not sure Easton feels the same way. He thought he was kissing you at Liz and Paul's rehearsal party and was pretty ticked to discover it was Chloe."

Cat winced at the memory. Vivi was right. The trading-places thing never turned out as planned. And it was always at Chloe's instigation, which was probably why. Cat may not be able to change the past, but there would be no more switcheroos in her future. And right now, thanks to the knowledge her friends would soon be here to help, Cat's future and her sister's were looking a little brighter. One of Cat's suspects would be behind bars before the shoot in Christmas wrapped up. She smiled as she put on her cat slippers, her bad mood lifting at the thought of not having to return to Hollyweird.

Cat did a happy-dance shuffle to the door in her red plaid sleep pants and black tee. "Wish I could continue the chat, ladies. But Her Majesty is summoning me," she lied. She wanted to hang on to her good mood as long as she could, and she had a feeling that if she stayed on the phone much longer, Vivi or Skye would say something to send her back to a not-so-happy place.

And she wanted to get something to eat before Chloe and their houseguests got up. A full stomach and a cup of coffee was required to face the three of them, especially Chloe. Cat figured she'd have to suck up to her sister if she planned to accompany her today. Cat didn't have a sucking-up bone in her body. But since they were identical twins, surely she had acquired some of her sister's acting gene. She hadn't messed up too badly when she'd subbed for Chloe as Tessa Hart.

"Poor you," Skye said. "Hang in there, and if you need us, we'll be on the first plane home."

"Thanks, but I'll be okay. Have fun at Disney World. Give Evie a kiss for me."

Skye said good-bye, and Vivi promised to text Cat as soon as they got home. She disconnected and opened the door. As she stuck her head into the hall, a piece of paper floated into the room. She picked it up, relieved that everyone appeared to be sleeping, and glanced at the paper. So much for her good mood. Chloe had left instructions for a four-course breakfast. One she expected Cat to make and serve to the three of them in their respective beds.

Crumpling the paper in her hand, Cat was tempted to open her sister's bedroom door and lob the menu at her head. Instead, she reminded herself of her goal for the day, and strode toward the gourmet kitchen to prepare a breakfast fit for their aristocratic guests. At this point, Cat wanted to kick their royal butts to the curb. She skidded to a stop at the entrance to the kitchen at the sight of an exceptional-looking royal butt clad in black sleep pants. Harry was bent over in front of the Sub-Zero refrigerator.

Her gaze moved to his bare feet, sexy, up his long legs, even sexier, to his...Before she could ogle any more of his royal hotness, she realized his attention was no longer focused on the refrigerator drawer but on her. He looked over his shoulder, then straightened with a pound of bacon in his hand.

She cleared her throat. "Morning." Her eyes were a couple of seconds behind her mouth. They were still working their way up his white T-shirt, appreciating the display of manly muscles and broad shoulders.

"Cat?"

She jerked her gaze to his. "Yes?"

He scratched the back of his neck, and she couldn't help but notice his impressive bicep. Then she realized she was staring again. His sculpted lips lifted at one corner, his eyes on her... head.

It seemed entirely unfair that while his lordship's dark waves were swept smoothly from his forehead, her hair was undoubtedly standing on end. She was a restless sleeper on a good night, and last night had been far from good. She lifted her hand, about to pat down her hair, then realized, without a mirror, it wouldn't do her any good. She probably looked like a cross between a rooster and a porcupine. Whereas Harry looked ready for a photo shoot with his perfect hair and chiseled jaw lined with scruff. It was the first time she'd seen him without a clean-shaven face. It was a good look on him. Okay, so it was exceptional.

She dropped her hand to her side as he held up the pound of bacon. "I hope you don't mind."

"No, not at all." She walked to the center island, smoothing the paper on the dark granite in an effort to keep her eyes and mind occupied before she embarrassed herself. "I was just going to make breakfast."

He moved in behind her, and she lifted her eyes to the coffered ceiling. He was so close, she felt the heat from his body. Which was not at all conducive to calming her overactive libido. And where had all this sexual desire come from, anyway? It was annoying. She was acting like a woman who hadn't...Well, yes, she supposed her twenty-month dry spell explained it. It had nothing to do with Harry. Any man would do. And any man who looked like Harry would really, really do.

She briefly closed her eyes, then forced an unruffled note to her voice. "If you don't mind, I need to get..."

From over her shoulder he read, "Bacon, sausage, eggs, grilled tomato, mushrooms, fried toast, marmalade, and tea. I say, Cat, that's quite the menu."

Okay, that was better. She'd been right about the accent. He made even a menu sound sexy. Thankfully, though, the comment that followed cooled his hotness factor. Then his arm brushed against hers as he reached for the paper, and she got an up close and personal look at his strong, tanned forearm and his masculine hands.

"You know, I don't recall ever being served in bed before. I think it's an experience I'd quite enjoy. As long as you're doing the serving, Cat." His voice was low and rough, and far too close to her ear.

Holding herself stiff so as not to rub against him, she shuffled her way along the island. "Since you're up," she said, shooting him a narrowed-eyed glance at what sounded like a muffled cough, "you can eat at the table. And maybe, seeing as you're an aficionado, you should make the tea."

"Actually, I prefer coffee in the morning. Pot's on if you'd care for one."

"You made coffee?"

He leaned his hip against the counter. "Title, but no

fortune, remember? I can hardly afford servants to do my bidding."

She twisted her mouth to the side. "I'm sorry about last night. I was mad at my sister and took it out on you. I know you're not interested in Chloe for her money. My crack was uncalled—"

He moved closer, a smile playing on his lips as he raised his hand and began to finger-comb her hair. She didn't know whether to be annoyed or amused that he felt the need to fix her up. But those strong fingers skimming along her scalp made thinking difficult, and then he stunned her with the next words out of his mouth.

"The accusation *was* uncalled for. Because, Cat, if I were interested in a relationship, it wouldn't be with your sister. It would be with you."

Chapter Ten

Cat closed the barn door after feeding the horses. Her mother had given the ranch hands the day off to attend the casting call. Cat didn't mind. At least it was quiet. She leaned against the barn, breathing in the cool, pine-scented air as she took a moment to enjoy the sun's warmth on her face before returning to the house. The cloudless azure sky reminded her of Harry's eyes, though they'd been a darker shade of blue when he'd made his stunning declaration earlier this morning. She'd barely had time to process what he said when her sister and Estelle sashayed into the kitchen, demanding their breakfast.

As Cat expected, those demands only increased as the morning wore on. Chloe made it clear she hadn't forgiven Cat for the night before. And Dame Alexander had jumped on the bandwagon with both feet. Even Fluffy had joined the I Hate Cat Club and peed on her slipper.

Cat sighed. She'd stalled as long as she could. They

were scheduled to be at the town hall in an hour. Pushing off the barn to head back to the house, she heard an engine turn over. Oh, no, she wouldn't. But of course she would, Cat thought as she raced along the snow-packed path.

Rounding the corner of the house in time to see the Range Rover pulling away, Cat ran after them. She waved her arms. "Chloe, don't you dare leave without me!"

Her sister, who was in the driver's seat, ignored her and pressed on the gas. A wave of wet snow splattered Cat from her head to her toes. She wiped the snow from her face, scowling after them as the Range Rover turned onto the main road without stopping. Cat brushed the iced mud from her hair. Typically she knew when Chloe was up to something, but this time she hadn't had a clue. The only explanation was that Harry's confession had thrown Cat for a loop, and she was off her game.

If he hadn't removed his fingers from her hair and stepped back seconds before Chloe and Estelle arrived in the kitchen, Cat had no doubt her sister would have run her over.

She pulled the damp wool from her body to shake off the snow from her sweater, then took the path back to the barn. She'd have to warn Harry to hide his keys from now on. As he would soon discover, her sister was a terrible driver.

Cat dug her cell phone from the pocket of her brown puffy jacket and texted Jill Flaherty, the deputy Chance's brother, Sheriff Gage McBride, had assigned to her sister. Once again Chloe had Cat second-guessing her abilities to protect her. Cat pushed her self-doubt aside as she rounded the red barn. She didn't have time for this. She had to get...Raul's pickup was gone. Of course it was, because their head ranch hand and his wife, Rosa, their housekeeper, had gone to visit their daughter for the holidays. Cat was stranded.

She debated calling her mother, but then she'd have to confess that Chloe had abandoned her. Forget that. Cat strode to the garage that housed the farm equipment, sleighs, and snowmobile and opened the doors. After pulling off the cover from a black-and-red Polaris, Cat maneuvered it outside. She went back in and grabbed a helmet and goggles off a shelf and put on her gloves, then closed the garage doors behind her. Straddling the black leather seat, she gunned the engine and took off.

Normally she'd take her time and enjoy the scenery as she traveled the backwoods trails through the forest into town. But today the winter wonderland was a white blur as she traveled at high speed. Though she had managed a brief glimpse of two elk a few yards away in the woods, and a bighorn sheep on the rocky cliff that soared above her. The sightings reminded her what she'd been missing being so far away from the beauty of her home. Nature recharged her, and she loved the changes in the seasons, how she could step out her door into a nature lover's paradise. No, not her door, she reminded herself, her sister's. Once again her anger from the night before ignited. It wasn't fair, but right now she had more urgent things to occupy her mind.

What typically would take twenty minutes by car took Cat an hour. She cut through a back road off Main Street to come up behind the two-story wooden building. She parked the snowmobile in a wooded area off to the side of the parking lot. Removing her goggles and helmet, Cat strode to the front of the town hall. There was a line all the way out the glass doors.

Wonderful. She fluffed her hair, but the tips were frozen, so it didn't have much of an effect. She didn't know why she bothered. "Hey," she said to the deputy at the door. She didn't recognize him. "If I can just get by..."

"Sorry, you have to get in line like everyone else, ma'am."

From behind her, several people muttered angrily, and she turned to reassure them. "I'm not auditioning for a part. I'm Chloe O'Connor's sister. I—"

"Yeah right," someone scoffed while the deputy smirked. Cat searched for a familiar face in the long line, but didn't find one.

She had to create a diversion. She couldn't afford to waste any more time. Pointing across the street, she waved her arms, nearly taking out a young girl with her helmet. "There she is! Chloe, over here! Tessa! Tessa Hart!"

"Where is she? Do you see her?" As she'd hoped, the deputy was as big a fan of Chloe's as the rest of the people in line. Cat took advantage of his inattention and scooted past him, ducking down as she made her way through the crowd waiting to get into the main hall.

"There! She's right there!"

Hoping they were talking about her sister and not her, Cat went up on her tiptoes to search the jam-packed room. Because of his height, she spotted Harry first. He was surrounded by people, mostly women, several of whom she knew. Cat made a beeline toward the group. She'd almost reached them when someone grabbed her from behind.

"Gotcha." The deputy took her by the arms, twisting them behind her back.

Harry, wearing a well-tailored navy suit, looked over.

He blinked, then a slow smile spread across his face. Her sister, who'd been standing beside him signing autographs, glanced over her shoulder and sent her eyes to the timbered ceiling. Jill was there, too, but she hadn't noticed Cat. She was too busy staring at Harry. "Jill, would you tell your friend here that I'm Chloe's sister?" Cat didn't trust her sister to. She'd probably tell him she was a stalker and to throw her in jail.

"Cat? What happened to you?" Cat pressed her lips together. Jill grimaced. "Sorry. Brad, you can let her go. She's Cat O'Connor, Chloe's sister."

"But I thought they were supposed to be twins. She doesn't look anything like Ms. O'Connor." He released Cat and extended his hand to her sister. "Hi there, Ms. O'Connor. I'm a big fan. Sorry about the confusion."

Chloe clasped his hand with a wide smile on her face. "Don't you worry about it, Brad. It's an easy enough mistake to make. Especially with my sister looking like she's been dragged through the mud. Really, Catalina, you think you could have cleaned yourself up before you came."

"I didn't have time, sister dearest, since you left me without a ride. I had to take a sled."

Harry scratched the back of his neck. "How exactly did you manage to get here on a sled?"

She raised her eyebrows and held up her helmet and goggles.

"Ah, I see, a snowmobile then." There was a warm glint in his eyes, but she didn't think it was amusement. "You are a resourceful woman, love. Filthy, but resourceful."

Odd, he made it sound like that was something he appreciated. Honestly, the guy could be weird sometimes.

And her reaction, the pitter-patter in her chest, was weird, too. She reminded herself that he wasn't interested in a relationship.

She drew her attention back to her sister, whose suspicious gaze sliced from Harry to Cat. She couldn't figure out what else she could have done wrong in the space of a few minutes, until she remembered Harry had called her *love*.

Since she didn't feel like getting reamed out in public, Cat said, "I need a cup of coffee. Jill." She lifted her chin in Chloe's direction, silently reminding the tall, dark-haired woman in uniform who she was supposed to be watching, then headed toward a table at the back of the hall. Grace, the owner of the Sugar Plum Bakery, was in charge of refreshments. Just what Cat needed to feel human again: cupcakes and hot coffee.

As she made her way across the room, she located her suspects. Both Molly and George were surrounded by adoring fans, looking happier than Cat had seen them in a while. Not that Harry's manager was a suspect, but Cat searched the crowd and found Dame Alexander set up at a table at the other side of the room beside Phil. Two of the director's assistants were attempting to manage a long line of would-be extras, including Nell and her friends. Good. Cat could eat in peace. As soon as she had a status update from Ty.

None of the crew appeared to be here, which wasn't surprising. Filming wasn't to take place for a couple of days. She put her phone to her ear, waiting for Ty to pick up.

He answered. "Arrived 0900 hours at the lodge. I'm on the job. Suspect is in bed watching *Good Will Humping* and drinking beer."

She pinched the bridge of her nose. "Ty, how do you know what he's watching on TV?"

"I'm peeking through...Oh my God! I think he saw me. What should I do?"

Cat heard a door slide open. "What the hell are you doing out here, man? You scared the shit out of me."

"I...ah, I went out to do a doobie. Got myself turned around. Sorry for freaking you out."

"You got any more?"

"Any more what?"

She was going to strangle him. "A joint. He wants a joint, Ty. Tell him no and get over to the town hall now."

"You have the most interesting conversations, Catalina," a familiar, amused voice said from behind her. Cat hated to be called by her given name, but hearing it in that deep, accented voice sent a heated quiver up her spine.

She disconnected and turned. "And you have an annoying habit of sneaking up on people. Shouldn't you be signing autographs instead of listening to conversations that are none of your business?"

His mouth quirked at the corner. "Methinks the lady doth protest too much. Do you have secrets you don't wish me to hear?"

"No, I..." She caught sight of the twins, Holly and Hailey, and groaned. They owned the Rocky Mountain Diner. But her groan had nothing to do with the food they served. It was because of their side job. They were Christmas's self-appointed beauty experts, and Cat didn't have fond memories of the last time they attempted to make her over. "Dammit," she muttered, and grabbed Harry by the arms, using his tall, muscular frame to hide behind.

He looked down at her, his eyes glinting with amusement. "So is this your secret? You want to ravish me?"

Yes. "No, I'm hiding from..." She went to bow her head at the sound of Hailey and Holly calling her name, but hadn't accounted for how close she and Harry were standing. She ended up doing a face-plant in his chest. She felt his silent laughter against her forehead.

"Cat, we've been...Oh, hello."

Cat lifted her head to see the twins staring at Harry. She took a step back. "Hey, Holly and Hailey, how's it going?"

Hailey waved her hand as though to tell her to be quiet and allow them to enjoy the splendor that was Harry in peace.

Cat had no doubt that once they finished ogling Harry, they'd turn their critical eyes on her. So in order to save herself from a twenty-minute critique, she had no choice but to throw Harry under the bus. "Harry, this is Holly and Hailey. Ladies, I'll let you in on a little secret. Harry has an in with the director. So if you're looking to be extras, he's your man." She winked at Harry, who looked like he wanted to strangle her, and headed for Grace and her cupcakes.

Cat was five feet from reaching her destination when she heard Chloe call her name.

Her sister's manicured hand closed over Cat's bicep just as she was about to make a run for it. "Kit Kat, I need to talk to you."

Chloe calling Cat by her pet name should have eased some of the tension in her shoulders. It didn't. It put her on instant alert. "What's going on?"

Chloe gave her a winning smile, one obviously intended

to butter her up, and looped her arm through Cat's. "We need to talk in private." Chloe led her toward the far wall.

Cat dug in her heels. "Let me get a cupcake first." She had a feeling she'd need one.

"We don't have time. Get one after we talk."

When they reached their destination, Cat leaned against the wall and crossed her arms. "Okay, spill."

Chloe moved closer and leaned in, her eyes sparkling, her color high. "I got the audition. They want me, Kit Kat. Can you believe it? They really want me."

"Of course I believe it. And I don't know why you don't. Honestly, Chloe, when are you going to realize how good an actress you are?"

Her sister stayed quiet for a moment, then bowed her head, shaking it slightly before looking up. "I'm sorry, Kit Kat. You're so supportive, and I'm… well, I'm not. But I'll make it up to you, I promise. As soon as I get back from London—"

Cat stiffened. "Hold it. What do you mean as soon as you get back from London?"

"Shush." Chloe cast a nervous glance over her shoulder. "No one can know I'm leaving. It'll be for only a day or two at most. You'll just have to cover for some of the publicity stuff. We're not filming—"

"No." Cat shook her head. She couldn't believe her sister was asking her to do this. "No way, Chloe. I'm not covering for you again."

"But this could be my big break. I feel it, Kit Kat." She patted her chest. "Right here, I feel it. This is my chance. I'm not getting any younger. I—"

"I'd like to help you, Chloe. But I can't. We can't do this anymore. It's not right."

"I'll do whatever you want. I'll tell Mommsy to change the will back. Please, Kit Kat, please."

"You're unbelievable. Don't try and manipulate me with the ranch, Chloe. You never should have asked Mom to change her will in the first place." She took advantage of her sister's desperation to ask the question Cat knew she'd never get a straight answer to otherwise. "Why did you do it?"

Her sister looked away, rubbing her chest with her fingers. When she finally returned her attention to Cat, her eyes shimmered with unshed tears, and she said quietly, "Because Daddy was proud of you and Ethan, and he was never proud of me. I wasn't smart like Ethan, or strong like you. I was just an actress. I—"

Cat sensed that Chloe was telling the truth. Her sister genuinely believed their dad hadn't been proud of her. She laid a hand on Chloe's shoulder. "That's not true. Dad—"

"Yes, it is. He...he called me the day you made detective. He was organizing a big party for you and wanted me to come home. I told him I couldn't get away. I was auditioning for the part of Tessa Hart, and I told him it looked like I was going to get it. I thought he'd be happy for me. Maybe even a little proud. But he said I needed to grow up and stop living in a fantasy world and get a real job like you and Ethan. A job that mattered." Chloe looked away again and surreptitiously wiped a finger across her bottom lashes.

"I'm sorry, Chloe. But you have to know Dad didn't mean it. He probably just—"

"He meant it, Kit Kat." Her sister cleared her throat. "I couldn't make him proud of me when he was alive, so I thought if Mommsy left me the ranch, I could make sure it stayed in the family. The taxes and upkeep are expensive, and you know how much he loved the ranch." Chloe frantically wiped at her face as tears began to slide down her cheeks. "This is so embarrassing, I didn't mean to cry."

Cat gathered her sister in her arms, feeling like a bitch for pushing back on the will. She was angry at her dad, too. He'd been a good man, a good father, but he'd also been competitive and driven. His expectations were tough to live up to. Chloe wasn't the only one in the family who thought she'd failed him.

Dammit, she didn't want to think about that now. This wasn't about her. It was about Chloe. And after her sister's emotional confession, she couldn't bring herself to say no. "Okay, I'll do it."

Chloe leaned back and rubbed her palms across her cheeks. "Are you sure? I'm going to tell Mommsy to change the will back anyway, so if that's why you're agreeing to—"

"I'm doing it for you. But Chloe, you have to be careful. Obviously, you can be you at the audition. But other than that, you have to pretend you're me. And absolutely no contact with Lord Darby." The more Cat thought about it, the more she realized this could work to her advantage. It would be easier to figure out who was trying to kill Chloe if she wasn't constantly worrying about her.

"I love you. You're the best sister ever."

Cat held up her phone. "Say that again. I want it on record."

Chloe grinned. "Sorry for leaving you behind today and splattering you with snow." She wrinkled her nose. "You really are a mess, Kit Kat." Chloe's eyes widened.

"Oh no, if I'm supposed to be you, I'll have to look like a hot mess, too."

Cat rolled her eyes. "How do you think I feel? I'm going to spend more time doing my makeup and hair in the next couple of days than I do in a year." Good thing Ty would be around to help. At the thought, she searched the room for him. Instead of finding Ty, she locked eyes with Harry, who'd obviously been watching her and Chloe's exchange. She felt a small twinge of regret at the thought there'd be no more flirting with his lordship. Given that he wasn't interested in a relationship—and he made her forget that neither was she—maybe it was for the best.

*   *   *

Grayson couldn't put it off any longer. He had to tell Cat who he was. If Chloe continued to pull crap like she did this morning, at least Cat would know he was there to protect her sister. Telling Cat who he was would be easier than what he had to do next. He had to make Chloe understand that he wasn't interested in her. As he'd discovered, she wasn't good at taking a hint. He'd kept an eye on the sisters while trying to shake off Holly and Hailey. They were about as shakable as drug-sniffing dogs on a dealer's backpack.

He lifted his chin and waved at Phil, then threw the director under the bus. "There's your cue, ladies. Phil will see you now. And rest assured, I'll put in a good word for you."

They thanked him profusely, then made their way to Phil. Grayson headed toward the refreshment table. He should be able to get a better idea what was going on between Chloe and Cat from there. He worried that once again, because of him, Cat was on the receiving end of her sister's jealous temper.

He frowned when Cat drew her sister into her arms. Maybe he'd misjudged the situation. They seemed to be getting along fine now. Unlike a few moments ago when he'd worried Cat intended to strangle Chloe.

Grayson smiled at the pretty blonde behind the refreshment table. He'd met her briefly last night at the party. "Hello, Grace. Lovely to see you again, my dear."

"Lovely to see you too, Your Highness." She curtsied. "What can I get you?"

Grayson drew in a breath and released it slowly. He was more than ready to end the charade. It was fine in LA, but it felt different here. They were nice people, and he didn't like lying to them. He smiled at Grace. "Please, it's Harry. And no need to curtsey. I'll have a coffee, if it's no trouble."

"No trouble. No trouble at all, Your High…" She blushed. "Harry."

A tall, dark-haired man wearing a black leather jacket came around the table. He angled his head, then waved his hand in front of Grace's face. "You going to get the man his coffee, sweetheart, or should I?"

"I was just going to ask what he takes in it, Jack."

"Sure you were." The man grinned and stuck out his hand. "You'll have to excuse my wife. She's got royal fever like the rest of them. Jack Flaherty."

"I do not." She looked at Harry and smiled. "Maybe just a little. What would you like in your coffee? Or I have tea, if you'd prefer."

"Coffee's good. Black. Thanks," Grayson said as he shook the man's hand. "I've read about you. It's an honor to meet you, Jack." The man had been a POW in Afghanistan for seventeen months before he'd escaped, leading his crew to safety.

"Thanks. Good to meet you, too."

Grace nudged her husband with her elbow while handing Grayson his coffee. "He's a lord, Jack. You should—"

"Are you using your title to get special favors again, Harry?" Cat asked, coming to stand beside him.

He took in her helmet hair, the way her sunburnt cheeks and nose stood out against her creamy white skin, and her mud-spattered green sweater, and wondered what it was about this woman that made every word out of her mouth a sexual turn-on. "What special favors did you have in mind, love?"

She snorted. "Obviously not the ones you're thinking about," she said, then turned and smiled at the couple behind the table.

The three of them began talking about mutual friends who were hoping to become extras. Grayson half listened to their conversation while studying Cat. Lifting the cup of coffee to his mouth, he contemplated the best time to reveal his true identity. There was a part of him that was anxious to get it over and done with, while concern for how she'd react to his deception had him wanting to put it off for another day. He didn't know what bothered him more, realizing how much her opinion mattered to him or realizing his attraction was more than physical. The two, he supposed, went hand in hand. But right now, watching as she took a bite of a chocolate cupcake, then wiped her full, kissable lips with a napkin, his reaction was purely physical. To the point of possibly becoming embarrassing.

"Maybe we could do it another night." Cat cast him a sidelong glance as she continued. "I'm leaving town for a few days."

He choked on his coffee, droplets splashing the front of his shirt. He reached for a napkin, but Cat intervened.

"Here, let me," she said, and began dabbing at the stain, only to smear chocolate all over his shirt instead. "Oops." She grimaced. "Sorry about that."

Now he wasn't as particular as Harry, but at any other time, at the hands of any other person, that would have ticked him off a bit. He covered her hand with his. "It's fine."

But he wasn't. All he could think about was her leaving town. She had a sister to protect, didn't she? "Where are you off to, love?" He intended to keep his tone light, but came off sounding a little growly. He cleared his throat.

Her eyebrows shot up. "Not that it's any of your business, but I'm heading to London to see a friend."

London? Friend? He didn't like the sound of that. Could she be looking into him? Jesus, he was beginning to think like Harry. Or more disconcerting, like a jealous boyfriend. Before he could question her further, he noticed Ty staring at Cat.

"You can't leave. We have—"

Shooting an anxious glance at Grayson, she grabbed Ty by the arm and started to walk away. As though as an afterthought, she turned and gave them a finger wave. "I'll, uh, see you all in a couple of days."

He heard her telling Ty to *shut it* as she hustled him out of the main hall. Grayson stared after her, wondering what had just happened. It was possible she didn't realize her sister was in danger. It was also possible that he'd scared her off when he told her that he was interested in her this morning. As several different scenarios crowded his brain, he realized it was probably for the best that she was heading out of town.

He was invested in the case now and wanted to see it through, but he had only eight days left of his vacation. Cat was a distraction. It would be easier to stay focused without her around. And if there were no further attempts on Chloe's life while Cat was away...

Chapter Eleven

Cat tugged on the white lace comforter. "You're a cover hog."

Ty, with his arm tucked behind his head, lay beside her on the bed staring up at the canopy. He'd been worried about Cat's safety and had arrived after midnight. At least he hadn't blown her cover by ringing the doorbell. He'd fired snowballs at her window until she'd woken up and hauled him inside. The last thing she wanted to do was arouse Harry's suspicions. As soon as she'd gotten Chloe safely out of town, Cat had retired to her sister's bedroom, pleading a headache.

"This room is kind of freaking me out. I feel like I'm in Sleeping Beauty's bed. Good thing you're awake or I'd have to play Prince Charming and kiss you."

"Good thing you didn't. I would have slugged you." She yawned, glancing at the princess clock on the bedside table. Her sister's room had been the same since she was four. Cat had redecorated hers when she was twelve. Ty was right, it was kind of freaky. "Well, Prince Charming, if you plan on putting those extensions in my hair, we better get up."

"This is the last time I'm doing this, Ty," he mimicked her voice, then nudged her with his elbow. "You're lucky I know you so well or I wouldn't have brought extensions to match your hair color."

"Extenuating circumstances. It doesn't look like Chloe's friend is going to live much longer. I couldn't say no," she lied. She trusted Ty to have her back, but not her sister's.

He rolled out of bed wearing Chloe's pink satin pajamas and stretched. "Color me shocked. I didn't know Chloe had any friends."

She didn't. Her sister was too busy clawing her way to the top to make time for anyone. Anyone other than Cat. Despite their problems of late, Cat had always known her sister was there for her. When the story about Michael broke, Chloe had immediately flown to Denver. She'd handled the press and the never-ending phone calls, making sure Cat got out of bed and ate when all she'd wanted to do was curl up in a ball and hide under the covers.

"Don't be bitchy," Cat said to Ty and headed to the en-suite bathroom. "I'm going to grab a quick shower."

"Your sister may not be my favorite person, but I will say one thing for her, she has exquisite taste in clothes." He stood at Chloe's closet, looking like he was having an orgasmic experience as he drew a silver lamé gown from its hanger.

"I'll be checking your makeup bag before you leave, buddy." It was the size of a suitcase.

"I'm a tactile gay man, not a cross-dresser." He waggled his eyebrows and smoothed his hand down the pajama top. "But I may have to steal these. I never knew how divine it was to sleep in satin."

Cat rolled her eyes, closing the bathroom door behind her. While she showered, Ty shoved outfits through the pink plastic curtain for her inspection. He'd taken it upon himself to dress her for the Christmas bazaar today. She'd tried to get out of attending, but the publicist was adamant that Chloe and Harry make an appearance. Cat had a feeling she'd be developing another migraine before the end of the day. Fooling the cast and crew was one thing, fooling the people she knew and loved another.

Slipping on Chloe's leopard-print robe, Cat tied the sash and stepped from the steam-filled bathroom. She frowned at the sight of Ty slumped in the pink slipper chair with a high school yearbook cradled in his hands. "What's up?"

"Have you seen this?" He flipped to the autograph page and held it up. "Cruel little bastards. Tell me you beat them up."

Cat walked over, took the book from him, and sat on the edge of the bed. It was Chloe's tenth-grade yearbook. "Where did you get this? I was sure I threw it out."

Ty jerked his thumb to the hundreds of books lining the white shelves behind him. "Top shelf. I feel sorry for her now. I know what it's like to have kids make fun of you. It hurts. You lose your self-respect and sense of self-worth. Takes a long time to get it back. Some of us never do." He took off his glasses, wiping the lenses with a corner of the pajama top.

Cat could tell he was embarrassed. And while she gave him a moment, her eyes went back to the yearbook. Chloe must have taken it out of the trash the day Cat had thrown it away. She didn't understand why Chloe would do that, because Ty was right. The kids had been cruel, taunting Chloe about her weight, her glasses, her headgear and braces.

Cat ran her finger over the hurtful comments as though she could erase them. "I didn't beat anyone up. Easton McBride did. He ended up being suspended for a week." And becoming Chloe's hero. "I found more creative ways to get back at the girls." She smiled at the memory of her payback, then raised her gaze to Ty. "I hope someone stuck up for you."

"No, they would have been beaten up if they did. You don't stick up for the geeky gay guy unless you want everyone to think you're gay, too."

She nudged his foot with hers. "I would have."

"I know you would." He gave her a small smile that broadened as he motioned for the yearbook. When she handed it to him, he flipped through the pages until he found what he was looking for. He pointed to a picture of Easton McBride. "And no offense, but if I had to pick a white knight, it would be him, not you. That boy is beautiful. Look at those shoulders and neck, that cleft chin, those eyes."

"Can't say I blame you." Easton had been white knight material even back then.

Ty cast her a hopeful look. "He wouldn't happen to be gay, would he?"

"Sorry, pal. Straight as they come. Ex–Special Forces and former CIA operative. He works for his brother Chance now. They have a security firm in Christmas."

"Be still my heart. You mean there's a chance I will see this man in the flesh?"

"Yep, and you should prepare yourself because all the McBride men are hot."

"I think I may just move here."

"And straight." She laughed when he threw up his arms with a dramatic sigh. "Come on." She took his hand, pulling him from the chair. "If I'm supposed to be ready by one, we better get started."

She sat on the pink-cushioned stool while Ty unloaded the contents of his bag onto the small antique table in front of her. "Too bad you cut your hair. All we'd have to do is your makeup. And I have to tell you, after seeing your class photo, I don't understand how you could cut those gorgeous, long locks. Your hair was even more beautiful than your sister's with that loose, natural curl. Poor Chloe, it must have been horrible growing up with you as a sister."

"Hey, I was a great sister. And we're identical twins, so..." She trailed off at his arched eyebrow.

"Your sister didn't keep only her tenth-grade yearbook. She has yours, too." He nodded at a second blue book by the chair. "Head cheerleader, top in your class, voted most beautiful and most likely to succeed. And from the number of people who signed your yearbook, most popular, too. You were a tough act to follow."

"What can I say, I peaked early." Wasn't that the truth, and a depressing one at that. "Chloe was a late bloomer. She came into her own in twelfth grade." And pretty much ruined Cat's life. Maybe she was being overly dramatic, but that's how it had felt to her eighteen-year-old self.

There was a polite rap on the bedroom door. "Chloe, is everything all right in there?"

Cat's startled gaze met Ty's in the mirror. She couldn't

risk Harry seeing her without the extensions in and makeup on. More importantly, he couldn't know Ty was here. Harry wouldn't buy that he'd arrived this morning without him seeing him. "Yes." She cleared her throat, and mimicked her sister's voice, "Everything's fine, Harry."

Ty covered his mouth with both hands, hair blower in one, his eyes filling with laughter. She lightly swatted his arm.

"You're positive, are you? Because I could have sworn I heard a man's voice."

She scowled at Ty, then forced a tinkling laugh from her lips. "That was just me going over an upcoming scene. I like to do both parts. It helps me get into character."

"Oh, I see."

She could tell from his skeptical tone that he didn't. Which wasn't a surprise because it was a lame excuse. "You should try it—"

"—sometime, it's quite effective," Ty finished for her in a disturbing voice. He shrugged when she gave him a what-the-hell look.

"It's an…interesting idea. I'll let you get back to it." She heard the sound of his retreating footsteps, then, "I'm about to make breakfast if you'd care for something to eat."

"Yes—" Ty began, and Cat reached up to cover his mouth while giving him a shut-it glare. "On second thought, I'm running late. I'll grab something at the church bazaar," she said as the beginnings of a tension headache blossomed behind her eyes.

There were a few beats of silence before Harry said, "All right, then. I'll see you in an hour."

"Yes, I'll—"

Ty cut her off. "Two. I'll see you in two hours."

As Harry's footsteps faded down the hall, Cat turned on Ty. "What was that? One minute you sounded like Pee-wee Herman, and the next Linda Blair in *The Exorcist*. And there's no way it's going to take two hours to—"

With an offended look, Ty turned on the hair dryer, blowing hot air in her face.

And he was right, it took two excruciatingly long hours to transform her into Chloe. She didn't know how her sister stood it. Cat was practically jumping out of her skin when Ty finally proclaimed his work there was done. Then again, Chloe had fake nails, didn't have extensions to put in, and, as Ty repeatedly informed Cat, her sister knew better than to go without sunscreen.

Cat tugged at the low neckline of the red cashmere sweater Ty had paired with a black pencil skirt that had a thigh-high slit. "Maybe I should wear a scarf."

"For the tenth time, Chloe likes to flaunt her girls. And you're supposed to be practicing your walk." Looking up from packing away his supplies, he wiggled his finger. "Let me see."

"Despite what you think, I'm perfectly capable of walking in high heels."

He snorted as he zipped his bag. "Right, that's why you nearly fell on your face two minutes ago. I hate to tell you this, but you drew the short stick when it comes to coordination. You're a klutz."

"I am not. A klutz wouldn't be able to dive, flip on their back, and take down a shooter at twenty yards, now would they?"

His mouth twitched. "Okay, let me rephrase. You lack *womanly* grace."

She sighed. He was right. If she wasn't determined to

discover who wanted her sister dead before she returned from London, Cat would pretend she had the flu and hole up in Chloe's bedroom. "I'll sit as much as possible."

"Probably a good idea." He dragged his bag toward the window. "Let's hope Tall, Dark, and Fifty Shades of Gorgeous isn't out for a stroll."

Cat opened the window and stuck out her head, surveying the snow-covered grounds. Ty was going to sneak around to the front door on the pretext he'd come to do Chloe's hair. He'd put the extensions in, but left them uncurled. "I'll give you five minutes to make your way around the house." Since he'd taken a cab last night, Cat had to be the one to answer the door, or Harry would wonder how Ty had gotten there.

Ty handed her his bag. She tossed it out the window. He stared at her, his mouth forming a horrified *oh* before he started yelling, "Are you crazy? That bag—"

She quickly covered his mouth. "Be quiet! He'll hear—"

Ty ripped her hand away. "Do you know how expensive—"

There was an insistent knock on the door. "Chloe, what's going on in there?"

"Nothing," she and Ty said at almost the same time. She glared at him, then made a zip-it motion with her fingers and shoved him toward the window. "Just give me a minute, Harry. I'm not decent."

Ty, shimmying out the window, hit his knee on the ledge and swore loudly. Cat put a hand over her face, then banged on the wall in hopes of covering the noise, releasing a dramatic "Ouch." At the sound of the doorknob jiggling, she whispered "Hurry up" to Ty, the top half of his body hanging out the window.

Her eyes widened when the door started to open. She

turned back to Ty and pushed him the rest of the way out the window. Rolling onto his back in the snow, he stared up at her with a shocked expression on his face. "Pu..." His gaze moved to the man now standing beside her, and he covered his almost-slip by yelling, "*Puta!* You *puta*! I came to do your hair and this is how you treat me?"

Harry's eyebrows drew together as he looked from Ty to Cat. "What's going—"

She channeled her sister, throwing herself in his arms. "Oh, Harry, thank goodness you're here. I was so scared. I thought he was a stalker." She added a tremble to her voice, stroking the corded muscles of Harry's back through his white dress shirt because that's what Chloe would do, or so she told herself. And her sister would probably take advantage of the two open buttons at his neck to rest her cheek against his warm skin. He smelled of fresh linen and expensive cologne, and Cat thought how pretending to be her sister might not be so bad after all.

*   *   *

As Cat walked into the church hall with Dame Alexander's arm looped through hers, she knew without a doubt that agreeing to trade places with Chloe had been a bad idea. Friends and neighbors looked up at their entrance, smiling and waving hello. Evelyn and Stella, wearing festive red aprons, stopped with white carafes in hand to curtsey. "Welcome, your ladyship. We're honored you have graced us with your presence," Stella said in a stilted voice.

"Yes, most honored. We have a special table set up for you." Evelyn beamed, pointing out a white linen–draped table with a ceramic Santa centerpiece holding a British flag.

Dame Alexander looked down her aristocratic nose. If she said something snotty, Cat was going to step on her toe. "How thoughtful. Thank you for your hospitality. I'm sure Lord Harry will be as touched as I am."

Cat would have relaxed if Estelle hadn't thrown in the bit about Harry. His lordship had dropped them off at the church and was currently en route with Ty to the lodge. Her nerves returned at the thought of the two men alone in the SUV. Harry had seemed suspicious of her story earlier. As soon as he'd set Cat away from him, which he'd done rather too quickly for her liking, he'd peppered them with questions while reaching out a hand to Ty. Harry had hauled the other man through the window with an ease that left Cat admiring his strength and Ty panting. If Harry questioned Ty further, Cat was afraid he'd cave. But Ty didn't seem concerned. Ignoring Cat's silent messages of warning when they'd arrived at the church, he'd practically dragged her out of the Range Rover to take her place in the front seat beside Harry.

Cat dug in the pocket of her sister's floor-length fur coat for her cell to text Ty. It pinged at the same time Stella said, "As soon as we serve our tables, we'll come and take your orders."

"Thanks, Stella, but you and Evelyn are busy. I can…" Cat paused at the look the two older women shared. "Is something wrong?" She squinched her right eye to see if the stupid fake eyelashes she wore had come unglued.

"No, we're just surprised you know our names," Stella said, and Evelyn nodded.

"Of course I do. I…" She trailed off, reminding herself she was Chloe, who could be as stuck-up as Dame Alexander. "We should probably take our seats. Fred and Ted are trying to get your attention." The two older men reminded Cat of Walter Matthau and Jack Lemmon in *Grumpy Old Men*. Today they both had on red shirts and black bow ties. From the ticked-off looks they were giving each other, they hadn't coordinated their attire on purpose.

"I think they're trying to get mine." Estelle preened, giving the men a royal wave. "I'll just go over and say hello. I'll meet you at the table, my dear."

Evelyn and Stella shared another look, one Cat had no trouble reading. They might be thrilled to have royalty in their midst, but they weren't thrilled that said royal was encroaching on their men. Out of the corner of her eye, Cat caught movement. Nell scooted from behind the table she manned, making her way toward them.

Wearing a red Rudolph sweater and antlers, she had a Santa hat and an apron in her hand. "Where's Lord Harry?"

Cat relaxed. She'd been worried Nell was going to ask her to man her gingerbread table while wearing a "Kiss the Cook" apron. Something she'd made Madison McBride do two years earlier in a bid to sell more cookies than Stella. The two friends had a long-standing competition, and Nell was a sore loser.

"Why do you want to know where his lordship is?" Stella asked with a suspicious look in her eyes.

Nell put her hands behind her back. "No reason." She nodded at a table in the opposite corner of the room with an elaborate gingerbread house on display. "I hear you asked Dr. McSexy to work your table."

"Yes, but he had an emergency. He'll be here soon," Stella said.

Nell grinned. Cat wouldn't put it past her to have

staged the emergency. And before either of them set their competitive little eyes on her, Cat decided to head for the table. "Well, ladies, I should probably take a seat before someone steals the table you kindly provided for us. The hall looks great, by the way."

It did. They'd obviously put more effort than usual into the decorations. A large white tree wrapped in strands of blue lights stood on the stage, and silver snowflakes hung from the ceiling. The Christmas scenes decorating the walls were framed with cotton batting to look like snow while giant blow-up snowmen waved from the four corners of the hall.

The three older women stared at her. Nell was the first to break the uncomfortable silence. "We've asked you to attend three years in a row, and you always refuse." An *aha* look broke across Nell's face. "It's because of Harry, isn't it? You're trying to put on a good show. Pretend you like your hometown. You're a better actress than I gave you credit for. But even if you don't like us, we appreciate what you've done for the town, don't we, girls?"

What was wrong with her sister? How could she be so rude to the people she'd grown up around? Cat had her own *aha* moment. Obviously, Chloe was taking her past hurts out on the entire town. While Cat empathized with her sister, she didn't like that people were thinking the worst of Chloe. "Don't be silly, Nell. I love my hometown. I wouldn't have suggested they film our holiday segments here if I didn't, now would I? I'm sorry I haven't been able to attend the Christmas bazaar. I'll be sure to put it on my calendar for next year." She smiled, furtively looking around the room for an excuse to make her escape. Her phone pinged again. "I better take this. Good luck to you both on the gingerbread sales."

As she started to walk away, she heard Stella say, "It must be love. She's never given us the time of day before."

"Do you think so, Stella? I was so hoping it would be Cat and Harry. Oh well, it looks like you have the couple for your next book, Nell," Evelyn said with a disappointed sigh.

"Time will tell, Evelyn. Time will tell."

There was something in Nell's voice that made Cat shoot a nervous glance over her shoulder. The older woman watched her with a speculative gleam in her eye, or was it a suspicious one? Cat didn't have time to think about it. Phil had just entered the church hall with George and the publicity team.

It was time to get to work. She checked her phone as she made her way toward them, stopping in her tracks as she read through Ty's texts. The first one was a selfie of Ty leaning against Harry, who was driving with a beleaguered expression on his handsome face, while Ty mouthed *hot*. In the second text he informed Cat that his lordship had been questioning him about her trip to London, but not to worry, he hadn't given anything away. Her phone rang just as she was texting him back. She wanted a word-for-word account of the exchange. Moving to a quiet corner in the room, Cat faced the giant snowman and answered, "Hey, Ty, are—"

"Oh my God, you are not going to believe this! Sam has a gun!"

"Okay, calm down. Where is he? Can he see you?"

"No, he's in his room at the lodge. Harry just dropped me off, and I thought I'd better have eyes on the suspect, you know. So I peeked through his patio door. What do you want me to do?"

"Nothing. Stay away from him. I'll figure out how to get him out of his room tonight and search it."

"Leave it to me. I'll come up with a plan."

"No, Ty, I'm serious..." She sensed someone approaching. "I'll call you back." She disconnected. "Hi, George."

The actor scanned the church hall. "Where's your lap dog?"

She stiffened. "Pardon me?"

"Your sister. I can never get a private word with you these days without her around." With a petulant look on his face, he shoved his hands in the pockets of his black pants.

Cat let his comment go. She had more important things to worry about than his rude remark. "She's out of town for a couple of days. But you know I always have time for you, George. How are you enjoying my hometown?"

"Feels like I'm in a time warp, but it's all right. People are friendly enough and big fans of the show. Which is what I wanted to discuss with you. I know what you're up to, and it has to stop."

At this point she'd expect to see some sign of anger on his face, but she didn't. He acted as though he was dealing with a recalcitrant child. "I'm not up to—"

He drew his hand from his pocket and stroked her hair, an indulgent smile on his face. "We're more alike than you know. We both have the same goal. But you're going about it the wrong way. The audience wants us together, not you and Rand Livingstone." His thin upper lip curled, and then he continued. "I've spoken to Phil. This past year hasn't been easy on me, and I've let you and the show down." A vein at his temple throbbed. Now there was the flash of temper she'd been waiting for. "Phil says—"

"Chloe, there you are, my dear," Estelle cut off George, nudging him out of the way to take Cat's arm. "Harry's arrived." She pointed her cane at Nell's table.

Trying to get a read on George, Cat hadn't noticed Harry enter the hall. But obviously he'd noticed her. Chloe, she reminded herself, when his intent gaze sent off a tiny tremor in her stomach. When he removed his black wool coat, Nell tied a white "Kiss the Cook" apron around his waist.

"If you don't mind, I was having a conversation with my...Chloe."

Cat had the oddest feeling he'd been about to say "wife." It wouldn't be the first time she'd wondered if George had confused fantasy with reality. Maybe as a way to cope with his wife leaving him, he'd transferred his feelings for her to his fake wife. But that wouldn't give him a motive for killing Chloe. Unless...Tessa Hart was having an affair with Rand Livingstone.

"You'll have to continue it at another time. As you can see, the publicist wants her."

It was true, the woman was waving them over to Nell's table. "We can finish our conversation as soon as I see what she wants, George."

His eyes narrowed at the publicist and Harry. "It better not be what I think it is, or heads will roll."

As soon as they were out of earshot, Estelle said, "There's something not quite right with that man."

"What do you mean?" At this point, Cat welcomed any insights into her suspect. Even Estelle's.

"We don't have time to talk about it," the older woman

said as she helped Cat out of the fur coat. "We have just been presented with the perfect opportunity to put our plan into action."

Great, Estelle and Chloe had a plan. Cat tugged the sweater's neckline higher. Her sister may like to show off her girls, but Cat's were going undercover. And since she didn't want Estelle to blow *her* cover, she hoped the older woman enlightened her about *their* plan.

They were a few feet from the table where Harry stood looking deliciously edible when Nell waved a gingerbread man in the air. "Get a kiss with your cookies, ladies. Two dollars for a kiss and a cookie."

A horde of women stampeded in their direction.

"Make it count, my dear," Estelle murmured, shoving Cat at the table.

The push caused Cat to wobble on her heels. If not for Harry reaching across the table, encircling her biceps with his strong hands, she would have fallen on her face. Something her sister would never do. So it was imperative that Cat put on a believable performance. She fluffed her hair, did a flirty head tilt, and batted her fake eyelashes. "I'll take two, Harry." She puckered her lips.

His mouth flattened, a muscle ticking in his clenched jaw. Then he leaned toward her. It's possible he said *bloody hell* under his breath as he lowered his head, but she couldn't be sure because everything went a little fuzzy the moment his warm, firm lips touched hers. She tasted mint, smelled his expensive cologne, and drew closer, placing her hands on his shoulders to avoid toppling over. Okay, so it was an excuse, but she was sure her sister would have taken advantage of the situation in exactly the same way.

Her mouth softened, her fingers tightening on his broad shoulders as her lips parted. She was just getting into the kiss, and it was some kiss, when his mouth left hers. He took what appeared to be a startled step back. She understood the reaction—the kiss had rocked her world, too.

"Hang on, I need a picture for the *Chronicle*," Nell said, putting down the cookie to pick up her cell phone. "Okay, go for it."

In the background, she heard George saying something to Phil about breaking his promise. Harry looked over her head, then back at her. An emotion she couldn't read darkened his blue eyes, then he brought his hands to the sides of her face and did as Nell suggested. He went for it.

Gently tilting her head so his lips slanted over hers at a precise angle, he gave her a deep, passionate kiss. It was long and lush, and breath-stealingly perfect. Her eyes were still closed, her head tipped up, when she realized she was kissing air. Blinking her eyes open, she stared at him. Acting as though he was completely unaffected, as if he hadn't felt the same emotional rush of desire, he handed her two cookies.

If that was a kiss from an uninterested man, she'd eat . . .

"That will be four dollars, Chloe." His words were cool and clipped, his back ramrod straight.

And her heart, that seconds ago had been dancing to a happy beat, froze. It wasn't her he was kissing. It was her sister.

Chapter Twelve

The pilot left them on the top of the mountain, the *thump-thump* of the helicopter's rotor blades drowning out Chloe's conversation with their guide. Last night, when they got word Phil wanted to film the heli-skiing scene today instead of later in the week, she'd seemed as pumped as Grayson was. But now faced with the reality of a two-thousand-foot vertical run, he wondered if she was having second thoughts. Which would have been the reaction he expected from her.

Then again, she'd surprised him a couple times in the last twenty-four hours. She seemed different since her sister left. An intriguing different. And the kiss they'd shared yesterday at the Christmas bazaar had him rethinking his vow to never date another actress. At least for the brief time he'd had his mouth on hers. Then he'd felt guilty for that sizzle of heat and desire that shook him from his head to his toes. As if somehow he was cheating on Cat with her sister.

He pushed the memory aside. The sooner he solved the case the better. Bad enough the O'Connor women were encroaching on his vacation time, he didn't need them messing with his head, too. As though she read his mind, Chloe turned to him with a wide smile that deepened the dimple at the corner of her mouth. He felt a possessive tug at the sight of that small, inward curve. It belonged to Cat, not her sister. Or had he simply not noticed that Chloe had one, too? He was slipping if that were the case. But in his defense, before yesterday, he hadn't looked at Chloe the way he did Cat.

Chloe's smile faded. "Are you okay?"

"I'm good." He adjusted his goggles. "What about you, are you nervous?"

"No, I...Well, maybe a little," she admitted self-consciously, then bent to fiddle with her skis.

He sidestepped closer, reaching out to place a comforting hand on her shoulder when she straightened. She wore a hot-pink ski suit that showed off her feminine curves. Curves that he hadn't paid much attention to until yesterday. But after seeing the way she filled out her low-cut sweater and the flash of her shapely leg, he hadn't been able to think of much else.

"Don't worry, love. I won't let you out of my sight. You'll be fine."

"Oh, Harry, I know you'll take care of me. I wouldn't have agreed to do this without you by my side." She rubbed her chest and took several gulping breaths. "But I'm a little worried about the altitude. My heart condition, you know. It's why I've never done this before."

Now this was the Chloe he'd come to know. And while it erased some of his earlier guilt, he resented the fact he'd have to babysit her instead of enjoying the run. "Do you need to take one of your pills?"

"I took three. But thank you for asking. You're such a thoughtful man."

"I don't want you to do something you're uncomfortable with, Chloe. I'm sure Phil would agree to have a stunt double take your place." He gestured to the tall Swede who was on his radio. "I can ask our guide to contact him." Phil was at the bottom of the run with the cameraman. Grayson waited patiently, hoping she'd say yes.

She chewed on her gloved thumb, taking in, he imagined, the sheer drop, the dark, rushing water to the right of the tree line, and the huge granite walls on either side. As an added incentive for her to bail, he said, "If you're concerned about an avalanche, don't be. Our guide is trained, and the conditions aren't conducive to one. At least I don't think they are."

"You know exactly what to say to a woman to make her feel safe, Harry."

He frowned, detecting a hint of sarcasm in her voice. But she gave him a wide, trusting smile, and he decided he'd been mistaken. "You're sure you want to do this?"

"Yes, positively. Anything for the show, you know. And it's not as if I'm a beginner."

"I bloody well hope not." Well that came out more forcefully than he intended, but this had disaster written all over it. He worked to clear the frustration from his voice. "Perhaps we should go over a few things first, my dear."

Before she could argue, he slid back on his skis to give himself some room, and then began instructing her on the basics. As he looked up from showing her a side-to-side move, explaining how to stay in control, he caught her mid–eye roll.

"Am I boring you?"

She pushed a finger under her pink-tinted goggles. "No, my eyelash got stuck."

Why the woman went skiing in full makeup was beyond him. It wasn't as if they were shooting a close-up. Her sister wouldn't. At the thought, he found himself wishing he was here with Cat instead of Chloe. Maybe before he left, he could convince her to ski with him.

He forced a smile. "Just one more tip. If you're going to fall, go with it. Don't try to correct yourself with your poles or skis, sit down. There's no shame in falling." He had a feeling she'd be falling more than skiing. And as someone trained to read a person's body language, at that moment, he had the unnerving feeling she wanted to push him off the mountain.

"You've been very helpful, Harry. I'll try my best not to hold you back." She gave him a tremulous smile, one that had him feeling somewhat guilty for his unkind thoughts.

The guide skied to their side. "All right, folks. We're good to go. I'm ready when you are."

Chloe waved her ski pole. "You two go ahead. I'll catch up."

"It's probably best if I follow behind."

"No, my lord. I don't think it is." She placed her hand on his back and gave him a light shove. He stared down at her. There was something odd... She rubbed her cheek against the arm of his black ski jacket, then tipped her head back to flutter her eyes at him. "I don't want to embarrass myself."

"All right, then. See you at the bottom." He pushed

off the edge of the mountain, and all thoughts of Chloe and Cat gave way to the thrill of the drop. He let the raw beauty of the pristine wilderness, the snow-blanketed tress sink in as he absorbed the peaceful stillness, exalting in the exhilarating sense of freedom. The only sound the whoosh of his skis cutting through the deep powder, the cold, fresh air whistling past his ears.

And then he heard an excited feminine whoop. Bloody hell, he'd forgotten about Chloe. He shot an apprehensive glance over his shoulder, only to have a blur of pink swish past him. Through a massive cloud of powder, he saw her black helmet. He watched in awe as she commanded the slope. Her body crouched over her skis as she expertly carved through the snow. Her movements were graceful and powerful, and he could almost feel her uninhibited joy. An overwhelming need came over him, and he crouched lower, increasing his speed. He wanted to see her face, experience this with her instead of being a spectator.

"You're a liar, Chloe O'Connor," he yelled as he closed in on her.

She swiveled her head in his direction and laughed, her cheeks pink, her eyes sparkling. "No, I'm an actress."

And before he could respond, she sent up a spray of snow that covered him from head to toe. By the time he cleared his goggles, she was yards ahead of him, taking a mogul with the finesse of a pro. A wave of lust hit him as hard as his skis hit surface crust moments later, as hard as the day he'd felt Cat's gun under her leather jacket and the day she'd taken down the head of Chloe's fan club. He lost control and flew into the air. He landed hard on his back, knocking the wind out of himself, his skis tangled together. He groaned, struggling to unlock his skis and sit up.

"Are you all right, Harry?" Chloe yelled from where she'd stopped near the bottom of the run.

No, he was not bloody all right. He was in lust with two women, two sisters. "Jolly good," he yelled back, like the idiot he was.

*   *   *

Cat stood in the stall in the ladies' room at the Penalty Box, staring at her cell phone, willing her sister to call. She'd talked to Chloe last night around eleven London time. Her audition had been delayed. Cat prayed that was the reason she was incommunicado. Better yet, she was on the damn plane and heading home. Not that it would help Cat now. Despite what Chloe had told her, they were filming today. And unlike the heli-skiing scene this morning, Cat actually had to speak. She could have used some tips.

She heard the outer door open and what sounded like someone hyperventilating. A male someone. It's too bad the brown leather pants and tight turtleneck sweater she currently had on made it impossible for her to conceal a gun. Setting the script on the back of the toilet, she placed a high-heeled boot on the seat, pulling herself up to peek over the stall. Ty leaned against the exposed log wall with the back of his hand pressed to his brow.

She hopped off the toilet and opened the stall door. "What's going on?"

"What's going on is I'm in hot guy heaven, and they're all straight. Which means I'm in gay man hell."

She pressed her lips together. The men of Christmas

had been roped into playing extras in the bar scene by their wives.

"Easy for you to laugh. You have Tall, Dark, and Fabulous following your every move with those true-blue eyes of his. It's not fair."

If she'd been laughing, her laughter would have died an untimely death at Ty's observation. She didn't like the way Harry had been looking at her since their morning on the mountain. Or more to the point, at her sister. Because that's who he thought she was. Until today, those amused, admiring looks had been for her and her alone. She'd been hoping it was her imagination, but obviously it wasn't if Ty had noticed, too.

"He's following Chloe's every move, not mine."

Ty's eyes widened behind his red-framed glasses, and he pressed his fingers to his mouth. "You're right. That no-good cheater. We should have known he was too good to be true."

"We'd have to be in a relationship for him to be a cheater, Ty. We weren't, we're not, and we never will be." She ignored the small pinch in her chest. It shouldn't be there anyway.

"You wanted to be, even if you won't admit it to yourself." He pushed off the wall and came to her. "If he can't see past this," he said, gently tugging on an extension, "he doesn't deserve you. But out there is a plethora of men, hot men, and it's time for you to get back in the game."

"I don't want to be in the game. Games are exhausting and—"

"Fun. You need some fun. You deserve some fun. And if I'm not going to have any, the least you can do is let me live vicariously through you." He took her by the shoulders and steered her to the counter beside the sinks. "Get your delicious leather-clad butt up there, and while I fix your makeup, you can check out the merchandise." He handed her his phone, thumbing through pictures of familiar male faces. "Why don't you start with this one? He has the face of a fallen angel, and his hands and feet are—" He broke off when Vivian Westfield, now McBride, popped her head in.

"Everyone decent?" she asked in her husky voice.

"Come on in, Vivi. Ty was just telling me how big Chance's feet and hands are. Not sure where he was going with it, but maybe you can enlighten us."

Ty pursed his lips at her, then pointed a makeup brush at Vivi. "Are you with Thor?"

At Vivi's confused look, Cat showed her the picture Ty had taken of Chance. Vivi smiled. "Yes, he's mine. But I call him Superman."

Ty patted the counter. "Park your butt over here and tell Uncle Ty all about him while I repair Pussy's makeup."

Vivi fought to keep a straight face. "Pussy?"

"Yes, that would be me."

Ty moved his brush between them. "So, you knew she's Cat and not Chloe?"

"Vivi is about the only one, besides you, who ever does. I should probably introduce you two. Vivi, this is my friend and stylist, Ty."

"Best friend," Ty corrected.

"Right, and, Ty, this is Vivi Westfield, owner and publisher of the local newspaper and Chance McBride's... fiancée."

Hopping up on the counter, Vivi leaned in to give Cat a hug. "Good to see you, and nice to meet you, Ty." She extended her hand.

Ty shook it while scrutinizing Vivi's long, dark hair. "I'm not surprised you snagged Thor, you're gorgeous. Wait a minute, did you say McBride? Is Thor related to the White Knight?"

Vivi looked from Ty to Cat. "White Knight?

"He means Easton. Yes, Ty, he's Thor's…Chance's baby brother."

Vivi arched an eyebrow at Cat. "White Knight, eh? So you do still have a thing for Easton. What did she say about him, Ty?"

"You and the White Knight had a thing, and you didn't tell me? Holding out goes against the best friend—"

"We didn't have a—"

Ty snapped his fingers and thumb together in front of her face. "Shut it so I can put on your lipstick." She sighed and pressed her lips together. While Ty lined her mouth with brown pencil, he said, "Okay, Vivi, give me the goods."

"Sorry, Ty, she's holding out on me, too. All I know—"

Cat went to open her mouth, and Ty pinched her lips between his fingers, instructing Vivi to go on.

"If you'd let go of my mouth, I'll tell you," Cat mumbled. Once Ty released her lips, she gave him the short-hand version of her and Easton's two-year relationship, glossing over the nightmare that had been their disastrous breakup. And Chloe's part in it.

"He's the one," Ty proclaimed with a dramatic slash of the bronze lipstick. "Young love reunited. I'm loving this for you, Pussy. Don't worry, Vivi and I will take care of everything."

"No, no one is taking care of anything. We have bigger things to worry about than my love life, or fun life, or whatever you want to call it. We have to figure out who's trying to kill Chloe, and I have to learn her lines, or she's going to kill me."

"You know?" he asked Vivi.

She nodded, taking out her phone from the purple, down-filled vest she wore over a matching long-sleeve knit top. She patted Cat's thigh. "Don't worry, you've got us on the job now. You don't have to do this on your own."

Ty, with an offended look on his face, pointed to himself with the makeup brush. "She hasn't been doing it on her own. I'm on the case, too. Tell her."

"Ty's been helping me—"

"Helping? I'm the one who discovered Sam has a gun in his room."

"You *think* he had a gun. I didn't find one when I searched his room last night." It hadn't been easy getting out of the house. It was as if Harry had bionic hearing. She'd finally managed to sneak out around eleven.

"Right now, my money's on Sam," Vivi said. "He has two assault charges and a break-and-enter on his record. And it looks like he has a drug habit."

"I'm surprised the studio hired him," Cat said.

Vivi thumbed through her phone. "They may not know. His file was sealed. He was under eighteen at the time of the arrests."

"Then how…ah, Easton." Cat saw Ty's face light up with interest. "Don't, okay?" she warned him before returning her attention to Vivi. "My gut says, if it is Sam, he's not in this on his own. He's working for someone. Either to cover the cost of his drug habit or they're black-mailing him. Now to figure out who."

"I'll e-mail you what I have on George and Molly, but

it's not much. No red flags. We need a motive—" Vivi began, then made a face when a familiar deep voice called through the door. "You okay, Slick?"

Vivi sighed and hopped off the counter, saying under her breath, "He's going to drive me insane," before answering Chance with, "I'm fine, honey."

Cat frowned, taking in Vivi's long, loose top and her yoga pants. She'd rarely seen her in anything other than jeans. She scanned the other woman's face. "You're glowing." She considered Vivi's reaction to Chance looking for her and grinned. "You're pregnant."

"Oh my God, you're having a baby Thor." Ty clapped his hands.

The door flew open, and Chance strode into the ladies' room wearing a black shirt, faded blue jeans, and scuffed brown cowboy boots. He looked over his wife as he reached for her hand, drawing her toward him. Once he had a protective arm wrapped around Vivi's shoulders, he turned his intent green gaze on Cat and Ty, who was making a humming sound in his throat.

Chance nodded at Cat. "Chloe." Then looked down at Vivi, jerking his thumb at Ty. "Who's this?"

Ty, his face flushed, his eyes glazed, sidled closer. "Ty. I'm Ty. And may I just say you have the most gorgeous hair." He raised his hand as if to touch Chance's head. "Is it real?"

Chance drew back, his eyes narrowed. "Did you just ask if my hair is real?"

"Ty's a hairstylist for *As the Sun Sets*, Chance. And it's me, Cat."

"Oh, okay." Rubbing his head, his gaze moved from Ty to Cat, and he smiled. Ty moaned. Chance frowned at him while saying, "Good to see you, Cat. Vivi fill you in on what we've got so far?"

"Yes, she did." Cat slid off the counter and walked over to give him a hug. "Congratulations, daddy-to-be. You, too, Vivi."

Chance raised an eyebrow at his wife. "You told them?"

"No, Cat figured it out. You always said she was one of the best cops you knew. Guess she just proved it."

"Yeah, she is." He gave Cat a considering look. "Any chance you'd come work for me? I could use someone with your experience."

Vivi's eyes widened, and she mouthed *no.* For a brief moment, Cat was offended until she realized what was going on. Chance had lost his first wife and their unborn child in a car accident six years earlier. Vivi already found him overly protective, and now that she was expecting, Cat imagined it had gotten worse. No doubt Vivi was worried Chance's job offer stemmed from him wanting to be with her 24/7. It probably did.

"Until whoever is trying to kill Chloe is behind bars, I can't entertain a job offer. But I appreciate your confidence in me."

"Keep it in mind. I...Is there something wrong with him?" Chance lifted his chin at Ty, who was staring at him with his mouth slightly open.

Cat nudged Ty with her elbow. "You're drooling."

He touched the side of his mouth, then said to Chance, "I'm interested...in the job."

"You have experience in security, investigative work?"

"Have you never heard the saying 'Only my hairdresser knows'?"

"Can't say I have," Chance said, fighting back a grin.

"People tell me things. I know more about what's going on behind the scenes at *As the Sun Sets* than anyone."

"Yeah? We should grab a beer, then, and you can fill me in."

Ty looked at Chance with an enthralled expression on his face. "Is it okay if I have a Chardonnay?"

"Sure, whatever floats your boat." Chance smoothed his hand down Vivi's dark hair and kissed her forehead. "Don't be long."

"Ty, what about my makeup?" Cat called when he followed Chance to the door.

He waved his hand without looking at her. "It's fine."

"But you were supposed to help me with my lines."

He pivoted, placing his hands on his narrow hips. "Do you want to find your sister's would-be assassin or not? The big guy and I will handle this. All you have to do is play your part." As he left Cat staring after him, they heard him say, "So, will the White Knight be working on the case with us?"

Vivi laughed.

"It's not funny. He's going to be worse than Nell, I just know it."

The door opened, and Chance popped his head in. "Slick, I'm going to grab you a burger. You haven't eaten in a while. I'll be back in fifteen. Stick with . . . On second thought, you better come with me."

"No, I'm staying here to help Cat with her lines." Vivi made a shooing motion with her hands. "Go."

"Cat." He nodded at his wife.

"I've got her covered, Chance." She worked to keep the laughter from her voice.

Vivi gave her head a frustrated shake as the door closed behind him. "I'm lucky if I can go to the bathroom on my own. Speaking of which…" She moved to the stall and stepped inside, closing the door. "And yes, I know where it's coming from, and I'm trying to be patient with him… Umm, Cat, you didn't happen to leave the script in here, did you?"

* * *

Everyone's eyes were on Cat as she stood beside the table. Harry wore a black leather jacket and sat with his long, denim-clad legs stretched out. He didn't look like the debonair lord today. A couple inches of dark scruff lined his jaw, his hair had that just-woken-up sexy look, and the scar bisecting his brow was more prominent. He looked incredibly hot and dangerous, and he was messing with her concentration.

She tried to focus, drowning out "Grandma Got Run Over by a Reindeer" playing on the jukebox, while avoiding looking directly at Harry. She searched her brain for her next line. She'd already flubbed one. She had to get this right and quickly went over the story line in her head to see if that helped.

Byron had taken Tessa away for the holidays in hopes of reviving their marriage and getting her away from Rand, who followed them here in a bid to win her back. But Rand's lying to Tessa. He wants to oust Byron as CEO of Hart Enterprises because he blames the older man for the hostile takeover of his family's business, and he's using Tessa to get back at Byron. And he's using Tessa's sister Paula to make her jealous. If that doesn't work…

Okay, she should be good now. She looked at the gorgeous man slouched in the chair. Harry had just propositioned her, so she says... "Harry, you shouldn't have followed me here. I'm a married..." She turned when Phil yelled "Cut!"

The director threw up his hands. "What the hell's wrong with you today, Chloe? Rand, it's Rand."

Standing beside Phil, Dame Alexander narrowed her eyes. *Dammit.* Cat fluffed her hair, trying to channel her sister... and the words for the scene. Harry must have noticed the panic on her face and pushed back his chair. "Phil, why don't you give us a minute?"

"Sure, no problem, Harry."

Phil was a nice guy, but he was no pushover, especially when it came to the show. So she found it odd that he would take direction from Harry. Maybe it was the title thing.

Harry came to her side and held out a chair. "Sit and relax, love. I'll get you a cup of tea."

"Thank you. That's very thoughtful of you, Harry. But I just need to get this over with. I have a headache. I can't think straight."

"This is the second headache you've had in less than twenty-four hours. Perhaps you should have your stepfather examine you." He glanced around the bar. "Ah, there he is. How about I—"

"No, it's fine. I don't want to worry my... Mommsy." She rubbed her temples.

He drew her hands from her head and smiled down at her. "Let me. I've been told I'm pretty good at this."

His long, strong fingers moved in small circles over her temples. He was close enough that his chest brushed against hers, her nipples tightening at that accidental touch. She caught her bottom lip between her teeth to hold back a needy moan. She kept her eyes on the planked floor, praying to God he didn't notice. His hands moved from her temples to the sides of her neck. "Your muscles are rock-hard, Chloe. No wonder you have a headache." As his fingers gently kneaded and caressed, her knees went weak. She reached for the back of the chair and hung on.

"The natives are getting restless," he said, his minty breath fanning her cheek. "I can work on you when we get home. We have a couple of hours before the tree trimming."

A breathy *yes* was on the tip of her tongue when someone loudly cleared their throat. Ty stood off to the side with a sympathetic expression on his face.

She briefly closed her eyes. Why did she keep forgetting it was Chloe Harry was looking at, not her? She pinched the bridge of her nose and stepped back. "Thank you. I'm good now. Phil, ready when you are."

Harry slowly removed his hands, his brow furrowed as he searched her face. "Are you sure you're all right?"

"Fine." She frowned. Why was Ty waving his hands at her? She glanced at her own and realized what she'd done. She pinched her nose harder, her voice coming out in a nasally whine. "Cat told me this helps. She was right. Headache's all gone now." She fluffed her hair and did a flirty head tilt. "But you know, a back rub sounds lovely." She'd hide out in the barn until they had to leave for the town square.

Harry stepped away from her, watching her with an odd expression on his face. He wasn't the only one. George, standing next to Molly, did the same. Cat needed to do a killer job with these last lines to avoid their suspicions. Ten minutes later, she'd murdered them. She was lucky Harry was a better actor than her and managed to save her butt. The moment the words *It's a wrap* came out of Phil's mouth, Cat wove her way through the crowd, intent on making her escape. As she walked past a group of people, she heard a woman's voice say, "Maybe we don't have to kill her off after all."

Chapter Thirteen

Snow lightly fell as Grayson walked beside Molly down Main Street. They were headed to the town square with what appeared to be half the town. Young and old carried lanterns to light the way along the cobblestone sidewalks as the old-fashioned streetlamps decorated with greenery and red bows had been dimmed. Strains of "O Christmas Tree" floated on the crisp night air mingling with sounds of laughter and excitement.

It would have been an enjoyable walk if Grayson wasn't trying to keep an eye on Chloe. He spotted her white fur hat several yards ahead. George walked alongside her while two cameramen filmed the scene. For the next five minutes, they were to be in character. Tessa and Byron trying to reignite their loveless marriage while Rand and Paula plotted to bring the couple down.

Molly, wearing a fur vest over a cream sweater, leaned toward the shop window to get a look ahead. "Chloe seems to be her bitchy self again. Did she tell you what the problem was at the taping? She's never messed up her lines before."

"She had a headache." Or so she said. Grayson didn't buy it. There was more going on. The tone of her voice, her speech pattern, even her walk were off. For a split second while he massaged her temples, he could have sworn it was Cat. Even his body had been fooled. The hint of her sultry citrus fragrance nearly put him in an embarrassing situation. And when she pinched the bridge of her nose, he almost called her on it, but her excuse seemed plausible. Then she did that flirty thing with her head and hair, and he realized he was mistaken.

"Please, I can't stand the woman, but it would take more than a headache to explain what happened today. I'm surprised she didn't have a meltdown. Miss Perfect isn't so perfect after all. I can't wait to rub it in. She was gone before I had a chance to give her a taste of her own medicine. If any of us makes the smallest mistake, we never hear the end of it. Karma's a bitch, and Chloe O'Connor's about to get hers."

The people in front of them glanced back. "It might be best if you lower your voice, Molly." Besides being in the middle of a throng of *As the Sun Sets* fans, Sam was a few feet away with the boom mic.

"Other than capturing a Currier and Ives moment, they aren't paying any attention to us. It's all about Byron and Tessa. Phil just wants a shot of us tailing them. I think we look like we're up to something nefarious, don't you?"

She certainly sounded like she was. Grayson needed to figure out a way to keep Chloe at his side. She'd left the Penalty Box directly after taping and completely disappeared off his radar until fifteen minutes ago. Which wouldn't have been a problem if he wasn't supposed to be protecting the bloody woman. As much as he hated to admit it, GG was probably right. He had to "woo" Chloe. His gut rebelled at the thought. If Cat hadn't left town, he wouldn't be entertaining the idea of seducing her sister, for several reasons, the main one being he'd rather be seducing Cat.

As the crowd crossed the street to the town square, he noticed Ty trailing behind Chloe and George. The hairstylist wouldn't have been Grayson's first choice for a bodyguard, but it had been obvious from the moment he caught Ty trying to sneak into Chloe's bedroom that Cat had instructed him to keep an eye on her sister.

No, Grayson's choice would have been the tall, blond guy Ty was trying to strike up a conversation with. There was something about the man's distinctive build and mannerisms, the way he scanned the crowd, that told Grayson he was ex-military or law enforcement.

On the street, the two cameramen lowered their cameras. Molly glanced at Sam and nodded. She tugged on Grayson's leather jacket. "Why don't you join us for a drink?"

"You're not attending the tree lighting?"

She laughed. "God, no. I've had enough Christmas cheer to last me through to next year. Unless it comes in a glass. Don't you find it a little much?"

"No, actually, I find it quite charming. It's a nice change of pace from LA." And he liked the people better. If he wasn't on assignment, it was exactly the type of place he'd choose to spend his vacation.

"To each their own, I guess." She bumped him with her shoulder. "I'll be at the Penalty Box if you get bored."

He watched as she joined Sam. She said something to the younger man, and they glanced in the direction of the town square. As though they sensed Grayson's attention, they looked his way. He smiled and raised his hand, then headed down the street. With Sam and Molly at the bar, it was the perfect opportunity to check their rooms at the lodge. The tree lighting shouldn't take more than a few minutes. After it was over, he'd insist Chloe let him take her home. Maybe suggest she have a hot bath that he'd follow up with an even hotter massage once he got back from running his *errand*.

The thought left a bitter taste in his mouth. What he should do is get his hands on Chloe's phone and tell her sister to get her ass back here. Then he'd tell Cat who he was. He needed someone other than Ty to protect Chloe while he worked the case. If there'd been another attempt on Chloe's life, he'd make the call. But there hadn't been, and that was worrisome on a whole other level.

His grandmother carefully made her way toward him. She'd brought Fluffy along, dressing the cat in a red velvet, fur-trimmed cape. "Chloe and George are to the right of the podium," she informed him.

A makeshift wooden stand had been set up to the left of the twenty-foot Douglas fir, which stood in the center of the town square. An attractive blonde in a white wool coat with a pink scarf around her neck adjusted the microphone. Two young girls stood behind her, the taller one holding a toddler dressed in a blue snowsuit.

"That's the mayor, Madison McBride. She's married to the sheriff, Gage. He's Dr. McBride's son, Chloe's stepbrother. I think they know."

"Know what?" Grayson asked as he took his grandmother by the arm, guiding her toward the podium.

She held up her pen. "I was behind them. Everything they said is on tape." She clicked the pen. All you could hear was people singing "O Christmas Tree," including a woman who sounded like a cat in heat.

GG scowled at the pen. "I'm going to send this back and demand a refund."

"Did you catch what they said?"

She nodded, stroking Fluffy under the chin. "The sheriff told his wife not to worry. That he and Chance had everything under control."

"I'm not sure why you think they know Chloe's in danger from that." He lowered his voice as they passed a group of people huddled by the tree.

"Chance is the sheriff's brother. The big, blond man following Chloe and George. He runs a security firm in town."

This was the best news he'd heard in weeks. He'd speak to the McBride brothers first thing tomorrow morning. He couldn't risk someone overhearing them. Grayson leaned down and kissed his grandmother's cheek. "Great job, GG. I'm impressed."

"I have a vested interest in the case, my boy. I can't have my future grand—"

Just when he was feeling like things had started to go his way. "For the last time, I'm not interested in Chloe."

She held up her watch from Spies Are Us. "I have it on film. Cameras don't lie. I knew, once her sister was out of the way, you'd see what I did. Chloe's perfect for you. The other one's bad news. Her last boyfriend ended up in jail, you know."

"I do know. And *he* was bad news, not Cat."

"Is that right? Well maybe you can explain to me why there have been no accidents since she's been out of town.

Don't look so surprised, my boy." She tapped her gloved finger on her temple. "I'm still sharp as a tack. Didn't play Miss Marple for nothing. I know all the tricks of the trade."

Sweet mother of God. "We'll save this for another time, shall we, Estelle?" he said as they rounded the stand, smiling his thanks to the family of five who made room for them.

He had a clear view of Chloe. She stood beside George. Her white fur hat matched her coat, and snowflakes glistened on her long dark hair. A small smile played on her lips as she watched Ty, who stood gazing up at the man Grayson now knew to be Chance McBride. The security specialist spoke to a dark-haired man wearing a brown leather bomber jacket with a sheriff's patch on the shoulder.

Interesting, he'd never found Chloe particularly friendly to the hairstylist. George was behaving oddly, too. Arms crossed over his navy wool coat, the actor looked bored—which wasn't odd. What was, was the way he seemed to be distancing himself from Chloe. For the most part, George was attentive to his costar, overly so. It was one of the reasons he'd been on the bottom of Grayson's suspect list. He couldn't get a handle on his motivation. But as George was good friends with Grayson's primary suspects, he didn't plan to take the actor off his list just yet.

The mayor tapped the microphone. "Welcome to the seventy-fifth annual lighting of the town tree." Once the crowd stopped cheering and whistling, she continued. "As you all know, along with hosting the wonderful cast and crew from our favorite daytime drama, *As the Sun Sets*, we're honored that Lord Harry Halstead and his manager

Dame Alexander have joined us." She clapped, smiling down at Grayson and his grandmother. He gave a slight bow, waving at the crowd with Estelle.

A few moments later, the mayor once again tapped her microphone, and the applause died down. "Now, we were going to have Christmas's favorite daughter, the incomparable Chloe O'Connor, light the tree this year, but she's asked that the honor be given instead to Lord Harry and Dame Alexander. So if you would both please step up to the podium."

"How lovely." His grandmother beamed. "She's such a thoughtful girl, isn't she, Harry?"

"Yes, most thoughtful." It was a considerate gesture, but it also seemed out of character for the attention-seeking actress. Then again, she was rather fond of him and his grandmother and the whole royalty thing. As he took Estelle's arm to lead her to the stairs, he turned to mouth his thanks to Chloe.

"What is the meaning of this? I was told that you and I would be lighting the tree," George blustered, glaring at Chloe.

She seemed as surprised as everyone else by her costar's reaction and took a step back. Grayson moved to intervene, but Chance McBride was instantly at her side, placing a hand on George's shoulder.

The actor seemed to realize he was making a spectacle of himself and tugged on his coat's lapels. "I just think after all the work you did to bring our show to Christmas, you should have the honor of lighting this spectacular tree. But if you prefer to give it to Harry and his manager, that's your business, I suppose."

"Never a dull moment in Christmas," Madison said from

where she stood at the base of the podium. She extended her hand with a smile. "It's lovely to meet you both."

They exchanged pleasantries, and then Madison got them sorted on the podium. Estelle held one end of the plug, placing Fluffy's paw on it as well. Grayson held the other end as the citizens of Christmas counted down from ten.

On one, they joined ends. An electric current buzzed through Grayson's arms. Fluffy, hair standing on end, flew from GG's now-lax hold and landed on Grayson's head. Digging her claws into his scalp, she launched herself into the tree. Estelle stood in front of him in wide-eyed shock with smoke spiraling from her hair, as all around them Christmas lights exploded, shooting sparks into the night sky.

*   *   *

One minute Cat was smiling as she watched Harry and Estelle light the Christmas tree, and in the next, she was yelling Harry's name. As she pushed through the panicked crowd to reach him, someone grabbed her by the arm. "What do you think—"

Chance lowered his mouth to her ear. "You're Chloe, remember. Your sister wouldn't run toward danger. She'd faint."

"No, she—" Cat began to argue when someone hit her in the back of her knees, and her legs gave way.

"Room, give us room! Chloe fainted," Ty yelled, pushing her the rest of the way to the ground. He crouched beside her, and so did Chance.

She glared at Ty. "I can't believe you did that. Let me up. I need to see if Harry is okay."

"He is. Gage is with them. And right now you're safer

here until we figure out if it was an accident." Chance kept his voice low, then he slapped Ty on the back, nearly sending him face-first into Cat's chest. "Quick thinking. I might just hire you after all."

When Chance got to his feet, so did Ty, completely forgetting about his supposed best friend lying in the snow at risk of being trampled. "Are you serious? Oh my God, I don't believe it. Did you hear that..." Ty glanced from her to George, who went down on his knees beside Cat, pulling her into his arms.

"Chloe, you poor darling. But for the grace of God, it could have been you up there." Was it her imagination or did he sound like he wished it had been?

She was about to tell him he could stop squeezing the life out of her, but realized that wasn't something Chloe would say. She let her body go lax and pressed the back of her hand to her brow. "Don't remind me, George. The thought of all those electrical currents going through my body." She shuddered, touching her hat. "I might have lost my hair. It's too terrifying to think about. I can't...I can't talk about it anymore."

Chance and Ty stared at her. Okay, maybe she'd overdone it a bit. "Can you help me up, please? I need to check on Harry and Estelle." Despite Chance's reassurances, she had to see that Harry was all right for herself. If something happened to him because he'd taken her place on the podium...

George released her, then stood and reached for her hand. He pulled her up with such force that she pressed a palm to his chest to avoid smacking into him. "Too bad about Harry, he seemed to be enjoying his time on our show. Phil will probably need to hire a replacement now," he said with a smile. In the dim light cast by the streetlamps, it looked more like a sneer.

She whipped her head around. Harry and Estelle were no longer on the podium. She went up on her tiptoes, but she couldn't see over the heads of the crowd. "I should go—" she began, fighting against a wave of panic.

"I don't think that's a good idea. You might step on a live wire, and where would the show be then? You are the star after all."

He was really starting to get on her nerves. "Thank you for your concern, George. But—"

"Chloe, oh darling, are you all right?" Her mother pushed people out of the way as she ran toward her with Paul on her heels.

Cat held back a groan. She'd done a good job of avoiding her mother up to now. "I'm okay, Mommsy. Just shaken up. But Paul should check on Harry and Dame Alexander. They were electrocuted." She choked back a fake sob, burying her face in her mother's suede coat.

"Chloe's being a little dramatic, Dad. They seem to be fine," Chance said.

Paul rubbed Cat's shoulder. "Are you sure you're okay, honey?"

"Yes, yes, I'm good. I'm just worried about Harry."

"I'll go check on both of them right now. Chance?"

"I think I'd better stay with Chloe in case she faints again, Dad."

Now, instead of wanting to strangle George, she wanted to strangle Chance. "I didn't faint, Paul. I just had a bit of a weak spell."

"That's twice in a couple of days, Chloe. I think it would be best if you came in for a complete physical."

Shooting Chance an are-you-happy-now look, she opened her mouth to assure Paul she was fine, but her mother cut her off. "Do not think about arguing."

George looked from Cat to her mother with a slight frown furrowing his brow. Then he said, "Seeing as you're in good hands, I'll head to the Penalty Box. I could use a drink after all the excitement." He leaned in and gave Cat a tender kiss on the check. "You take care of yourself. I wouldn't want anything to happen to my Tessa."

Cat stared after him, totally confused. From the looks on Chance's and Ty's faces, she wasn't the only one.

* * *

"Are you sure you're all right, Harry?" Cat asked as she turned onto the one-lane road to the ranch. After his ordeal, Cat insisted she drive. Paul had checked both Estelle and Harry over before giving the okay to take them home. Neither had been burned, and other than Estelle being shaken up and her hair singed, they were all right.

"Chloe, I told you I'm perfectly fine. But how are you, my dear? I heard you fainted."

He sounded irritated. She supposed she couldn't blame him. After all, he'd been the one who had nearly gotten fried, not Chloe. "Ty overreacted. It was just a weak spell."

It was time to end the charade. She couldn't keep up the pretense any longer. At least not with Harry. Wondering if it was her he was interested in or Chloe was driving her crazy. She glanced in the rearview mirror. She had to go with her gut. She could trust Harry to keep her secret, but she wasn't sure she could trust Estelle. If she was asleep... The older woman's eyes met hers in the mirror. Okay, so she'd have to wait until Estelle went to bed.

"How are you and Fluffy doing back there?"

"I'll be all right, my dear. I'm tougher than I look. But I'm concerned about Fluffy."

Once the firefighters had finally managed to get the cat out of the tree, Paul had examined her, too. "I can call the vet if you'd like. I'm sure he'd make a house call."

"Thank you. But Fred already called him. We have an appointment in the morning."

Ted and Fred had been beside themselves with worry over Estelle. So much so that Cat was surprised they weren't following them to the ranch. "I'm sure the three of you will feel better after a good night's sleep," Cat said as she drove through the gates. She sensed Harry watching her as she shut off the engine. "Is something wrong?"

He studied her intently. "You seem…" He gave his head a slight shake. "No, it's nothing. Done in is all."

Maybe it was selfish of her, but she wanted to get this over with. She joined him at the passenger-side door as he helped Estelle out of the SUV. "Harry, I, uh, have something I need to talk to you about. In private. Do you think you could spare me a few minutes?"

"I really am knackered, Chloe. Can it wait until morning?"

"Harry, where are your manners? Of course he can…" Estelle trailed off when the front door flew open.

Chloe, as Chloe, ran down the steps. "Where have you been? I've been trying to reach you for the last hour."

Chapter Fourteen

He'd been played. Again. Only it was worse this time because he liked Cat. He really liked her and had been beating himself up because he thought he was attracted to her sister, too.

Chloe, the real one, flung herself into his arms. "Oh, Harry, I never should have listened to Cat. I never should have gone to London."

He glanced at Cat, who stared open-mouthed at her sister. She raised her gaze to his and winced.

Yeah, guess he wasn't doing such a good job hiding that he was pissed. Everything began to make sense. His reaction to her at the Penalty Box during taping, her sultry citrus scent, the way he'd responded to watching her ski. Jesus, the way she skied, and that kiss they shared. And there must be something seriously wrong with him, because right now he wanted to kiss her again, wanted to strip her down to bare skin and memorize every inch of her. Maybe it was the relief that it was her, and her alone, that fueled his insane desire.

He needed to get a grip. Because despite the relief that he no longer had to feel guilty, he had to put Cat back on his suspect list. And that really grated. He wanted to trust her. But there were questions that needed to be answered, and they needed to be answered now.

"I don't understand," his grandmother said, rubbing her eyes. Obviously worried that she was suffering double vision after her near-electrocution. Something else that put Cat under a cloud of suspicion as she had been the one to insist they have the honor of lighting the tree.

"It seems the O'Connor sisters put one over on us, Estelle." It didn't escape him that he and his grandmother were doing the same. But at least they had a legitimate reason for doing so.

"This had nothing to do with you and Estelle, Harry. Well, not really. And Chloe, how—"

"I see." Grayson cut her off, looking down at Chloe. "So it really is you. And you would be the imposter, then." He lifted his chin at Cat.

"Of course I'm me. Surely you can tell the difference now that you see us together," Chloe said, seemingly offended.

"To be honest, no. You're identical twins. I can't imagine anyone being able to tell you apart." It may be perverse of him, but he wanted to get a reaction from Cat.

She averted her eyes before he could read the emotion in them, and gestured to GG. "Look, you want to talk about this, let's do it inside. Estelle had a shock earlier, no pun intended, and should probably be resting." That said, Cat moved past them to walk up the front steps.

"Cat, what did you do, roll around in the dirt? My coat is filthy."

Standing on the front porch, Cat whipped off the hat then the coat. She turned, stomping back down the steps, her face flushed, her eyes flashing with temper. "No, I was forced to pretend I fainted, because that's what *you* would do, instead of checking on Harry and Estelle like I wanted to." She shoved the coat and hat at her sister. "I also had to go heli-skiing in your place, but I bet you knew that, didn't you? And let's not forget the scene we taped today that I totally blew."

All Grayson could think as she stalked away in the high-heeled boots, brown leather pants, and tight sweater, was that the burst of fiery temper suited her. She was magnificent.

Chloe apparently disagreed. "What do you mean, you blew it?" she called to Cat who ignored her and stormed inside the house. Chloe looked up at him. "How bad was it?"

"I wouldn't say it—"

His grandmother cut him off. "It was a bloody disaster. I should have known it wasn't you, my dear. You would never be so ill prepared."

Chloe fisted her hands in her hair, wailing, "I'm ruined. She ruined me. Everything's ruined. I'm washed up at thirty-one."

"Now, now." GG moved to her side. "Nothing is ever as bad as it seems."

"You don't understand. The role I auditioned for in London—the one guaranteed to win me an Oscar—they gave it to a twenty-two-year-old. It was written for me, not for some nobody who can't act her way out of a paper bag."

It was becoming clearer to Grayson that Cat had nothing to do with Chloe's trip to London. As he'd noticed, every time something didn't go her way, Chloe threw Cat under the bus. He guided the two women up the steps. "I'll make us a cup of tea." He had a feeling he'd need something stronger before the night was out. "And you can tell us all about it, Chloe."

She sniffed. "I don't know if I can. It's too depressing. I never should have listened to my sister."

Grayson was about to defend Cat, then realized he didn't want to deal with the fallout. He helped his grandmother out of her coat, then hung it up before crouching to unzip her boots. Both she and Fluffy were shivering. "How about I put on a fire? The three of you can curl up on the couch while I make you something to eat."

"Nonsense, you forget your place, my boy. The other one can take care of the food and drink," Estelle said, leaning heavily on her cane as she followed a sniffling Chloe to the great room.

"The other one is going to bed." Cat's voice came from the kitchen, followed by the banging of what sounded like pots and pans.

"That was uncalled for, Estelle." He settled her on the brown leather couch. Chloe sat at the opposite end, curling her feet under her, looking as if her world had crashed and burned. Which made him think about his and GG's close call. He found it interesting that Chloe hadn't bothered to ask what happened. Even more interesting was Cat's admission that she'd been preparing to come to their aid before she remembered who she was pretending to be.

GG shrugged in response to his reprimand, pulling the orange afghan from the back of the couch to wrap around

Fluffy. "The girl pulled a fast one on us. I don't appreciate being made to look like a fool."

Neither did he, but really, what did he expect. It's not like he and Cat were in a relationship. She didn't owe him an explanation. At least on a personal level. But as it pertained to his case, she did.

Without responding to his grandmother, he walked to the floor-to-ceiling fireplace in the center of the room. From where he crouched, he could see into the kitchen. Cat stood at the island, wincing as she pulled at her upper eyelid. He held back a laugh as he lit a match, holding it to the kindling beneath the logs. It must have been torture for her to have her hair and makeup done every day. And now, he thought, as he stood up, he'd find out why she'd agreed to the charade in the first place. From her, not Chloe. He wanted the truth.

His grandmother looked up from her conversation with Chloe. "Where are you going?"

"To get our tea."

"I suppose that might be for the best given that girl couldn't make a decent cup to save her life. Add a little extra sugar in mine."

"Mine too, Harry. And tell my sister when she's done with her hissy fit that I need to speak to her. I want to know how bad the situation is."

He made a noncommittal sound in his throat and headed to the kitchen. Cat stood at the stove with her back to him. She'd removed her boots, and from the looks of the island, hunks of her hair. Without looking at him, she pointed to a teapot on the stove. "Tea's ready."

He moved behind her. "I thought you were going to bed."

"I am, but I was hungry." She sighed, resting the wooden

spoon on top of the pot. "Look, I'm sorry for not... Why are looking at me like that?"

"Your"—he leaned into her, plucking the false eyelashes from her lid—"lashes are falling off. What should I do with it?"

"Toss it." She pulled at her other eyelid.

He took her by the shoulders, turning her to face him. "Let me." She squinted as he pulled. "Your own lashes are as long as these. Why do you wear them?"

"I don't. Chloe does."

"Ah, I see. Hang on, one more." He tugged, then offered the sticky lashes to her on the tip of his index finger.

"Thank you."

She went to move away, and he held her in place. "You could have told me, you know. I would have kept your confidence."

"I wanted to. But if anyone found out, Chloe would have been in breach of her contract. And then she'd blame me for her losing her job." Her shoulders lifted on a half laugh. "Which she obviously thinks I have. I can't win with her."

"So why do you keep trying?"

She wriggled from under his hands and turned back to the stove. "She's my sister. It's my job to protect her."

"Is that what you were doing, protecting her?"

"Yes, from... being fired, yes."

So not quite ready to open up to him. "You know, Cat, it is her career. It was her choice to audition for the role. What would you have done if she got the part? Pretend to be Chloe for however long production lasted?"

She stared at him, then briefly closed her eyes. "You're right. I didn't think that far ahead. I guess I should be thankful she didn't get the role."

"How can you be so selfish?" Chloe said from behind them. "I'm heartbroken. Completely devastated, and you're happy I didn't get the role."

"Chloe, that's not what I meant. I'm sorry you didn't get the part. But we didn't think it through. Harry's right. I couldn't—"

"What else have you been up to besides ruining my acting reputation?" She interrupted Cat, her eyes narrowed. "Did she make a move on you?"

"Pardon me?" He groaned inwardly when GG entered the kitchen. Surely she'd keep her mouth—

"She kissed him. At the Christmas bazaar. But Harry only kissed her back because he thought it was you."

Chloe shrieked, lunging for Cat. Grayson stepped between them. "Stop it, Chloe. There's no reason—"

"You're trying to steal my boyfriend just like I stole Easton from you. That's it, isn't it?"

"You didn't..." Cat slammed the wooden spoon on the pot. "It was fourteen years ago, Chloe. Get over it. I have." She flicked the knob on the gas stove to off. "I'm tired. I'm going to bed. Harry, if you're hungry, you can eat my Beefaroni."

*   *   *

Thanks to the O'Connor sisters, Grayson missed his opportunity to do a thorough search of Molly's and Sam's rooms. Actually, it was not so much Cat's fault as it was Chloe's. It took forever to calm the damn woman down. Twenty minutes in Chloe's company reminded him why he'd sworn off actresses, and why he preferred her sister. It was close to eleven by the time he snuck out of the house.

Sam and Molly had arrived back from the bar just

moments after he'd entered her room. Luckily, they were
loud enough that he had time to escape through the patio
door. From what he did find, the connection between
Molly and Sam appeared to stem from an affinity for rec-
reational drugs.

Grayson turned off the headlights as he drove through
the wrought iron gates. He didn't want to wake the residents of the house. Actually, he didn't want to wake Chloe
or GG, but he most definitely wanted to wake Cat. He was
tired of playing games. He wanted to take her off his list
once and for all. Who was he trying to kid? He wanted
her, period.

If he expected her to trust him, he had to trust her
enough to tell her who he really was. So he would.
Tonight. But first, he had to make it clear to her that she
was the one he wanted, not Chloe. And that somewhere
inside of him, he'd known it wasn't Chloe he was kissing
at the Christmas bazaar, but her. Given Cat's past experience with the FBI, he had to make sure she believed at
least that before he revealed his true identity.

Getting out of the parked SUV, he quietly shut the
driver's-side door. The only way to ensure his grandmother and Chloe didn't hear him and wreak havoc with
his plan was to sneak in Cat's window. Trudging through
the snow to the back of the house and her bedroom, he
stayed in the shadows. Her lights were off. He blew on
his hands, weighing his options. He didn't want to leave it
until tomorrow. Slowly, he eased the window open.

*   *   *

Cat rolled over and reached for her ringing cell phone.
"Ty, it's midnight. What—"

"We were right. He's a cheater."

She rubbed her eyes, then propped herself up on the pillows. "Okay, I'm not following you. Who were we right about?"

"Harry. He's cheating on you with Chloe, and on Chloe with you, and now he's cheating on the two of you with Molly."

She was going to go through the whole "he can't be cheating with anyone because he's not in a relationship with them," but the fact Harry might be seeing Molly was relevant to her investigation. And yes, dammit, she didn't have a right to be ticked, but the thought he might possibly be getting it on with Molly bothered her. So she did want this information, even though she kind of didn't. "All right, I'll bite. Why do you think he's with Molly?"

"Because, not thirty minutes ago, I saw him sneaking out of her room."

Before she had a chance to let the information sink in, she heard a scraping sound outside her window. "Ty, are you here?"

"No, do you need me to be?" He blew out a noisy breath. "I've upset you. I shouldn't—"

"Quiet, I hear... I gotta go. I think someone's trying to break in."

"Oh. My. God. Should I call the police?"

"I am the police. Well, I was." She almost hoped someone was breaking in and that that someone thought this was Chloe's bedroom. After the episode with her sister tonight, Cat wanted Chloe's would-be killer caught yesterday.

Cat rolled over, quietly easing open her nightstand drawer to reach for her gun. It wasn't there. She was sure... She racked her brain. The last time she remembered seeing it was the night of the party for Harry and Estelle. Maybe she'd left it in Chloe's room. A bump against the outer wall drew her mind back to the more immediate problem. "Ty, I'll call you back."

She disconnected and tossed her phone. Staying low, she crawled out of bed, moving silently to the window. It was a moonless night, making it difficult to see anything but a dark shadow. The window opened soundlessly. She'd wait until they were fully in the room before making her move. There was no way she was giving them an opportunity to escape.

It was a man. He was powerfully built, had dark hair, and was more than six feet tall. There was something oddly familiar about him. But she didn't have time to give it more thought as he pulled himself all the way into the room. He quietly lowered himself onto the floor. Once he was on his knees, she made her move.

She jumped him from behind, bringing him down to the hardwood floor. Before she had a chance to utter a word, he flipped her effortlessly onto her back. His large body covering hers, the cold from his leather jacket and jeans seeped into her body, making her shiver. Or maybe it was the realization that her intruder was Harry, a man she'd wanted to be underneath for a couple of weeks now.

His white teeth flashed in the dark. "I must say, I prefer being on top."

Heat radiated through her. She ignored it. "Dammit, Harry." She pushed on his chest. "What were you thinking breaking into my room? I could have shot you." Maybe it was a good thing she hadn't been able to find her gun.

"Did I ever tell you how sexy you look holding a

weapon?" His eyes glittered down at her as icy cold fingers moved to her lower spine. "I wanted to talk to you. Alone. This seemed the only way."

"I can think of a couple of others." Ones that didn't involve her lying on the floor beneath a heavy, muscular body. A man who smelled of fresh air and wood smoke and thought she was sexy. Apparently he thought her sister and Molly were, too. "Harry, it's after midnight. I'm tired. Can you get off me now?"

"I will. But first I have to be sure you're you."

She blew out an aggravated breath. "Of course..." Her words stuttered in her throat when he lowered his mouth to hers. Teasing her lips open with his tongue, he wrapped an arm around her waist. His other hand cradled the back of her head as he rolled to his side, bringing her with him.

She was still processing that Harry was actually kissing her when his mouth left hers. He drew back, gently tugging on her hair. "Real, and very beautiful."

"Harry, I—" Her voice came out a throaty whisper, and she forgot what she was about to say when he moved his hand to her face, trailing his fingers down her cheek to her mouth. He rubbed his thumb over her damp bottom lip. "No makeup, and naturally gorgeous. Yes, I think it is you, love. But just to be sure." He replaced his thumb with his mouth.

Desire stole through her as much from his words as his kiss, leaving her helpless to deny the attraction. She wanted him, wanted this, had wanted it for weeks, if she were honest. This kiss was real and deep and passionate. So much more than the one they'd shared at the Christmas bazaar. Her arms went around his neck, her fingers tunneling through his thick hair as she touched her tongue to his. He groaned into her mouth, moving his leg between hers, smiling against her lips when she released a helpless moan. She needed to get closer, feel more of him, and she removed her hands from his hair, placing them under his leather jacket to explore his broad chest and taut abs. As though sensing her need, he rolled her to her back. Their kiss turned hotter, more frantic. And then her cell phone rang. It was as effective as a cold shower, wrenching her from her lust-filled state.

She pulled back, breathless. "I have to answer. It's probably Ty. If I don't, he'll call the police."

"All right, then," Harry said, his accent thick and sexy. Releasing her, he sat up and shoved his fingers through his hair.

She scrambled to her feet and hurried across the room to grab her phone. "Everything's fine, Ty. No, no one was there."

Listening as Ty gave her crap for not calling him back, she watched Harry close the bedroom window. He turned, shrugging out of his leather jacket, which he carefully draped over the black beanbag chair in the corner of her room.

Ty huffed in her ear.

She dragged her gaze from the man prowling toward her bed and turned on the bedside lamp. "What? I know. I'm sorry, I fell asleep. No, there's nothing wrong with me. Maybe I'm getting a cold." She frowned when Ty told her of his plan to catch the three-timing Harry, who, at that moment, was stretching out beside her on the bed. Harry tucked an arm behind his head and smiled, crossing his feet at his ankles, looking like he intended to stay the night.

A minute ago, she'd thought Ty's call couldn't have come at a worse time. But now, after being reminded about her sister and Molly... At least Cat hadn't done something stupid like making mad and passionate love with him on her bedroom floor. "We'll talk about it in the morning. Okay. Night." She disconnected, leaning over to place her phone on the nightstand.

"Ty feeling better knowing you're tucked safely in your bed?"

Hearing Harry's deep, suggestive voice didn't make her feel safe. Nor did seeing his gorgeous face and dangerously powerful body taking up two-thirds of her bed. Before Harry had a chance to distract her, she said, "Yes, but I should warn you he plans to investigate you tomorrow."

"Whatever would prompt him to investigate me?" There was a hint of tension beneath the amusement.

"He thinks you're a player, and that you're three-timing my sister with me and Molly."

He glanced at Cat, his hesitation causing her heart to skip a beat. She stiffened when he pulled her down beside him on the bed. "I'm not three-timing anyone." He pressed a finger to her lips when she opened her mouth to ask about his visit to Molly's room at the lodge. "Just give me a chance to explain. I'll tell you about Molly, and it's not what you think. But before I do, it's important that you believe I'm not interested in your sister. I'm not, love. Not in the least. Granted, she can occasionally be sweet, and there have been times I felt sorry for her. But more often than not, she's demanding and self-centered. You're the one I'm interested in. You, and only you."

She crossed her arms. "So how do you explain the kiss

at the Christmas bazaar? And what about yesterday? I saw the way you looked at Chloe. I mean me pretending to be Chloe."

"How do you explain the kiss we just shared?"

Brain freeze. Stupidity. Lust. Hope. Sadly, it was probably the latter. "You don't answer a question with a question, Harry. It doesn't work that way."

"All right, if you won't answer, I will. We have something, Cat. A connection, chemistry, whatever you want to call it."

"But you said you didn't want a relationship." She should have stuck with the Cat-Chloe thing because what she just said made it sound like she wanted something more than a fling.

"I didn't, until I met you."

Okay, that was nice, and more than she expected. "So, what you're saying is, because of the connection thing, you knew it was me all along."

He made an apologetic face. "Well, no. I thought I was interested in Chloe, too."

She supposed she should appreciate his honesty. But really, she wouldn't have minded if he'd kept that to himself.

"I wish you wouldn't look at me like that. I feel bad enough as it is. And while in here"—he pointed to his head—"I thought you were Chloe, in here"—he placed his hand over his heart—"I knew it was you. And another part of me did, too, but it's probably best if I don't put my hand there." He waggled his eyebrows. "But you're welcome to."

She started to laugh, and he smiled, turning on his side. "Now, to explain about Molly." He stroked her hair, tucking it behind her ear in teasing sweeps. "There's something I should have told you for a while now, but I've been—"

At a quiet knock on her door, she covered his mouth with her hand.

"Kit Kat, I need to talk to you."

She bowed her head, giving it a slight, frustrated shake. "Chloe, it's late. We'll talk in the morning."

"I'm on London time. And I need—"

Harry removed her hand from his mouth and whispered, "Do not give in to her."

She gave him an I've-got-this smile. "Well, I'm not. I'm tired."

"You don't sound tired. And it's important. I know I wasn't very nice earlier, but I'm scared. I don't have anyone else to talk to. Please, Kit Kat. My heart is acting weird. It keeps skipping a beat."

She glanced at Harry and made a face.

He sighed, then leaned over and pressed his mouth to hers. "You're a pushover. One I'm very fond of. I'll go now, but first thing tomorrow, we talk."

Chapter Fifteen

Early the next morning, Cat was in the barn mucking out the stalls. Her mother had called to ask if she'd mind. Their ranch hands had been cast as extras for the scene being filmed today. Of course sister dearest hadn't been asked to help. She was snuggled under the blankets in Cat's bed, snoring away. At least one of them was getting some sleep. Cat's sympathy for Chloe's imagined heart attack had evaporated around two this morning. If Cat hadn't been on a high from her romantic interlude with Harry, her sympathy well may have run dry earlier. But even the memory of their hot make-out session couldn't withstand the shot of good old-fashioned guilt her sister had delivered.

Chloe was delusional...and relentless. Every time her sister brought up Harry, Cat changed the subject. But Chloe kept sliding him back into the conversation. No matter what Cat said, her sister held fast to the notion

Harry was *the one*. Chloe's one, not Cat's. Maybe if her sister hadn't just lost her dream role and Cat hadn't messed up at yesterday's taping, she would have told Chloe the truth. That while Harry might not be Cat's one-and-only yet, there was a possibility he could be.

She didn't know how Harry would feel about it, but until Chloe was in a better place, this thing they had, whatever this thing was, had to be kept between the two of them. She smiled at the thought of long walks in the snow and kissing under the mistletoe. And then she remembered he'd be heading back to California in less than a week.

She stopped shoveling and leaned against the rail. Well that just stole the fun out of sneaking around. Their relationship was doomed before it got started. Maybe she was the one who was delusional. The man was ninety-eighth in line for the British crown. Chloe would fit right in with the royal crowd, but Cat wouldn't.

No doubt his friends and family were as snotty as Dame Alexander. It was probably for the best he was leaving soon. They'd keep it light, enjoy each other's company for a few days, and then that would be it. He'd be her rebound guy. She hadn't had any interest in dating until Harry, so all in all it was a good thing. Like Ty said, she could use some fun.

A warm, wet puff of air brushed Cat's cheek, and then her knitted brown hat disappeared from her head. "Hey," she laughed, turning to see Bandit, a gorgeous black Appaloosa with white spots on his hindquarters, happily chomping on it.

Cat stepped onto the bottom rail of the stall and tugged on the hat. Blossom, a brandy-colored thoroughbred, nudged Cat's hand as though telling her to back off. The two horses were inseparable. It's why Cat had felt comfortable putting them together while she cleaned Blossom's stall. They were rescue horses, and a wedding present from her brother to his wife Skye.

Since Skye had convinced their mother to get involved with animal rescue and retraining, at least half of the fifteen horses in the stable were now rescue horses. A gorgeous bay-colored stallion over seventeen hands double-kicked his stall. A recent addition, he was aptly named Blackheart. Even Skye was having a hard time getting through to the animal. Bandit had been as difficult, so she imagined her sister-in-law would eventually win the stallion over. But that was one stall Cat wouldn't be cleaning today.

"I'll get you both an apple once I'm done here. Now give over," she said, tugging her hat from Bandit's mouth. "Good boy." She patted his muzzle, then grimaced at the condition of her hat. She tossed it on the bales of hay stacked to the right of the stall. Picking up her shovel, she surveyed the state-of-the-art stable. Being here, being home, reminded her of what was missing in California. This was the life she wanted. And if she accepted Chance's offer to work for him, she could have it. Once Chloe's would-be killer had been caught, she'd give the offer some serious thought.

At least with Chloe back from London, Cat could now devote herself to the investigation full-time. She planned to confide in Harry this morning. After he talked to her about whatever he'd been putting off. She wondered if, once he woke up to the cold light of day, he'd have second thoughts about them, too. Looked like she was going to find out sooner rather than later; she heard him talking outside the barn.

She frowned. It was Harry's voice but without the accent. He sounded tougher, edgier—a little like Rand Livingstone. Snippets of his conversation reached her as he entered the barn. He leaned against the door with his leather-clad back to her.

"Trust me, Jamie. Cat didn't have anything to do with the attempts on Chloe's life. I know I did, but that was before I—"

Her knees went weak, the shovel hitting the ground as she reached for something to hold on to.

Harry, or whoever he was, slowly turned. His eyes met hers, and he briefly closed them. "Jamie, I have to go." He shoved his phone in the pocket of his leather jacket and started toward her. "Cat, I can explain."

She stared at him. "Who are you?"

With his wind-blown hair and his jaw darkened with stubble, the angles of his face appeared sharper, the scar bisecting his dark eyebrow standing out in stark relief. He looked dangerous, all predatory male, as he stalked toward the stall. Nothing like the gentle, kind, and funny man she'd come to know. A man she thought might possibly, in the not-so-distant future, be *the one*. Her one. Just like she'd thought Michael was.

Her stomach cramped, and she leaned heavily against the rails. She wanted to hit something, scream at her stupidity for not listening to her gut. She'd known all along he wasn't who he pretended to be. She raised a gloved hand. "Don't come any closer."

He stopped a couple feet from the stall. "Cat, listen to me. I—" His pale blue eyes roamed her face, then he nodded a couple times as if he realized any attempt to placate or con her would fail. "I was hired by a security firm to protect Chloe."

As far as she knew, no one had been suspicious about the accidents, so why . . . "Who hired you?"

"The executive producer. Chloe's agent found a threatening note in her dressing room about a month ago."

"What? Why wasn't I informed? Her agent knows I act as my sister's bodyguard, as well as her manager. If they would have brought me in—"

"They were afraid, if Chloe found out, she'd refuse to work. They couldn't afford for that to happen." He took a step closer, reaching for the stall door. "Cat, I wanted to tell you. I was going to—"

As she thought about the brief snippet of conversation she'd just overheard, she took a step back, bumping into the wall. "You thought it was me. That's why you didn't tell me, isn't it? You thought I was behind the attempts on my sister's life." She glanced away, then looked back at him as she realized it was even worse than that. "You used me. That's what last night was about. Why you pretended to be interested in me." And she'd fallen for it. Just like she'd fallen for Michael.

"No, dammit." He threw open the gate and was on her before she could move. He grabbed her by the shoulders, giving her a light shake. "It wasn't an act. I didn't play you, Cat. I wouldn't do that."

"You honestly expect me to believe that after you—"
He cut her off with a word-stealing kiss. Every single thought flew out of her head at the feel of his mouth crushing hers. It wasn't like last night when he explored her with a heated tenderness. No, this kiss was angry,

passionate, frustrated. He pressed against her as though to offer more proof that he was interested. And he was very interested, and maybe if she trusted him, she would be, too. A small voice in her head said that she could, but it was the louder one of past experience that she listened to. She moved her hands between them and pushed him away.

He tore his mouth from hers, staring down at her. His eyes a fiery blue. "Don't do this." He grabbed her hand and held it to his chest. "I may have been pretending to be a British lord to get close to your sister, but I'm still the man you kissed last night, the man you wanted. Just like I knew you were *you* when you were pretending to be Chloe."

"Who are you...the real you?"

His gaze slid to the left, then back to her. "Grayson Alexander."

She forgot about the evasive slide of his eyes when she heard his last name. "Wait a minute. So Estelle is actually related to you?"

"Yes, she's my grandmother. And she really is a former Broadway star, who at the moment thinks she's Miss Marple. She's also as big a pain in the ass as your sister."

Trying to keep a straight face after the Miss Marple reference, Cat said, "You brought your grandmother on assignment?"

"My cousin owns the security firm, so I have some leeway. And I couldn't find anyone to look after Estelle while I was away."

She had to admit that it was kind of sweet that he'd brought his grandmother with him. Something the man she thought of as Harry would do. Her guard lowered a bit. "So Estelle is faking her accent, too?"

He angled his head. "Now that you mention it, I guess she is. She was born in the UK, but her family moved to the States when she was five. Although, like your sister, she had a thing for British aristocrats and married three of them, one of whom was my grandfather. I think she liked the titles and the accent more than she ever liked her husbands. Her marriages never lasted more than two years." His mouth kicked up at the corner as he looked down at her. "Don't try to hide it. I know you want to smile."

"Fine." She bared her teeth. "Happy?"

"No." He tucked her hair behind her ear. "Not until I get a real one. I want to see your adorable dimple."

She touched her cheek. It wasn't as if she didn't know she had a dimple, but she never gave it much thought. She should have, since her sister's was barely noticeable. And that small indent could have easily given Cat away on the set. Obviously she hadn't smiled or it would have. "Is that why you thought I might be me and not Chloe, you noticed my dimple?"

"No. I didn't look at your sister the way I looked at you, so I just assumed I hadn't noticed." He stroked her cheek and smiled. "There it is."

"Stop it," she said, fighting a laugh, her earlier anger and hurt subsiding into a wary acceptance. It helped that Grayson Alexander was, of course, as hot as Harry, and his sense of humor and warmth seemed to be real as well. She kind of hoped the things that annoyed her, like his habit of saying *jolly good* and the way he crossed his legs like a girl and raised his pinkie while drinking tea, were part of his act. She liked Grayson's sexy, casual look better than Harry's put-together one. And his real name did it for her, too. Geez, could she be any more superficial? Or distracted from what really mattered?

He smiled down at her. "So, are we okay?"

"Yeah, we're good."

"How good?" He stepped into her, wrapping his arms around her. "Last night good?"

"I don't know. I liked Harry, and you're not him anymore."

"Harry was an idiot. But just for curiosity's sake, how much did you like him?"

"A lot."

"Good. You'll like me even more."

"You're—" She went to say "cocky," but once again he stole the word by slanting his firm, warm lips over hers. And this kiss was even hotter than the last. Though it wasn't angry or frustrated. More like the kiss of a man trying to make a point. And he made it very well. So well she thought he might be right and poor Harry didn't stand a chance against Grayson Alexander. Which was a little scary because after *a lot* came *love*, at least for her it did. And she wasn't ready to trust her heart to a man she'd met five minutes ago.

As she took two steps back, he released a frustrated groan, one she echoed in her head. "We have to talk before Chloe comes looking for us, Grayson." Her voice was a little breathless.

"I like hearing my name on your lips." He didn't release her, drawing her closer. "Only next time, I want to hear you moaning it."

Didn't seem to matter whether he had an accent or not, every word out of his mouth sent a warm tingle to her girl parts. It's like he had them on speed dial. But he'd just given her the opening she needed. "Well, if there's going to be moaning, it has to be done quietly. Chloe can't know there's anything going on between us."

"I disagree. Look, Cat, I don't know why, but your sister…" He scratched the back of his neck. "She acts like there's something's going on between *us*. I'm sure GG, my grandmother, isn't helping matters. But I've made it clear to Chloe that I'm not interested. Maybe if they realized we were together, they'd back off. And I have to tell you, I'd be a happy man if they did. They're bloody exhausting. Annoying, too."

"Trust me, if you think they're exhausting and annoying now, I guarantee it would be a hundred times worse if they thought we were…" She trailed off, unsure what they were doing.

He cocked his head. "I think the word you're looking for is dating, love."

Love? Hmm, so that hadn't changed, either. "We're dating?"

"We would be if we weren't sneaking around. So the sooner we catch your sister's would-be killer the better."

Cat moved out of his arms and reached for the shovel. "I hope you're having more luck with that than me."

"I was just about to say the same thing to you." He looked from her shovel to his feet and raised his boot. He grimaced. "You might have warned me you hadn't finished this one yet."

"City boy," she scoffed. "I have four more stalls to go. Grab a shovel, and we'll talk while we work." She was kind of teasing, maybe testing a little, too.

Michael hated the ranch. No, she reminded herself, he'd loved the house and the six hundred acres they owned. He just didn't want to have anything to do with the running of it. She wouldn't be surprised if he'd contacted a real estate agent after their first visit to get an evaluation of its worth. Grayson had already spent more time in the barn than Michael had in the two years they were together.

Bandit shoved his nose into the stall, nuzzling Grayson's hair. He smiled, patting the horse's muzzle. Blossom, feeling left out, did the same. "Beautiful animals."

"They are, and they like clean stalls, so are you going to help or not?" She hadn't realized how much she'd hoped he'd say yes until it looked as though he was trying to get out of it.

With one last pat to both Blossom and Bandit, he walked over and took her shovel. "I may live in LA, but I'm a country boy at heart."

Grayson wasn't kidding. He actually seemed to like getting dirty and spending time around the horses. And she had to admit, it was a pleasure watching him work. He was in great shape, and it showed. It wasn't until they'd finished up the last stall that she realized they hadn't even talked about the case. They'd spent the entire time talking about the ranch and her hometown.

"Thanks, you were a big help," she said as she filled the buckets with hay.

"Anytime. I don't know when I've enjoyed myself as much." He grinned. "Who knew shoveling shit could be so much fun."

She laughed, handing him a bucket. "I'm glad you enjoyed yourself."

He closed his hand over hers and said, "I enjoyed spending time with *you*," and leaned in and kissed her. This time she was the one who groaned in frustration when he lifted his mouth. "Hold that thought until tonight." He glanced at his watch. "We have to be in town in an hour and a half. If you're okay with it, I thought that since I can handle Chloe's security, you could use the time to search the rest of the cast and crew's rooms at the lodge."

She should be okay with it. Grayson obviously was more than capable of keeping her sister safe. But Cat had spent a lifetime protecting Chloe, and the thought of leaving her sister's life in the hands of a man she didn't know that well made her nervous. Then she remembered he'd have backup. She told him about Chance and Gage's involvement, and while they fed the horses they talked about the case. Sadly, Grayson wasn't any closer to solving it than she was. But they did agree that Molly, Sam, and George were the most likely suspects. And Grayson did have one piece of evidence she didn't—the letter.

"So when exactly did the agent find the letter?"

"The twelfth of November. The same day the banister gave way. They didn't take the threat seriously until two weeks later when the chandelier fell."

Now it kind of made sense why he'd initially considered her a suspect. Since she'd been the one playing Tessa Hart in both incidences, her absence on the sidelines would have been noted. "Do you have a copy of the letter?"

He nodded. "In my room. But basically it said 'I know what you've done and you're going to pay. I'm going to destroy you like you destroyed me, you greedy bitch. You think you got away with it, but you didn't. I'm the judge and jury and your sentence is death.'"

She rubbed the bridge of her nose. "Kind of dramatic

and over-the-top, but we're dealing with actors, so it's to be expected, I guess." That was one more check in the Grayson box: at least he wasn't an actor. Though he certainly could be one given what she'd seen of his abilities over the past couple weeks.

"What we need to find out is which of our suspects has the strongest motive. Something must have happened a few weeks prior to the twelfth to trigger the death threat."

"Right." She remembered her conversation with Ty the day the chandelier fell. "Molly. Ty said Chloe had asked for a cut in Molly's on-air time."

"I heard the same. But do you think that alone would be enough for her to commit murder? Whoever is behind the death threat is serious. They've tried to kill Chloe four times. Possibly five if you include last night."

From behind them someone gasped. They turned to see Chloe, her fur coat draped over her leopard-print robe with a pair of white fur boots on her feet. Her sister grabbed the stable door. "Kill me? Someone's trying to kill me! Oh God." She pressed the back of her hand to forehead. Grayson reached her, catching her before she crumpled in a heap at his feet.

Wearing her fur coat and carrying Fluffy in her arms, his grandmother came up behind them. "Don't worry, my dear. No one will get near you with my grandson on the job. He's a special agent with the FBI."

Chapter Sixteen

Cat was heartily sick of riding into town on a snow-mobile. She raised a gloved hand to clear the helmet's visor as she took the path through the park from the lodge. The wet snowfall had added an extra thirty minutes to the ride into town. But at least she'd taken the time to dress appropriately in a black-and-pink one-piece snowmobile suit. Unlike four days earlier, she didn't have to worry that her sister was unprotected. No, she had Special Agent Grayson Alexander providing security.

Her stomach cramped at the thought, just as it had when his grandmother dropped the bomb four hours ago. It was the reason Cat took the snowmobile instead of hitching a ride into town with Grayson, Chloe, and Estelle. Cat didn't want to be anywhere near the man. She was afraid she'd punch him, or worse, cry. No wonder she'd been his primary suspect. In the suspicious minds of Grayson and his counterparts, the next step for someone who'd gotten away with bilking two hundred people out of their savings was murder. No doubt he'd spoken to Special Agent in Charge Turner.

At least Grayson was good for one thing; instead of having a full-blown meltdown upon learning she was in the crosshairs of a murderer, her sister had a mini one. The Alexanders had managed to calm Chloe down in under twenty minutes. Though Cat imagined it was being held by Special Agent Alexander while he spoke in deep, soothing tones that had really done the trick. Once Chloe was calm enough to speak and Cat had her anger and hurt under sufficient control, she'd offered her own comfort to her sister, assuring Chloe she wouldn't let anyone close enough to harm her. Her sister waved off Cat's offer. Hardly surprising. After all, why would she need a disgraced ex-cop when she had an FBI agent protecting her. A hot FBI agent, who, although he may not be a true Brit with a title or sexy accent, was actually ninety-eighth in line to the throne and heir to the title once his father died. Chloe had perked right up at that piece of news, and Cat had left the barn.

Cat turned the snowmobile onto Main Street. The one benefit of the two inches of snow they'd received in the last few hours was that the sidewalk hadn't been cleared. Sam, Phil, and several grips turned to scowl at her when she drove along the sidewalk, pulling into the alley beside the Sugar Plum Bakery. Cat took off her helmet and got off the snowmobile. As she walked out of the alley, their reaction made sense. They were filming a scene, and she'd drowned out the carols being piped onto the street.

Chloe and George sat in a white horse-drawn carriage

in the middle of the road half a block away while the residents of Christmas went about their holiday shopping. One in particular caught her attention: Grayson leaned against a decorated shop window looking utterly bored and devastatingly handsome. It was an act. And she'd learned the hard way that the man was one hell of an actor. When his head turned in her direction, she ducked into the bakery.

The shop smelled like cinnamon and coffee. Owner Grace Flaherty and her silent business partner Madison McBride stood behind the glass display case. Ty, in a black fur jacket, black pants, and black fur boots, dabbed at first Grace's cheeks with a makeup brush, then Madison's. From the slush on the black-and-white-tiled floor, they'd been busy. Not surprising, with the cast and crew stationed down the street. Plus, Grace made the best cupcakes and cookies in all of Colorado.

"Hi, Cat," Grace said as she approached the counter. Madison smiled, earning her a "Stop that till I'm done" from Ty. She widened her eyes at Cat.

Once he'd finished, Ty turned. He slapped his open palm to his face. "Good God, why are you wearing that? And look at your hair." He grabbed her by the arm, dragging her toward a nearby table covered with what looked to be the entire contents of his makeup bag.

She pulled her arm free. "Wait a minute. I have to place my order."

"Make it snappy. I don't have all day. The cast will be coming in for their touch-ups. And they're filming a scene here."

Maybe she shouldn't have stopped in after all. But she wanted to pick up a coffee for Vivi. Cat had come up empty at the lodge, and they were going to work on the case at the *Chronicle*. *No sense leaving now*, she thought, her order would take all of a few minutes. "So, you two are making your on-screen debut today, are you?" she asked, smiling at Grace and Madison.

"Yes, it's the scene where Tessa bumps into Rand. I think they kiss." Grace sighed. "Your sister is one lucky woman."

Cat forced her smile to stay in place. "She sure is."

"Harry isn't. This is the scene where Byron finds out Rand followed them on their holiday and punches him," Madison said.

Cat's smile widened. Best news she'd heard today. She hoped George didn't hold back. Madison and Grace gave her an odd look. "Sounds exciting. Um, I won't keep you, then. I just need a decaffeinated latte with whipped cream and chocolate sprinkles and a large regular latte, no whip, no sprinkles." She glanced in the display case. "And four of those." She pointed at a chocolate cupcake with a swirl of creamy icing on top and a chocolate tree standing in the center.

Grace went to fill the coffee order while Madison took care of the cupcakes. "These are amazing. They're filled with a raspberry ganache." She lowered her voice. "I'm guessing the decaf latte is for Vivi? Cupcakes, too?"

Cat nodded, wondering why she was whispering, then realized they must want to keep the baby news on the down-low, just like their marriage.

"Okay. Then you better double your cupcake order. Chance is driving her crazy."

"Make it a dozen." Vivi wasn't the only one being driven crazy by a man. And Vivi's was a good crazy, even if she probably didn't see it that way.

"Pussy, I don't have all day."

Cat sighed, unzipping her jacket to pull out forty dollars. Madison laughed. "You go, and we'll get this boxed up for you."

"Thanks," she said, placing the money by the cash register. Ty pointed at the chair.

"Ty, I—"

"Sit." He leaned forward once she did. "Rumor has it the White Knight is in town."

Leave it to Ty to know more about what was going on in Christmas than she did. "Okay, that's good, but what does Easton being home have to do..." He made a duck face. "Why are you doing that?"

He held up a lipstick and pencil. "I can't do anything about the outfit, but I can at least make you presentable. Pucker up."

"I'm not puckering..." She frowned as a dazed expression came over his face, his mouth hanging open.

"Easton!" Madison rounded the counter, rushing to the front of the shop.

Cat twisted to see Easton McBride coming through the door. Snow dusted his inky black hair and his brown aviator jacket. He gave his sister-in-law a tired smile, his usually tanned skin pale. It was then that Cat noticed he was leaning heavily on a cane.

"Careful," Madison said, holding the door open for him. Once he was inside, she gave him a one-armed hug. "I'm so mad at you. Why didn't you tell us you were having the surgery?"

He hugged Madison, his sapphire blue eyes meeting Cat's. Ty sucked in a breath.

Easton glanced at Ty, a slight frown furrowing his brow,

then lifted his chin at Cat before returning his attention to Madison. "I didn't tell you because it wasn't a big deal. So don't make it one, okay?" His voice was low and raspy.

Madison sighed. "You're as stubborn as your brothers. Come on, I'll get you a coffee."

The lipstick and pencil landed on the table with a clatter. "He...He's coming this way."

"Hey, Cat." Easton placed a hand on her shoulder, leaning down to kiss her cheek. "How are you doing?"

Awful. "Good." She stood up and offered her chair. "Here. Sit down."

He cocked his head. "Really?"

She laughed. "Okay, tough guy, I won't—" She broke off when Phil, Sam, and three other members of the crew entered the bakery.

"Folks, hope you don't mind, but we have a scene to film." Phil didn't so much as look Cat's way. The director had been standoffish since the night of his birthday party. His gaze cut past her to Easton. "If you'd like to be an extra, we—"

"No thanks. I'll just grab my coffee and get out of your way," Easton said.

That was her cue to leave. She joined Easton at the counter and picked up her order and change. "You heading to the *Chronicle*?" he asked once they'd said goodbye to Madison and Grace.

"Yeah, are you coming?" She turned with the cake box and coffee tray in her arms and walked straight into Ty. Easton's hand shot out, saving the coffees.

"You have amazing reflexes," Ty said, his eyes glazed behind his red-framed glasses.

"And you would be?" Easton asked.

Ty looked wounded. "I thought Thor would have mentioned me. I'm Ty." He lowered his voice. "I'm helping on the case. So I guess that makes me your partner?"

Easton raised an eyebrow at Cat. "Thor?"

"Chance," she said, fighting back a laugh. She wondered if she should tell him he was the White Knight, but thought better of it. Through the front window, she caught a glimpse of George and Molly. "Ty, we have to get going. As soon as you're finished here, stop by the *Chronicle*." She gave him directions.

"I'll be there with bells on." He beamed at Easton, then raised his hands to Cat's hair and tried to fluff it. He sighed. "I can't do a thing with it. I forbid you to wear that again, Pussy." He flicked his finger at her helmet. "That too," he said, pointing at her snowsuit.

"Pussy?" Easton chuckled as they walked to the door.

"Yeah, and you don't want to know—" She broke off when George and Molly walked in, followed by the Alexanders and her sister. Cat and Easton stepped aside to let them pass. "So, how do you like being back in Christmas?" she asked, focusing on Easton to avoid making eye contact with Grayson.

Before Easton could answer, Chloe stopped in front of them. "I didn't know you were home." She noticed his cane, and her gaze jerked to his face. "What happened?"

His jaw tightened. "Skiing accident." He turned to Cat. "Ready to go?"

"Cat, I need a moment of your time," Grayson clipped out, laying on a thick, fake British accent. He reached for her arm at the same time he sized up Easton.

"Sorry, we have somewhere to be." Cat turned to Easton, giving him a flirty smile. "Don't we, baby?"

Cat didn't know who was more shocked: her, Easton, Chloe, or Grayson.

*   *   *

Baby. Grayson hadn't been able to get the damn word or the image of Cat saying it out of his head. He got that she was mad. She had a right to be. He should have told her. But the way she'd found out he was undercover hadn't been ideal, so he'd decided to put if off until tonight. Once Estelle and Chloe were in bed, he'd planned to take Cat for a walk under the stars. Maybe go back to the barn with a blanket and a bottle of wine. Best-laid plans...Leave it to his grandmother to out him.

Following Nell McBride's directions, Grayson looked for the pale yellow wooden building on Main Street that housed the *Chronicle.* The older woman had been waiting for them at the town hall. After the taping was over for the day, Grayson, Chloe, George, Molly, and Phil were sent off in a horse-drawn sleigh to judge the best-lit house. Nell had been hoping to find out if she'd won, but they'd been sworn to secrecy. The winner would be announced tonight after the Parade of Lights.

And the parade was the reason Grayson was looking for Cat. Actually, it was more of an excuse to talk to her. But he also had a legitimate reason for seeking her out— he wanted her to provide added security for Chloe. Gage McBride, the sheriff, had already informed him he'd be busy with crowd control. With the cast of *As the Sun Sets* appearing in the parade, they were expecting a record turnout. The parade was still three hours away, and people were already lining up along the route.

He spotted the yellow building up ahead and pulled

into the only parking spot available four shops down.
Gage was with Chloe at the warehouse, but he had to take
off in twenty minutes. So Grayson didn't have a whole
lot of time to convince Cat to come with him. He caught
a glimpse of her through the window of the *Chronicle*.
She was laughing with Chance McBride, his fiancée Vivi
Westfield, and the man Cat had called *baby*—Easton
McBride.

Grayson hadn't known he was a McBride until he
talked to Ty while having his hair and makeup retouched.
He'd remembered hearing the name when Chloe accused
Cat of using him to get back at her for stealing Easton.
Clearly what Grayson had assumed was a love triangle
from the past wasn't over. At least if Ty was to be believed.
Grayson didn't. A woman like Cat wouldn't kiss a man
like she'd kissed him if she was involved with someone
else. The word *baby* taunted him as he opened the door.

Four pairs of eyes turned in his direction as he walked in.
None of them appeared to be happy to see him, especially
Cat. Chance, who stood behind Vivi with his hands on her
shoulders, cocked his head. "What happened to you?"

He rubbed his jaw and winced at the bite of pain.
"George. It was in the script." Though the actor wasn't
supposed to actually hit him. George said he slipped on
the floor, but Grayson didn't buy it.

Easton, who sat sprawled in a chair in front of Vivi's
desk, said, "Interesting. Maybe you're right, Cat, and
George really does think he's Byron Hart."

Grayson was aware of Cat's transference theory. She'd
shared it with him this morning. He stepped closer to
the desk. "Or he's unhappy that it's looking like Harry is
going to cut into his on-air time. Grayson Alexander, by

the way," he said, extending his hand first to Easton, who was closest, then to Vivi and Chance, who introduced themselves.

"*Special* Agent Grayson Alexander," Cat added, putting extra emphasis on the *special*.

She sat in a chair a couple feet from Easton, wearing a green sweatshirt, the upper part of her snowmobile suit down around her waist. She held his gaze, both eyebrows raised. Oh yeah, she wasn't going to make this easy. "Cat, I have to get back to the warehouse, and I was hoping you'd come with me. I need an extra pair of eyes tonight. Gage and his deputies will help out as much as they can, but they'll be busy managing the crowds."

Vivi, Chance, and Easton turned to look at Cat, waiting for her response.

She studied her nails, then finally muttered, "Fine."

He released the breath he'd been holding. "Great. Nell says there's an extra ATV you can use to ride beside the float."

"I've already volunteered to drive the float Chloe will be on, so I'll have you covered, too," Chance said.

"I'm sure I can hunt down another ATV," Easton said.

"No way, baby brother. You're going to go home and get some rest. And my...fiancée's going with you to make sure that you do. Right, honey?"

Vivi scowled up at him. "I know what you're doing, and it's not going to work. Easton doesn't need a babysitter, and I have to cover the parade for the paper."

Since it appeared both Easton and Vivi were about to argue with Chance, who didn't look like a man who backed off easily, Grayson lifted his chin at Cat. "I don't want to rush you, but we should get going."

Her lips were pressed into a thin line as she leaned forward and put her cup of coffee on the desk. Then she stood up and shrugged her snowmobile suit on, grabbing the helmet off the floor. "Thanks for the help, guys. I'll talk to you tomorrow, Vivi. Take care of yourself, Easton." She nodded at Chance. "I'll see you later."

"You'll see me, too." Easton ignored his brother, who was muttering under his breath. "Find a way to get Chloe to turn on her phone. That way I'll be able to hack into it."

Before Grayson could ask why Easton wanted to access Chloe's phone, Vivi said, "We'll talk," then mouthed *at the parade*. She didn't realize her husband had leaned over to look down at her.

"Dammit, Slick, I'm not fooling—"

She tipped her head back and, smiling up at him, patted his cheek. "We'll discuss it later." Then she said to Cat, "Word of advice, Nell's a stickler. No one is in the parade unless they're in costume. So if you don't want to end up as an elf, I'd avoid her."

Chapter Seventeen

I am not going to be an elf," Cat grumbled as Grayson held open the *Chronicle*'s door.

"I don't know, I think you'd make a cute elf." He smiled, joining her on the sidewalk. From the look on her face, he should have kept that comment to himself. "I'm parked over here." He indicated the Range Rover down the street.

She looked in the opposite direction and held up her helmet. "My snowmobile is that way. I'll meet you at the warehouse."

He reached for her as she started to walk away and got a narrow-eyed stare in return. He needed time alone with her, so he figured he'd better talk fast and make it good. He removed his hand from her arm. "They're calling for more snow. It'll be late by the time the parade wraps up. Do you really want to be heading to the ranch in the middle of a snowstorm? I'll bring you into town first thing tomorrow." He held back a relieved smile when she agreed and pivoted in the direction of the Range Rover.

Now might be the time for that apology, but he decided to wait until they were on their way to the warehouse. That way he could lock her in and she'd have to listen to him. "How did it go at the lodge? Did you find anything incriminating?"

"No. But you should probably check out the rooms for yourself. You know, since you're an FBI agent."

So much for waiting. He followed her to the passenger side and pressed the unlock button on the key fob, opening the door for her. "I screwed up. I should have told you. I'm sorry you had to hear it from my grandmother and not from me. I was going to tell you tonight, Cat."

"I'm having a hard time buying that," she said as she got in the Range Rover.

"Why? I'm not working this case as a federal agent. And initially, I had a good reason not to tell you who I was."

"Right, like suspecting me of trying to kill my sister." She dropped her helmet at her feet, then reached for her seat belt.

He covered her hand with his. "And in my place, you would have done the same."

"I...Okay, I would have. But you being an FBI agent changes everything."

"No, it doesn't." He shut her door. He wasn't going to argue with her about this in the middle of Main Street.

"Yes, it does," she said as soon as he got in the SUV.

"Look, I get, with how Turner handled you, the last thing you wanted to hear is that I'm an agent. It's the reason I put off telling you. But I'm not him, Cat. I don't believe you had any idea what Upton was up to. You were as much a victim as the others."

"You talked to Turner about my case, didn't you?"

He backed onto the street. "I've spoken to him twice. The night I took the case, and the day after you told me about Upton. I've asked Turner to take another look at the business partner's death."

Her silence made him uncomfortable. He glanced at her. She had her eyes closed. "Cat—"

She turned her head. "So now not only did I miss he was running a Ponzi scheme, you think the man I was going to marry was a murderer. Which would mean he was using me from the very beginning."

"It's just a hunch. I could be wrong."

"But you don't think you are."

"No, I don't. I think his partner figured out what he was up to and was going to go to the Securities and Exchange Commission." He reached for her hand. "We're human, Cat. We all make mistakes. But you weren't primary on the murder investigation, I checked, so this won't come back to you."

"Maybe not as far as the department is concerned, but here"—she pointed to her head and then her chest—"and in here, it will."

"Only because you're a good cop, a good person. But none of us are infallible."

"Even you?"

He released a dry laugh and told her about his last case. About how badly he'd misjudged Valeria Ramos.

"But in the end, you put her away, shut down her operation, and saved those girls. That's all that matters," she said.

"My cousin and my partner had my back. Someone should have had yours. If you'll let me, I'd like to be the one who does."

"Well, you kind of already do, since you're the one who's been keeping Chloe safe all day." She shifted in the seat to face him. "I'm sorry I overreacted. Maybe we can start over." Her lips turned up, her adorable dimple making an appearance as she held out her hand. "Hi, I'm Cat O'Connor."

He laughed as he turned into the warehouse parking lot. "No way. I already got to first base, and I plan to get to second...tonight." He pulled into a space and turned off the engine. "Unless you and Easton McBride are—"

Her cheeks pinked. She lowered her hand and undid her seat belt. "Yeah, about that, I shouldn't have said what I did. I—"

"So he's not your *baby*?" He reached out, running a finger along her now-fiery red cheek.

"I don't need to be reminded of what I said, thanks. It was stupid." She picked up her helmet.

"I don't know if I'd go so far as stupid, just not the kind of thing that a man who you're supposed to be *dating* wants to hear."

"We weren't dating at the time."

"Ah, I guess I didn't get the memo. Are we dating again? Because if we are, we should probably kiss and make up."

A car door slammed and several people walked behind the SUV. She patted his chest. "Probably best if we save the making up for tonight when we're alone."

The relief that coursed through him at her answer made him nervous. If he'd thought a casual relationship was all he wanted from her, that reaction had just proved him a liar. Might be a good idea to lighten things up a bit. He adjusted his sleeves beneath his coat, then gave her a smoldering look along with a British accent. "And my chances of getting to second base, how's that looking, love?"

"Lose the Harry act, but keep the accent, and the odds go up exponentially." She got out of the SUV.

Lighten the mood? He hadn't thought that through very well, had he? He rubbed his face, wincing when his hand slid over his jaw.

He was still sitting there when Cat came around to his side and opened the door. "Are you okay?"

"Old George packed a harder wallop than I gave him credit for." So did Cat.

"Maybe we should be worrying about you and not Chloe. You better be careful he doesn't push you off the float." She put her hands on her hips and looked around the parking lot, then back at him. "I can't figure out what George's angle is."

"And here I was hoping you'd say you'll kiss it better when we're alone."

"Focus, Gray…Harry," she corrected when another couple walked past. She lowered her voice. "I've been racking my brain, trying to come up with a reason why George would want to get rid of Chloe, and I can't. Easton's going to look into his, Molly's, and Sam's financials. Maybe something will pop."

She was right. He had to stay focused, and not on her. "I may not be on the case in an official capacity, but all the same, I'd prefer if we didn't break the law. I'll talk to Easton, find out how he's going to go about digging into their financials. Same goes for him hacking into Chloe's phone. What was he hoping to find?"

"It's not good news. We have another suspect. Lady Darby."

"The woman who threatened to kill Chloe after she'd been caught with her husband?"

"One and the same. The Darbys split up a month ago, and she moved back to LA. She's been laying low, or I would have known."

"And Chloe was in London. Any chance she met up with him?"

"Since I'd warned her not to see him, she won't cop to it. That's why Easton was going to hack into her phone."

"I'll take care of it while she's getting ready for the parade." He placed his hand at the small of her back. "We better get in there and get you suited up. You'll make an adorable elf." He opened the doors to the warehouse.

Whatever she said was drowned out by a wave of noise. People were running around half in costume and half out. Phil was yelling directions, as were Chloe and Nell McBride. While Nell's great-nephew Sheriff Gage McBride looked about ready to tear his hair out. He spotted Grayson and Cat and headed toward them, barely avoiding a ten-foot snowman that careened in his direction.

"Geezus, I didn't think you were going to show. I'm outta..." Gage trailed off when a fight broke out to the right of them.

Ty, standing in front of Molly, wielded a curling iron as if it were a sword, warding off the twins Hailey and Holly. "Do not come near her. Beehives went out in the fifties. We're not in Texas, you black-haired Medusas."

"We're in charge of hair and makeup, you, you—"

Cat put four fingers in her mouth and whistled loud enough to blow out Grayson's eardrums. Everyone fell silent and turned in their direction. "Phil and Chloe, this is Nell's show; leave her to the directing. Holly and Hailey, Ty will take care of the cast, you look after the rest. And would someone please help the snowman."

Gage chuckled. "You always did know how to get a crowd's attention. I'll head out now." He started for the doors, then turned to Cat. "My wife said to tell you the zipper on the elf's costume gets stuck halfway, but all you have to do is give it a good tug."

Cat turned to follow Gage out the doors. Grayson grabbed her by the back of her snowsuit. "Oh, no, you don't. We're in this together."

*   *   *

Cat was an elf. And from the horrified look on Ty's face, not an attractive one. This didn't cause Cat much concern, since Ty looked at her that way on a regular basis. But Holly's and Hailey's reactions? Yeah, that was somewhat worrisome. Ty stood in front of Cat like a warrior about to go into battle, with his black fur boots shoulder-width apart. He flipped out his right hand. "Tissues," he said to Holly, who immediately jumped to do his bidding. Then he flipped out his left. "Makeup remover." When Hailey, the twin who typically had an attitude, immediately did as he asked, Cat said, "Give me a mirror."

"No, not until I turn you from porno elf into cute elf."

"Ty, I've been sitting in this chair for thirty minutes. I don't have time for you to redo my makeup," she said. "See?" she added when Nell yelled, "Places people, we roll out in fifteen minutes."

"Hails, we better check and make sure we got everyone," Holly said.

"Okay. Ty, can we borrow your gold dust? We ran—"

"Because you used it all on my poor Pussy." He riffled through his makeup bag and handed her a container and brush. "Light touch, ladies. Now let the master get to work." He licked the tissue. "All right, just let me..." he said, and went to dab Cat's cheeks.

She blocked his hand. "You are not wiping spit on my face. Don't pout," she said as she got to her feet. "It's dark out. No one will see me."

He lifted his nose and sniffed. "Tell that to your sister. I practically had to pry her from my chair." He gave Cat an up-and-down look. "At least you are totally rocking the costume. Tall, Dark, and Delicious hasn't taken his eyes off you."

She glanced to where Grayson stood in front of *As the Sun Sets*'s float, a replica of the Harts' living room, with a decorated Christmas tree standing to the side of a cardboard fireplace. He was talking to Chance, who'd arrived a few minutes ago. She'd been getting changed while Chloe was having her makeup done, but Cat was pretty sure Grayson had lifted her sister's cell phone then. Afterward, she'd seen him standing off by himself at the back of the warehouse.

She drew her attention back to Ty. "What happened? I thought you'd set your matchmaking sights on me and Easton." She still couldn't believe she'd called him *baby*.

Easton had laughed off her apology and her attempt at an explanation, but she sensed his disappointment. Which sucked, because she cared about him, a lot. And the last thing she wanted to do was hurt him. Besides being jaw-dropping gorgeous, he was warm and funny and smart. Maybe too smart. Because once Cat finished venting about Grayson's subterfuge, Easton looked at her and said, "You're in love with him." And if that wasn't enough to send her into panic mode, he also told her to be careful she didn't let her trust issues ruin what could be a good thing. She wasn't sure if he was referring to their high school romance or to Michael. To say she was shocked was an understatement, but she also had a feeling he might be right.

"Yes, but that was before you told me he's a special agent..." Ty patted his chest with both hands. "Be still my heart. You and James Bond are perfect together. He should keep the accent though. Just imagine when you're in bed with—"

"Shut it," she said as the words *second base* ran through her head and a tiny thrill quivered in her stomach.

Ty grinned. "I'll be expecting details. Lots and lots of details."

In an attempt to hide her flushed face, she bent down to pull up the red-and-black-striped leotards that bagged at her knees. The bell on her red hat jingled. She straightened, tugging it down around her ears. "I can't believe I'm doing this. I could have jogged along the parade route."

"At least you would have kept warm. You're going to freeze to death," he said, taking in the thin, long-sleeved red top and short black skirt. He grabbed his black fur jacket off the table behind her. "Here. Wear this."

She was about to politely refuse, then realized that not only would it keep her warm, it would cover her up. "Okay, thanks." She nodded at her snowsuit and helmet sitting on the other makeup chair. "You can wear mine."

He looked like he'd sucked on a lemon. "I wouldn't wear that thing if you paid me... Uh-oh, a cat fight between Dame Alexander and Nell McBride. My bet's on Nell. She's a feisty little thing." He tapped his chin with his finger. "I should talk to her about that red streak. She has gorgeous hair... Where are you going?"

"To save Santa." The bells on the curled-up toes of her black slippers jingled as she jogged toward Santa's float. The two older women were having a tug-of-war, with Santa as the prize. Coulter Dane with his snow-white hair and beard and handsome pink-cheeked face, looked like the man he was pretending to be. He also looked like his arms were being torn from their sockets.

"Ladies, let go of Santa." Surprisingly, they did as she said. Must be her cop voice. "What's the problem?"

Estelle smoothed her hair back. "Santa invited me to ride on his sleigh tonight, and this—" She jabbed her finger at Nell.

Coulter interrupted her before she finished. "Now, ma'am, I—"

Nell cut him off with a stubborn jut of her chin, her Rudolph earrings swinging and blinking. "I don't care if you're the Queen of England, you're not riding on Santa's float."

Rumor in town was that Nell and Coulter had been romantically involved years before, and if Cat wasn't mistaken, Nell was jealous of Estelle spending time with her old beau. Even if he wasn't her beau now. Estelle had already stirred things up with Fred and Ted, so this wouldn't go over well. Since both women had the personality of a Rottweiler, it took a second for Cat to figure out what to do. "You know, Estelle, the kids would probably find it odd if you were on the sleigh with Santa. They might think he's stepping out on his wife. But I'm sure we have a Mrs. Claus costume somewhere, and we can stuff some pillows—"

"I think not." She lifted her nose. "I'll ride in the sleigh with the mayor. Mr. Dane, it was a pleasure speaking with you. I hope we can do so again."

Nell grumbled something under her breath, but Cat didn't catch it because, from behind her, she heard George yelling at Grayson. As she pivoted and headed in their direction, the high school band started to line up. By the time she finally reached the daytime drama's float, George was stomping off, with Phil chasing after him.

"What happened?" Cat asked her sister and Grayson.

Chloe laughed. "I think a better question is, what happened to *you*? You're not really going out in public looking like that, are you?"

Cat glanced at Grayson, a little surprised when he didn't immediately come to her defense. Then again, she looked like a porno elf, and her sister looked like a fairy princess in her white fur coat with a shimmery, silver gown underneath. All she needed was a crown.

"I don't have much choice, Chloe." Just once she'd like her sister to show some appreciation. She was doing this to protect her after all. She lifted her gaze to the man at Chloe's side. He was watching Cat with a pensive look on his face. Something was wrong. "Harry, what happened with George?" She didn't want to use his real name in case someone overheard.

He glanced at the doors, then back at her. "He didn't want me on the float. He thinks it should be just him and Chloe. Obviously, I couldn't share why I had to ride on the float with her, and neither could Phil."

Chloe hugged Grayson's arm and beamed up at him. "My protector."

He gave her sister a tight smile. "Chloe, I'd like a word

with your sister. Chance will help you get on the float."
His voice was clipped, tense.

Cat rounded on him as soon as her sister was out of
earshot. "What's going on?"

He drew Chloe's cell phone from the pocket of his
black wool dress coat and held it out to her. "Do you have
an explanation for this?"

She took the phone from him and glanced at the screen.
"It's the e-mail I sent to Molly the day we got stuck in the
closet. Why?"

His ice-blue eyes held hers. "Read it."

"Grayson, I don't under—"

"Read it."

"It says 'I know what you've done. You won't get away
with it.' " She lifted a shoulder. "I don't know—"

"The phrasing is identical to the first line in the letter
left for Chloe."

Chapter Eighteen

Grayson didn't believe in coincidences. The two sentences were the same, and that's what he'd focused on. Just like he'd been trained to do. Admittedly, the wording was common enough. Cat had been genuinely shocked when she realized what he was accusing her of. Then her shock turned to hurt, which she covered with anger. But she was right when she said that if he didn't trust her, they had no business working the case together, let alone contemplating a relationship.

While standing beside Chloe on the float, Grayson went step-by-step through the investigation in his mind. He took his feelings for Cat out of the equation, looking at the evidence objectively. About ten minutes into the parade route, he'd decided that his screwup with Valeria was still messing with his head. He trusted Cat. And he stood a better chance of wrapping up the case partnering with her and the McBride brothers than on his own. He had four days left of vacation time. If he had to, he'd put in a request for an extension. As for their "relationship," it was probably for the best if they didn't take it any further.

As though the thought conjured her up, Cat drove past them on a red ATV. She'd been circling the float since they turned onto Main Street, scanning the excited crowds at the same time waving and throwing candy canes. Despite the makeup job from hell, she looked adorably sexy in her costume. A fact that had him regretting his decision of moments ago. And not just because he wouldn't be spending the rest of his nights with Cat making his way to home base.

He was a thirty-five-year-old, all-American male with a healthy appetite for sex. He enjoyed women, liked and respected the women he'd gone to bed with. But Cat was different; he wanted more from her than sex. He wanted to spend time with her, sit under the stars holding hands, ski off the top of mountains, clean out horse stalls. Whatever, he didn't care, as long as he was with her. It wasn't a comforting thought. It scared the hell out of him.

Chloe covered her face with a fur-trimmed gloved hand. "Look at her. I'm so embarrassed. She looks ridiculous."

"She looks adorable," Grayson said through a clenched-teeth smile as he waved at the crowd. "But you do realize, don't you, Chloe, that the only reason your sister is riding around on an ATV in an elf costume freezing her buns off is to protect you?"

She shrugged and blew kisses to her cheering fans. "She doesn't have to," she said, smiling up at him. "I have you to protect me."

Once Chloe had calmed down after learning someone wanted her dead, she'd seemed to romanticize the threat. This afternoon, he'd heard her and his grandmother rattling off stalker movies. He'd told them to cut it out when they started freaking each other out. But five minutes later, they both were sighing with dreamy smiles on their faces over a movie entitled *The Bodyguard*. He'd Googled it, and that's when he got nervous. Bloody actresses, they were a pain in the ass.

As they passed the Sugar Plum Bakery, the flatbed hit a pothole. Chloe stumbled in her heels. Grayson steadied her. Chance stuck his head out the truck's window. "Sorry about that. You guys okay back there?"

"Jolly good," Grayson called out and heard Chance's amused snort.

"I love when you say that." Chloe smiled. "It's so cute."

Cat, who was across from them, looked his way and rolled her eyes. Grayson was about to yell out to her that she looked "jolly good" just to bug her, or better yet, make her laugh, but she'd already driven past. The flatbed slowed as Chance allowed her to cut in front of them to come around to the other side. Easton stuck his head out the passenger-side window to say something to her, something that made her laugh. Grayson wished the guy had done as his brother asked and stayed at home. The wanker.

Chloe stamped her feet, then looped her arm through his, snuggling against him. "It's freezing. I can't wait to get home. We can sit by the fire and drink mulled wine. How does that sound?"

No doubt Cat would be pouring the wine. "Great," he said, scanning the crowd. He frowned when he spotted someone wearing a snowmobile suit and helmet identical to Cat's move toward the front of the crowd. As a gloved hand started to rise, Grayson yelled, "Shooter! Hit the gas," at the same time he grabbed Chloe and took her down with him.

He'd just covered her with his body when the first shot rang out, the second shot almost drowned out by the terrified screams of the crowd. The flatbed lurched to a stop. He looked up to see Chance leap from the truck and start running, his gun drawn. "Call for an ambulance! Cat's been hit."

And that's when Grayson saw her ATV on its side directly across from them. His pulse raced, the sound of his heartbeat pounding in his ears. "Stay down," he ordered Chloe, fighting against his panic. With a shooter on the loose he had to protect her, but everything inside urged him to go to Cat. He raised himself on his elbow, whipping his head around when Easton dragged himself onto the flatbed.

"You armed?" Grayson asked the other man. At Easton's tight nod, he said, "Look after Chloe," and vaulted to his feet. He jumped from the float, racing to Cat's side. Chance had righted the three-wheeler and was on his knees beside her. All around them, people were shouting, pointing in the direction the shooter had gone. Three deputies in tan uniforms and brown leather jackets ran toward them. Chance waved them on.

Grayson dropped down beside Cat. Her eyes were open. She was alive. He silently repeated the words in his head, willing his pulse to slow, the suffocating ache in his chest to release. She turned her head and frowned at him. "Are you going to faint?"

She was talking. She was going to be okay. He wasn't going to lose her. "Oh no," she groaned.

He finally managed to get his voice to work and took her hand. "It's all right, love. You're going to be fine. Where were you hit?"

She tried to sit up and winced. He gently pressed a hand to her chest, pushing her back down as he searched her for some sign of injury. He thought she may be in shock.

She scowled at him. "Stop it. I'm fine. I can't let my mother see me lying on the ground." Gage, with his gun drawn, was escorting Cat's mother and Dr. McBride to them.

Chance, who'd risen to his feet, looked down at Cat. "Stay put until Dad checks you over." He grinned. "Harry, you look like you should lie down beside her."

Grayson ignored him, even though he thought he might be right. "Cat—"

"Oh my baby," Liz O'Connor cried, going down on her knees beside her daughter, carefully taking Cat's hand in hers. "Thank God, you're alive."

"Mom, don't cry. I'm okay. Honest." She pushed away Grayson's restraining hand to sit up and put her arms around her mother.

Grayson hadn't taken his eyes off her and said, "Right arm. Bicep. Cat, I'm going to remove your jacket." He carefully eased the fur coat off her shoulder and down her arm. She was bleeding; not a lot, but she was bleeding.

"Son, do you mind if I take a look?"

As he got to his feet to give Dr. McBride room, across the street Chloe broke free from Easton. "I need to go to my sister," she screamed, racing toward them. She collapsed beside her mother and Cat, tears streaming down her face. "Do something, please do something, she's bleeding! You can't let her die."

"Chloe." Cat sighed. "Chloe, look at me. I'm fine. It's just a scratch."

Chloe flung herself at Cat. "You took a bullet for me. You nearly died trying to protect me."

"What a freaking drama queen," Easton muttered as he limped to Grayson's side. "Cat gets shot, and it's all about her."

He was being a little harsh, but Grayson had to agree with him. Dr. McBride calmed Liz and Chloe in a quiet, soothing voice as he examined Cat, who grumbled she didn't have time for this. Gage and Chance, who were talking to the right of them, looked up when Jack Flaherty jogged in their direction with a wadded-up towel in his hand. "Shooter took off on a snowmobile that was parked in the alley beside the bakery. He went through the park. He dropped this." Jack opened the towel to reveal a Glock 22. "Your deputies went after him."

"Good job," Gage said, patting Jack on the back. He took the gun from him.

As people sensed the danger had passed, several made their way toward them. His grandmother, Nell McBride; Gage's wife, Madison; and Chance's fiancée among them.

When Vivi approached with a camera in her hand, Chance crossed his arms. "You've got some explaining to do, Slick."

She went up on her tiptoes and kissed his cheek. "Relax, okay? I was careful, but you're going to want to see this. Just give me a minute."

She went to walk around him, but Chance stopped her, lifting her off her feet to plant a kiss on her mouth. "I know you're careful, Slick. But you can never be too careful for me." He lowered her to her feet, and Grayson didn't miss the tender pat he gave to her stomach. She whispered something to Chance, and he laughed. "It would serve you right if she did."

Vivi rolled her eyes, then joined the women now

crowded around Cat. They heard her say something to Cat, and then she returned. She held up her camera, angling the screen toward them. She'd gotten several shots of the shooter: before, during, and after. And with each one she revealed, Chance McBride's face darkened. Grayson didn't blame the man. For all her talk of being careful, Vivi had moved closer to the action with each successive shot. Obviously unaware the man beside her was seething, Vivi said, "Wait until you see this one. You won't believe it."

They leaned in. It was a photo of Cat. She'd seen the shooter and purposely tipped the ATV onto its side. Driving with the skill of a professional on two wheels, she leaned forward, head down. In the next frame, you could see the bullet hit her arm, the fur on the jacket part, a puff of smoke. If she hadn't leaned forward... Grayson's chest tightened to the point he could barely breathe. He'd seen people die an ugly death in front him, some by his own hand, and he'd taken a bullet himself, but nothing prepared him for how he felt at that moment, knowing how close Cat had come to being killed.

Chance gave him a look of understanding and placed a hand on his shoulder. "Don't even go there," he said quietly.

"Cat O'Connor, you're the shit," Vivi called over her shoulder. "You're going on the front page of the *Chronicle* tomorrow."

"And you're in shit up to your gorgeous violet eyes, Slick," Chance McBride muttered.

Behind them, Cat argued with Dr. McBride. When her stepfather gave in, agreeing that she was okay to go home, a cold calm settled over Grayson. Now that he knew she was all right, it was time to get to work. "Gage, have your deputies round up the cast and crew from *As the Sun Sets* and bring them to the station for questioning. Put an APB out on Sam Redding. If my hunch is correct, he's the shooter and won't return to his room. And to avoid raising suspicions, bring in anyone from Christmas who might hold a grudge against Chloe."

Easton snorted. "He doesn't have enough room in the station to hold them all."

"Including your brother." Grayson ignored the McBride brothers' shocked expressions and continued, "Question Easton first. I'd like him to provide security at the ranch while I sit in on the interrogations. You do have a two-way mirror, don't you?"

Gage didn't appear to appreciate his running the show, but nodded.

Jack Flaherty stared at Grayson. "Who are you?"

"Special Agent Grayson Alexander." He extended his hand. "Sorry for the deception, but I'm undercover. I'd appreciate your keeping the information to yourself for the time being. That goes for all of you, by the way."

Nell McBride sidled out from behind her great-nephew Gage. "Well, I'll be. I was right after all."

"Aunt Nell—" Gage began.

"Puusssy!" Ty pushed his way through the throng of people on the sidewalk, his arms in the air as he screamed for Cat. He sounded like Stallone calling for Adrian in *Rocky*. GG and Chloe were rubbing off on Grayson. His life had become a movie track. And now the woman he'd just realized how much he wanted in that life, joined them.

She raised her hand. "Ty, over here." Then turned to Grayson. "What are you all doing standing around? Let's get this show on the road. Gage, my gut says it was Sam. I doubt he'll stick around, so might be a good idea to put out an APB on him. Bring in the cast and crew for questioning. Maybe throw in… Why are you all looking at me like that?"

"Despite what you and Special Agent Alexander seem to think, this isn't my first rodeo," Gage said with a disgruntled shake of his head. "So if you don't mind, I'm going to get this gun processed."

"You have the gun?" Cat asked.

"Yeah." Gage opened the towel.

She looked from the Glock to Grayson. "It's mine."

*　　*　　*

Cat stared up at the ceiling in her bedroom. It was one in the morning, and she was wide awake. Her arm ached, but that wasn't the reason she couldn't sleep. Her brain wouldn't shut off. She'd nearly been killed by her own gun. Grayson was right, she should have told him or at least notified Gage that it was missing. She expected to see the same look of suspicion in Grayson's eyes that she had earlier. This time, it would have been warranted. But he'd seemed more concerned than anything else—concerned about her. Everyone was, but unlike her sister, Cat didn't like the attention. And since she'd been getting a lot of it, especially from her mom, Chloe hadn't been happy.

Once her initial worry had passed, Chloe made sure Liz and Paul understood that she had been the target, not Cat. That it was her life that was in danger, not Cat's. Yeah, the ride home in Paul's SUV, stuck between Estelle and Chloe in the backseat, had been about as fun as getting shot at. The only thing that had calmed her mother down was learning that Grayson was an FBI agent and Chloe's bodyguard.

Estelle was only too happy to share stories of her grandson's heroics to set Liz's mind at rest. Chloe's ooh-ing and aahing encouraged the older woman to get a little dramatic in the telling of her tales. Cat knew she was in trouble when Estelle started to act out a particularly violent confrontation Grayson had with a Russian mobster. Cat's encounter with the snow-covered pavement earlier must have compromised her reaction time because she hadn't moved fast enough to avoid an elbow in the cheek.

Which of course led to more attention from Paul and her mother…and Chloe's attack. If not for the timely arrival of Ty and Easton, Cat wagered it would have been the mother of all attacks. Even Estelle had been mildly dismayed. But all it took was for Easton to stand in front of Chloe with his arms crossed and a sardonic eyebrow raised. Too bad they couldn't bottle that look. It worked even better than the sugar pills.

A gust of wind rattled her bedroom window, and Cat pulled the covers over her shoulders. She thought about making herself something hot to drink, but that would mean getting out of her warm bed. She'd also run the risk of waking her sister or Estelle, or worse, Paul and her mother.

Who, like Ty and Easton, were spending the night. Cat was kind of surprised Ty hadn't crawled in bed with her. Then again, she couldn't compete with the White Knight.

Or maybe she could, she thought when the knob turned on her bedroom door. But the tall, broad-shouldered shadow was definitely not Ty. The intruder had something in his hand and moved with a stealthy grace, quietly closing the door behind him. Surely if someone had broken into the house, Easton would have heard them. Unless... She sat up, made a gun with her fingers, and said, "Don't move or I'll shoot."

"How many bullets in your finger, love?"

Her shoulders sagged with relief at the sound of Grayson's amused voice, and she fell back onto the pillows. "One. But I'm a crack shot." She reached across her nightstand to turn on the lamp, blinking as her eyes adjusted to the light. Or maybe it was the sight of the dangerously handsome man standing beside her bed in his black suit. His hair looked like he'd been dragging his fingers through the dark chocolate waves, a heavy scruff shadowing his jaw.

He crouched beside her, setting a thermos and mug on her nightstand as his gaze roamed her face. "How's the arm?"

"Fine as long as I don't roll on it."

"Easton didn't think you were getting much sleep. I thought this might help." He unscrewed the lid, the smell of citrus and cinnamon wafting past her nose as he poured the steaming red liquid into the mug. He held it out of her reach. "You haven't taken any pain meds for a while, have you?"

"Four hours ago, I'm good."

"Careful, it's hot."

"Are you going to join me?"

He smiled. "I was hoping you'd ask." He stood and shrugged out of his jacket, laying it on the end of her bed. His eyes on her face, he undid the top two buttons of his white dress shirt, then rolled up the sleeves to bare his tanned, corded forearms. She felt the heat rising to her cheeks, and it had nothing to do with the mulled wine.

She cleared her throat. "I take it there's been no news since you last texted me?"

Pouring the wine into the thermos cup, he shook his head. "Nothing. Still no sign of Sam. And Molly and George had airtight alibis." He rounded the bed and set his cup on the other nightstand. "Sit up for a sec." She did as he asked, and he propped two pillows behind her back, placing two more against the headboard before stretching out beside her. He grinned at what she imagined was her look of surprise. "You don't mind, do you?" he asked as he carefully slid an arm around her shoulders.

"No, not all." She kind of did. It was difficult lying this close to him knowing they'd do nothing more than talk. It wouldn't be like the last time when he'd rocked her world with his kiss. After he'd questioned her about her e-mail to Molly, Cat had made it clear that without trust, there was no future for them. "You must be tired."

He played with her hair. "More frustrated than tired. I want this case over. I want you out of the line of fire. Tonight was too close."

She felt the tension in her arm, the muscle flexing behind her neck. That as much as his words made her think that maybe Grayson cared as much about her as she did about him. It's why she set the mug on the nightstand and turned to face him. "I'm used to being in the line of fire. I can handle myself."

"Do you know what it was like, seeing you on the ground, knowing I had to stay with Chloe when I wanted to be with you?"

She stroked his clenched jaw with the pads of her fingers. "It wasn't your job to protect me. You—"

"This isn't about a job anymore. I care about you, Cat.

I want you safe. Your sister is a target, which makes you one, too. As tonight proved."

She felt a twinge in her bicep where the bullet had sliced through her skin, and lowered her arm, placing her hand on his chest. "So when you say you care about me, does that also mean you trust me? Despite the shooter having my gun and wearing my—"

"I wouldn't be here if I didn't. We had this conversation at the warehouse, remember?"

"I do"—she nodded, trailing the tip of her finger along the buttons of his shirt—"and I also remember our earlier conversation. The one where we were going to kiss and make up. I think you might have said something about going to second base, too."

He gave a startled laugh and placed his hand over hers. "You were just shot. So no matter how much I—"

"I was shot at, not shot. A scratch doesn't count."

He turned to face her, the heavy weight of his leg trapping hers between his as he gently drew her closer. "You're a very demanding, beautiful, sexy woman, but I won't risk hurting you. So for now, you'll have to be satisfied with a kiss." He touched those firm, perfect lips to her eyelids, the tip of her nose, then her mouth.

She groaned when he lifted his head. "It's not fair to tease a wounded woman."

"I thought it was just a scratch?" His laugh was low and strained.

"You know, there're studies that show sex after a near-death experience is very life affirming."

"How did we go from kissing and second base to a home run? Are you sure you took your pain meds four hours ago?"

Okay, this was getting embarrassing. She was practically begging him to make love to her. Maybe she'd misread his feelings for her. "You're right. I should probably get some sleep." She tried to move her leg and gave him a light push when he didn't release her. "Grayson, I—"

"I was taught never to argue with a woman. Especially a beautiful woman who I've wanted in my bed since the day she jumped me."

She laughed, the tension in her chest releasing. "That was the first day we met."

"I'm a guy, and you're hot. But now I want more from you than just sex." He gave her a slow and mind-blowing kiss. "And seeing that I do, it's probably a good idea to find out if we have chemistry sooner rather than later."

"Yes, I ... ah," she moaned as he pressed his lips to the sensitive spot beneath her ear, his hand sliding underneath her pajama top.

He nipped her earlobe. "One whimper, one pained grimace, and we stop."

"If you stop, I guarantee there'll be some whimpering and grimacing."

"Cat, I'm not kidding—"

She tugged on his head, drawing his mouth to hers. "Shut it and kiss me."

Chapter Nineteen

Cat never thought she'd enjoy spooning, but Grayson had changed her mind. He'd changed her mind about a lot of things. And right now she was enjoying being woken up by the slow, warm kisses he pressed to the back of her neck while he wrapped his big, hard body around her. She shivered as his hand swept over her, teasing and caressing with a maddening expertise. In only a few hours, he knew better than she did how to make her body hum.

He moved his mouth to her shoulder and kissed it. "I think we can put any worries about our chemistry to rest, don't you, love?"

Her laugh turned into a moan when he . . . "Darling, are you all right?" her mother called through the locked door. Cat turned her head into the pillow and groaned while behind her Grayson released a low laugh.

She lifted her head, nudging him with her elbow. "I'm good, Mom. I'll be up in a minute."

"No, you need your rest. Open the door, I have your breakfast."

"Um, breakfast in bed sounds good," Grayson murmured against the shoulder he continued to kiss.

"Since that's my mother out there, and we're keeping this between us, no breakfast in bed for you. If I can't get rid of her, you're sneaking out the window," she whispered, then reached for her cell phone. "Mom, it's only seven. I think I'll try to sleep for another hour."

"Two," he murmured, nipping her shoulder.

"You can go back to sleep after you eat. Paul has to leave for the hospital, and he wants to check you over before he goes." The doorknob rattled. "You don't even have to get out of bed. I know there's a key somewhere. I'll be right back." They heard her retreating footsteps.

"Out, out," Cat said, turning to push at Grayson's muscled chest.

He stared at her. "You can't be serious?"

"As a heart attack."

"All right, all right," he grumbled, rolling out of bed. "I'll hide in the closet."

At the sight of his naked body in the light of day, she swallowed, then forced herself to say, "No, you don't know my mother. You'll have to go out the window and sneak back in through my mother's. Just make sure Paul's not in there before you do."

"Eyes to mine, love. You're making it hard to concentrate."

Yes, he was hard, very hard. Which made it difficult to stay focused. She dragged her gaze up his sculpted body to meet his amused eyes. "Get dressed. She'll be back any minute," Cat warned and got out of bed, scooping her pajamas off the floor. She straightened, glancing over her shoulder to see him staring at her while he pulled on his pants. She made a frustrated sound in her throat for several reasons; not the least of which they were going to get caught. She grabbed her phone and texted Ty, telling him to distract her mother.

"Cat, I don't have shoes." Grayson's unbuttoned pants hung loosely at his hips as he pulled on his shirt, her gaze stuck on his sun-kissed abs and the dark line of hair disappearing under the waistband of his black boxers. Her mother's timing sucked.

"You can borrow my slippers," she said, stepping into her pajama bottoms. Her cell phone pinged with Ty's response: *Aha! I knew it! You have James Bond in your bed! Got your back but I want DETAILS.*

She groaned, tossing her phone on the bed. Sharing details with Ty would almost be as embarrassing as getting caught by her mother.

Grayson moved toward her with a frown, taking her pajama top from her. "Did you hurt yourself?" he asked, gently guiding her arms into the sleeves.

"No, I…" She trailed off when his warm fingers brushed against her bare skin as he slowly did up the buttons of her top. "You have to go," she said, her voice breathy. "Ty will only be able to stall her for so long."

He leaned in, kissing the underside of her jaw. "You don't really want me to go, do you?"

"No." She arched her neck to give him better access, then heard her mother's and Ty's voices coming down the hall. "Yes, yes, I do." She stepped away from him, grabbing his jacket from the end of the bed. She shoved it at his chest, pushing him toward the window. Her arm twinged, and she swallowed a pained gasp.

"Stop pushing me. You'll hurt yourself." He framed her face with his hands and gave her a hard kiss. "You owe me for this," he said, turning to the window. As he opened it, a gust of cold mountain air blew into the room, and snow swirled across the field outside her window.

She took in his black-stockinged feet and grimaced. "Hang on." She ran to her bed, grabbing her cat slippers from beneath it.

He looked from the slippers to her. "You can't be serious."

"It's better than nothing." Not much, she realized when he put them on. Half his foot hung over the end. He gave his head a slight shake, lifting his long leg over the ledge.

Unlike Ty, Grayson had a talent for climbing out windows. But like with Ty, at the sound of the doorknob rattling, Cat panicked and pushed him the rest of the way out. Lying on the ground beneath her window, Grayson lifted his snow-covered face to look back at her. "Really?"

"Sorry," she whispered. Then slammed the window shut, pressing her back against it as her mother entered with a white breakfast tray in her hands and a suspicious look on her face.

*   *   *

Despite Paul declaring her good to go, her mother had insisted Cat stay in bed for the day. Cat wasn't the type to lie around. Now if Grayson was in her bed, that would have been a different story. But they had a case to solve.

Twenty minutes after her mother and Paul left for town, Cat stood at the stove, making omelets for her sister, Ty, and Easton. She felt Chloe's eyes drilling into her back.

Her sister's suspicions wouldn't be as easy to alleviate as her mother's. It's why Cat had refused Easton's and Ty's offers to make breakfast. It made it easier to avoid Chloe.

Cat's cell pinged on the counter. She and Ty had been communicating via texts since she'd come into the kitchen. She glanced at his message. *She's on to you. Stop humming Have Yourself a Merry Little Christmas.*

"Ty, are you sure those aren't my pajamas? I have a pair just like them," Chloe said.

Easton, who'd been on his computer the entire time Cat had been in the kitchen, snorted.

Cat texted back. *Looks like she's on to you* :)

"No, Pussy bought them for me. Well, look who finally graced us with his presence. Ouch, what happened to your face?"

Cat glanced over her shoulder. Grayson walked into the kitchen wearing a V-neck sweater that matched his eyes and a pair of well-worn jeans. Looking as tall, dark, and delicious as Ty proclaimed him to be. He also had a scratch on his cheek.

Grayson raised his eyebrows at Cat. She winced. He must have scraped his cheek on the rosebush beneath her window. "Nicked myself shaving," he said, returning Chloe's good morning. Easton's knowing gaze slid from Grayson to Cat.

Ty texted her. *You're not supposed to leave your marks where everyone can see them.*

"I didn't hear you come home last night, Grayson. Where did you sleep?" Chloe asked with a suspicious edge in her voice.

Afraid she'd give them away, Cat whipped her head around and loaded shredded cheddar cheese on the omelets. She hoped Grayson had a good answer for her sister.

"He slept with me on the couch," Ty said. Cat had just released a sigh of relief at his plausible excuse when he added, "Not that I got much shut-eye. He moans in his sleep, talks, too. But he's an incredible spooner, and he does this—"

Cat's cheeks heated and she briefly closed her eyes, then texted Ty. *Shut it.*

But Chloe had cut him off with a fake giggle. "You didn't have to sleep with Ty, Grayson. I have a queen-size bed."

"I don't think he would have been comfortable in your room, Chloe. All that lace and…" Ty trailed off. Cat could practically hear the *oops* in his voice. "You know, I probably should get dressed."

"How do you know—"

Cat interrupted her sister. "Okay, omelets are almost ready. Who wants toast?"

Grayson moved in behind her, reaching over her for a mug. He stood close enough that she could feel him against her back. "Incredible spooner?" he said under his breath, then bent over her. "Smells delicious, Cat." He nipped her earlobe, whispering, "And so do you." Straightening, he took the spatula from her. "Go sit and rest your arm. I'll take care of breakfast."

"It's okay, I—"

He gave her a look. "Sit."

"Thanks," Cat murmured and took a seat at the island, avoiding meeting her sister's eyes. "Anything new?" Cat asked Easton.

He looked up from the screen. "Redding dumped the

snowmobile and stole a pickup at a truck stop ten miles out of town."

"It's terrifying knowing he's still on the loose." Chloe plucked at her pink robe, blinking her false eyelashes. Of course her hair and makeup were perfect. Easton and Grayson were here.

Cat self-consciously finger-combed her hair. "You're in less danger now than you were before, Chloe. He's on the run. We just have to figure out who hired him."

"Cat, I appreciate you trying to make me feel better. But I'd rather hear what Grayson thinks. He is the expert after all."

"I agree with your sister." Grayson put a platter with the omelets and one with toast in the middle of the island. "Dig in." He pulled out a stool beside Cat, placing her cell phone by her arm. She could tell by the twitch of his lips that he'd read the texts between her and Ty. Her cheeks flushed, and he chuckled.

Her sister's eyes narrowed. "What's going on?"

"Nothing," Cat said quickly. She didn't entirely trust Grayson not to spill the beans. She knew he didn't fully agree that they keep their relationship on the down-low. But that was only because he didn't know her sister like she did. Cat cleared her throat and thought of something that would put the smile back on Chloe's face and hopefully distract her. "Grayson, since you and your grandmother will be with Chloe today, Easton and I will do another search of the lodge."

Great, from the look on her face, that didn't make Chloe any happier.

But Cat didn't have time to ponder the reason for her sister's disgruntled expression because Easton said, "I'm going to dig deeper into Molly's, George's, and Sam's financials." Grayson had okayed a standard search of their financials, so he wouldn't be pleased Easton meant to cross the line, but she and Easton had discussed it last night. They had nothing, and they needed something.

Grayson lowered a piece of toast from his mouth. Before he could shut them down, she said, "Don't ask. That way you have plausible deniability."

He chewed his toast, mulling it over, then nodded. "Okay. Do what you need to do. Did you ask Chloe about Lord Darby?"

Chloe bent over her plate, forking a piece of omelet into her mouth.

"No, I didn't. Chloe?" Her sister raised her gaze, looking like a deer caught in the headlights. "Oh, come on, you promised me you wouldn't see him."

"It wasn't my fault. I didn't seek him out. He…he's backing the movie I auditioned for. I honestly didn't know, Kit Kat." Her chin quivered. "The teenager who got the part is his new girlfriend."

"I'm sorry, Chloe. But you should have told me." Her sister had honestly believed she was in love with Darby. It didn't escape Cat that Chloe also thought she was in love with Grayson. "You haven't had any contact with his wife, have you?"

"No, why?"

"Because she's back in LA, and she threatened you last year. We have to rule her out as a suspect."

Beside Cat, Easton studied Chloe, and for a split second he looked sympathetic. But then his scruff-darkened jaw hardened when her sister gave Grayson a little-girl-lost look. "I don't understand why anyone would want to kill me."

Estelle swanned into the kitchen with Fluffy in her arms. She was as perfectly made-up as Chloe and dressed in a bronze silk pantsuit. She'd obviously overheard Chloe and moved to her side, patting her arm. "Don't worry, my dear. You have Grayson to protect you. As long as you're in danger, he'll be on the case."

"But you said he had only a few days left of his vacation time."

Something told Cat this was a setup. It seemed rehearsed.

"I put in for more time this morning. I'm off until after the holidays." He glanced at Cat, his eyes warm and full of promise.

Her sister clapped. Cat wanted to do the same, until Estelle said, "You see, my dear, I told you Grayson wouldn't leave you unprotected. Now you better get dressed. You two have a very important scene today."

The two women shared a look. Chloe patted Estelle's hand. "You're right, we do."

"Where are you filming today?" Easton asked. "I'll go check out the locations."

"Santa's Village," her sister said. "I'm going to tell Santa my Christmas wish." She glanced under her lashes at Grayson. "And if I've been a very good girl, my present will be unwrapped and lying in my bed at the lodge."

"Maybe you didn't hear me. I asked where you're filming today, not what you're doing," Easton clipped out.

Chloe sighed. "Santa's Village and the lodge."

"What about tomorrow?"

"Oh." Chloe plucked at her robe. "There's been a change in plans. Today's the last day of filming. But there's a wrap-up party at the Penalty Box tomorrow."

Grayson frowned. "I didn't hear anything about this. When did Phil decide to—"

"It was a last-minute decision. Phil and I came to an..." Chloe trailed off, then waved her hand. "It's nothing to worry about."

"Nothing at all, my boy. It'll be just like *Miracle on 34th Street*." Estelle sighed, rubbing her cheek on Fluffy's head. Cat didn't like the smug look on Estelle's face or on Fluffy's.

*   *   *

Grayson rubbed his jaw as he ended his call with Turner. As frustrated now as he had been after Googling *Miracle on 34th Street*. His grandmother and Chloe were up to something, and he couldn't get a handle on it. He couldn't get a handle on Turner, either. Other than the man was a wanker.

Since the shooting in Christmas had made the news, Turner had called Grayson for an update on the case. He'd had no choice but to tell him the gun was Cat's. He'd find out anyway. No matter what Grayson said, Turner believed that Cat was somehow involved with the shooting.

Something didn't sit right with Grayson. It was as if Turner had a personal vendetta against Cat. Grayson sent Easton a text, asking him to look into Turner and see if Cat and the agent had any history they were unaware of. He could ask Cat, but he didn't want to worry her. Then he remembered her brother had been an ADA in Denver a few years back and sent Easton another text, telling him to look over any cases Ethan O'Connor had persecuted that involved Turner.

Leaning against the white picket fence outside the red chalet-style house in Santa's Village, Grayson shoved his cell phone into his pocket. Chloe was inside, sitting on Santa's knee, telling him her Christmas wish with Phil and a cameraman present. Another cameraman and several of the crew stood down the way filming the extras meandering through Santa's Village, his grandmother among them. She walked Fluffy—on a diamond-studded leash, wearing red booties and a red, fur-trimmed cape—along with Estelle's constant companions, Ted and Fred. George and Molly stood off a snow-covered path beside a giant plastic candy cane. They looked as uneasy as Grayson felt.

Phil was playing the last scene close to the vest. If it went down the way Grayson expected it to, he was going to be the guy lying in the bed at the lodge. Which meant Tessa Hart had chosen Rand Livingstone, and where that left Byron Hart was anyone's guess. But if Grayson was a betting man, he'd wager Byron Hart had a fatal accident in his future and George would be out of work. And with Rand choosing Tessa, Molly's future as Paula was at risk as well.

He walked over to Molly and George. "Bloody terrifying about Sam, eh? To think we had a murderer in our midst and didn't know it." He was getting real tired of being Harry. If he didn't think he'd get more out of Molly and George playing a British lord, he'd drop the act.

George rolled his eyes.

Molly shoved her gloved hands in the pockets of her fur-lined leather coat. "Too bad he missed. He would have done us all a favor. Us, at least. You don't have anything to worry about."

"What do you mean?"

"Oh, don't play the fool, Halstead. You've been after

Tessa since you stepped foot on the set. It won't work, you
know. If Phil thinks he'll get away with it, he won't. The
fans will revolt. They'll picket the studio."

"I'm not sure I'm following you, George."

The actor looked away. Molly rubbed his arm. "George
thinks that instead of Tessa picking Byron, she picks
Rand."

"So the scene at the lodge today, I'm in it and not you?"
he asked the older man. He could alleviate George's worries
by telling him, no matter what Chloe and his grandmother
wanted, this was his last episode. But this might be what
they needed to force George or Molly to show their hand.

"Over my dead body," George said and stomped off.

"Sadly, for poor George, I think that's exactly what's
going to happen." Molly sighed, then patted his shoulder.
"No hard feelings, Harry. I know it's not your fault." Her
delicate jaw tightened. "If anyone's to blame, it's Chloe.
I'm sure she's the one behind this. Numbers start to fall,
and she has a meltdown. If she would have just left it
alone, none of this would have had to happen."

"None of what?"

"Hmm?" She looked distracted. He repeated his question, and she gave her head a slight shake, lifting her
shoulders. "Don't pay any attention to me. I should probably get to hair and makeup in case I'm in the next scene.
Who knows, Harry, maybe I'll get _my_ Christmas wish,
and it will be me and you in bed at the lodge." She winked
and walked away.

*   *   *

Chloe got her Christmas wish. Molly didn't. And Grayson
now understood the lack of a script. Rand and Tessa had

exchanged less than four words before falling into bed. Maybe if Grayson really was an actor, the scene wouldn't have bothered him as much as it did, but he wasn't. Making out with Cat's sister was more than a little uncomfortable. He kept reminding himself it wasn't real. The problem was, he had an uneasy feeling Chloe had confused fantasy with reality.

Phil yelled "Cut."

Chloe, as if she didn't hear him, writhed on top of Grayson, moaning.

"Chloe, get—" She smashed her mouth on his, drowning out the words.

"Cut," Phil yelled again.

Grayson wrenched his lips from hers, flipping Chloe onto her back. But instead of stopping like he assumed she would, Chloe wrapped her legs around his waist, fisting her hand in his hair to drag his mouth back to hers.

"All right, I give up." Phil laughed.

Grayson didn't want to hurt her, but he'd had enough. He grabbed her wrist, forcing her hand from his head and drew back. "Stop it, right now."

She looked taken aback by his anger. Surely she couldn't actually believe he'd been into it. "Get off me." She moved mechanically, and he rolled off the bed. He hadn't had a chance to talk to Phil, but he had to do that now. The director needed to start looking for a replacement or change the story line. Just as long as he didn't tell Molly or George, at least until they'd discovered which one of them wanted Chloe dead.

Grayson looked for Phil in the group of people congregated behind the cameras. He spotted the director, and to the left of him, Cat and Easton. She had to be upset by what she'd just witnessed. It didn't matter that she knew Grayson was acting, she knew her sister wasn't. "Cat." He started toward her, then realized he had on nothing but a pair of black satin briefs. Searching the floor by the bed, he spotted the black robe, walked over, and picked it up. By the time he had it on, Cat was gone.

After the night they'd spent together, he didn't want something like this to come between them. He had to find her.

"You're in love with my sister, aren't you?"

He turned to Chloe. She'd put on a robe and was standing by the bed. He dragged his hands through his hair. It was too early to say if he was in love with Cat. Falling for her? Probably. "We're seeing each other."

"But I thought... Everything you said to me..."

"Why don't you get dressed, Chloe. We'll talk then, all right?"

She searched his face, then gave a small nod. She walked into the adjoining room and quietly closed the door. He headed for the bathroom where he'd changed for the scene and got dressed. As he left and strode to the door, a scream tore through the room. *Chloe.* Grayson ran across the room, throwing open the door. "Chloe, what happened?"

She was on the floor in front of the bed, her hands at her throat. "Someone... someone tried to kill me. They choked me." She started to cry, and he crouched beside her to take her in his arms.

"I've got you now. No one's going to hurt you," he said, scanning the room while he held her trembling body close. He gave her a couple more seconds to get it together before he drew back to examine her neck. Tipping her chin, he studied the red marks. They appeared to be left by bare fingers, with tiny gouges from nails. "Chloe, did you see who did this?"

"No, she must have come in through the sliding door. She came from behind and strangled me. I couldn't breathe. I think I blacked out. She must have thought I was dead and left."

He pulled out his cell to call Gage. Chloe closed her hand over his. "D-don't call the police. I think..." She swallowed, touched her throat, and lifted tear-filled eyes. "I think it was Cat."

Chapter Twenty

Cat saw the look in Grayson's eyes when he called her name and knew she had to leave before he outed them. No doubt he thought she was upset seeing her sister sprawled on top of him, moaning in ecstasy as she ate his face. Admittedly, it had been uncomfortable, and she'd spent the last fifteen minutes with her eyes averted. She would have covered her ears, but that would have looked weird.

Part of her discomfort came from knowing that while Grayson was acting, her sister wasn't. Which was why Cat had to leave. Because if Grayson reacted the way she expected him to, her sister would know they were together. Something Cat wanted to avoid at all costs, especially now. They had enough to deal with.

She'd witnessed a confrontation between Molly, George, and Phil in the lodge's parking lot when the director broke the news about the scene Cat had just watched.

It's why she'd been at the taping in the first place. She'd been afraid one of them would make their move. But they hadn't shown up. So when Grayson turned to pick up his black robe, she figured she'd kill two birds with one stone and check on their whereabouts.

As she started to walk away, Easton stopped her with a hand on her arm. "You okay?"

"Yeah, I'm good." She almost asked the same of him. She'd sensed his tension while he watched the scene.

"I'm going to grab us a couple of coffees. I won't be long."

She nodded, catching Grayson's grandmother's smirk. The older woman was a pain, and worse, she was encouraging Chloe. Cat opened her mouth, then closed it. She turned away. She'd let Grayson deal with his grandmother.

Cat jogged along the walkway, past the last room, and rounded the corner to the back of the lodge. She'd get a better view into Molly's and George's rooms through the patio doors. Obviously, she wasn't the only one who'd taken the path as the snow was well trampled. George's room was first up. She could hear him talking. Edging closer, she peeked past the curtains. He was on the phone, his face pale as he ran an agitated hand through his hair and paced the room. No doubt talking to his agent about the new development on *As the Sun Sets*.

She waited until his back was turned and moved on to the next room. Blowing on her bare hands, she gave a cursory glance through each patio door until she reached Molly's. As far as Cat could tell, the actress wasn't in her room. She waited a couple of minutes with her ear pressed to the glass, then tried the patio door. Finding it unlocked, she entered Molly's room. Cat gave up her

unproductive search and opened the door to leave when
a blood-chilling scream stopped her cold. It was Chloe.

Slamming the patio door shut, she stumbled along the
path as she raced to the room. She pressed her face to the
glass where they'd taped the last scene. No one was there,
but the door to the adjoining room was ajar. She ran to
the next set of patio doors and shoved them open. Grayson looked up from comforting Chloe on the floor. Her
sister's flimsy white robe slipped off one shoulder as she
twisted at her waist.

She stared at Cat with wide, distrustful eyes, then buried her face in Grayson's chest. "Keep her away from me,"
she whimpered.

Cat's shoulders rose and fell on a resigned sigh. It was
too late. Grayson had told Chloe about them, and now her
sister hated her. She ignored the stab of guilt in her chest
and took a step forward. "Chloe, I can explain—"

The outer door flew open, framing Phil, a couple of
grips, and Easton, who all took in the scene. "I have it
handled, Phil," Grayson said in an authoritative voice.
"Easton." He lifted his chin at the door.

"Out." Easton closed the door on their shocked faces,
then rounded on Grayson. "What the hell happened?"

"Chloe was attacked," Grayson answered Easton, but
his eyes remained on Cat.

She moved toward her sister. "Oh God, Chloe, are you
all—"

Grayson cut her off. "Cat, where were you?" He dis-
tractedly patted Chloe's shoulder when she once again
whimpered.

Cat frowned. "I was searching Molly's room. Why?"

"Did anyone see you?"

"No." She placed her hands on her hips, irritated by his line of questioning. "I may not be a cop anymore, Grayson, but give me some credit, I know—"

"Chloe was attacked by a woman. She thinks that woman was you."

Cat's arms fell limply to her sides as the emotion in his eyes finally registered. It was suspicion. He actually thought she was capable of this. She shouldn't be surprised or hurt. After all, she'd been his primary suspect from the beginning.

"Bullshit," Easton snapped, moving to Cat's side. He put a hand on her shoulder. "Chloe, you look at your sister right now and make that accusation to her face."

Cat was startled at what Easton seemed to be implying. Did he honestly believe her sister would do something so heinous as falsely accusing Cat of attacking her? There would be no reason for Chloe to do such... Other than the man comforting her.

Cat didn't know what made her do it. Maybe it was because she was sick to death of being accused of something that she didn't do. Or maybe it was because the man she'd been falling in love with wasn't the one calling bullshit. But whatever the reason, she strode to where the couple sat on the floor.

"You told her we were together, didn't you?"

"Yes, but Cat, you can't actually believe that she..." He lifted Chloe's chin, revealing the faint outline of two thumbs. Chloe wrapped her arms around her waist, tears sliding down her cheeks as she averted her gaze. "...would do this to herself for attention?"

No, she didn't want to believe it. And faced with the evidence, she started to doubt herself.

Easton walked over, crouching down to skim his fingers over the marks. Chloe shivered and bit her bottom lip. "What were you doing when you were attacked, Chloe? Where were you standing?"

"Here, and I was listening to an audiobook." She pointed to her earbuds and iPad lying on the floor. At least that explained how she could be taken unawares. Cat had given her sister lessons in self-defense, at which she'd excelled. When she wasn't worrying about having a heart attack from overexerting herself.

Grayson helped Chloe off the floor, guiding her to the end of the bed. "Sit down," he said, draping the comforter over her shoulders.

"Thank you," Chloe whispered, touching her throat.

"So you're saying the person came in through the patio doors, attacked you, then left that way, but you didn't see them. Or you did see them and it was Cat?"

"I didn't see them. I must have blacked out, and they left me for dead." She stared at her hands folded in her lap.

"How do you know it was a woman? Seems odd they didn't speak to you." Easton grilled her while Grayson watched her closely. Cat did the same.

"They were the same size as me. I smelled their perfume. They may have said something, but I didn't hear it." Chloe's fingers whitened as she clutched the comforter, her chin lifting. "I was the one who was nearly murdered. Shouldn't you be out looking for whoever did it instead of questioning me, the victim?"

Easton muttered, "Victim my ass."

"That's enough, McBride," Grayson said. "So the perfume was the reason you thought it was Cat?"

"Yes." She gave two quick nods.

"Chloe, you know I don't wear perfume, unless it was my shampoo you smelled. Did they have gloves on?"

"Stop it. All of you just stop it. Maybe I was wrong and it wasn't you, Kit Kat. But I saw how you looked at me after the taping. You were jealous, and angry, really angry. I could see it in your eyes. So when I...was attacked, I immediately thought of you. I was in shock." She flapped her hands in front of her face. "I feel...faint." She swayed on the end of the bed.

Automatically, Cat reached for her.

"She's playing you, Cat. She's not going to faint," Easton said.

Chloe's gaze jerked to Easton, and she lurched off the bed. The comforter fell at her feet as she got in his face, stabbing him in his chest with her finger. "You have no idea what it's like to know that someone wants you dead. That any second may be your last. So excuse me if I'm a little emotional."

He looked down at her, and with the tip of his finger, moved her robe back onto her shoulder. "Preaching to the choir, Scarlett. You're talking to ex–Special Forces, ex-cop, and an FBI agent. Now drop the act and tell the truth."

"I don't know why you're all so mad at me. You all agree someone is trying to kill me yet you haven't arrested anyone, and I'm still a target." She moved away from Easton and turned her back. "Cat, choke me."

"I'll do it," Easton said.

"McBride." Grayson shook his head. "Do it, Cat. Chloe's judgment won't be impaired by fear or surprise."

Chloe smiled at him over her shoulder.

Cat stepped up behind her sister, placing her hands

around her neck. A few minutes earlier, she would have
been tempted to squeeze. Grayson came to stand in front
of Chloe and traced the outline of Cat's fingers, holding
her gaze as he did. She wondered if he felt the same electrical buzz she did when his fingers brushed hers. A buzz
she wished she didn't feel. If she had her hands around *his*
neck, she'd give in to the urge and choke him.

"Chloe, close your eyes. Put yourself back in the moment.
Was the person of similar height and build to Cat?"

She shook her head. "No, taller and more voluptuous.
I'm sure it was Molly. She's already a suspect, so it makes
sense she'd try to murder me now that she's found out
Paula is going to be killed off."

Cat groaned. "Don't tell me you were behind the
change in the story line." She felt her sister tense. "Dammit, Chloe, you didn't need to give Molly and George
another reason to want you dead."

Chloe ignored Cat, biting her thumbnail. "You know, I
think I might be mistaken. It could have been Lady Darby,
she's tall and curvy, too." She shrugged, turning with a
smile. "See, everything worked out for the best. I stopped
Grayson from calling the police, so no one knows—"

"You falsely accused your sister," Easton finished
for her.

She ignored him too and continued. "...I thought it
was Cat. And now you can arrest both Molly and Lady
Darby based on my testimony. Once you interrogate
them, they'll break down and confess to hiring Sam to
kill me." She held up her hands. "Ta-da, case is solved."

The door flew open. "Phil said something happened
to...Why are you all looking at me like that?" Ty, wearing
a dark wig, short skirt, tight sweater, and thigh-high boots,

placed his palm on his cheek and laughed. "Oh right, I forgot. I decided to go undercover. I wanted to see what Sam had been saying to the crew. Thought they'd be more likely to open up to a hot woman than me. What do you think?"

That he fit Chloe's description. He also had access to Cat's snowmobile suit, helmet, and gun. Cat pinched the bridge of her nose. She couldn't believe the thought had crossed her mind. She was as bad as her sister. The case was getting to her, and so was the man she thought she was in love with.

"Okay, I've seen and heard it all now. I'm outta here. Do you need a ride, Cat?" Easton asked as he opened the door.

"Yeah, just give me a minute. I need to speak to you," she said to Grayson.

"Ty, is that my sweater?" her sister asked.

"Umm, no. Hey, what happened to your…Oh my God, someone tried to choke you to death. You poor thing." He took Chloe in his arms, rocking her back and forth.

Chloe sniffed. "Are you wearing my perfume?"

Grayson rubbed his hand over his face. "Ty, stay with Chloe while I talk to Cat." He took her hand and led her out the door, closing it behind him. "Look, I know what it sounded like, but I didn't believe you attacked Chloe."

"No, you were just going to call the police without giving me a chance—"

"No, I wasn't. Chloe hadn't accused you yet."

They both turned at the sound of a car door slamming. Gage walked toward them, his expression grim. "Cat, you're going to have to come to the station with me."

"Gage, I don't know who called you, but it was a misunderstanding—" Grayson began.

"We just brought Sam in. He said Cat hired him to kill Chloe."

*   *   *

In all his years as an agent, Grayson had never been involved in a case that was as big a shitshow as this one. He shrugged off his jacket and rolled up his sleeves, staring at Sam across the table as he did. "All right, Redding, let's take it from the beginning again." Grayson pressed the record button. He'd been interrogating Sam for more than three hours, and his story had changed every single time.

"I already told you she hired me. What more do you need? At least let me have a smoke. I'm dying here, man."

Grayson lifted the pad he was taking notes on. "What I need is the truth. You've changed the date, the time, and the place you were allegedly hired, the amount of money involved, and the motive behind the contract. So why don't you just tell me who really hired you, and we'll get you that cigarette."

At a knock on the door, Grayson inhaled a deep, frustrated breath and shut off the recorder. This wouldn't be taking as long if he didn't have to deal with the constant interruptions. "I'll give you a few minutes to think about it."

Grayson stepped out of the room. Surprised to see Deputy Jill Flaherty and not the McBride brothers. "We have a situation," she said. "Gage wants you in his office. Suze, our dispatcher, went to get a couple of burgers and fries for the prisoner. You okay with us giving him something to eat?"

Might not be a bad idea. So far nothing else had

worked. He nodded. "Take another deputy in with you and question him while he's eating."

Her eyes lit up. "Can I be the bad cop?"

"Go for it. Just be sure to record the interrogation."

"You know Cat's innocent, right?"

"Yeah, I do." He'd told Cat the same thing, several times, but she knew as well as he did that unless they got Redding to tell the truth, they had an uphill battle. And if Turner got wind of the new development, it would get a whole lot worse. But he didn't have time to worry about that now. "How's Cat holding up?"

Jill made a face. "She put herself in a cell. Don't worry, the door's open. She just got tired of Liz and Chloe going at it. That Chloe's a real piece of work. Family's supposed to stand up for family, not turn on them the way that she did. Can you believe she actually thinks Cat hired a hit man? She's protected Chloe since as far back as I can remember. And if Cat wanted someone dead, she'd do it herself."

After today, he could believe just about anything. And if Chloe wasn't lying about the attack this afternoon—the jury was still out on that since Molly had an airtight alibi, and from the information Easton had gathered so far, Lady Darby hadn't left LA—then he understood why she might question her sister's innocence. "Maybe we'll keep that last bit between us." He smiled and headed to Gage's office.

As he rounded the corner, he stopped in his tracks. It looked like half the town had staged a sit-in. A quiet sit-in, but there was no doubt they were here to support Cat. Several people held signs that read FREE CAT. So much for keeping this under wraps.

As Grayson stepped around the people sitting on the floor, he skirted the woman in uniform that he assumed was Suze, carrying a to-go bag and a tray of coffees. He turned at her gasp, she'd tripped over someone and spilt the coffee. Several people reached out to help her, so Grayson continued on his way. Dr. McBride came out of Gage's office. The older man shut the door and leaned against it with a beleaguered expression on his face. When a tall blond man swept in through the front doors of the station wearing a black wool coat and carrying a brief-case, Dr. McBride's expression changed to one of relief.

"Ethan, thank God." He took the man's hand and patted him on the back.

Grayson walked over and extended his hand. "Gray... Harry Halstead," he introduced himself to the man he knew to be Cat's brother. Grayson didn't want to break his cover just yet. He glanced around the room as the crowd went quiet. "We should probably talk in private."

Ethan nodded, then addressed the room. "Folks, Cat appreciates your support, but it would be best if you went home and let us do our job." He searched the crowd, blinked, then looked past Ty to find whoever he was looking for. "Nell, that goes for you, too." The older woman pretended not to hear him.

The twins, Holly and Hailey, stood up and waved their signs in the direction of the exit. "Come on, people, piz-za's on the house at the diner. We'll come up with a plan to free Cat."

"Oh, I am so down with that." Ty rose from the cor-ner of a desk and straightened his skirt, patting Grayson's chest as he walked by. "You take care of our girl, you hear." He stopped in front of Ethan. "I'm Ty, your sister's best friend. And"—he leaned in to whisper—"if she needs an alibi, just tell me the date, time, and place, and I'll say I was there."

Ethan rubbed the bridge of his nose between his fingers. "It's actually a federal offense to perjure yourself, Ty. So I'm—"

Ty sunk his teeth in the tip of his finger. "Can you repeat that?"

Hailey grabbed him by the hand. "Stop flirting with Ethan." As they walked toward the doors, they heard Ty say, "How hard do you think it would be to break someone out of this place?"

"Don't even think about it, Ty," Cat said, coming through the door leading from the cells.

That was it; the room went wild. Everyone converged on Cat as if she were a rock star. The door to Gage's office opened, and Chloe walked out. She took one look at her sister's reception and burst into tears.

Chapter Twenty-One

Cat heard her brother, Grayson, and Paul trying to reason with Chloe while friends and neighbors crowded around her. She forced her lips to curve while accepting their offers of support, their hugs and pats on the back. She couldn't believe that once again she was the center of a police investigation. Initially, she'd been in shock. It felt like a horrible joke. But as the seriousness of the situation sunk in, fear and self-doubt took hold. She felt herself shutting down, and this time Chloe hadn't been there to snap her out of it. No, this time her sister was the one holding the shovel, ready to bury her.

But as she met Grayson's eyes across the crowded room, some of Cat's fear and self-doubt faded. He had her back in more ways than she'd realized until Easton shared what had been going on behind the scenes. Easton had joined her in the cell to give her the butt kick she needed. He was a good and supportive friend. Someone she could count on, as he continued to prove to her time and time again.

She could count on Grayson, too. Even with the evidence building up against her, he believed in her. She wouldn't be fighting this on her own. But if he was smart and valued his career, he should be distancing himself from her, not putting himself in the middle of the investigation. She realized then that Grayson and her friends and family, other than Chloe, were putting up a bigger fight for her than she was, and that kicked every ounce of self-pity out of Cat. This time she wasn't going to roll over and play dead. Even if it meant protecting herself instead of her sister.

"All right, everyone. If you want us to get Cat out of here, let us get back to work," Easton said, moving toward the exit.

Ty clasped his hands against his fake boobs as he watched Easton usher people out the doors, then he drew her in for one last hug. "You've got James Bond, the White Knight, and Thor on the case. And if all else fails, you've got me and the gang from Christmas." He waved his hand at his newfound friends heading out the door.

"I hate to tell you this, Dolly, but that makes me more nervous than comforted. But thanks, I appreciate all the support."

Ty finger-combed her hair. "I just wish all of this was over. This is our first Christmas together. I don't want to celebrate it with you in jail." He frowned, pulling his vibrating cell phone from his cleavage. He read the message and stomped his booted foot. "Phil canceled the wrap-up party at the Penalty Box. There's a heavy snowfall warning, and he wants the cast and crew to leave now.

The nerve of the man, he's scheduled a mandatory meeting at the studio for tomorrow afternoon." He lifted his eyes. "What am I going to do? I can't afford to lose my job."

"I guess we'll be celebrating Christmas in LA together," she said, unable to hide her disappointment. She wanted to spend the holidays at home this year. But she also wanted to spend it with Grayson, so she'd have to suck it up.

Since her supporters had pretty much cleared out by then, her voice traveled, and her sister stared at her from across the room. "You can't actually believe you're coming back to LA with me? You tried to have me killed! I don't want you anywhere near me. You're dead to me," Chloe yelled, dramatically trying to rip the sleeve of her fur coat.

Cat rubbed her forehead. What had she been thinking? Of course she'd have to stay here and clear her name. And that was something she'd start to do right now. But before she had a chance, her mother took Chloe by the arm and spun her to face her. "I am ashamed of you, Chloe O'Connor. All your sister has ever done is protect—"

"She tried to kill me in the womb!"

"Oh, for chrissakes," Easton muttered as he returned to Cat's side.

"Stop that right now. This is not a scene from a silly little soap opera. This is real life, and your sister is in trouble. I expect you—"

"You think what I do is silly? You all do, don't you?" Chloe looked around the station, and her face crumpled. "No one cares that someone is trying to *kill me*. Everyone loves Cat and hates me. Well, looks like she had you all fooled, doesn't it? She's a murderer and a thief. Or do you not even care that she wanted me dead?"

Her mother lifted her hand as though to slap Chloe. Paul grabbed it. "That's enough. Everyone's upset and saying things they don't mean. It's been a difficult time for you, Chloe. But you know your sister—"

"I know that she's jealous of me. I know that she's broke—"

Cat walked toward Chloe, noting her brother and Grayson go on high alert as she did. They needn't worry that she'd resort to physical violence. She didn't need to. "I'm not jealous of you, Chloe. I feel sorry for you. You're self-absorbed and don't care who you have to step on or hurt to get to the top. I get that you're scared, and I'll give you the benefit of the doubt that you're not thinking clearly or acting rationally because of that fear. But you know Sam's lying, and I can prove it. I was pretending to be you the day of the first accident and the day the chandelier fell. That was me on the set, not you. And maybe you'd like to explain why, if I wanted you dead, I was the one who got shot. As to being broke"—she shrugged—"I'll get another job. A job where the people I work for respect me and don't treat me like crap and pay me below minimum wage."

"I did everything for you, everything, and this is how your treat me? You're fired!"

It was such a classic Chloe reaction that Cat was tempted to laugh, until her sister reached for Grayson's hand. "We have to go. The cast and crew are flying out today, and I have a meeting tomorrow."

"You're not going anywhere until I have a statement from you confirming that Cat was the one on the set at the time of the first two attempts," Ethan said.

Chloe dropped Grayson's hand and rounded on their brother. "I can't do that! They'll fire me!"

Ethan's jaw clenched. "Get your ass in Gage's office now."

"You can't speak to me—"

Her mother grabbed Chloe by the arm. "You will do as your brother says, and you will do it now, young lady. And then you and I are going to have a much-needed talk." She turned to Cat. "I'm sorry, darling. I had no idea it had gotten this out of hand."

"Cat, can anyone else corroborate your story?" her brother asked.

Ty raised his hand. "I can."

Ethan narrowed his eyes at Ty. "You're not making this up to protect my sister, are you?"

"No, sir."

"All right." He waved Ty into the office.

Grayson scratched the back of his neck. "I wish you would have told me this earlier, Cat."

"I was so focused on Chloe and protecting her that I honestly didn't think about it until ten minutes ago." She glanced from the closed door of Gage's office to Grayson. "Do you have to go back to LA?"

"No, I'm not leaving you to face this on your own. I—"

Easton interrupted him. "I hate to be the bearer of bad news, but you don't have much choice. Chloe's still in danger, and while everyone is rightly pissed off at her at the moment, if something happened to her…"

Cat briefly closed her eyes. "Easton's right."

"I don't want to leave until I know you've been cleared. As long as Sam doesn't ask for a lawyer, we have seventy-two hours before we have to officially charge him and it becomes public record."

"We're not going to let anyone railroad Cat, Grayson.

You can count on us to protect her. She's got the whole town's support."

"I know she does." He bowed his head and gave it a frustrated shake. "Okay, I'll go with Chloe. I might be able to get my cousin Jamie to take—"

Cat appreciated what he was trying to do, but she knew her sister all too well. "She won't let you pass her off to someone else. Besides, Christmas is only a couple days away, and you have your own family to think about."

"Excuse us for a minute," Grayson said to Easton, then pulled Cat through the doorway to the cells. He shut the metal door and pressed her back against the cold surface. "The only reason I'm agreeing to this is because Chloe is your sister, and if something happened to her, no matter how you're feeling right now, you'd never forgive yourself. But Cat, there's only one person I want to be with, and that's you. Even with the investigation hanging over our heads, I was looking forward to spending the holidays with you."

"So was I. I'll miss you."

He stroked her hair. "I don't plan on being away from you for long."

"I'm not going back to LA, Grayson."

"Yeah, I didn't think you would be. Maybe I'm getting ahead of myself, but LA isn't the only place I can work, you know."

A warm, happy glow expanded in her chest. "You'd move to Colorado?"

"I'm tired of LA, have been for the past couple years." His mouth curved as he looked into her eyes. "And there's a beautiful woman I'm falling for who happens to live in the state."

She smiled and kissed the underside of his beard-stubbled jaw. "You just made a really crappy day wonderful."

"Good. Now give me something to get me through the next few days."

Cat was giving him something when they heard her sister call his name. He groaned, breaking the kiss to press his forehead to hers. "I want this case solved yesterday." With one last lingering caress to her cheek, Grayson held the door open.

Chloe stared out the front doors of the station while everyone said their good-byes. Ty, of course, took forever, and Grayson had to practically drag him away. And after Grayson indulged in a very public display of affection, Cat was sure she'd endure an interrogation of another kind shortly. Then again, her mother was so upset at Chloe that Cat didn't know if she had any energy left to question her.

Ethan nudged her after the three of them had left. "So, is he *the one*?"

Cat snorted. "You're starting to sound like your wife."

"Who do you think told me to ask?"

She rested her head against his shoulder. "I'm glad you're home."

He kissed the top of her head. "Me too. And, Cat, this time is going to be different. We go in fighting and we don't stop until we win."

"Wouldn't have it any other way, big brother."

"Okay, let's get this over with. Since Redding hasn't been formally charged yet, Gage is going to interview you off the record, and then you'll be free to go."

Twenty minutes later, as her brother led Cat out of Gage's office, they heard Jill yelling, "Call for an ambulance. Redding collapsed. He's unconscious."

A male voice shouted from the interrogation room. "He's stopped breathing! Get me the defibrillator."

*   *   *

Cat stood by the window in the great room watching the snow fall. Behind her, the fire crackled, casting the room in a warm, amber glow. She sipped on a cup of hot cocoa, startled when the sky lit up followed by the rolling roar of thunder. She'd seen thundersnow once before and knew what it meant. She'd probably lose power.

Her mother and Paul had wanted her to stay in town. But with the ranch hands off for the holidays, someone had to be here for the horses. Might as well be her; she needed something to occupy her time and she wanted to be alone. She didn't want to rehash the case with her family or discuss her sister's bad behavior.

The only person she really wanted to talk to was on a plane to LA. Grayson had been two hours from the Denver airport when she texted him the news about Sam. Until they'd done several rounds of blood and urine analysis, they couldn't be sure, but Paul thought he'd gone into anaphylactic shock. His burger had a thick peanut sauce mixed with the mayo, and as they'd since discovered, Sam had a peanut allergy.

Both the short-order cook at the diner and Suze the dispatcher swore there'd been no peanut sauce on the initial order. Cat told Gage what Grayson had witnessed at the time Suze was delivering the order to Sam. There'd been an opportunity for someone to add the sauce when Suze had put down the order to clean up the spilled coffee. Since at least fifty people had filled the station, it would have been easy enough for George or Molly to blend in with the crowd. Especially if they were as creative with their disguises as Ty.

Whoever hired Sam wanted to get rid of him. Easton and Jill were at the hospital to ensure he remained alive. As everyone agreed, the attempt on Sam's life was a lucky break for Cat. Once he recovered enough to talk, the likelihood he'd roll on his partner was good.

Since Molly, George, and Sam's financials hadn't given them their smoking gun, they could use the break. As another flash of lightning lit the night sky, Cat walked to the kitchen and put down her mug. Loading her arms with flashlights and candles from the well-stocked pantry, she laid them out on the island. Her head jerked up at another loud bang. It didn't sound like thunder. Cat wasn't a nervous person, but she felt a shiver of unease as the bang was followed by another. The sound was coming from the front of the house. She considered grabbing a knife, but grabbed the flashlight instead. When she reached the front foyer, the door flew open.

"We're home! It's a Christmas miracle!" Ty, as Ty, stood in the doorway with his arms flung wide and an ecstatic expression on his face. Before she could take it all in, he ran to her, lifting her up to spin her around. Mid-spin, she spotted Grayson helping his grandmother up the steps, the older woman obviously upset. Cat wasn't thrilled to see her either, but she was delighted to see the man at Estelle's side. She returned Grayson's smile, but her own fell when she spotted her sister trudging through the snow to the front door with George and Molly.

"What the hell?"

Without setting her on her feet, Ty walked her through the house whispering, "Our flight was grounded. It doesn't look like anyone will be flying out for the next couple of days, and there's no room at the lodge." He lowered his voice, "Grayson's staying undercover while they're here. He thinks it works to our advantage. Keep your enemies closer and all that." They heard Estelle sobbing in the foyer. "Oh, and Fluffy's carrier got put on the last flight by mistake. Grayson's trying to reach his cousin to pick her up at the airport."

Well, at least Cat's slippers were safe. She couldn't say the same for her sister.

Grayson gave Cat a sweet-mother-of-God look as he walked his grandmother to the couch in the great room. "She'll be fine, Estelle. Jamie just texted that he'll be there when the flight lands. Yes, we'll call, and you can talk to her."

"I need a drink," George said, brushing a thick layer of snow from his hair as he walked toward the fireplace.

"If we have to be stranded, I'll take this over the lodge or the airport. Nice digs, Cat." Molly smiled and followed George into the great room.

When Chloe appeared, Cat prepared herself for a cutting remark, but her sister pulled out a stool at the island and sat down. She cast a nervous glance over her shoulder, then turned back to look from Ty to Cat and whispered, "You won't protect me from them, will you? Everyone hates me. No one cares anymore if I live or die."

Cat was done with the drama. She couldn't bring herself to sympathize with her sister, but Ty did. Ever since he'd read Chloe's yearbook, he'd developed a soft spot for her. "Even if your sister hates you right now, she'll protect you. That's what she does. Right?" He nodded, and kept nodding until Cat reluctantly agreed. "See?" He smiled at Chloe. "And you have me and Grayson to look after you, too."

"I guess you're right." She looked at Cat from under her clumped false eyelashes. "I'll be safe with Grayson here. At least I won't have to sleep alone."

"Of course you won't be sleeping alone, Chloe. Ty or Estelle can bunk with you," Cat said sweetly.

Chloe stared at her and opened her mouth, but didn't get a chance to voice what Cat assumed would be a heated objection as Grayson entered the kitchen. He slid an arm around Cat's waist and drew her close. "Hi." He smiled down at her, lowering his head to give her a brief but warm kiss. "Sorry for not giving you a heads-up. I lost cell service."

He angled his head, a slight frown furrowing his brow as his grandmother handed Molly and George each a glass of wine. The actor and actress stood by the window in the great room, but Grayson lowered his voice anyway. "As far as George and Molly know, none of us suspect they had anything to do with the attempts on Chloe's life. We're playing it as if Sam acted on his own. So no more talking about the case when they're around."

The front door opened. "It's just me," a familiar voice called out. It was Easton.

"I called him before I lost service. He'll be staying here. Don't worry, Gage assigned another deputy to Sam."

"No change?" Cat asked.

He shook his head, his hand tightening at her waist. "Another day or so and this will be over, love."

"I hope so," she said, leaning into his strong, protective embrace.

"*You* hope it will be over? I'm the one in danger, not

you. Honestly, since when did this become all about you, Catalina?" her sister asked in a fierce whisper.

"You wanna tell me again why I agreed to do this?" Easton—water dripping from his dark hair, the heavy scruff lining his jaw iced with snow—looked at Grayson and Cat as he limped into the kitchen and dropped a duffle bag by the island.

Cat grinned. "Because you want to keep me safe."

Easton chuckled.

"I hate you all," Chloe said, and got up from the stool. She started to walk away, then pivoted. "My bags are in the entrance."

Easton quirked an eyebrow. "And?"

A loud bang drowned out Chloe's response, and then the lights went out. Four people screamed: three female and one male. The screams were followed by one thud, and then another.

Chapter Twenty-Two

Cat shivered, pulling the covers over her bare shoulder. "Remind me why we have to get up again?" she asked, playfully rubbing against Grayson.

He placed his hand on her naked backside, drawing her closer, providing her with the evidence that he didn't want to get out of bed any more than she did. "For starters, I don't trust GG not to drug George and Molly again."

Cat laughed. "Not that your grandmother and I see eye to eye on much, but slipping her sleeping pills into George's and Molly's wine wasn't a bad idea. At least we didn't have to worry about them last night."

He still couldn't believe GG had done it. He certainly didn't buy her excuse she was distraught over her and Fluffy's separation and wasn't thinking straight. Her second reason, that she wanted to protect Chloe, was a little more believable. But more likely than not, it had something to do with the movie she and Chloe had been discussing on the drive back to Christmas.

"You're right, we didn't," he agreed with Cat. "But now we have to come up with a reason for them passing out. Otherwise, they'll think someone is trying to kill them. Which could end up with the innocent party calling the police."

"Or the guilty party will have something else to accuse me of." She thunked her forehead against his chest and groaned.

He chuckled and stroked her hair. "Don't worry, if it comes to that, I'll throw GG under the bus."

She pressed her warm lips to his chest. "You're my hero. So what's the other reason we have to get out of bed, because that one didn't really work for me."

"Okay, how about this. Whenever Easton is around your sister, he looks about this close"—he held his thumb and forefinger a quarter inch apart—"to strangling her. What's the deal with those two?" He didn't actually care all that much what was going on between Easton and Chloe. He supposed he would if he thought Easton would act on his urges, but he didn't. What he did care about was the past between the man and Cat. It was obvious they had one. The guy cared about Cat, and Grayson wanted to know if that was something he needed to worry about.

He'd meant what he said about moving to Colorado. He was ready for a change. And thanks to the woman lying in his arms, he was ready to take their relationship to the next level. He wanted her in his life. Whether that led to marriage was a question for another time. It was still early days. But he'd finally met a woman he could see a future with, and he wasn't about to let anything or anyone stand in their way.

She glanced up at him, then pulled back. "It's more what's the deal with the three of us."

"Should I hear this dressed and with a drink in my hand?"

"No." She gave a half laugh, then shook her head. "The way people around here talk about it, my mother and sister included, you'd think it happened last week, but Easton and I dated in high school."

"Were you together a long time?" He propped himself on his elbow.

"Two years. A long time for teenagers, I suppose. I didn't know it at the time, but Easton planned to propose the night of our senior prom."

"Would you have accepted?"

"Probably. But I wouldn't have been accepting for the right reasons. Our families were close, and I wouldn't have hurt either them or Easton by saying no. Maybe Chloe did us all a favor."

"Ah, so your sister was involved with the breakup."

"Oh yeah, she was involved. And it took me a while to forgive her. I don't think Easton has." She turned on her side to face him. "Up until grade twelve, Chloe had a difficult time in high school. Easton protected her as much as I did. He felt sorry for her. But Chloe mistook his sympathy for something else. She's always been a bit of a dreamer. The little girl who wanted to be a fairy princess. Easton was her hero, her knight in shining armor.

"The summer before our senior year, I hardly saw her. She was busy reinventing herself, becoming the queen who'd win the prom king. And when she couldn't win him as herself, she decided she'd win him as me."

"You had no idea?"

"None. When Easton started missing our dates, I figured he was busy with football practice, or school, and I didn't want to make a big deal about it and come across as the needy girlfriend. Plus I was busy, too. But then things got a little weird. He'd bring up books and English assignments we'd supposedly talked about that I had no memory of and no interest in. Around that time, I'd fallen from the pyramid during cheerleading practice and I began to think I had a traumatic brain injury."

"A cheerleader," he said, waggling his eyebrows at her, trailing his finger down her side and over her hip. "That explains why you're so flexible."

She smiled, showing off her dimple. "No, that would be from Tae Kwon Do, not cheerleading."

"What level do you have?"

Her dimple deepened. "Black belt, fifth dan."

Could the woman get any hotter? "If I wasn't already falling in love with you, that would have done it."

"You're easy."

He smiled. He wasn't. "Okay, continue your story. I'm guessing it didn't have a happy ending."

"No, it didn't." Her cheeks pinked. "Easton and I, we, uh, we were never intimate. So one night when he started to, well, anyway, I slapped him across the face. He couldn't understand what he'd done wrong since..." She shrugged.

"Since he and Chloe had done the deed."

"Right. Everything came out then. It was awful. Chloe had convinced herself that Easton knew it was her. Easton was furious. He said some really hurtful things to Chloe. She was devastated. She pleaded with me to tell Easton that I'd been in on it."

"Cat, you didn't?"

She winced. "I did. I was stupid and young and hurt. You don't know what it's like to be an identical twin, Grayson. To know that even your own family can't tell you apart from your sister. I thought Easton out of anyone should be able to, and I was angry that he couldn't." She raised her hand to her head. "I chopped off my hair that night."

"Were you angry at me when I thought you were Chloe?"

"Yes, and no. With you, I was pretending to be my sister. And you made it up to me that night."

"I'd know you now, even if you were impersonating Chloe." He traced her brow. "Your right eyebrow has a higher arch than your left, and you have more yellow flecks in your irises than your sister." He drew the tip of his finger down her nose. "And your nose doesn't turn up at the tip as much as hers." He caressed her cheek. "Your cheekbones are sharper, more defined." He turned her face and kissed her dimple. "And your sister's dimple isn't as adorable or as pronounced as yours."

He trailed his fingers over her body, lowering his head once she began to moan. "I know you inside and out. I love the heart of you, Cat O'Connor." He lifted his head. "And love, your sister needs professional help."

*   *   *

Cat took the rifle from the locked case in the den, loaded it, and checked the sight. She looked up at him and laughed at what he imagined was the entranced expression on his face. "It's not funny. You know what it does to me when I see you with a gun. Let's go back to bed. GG and Molly are having a nap. George is playing chess with Easton, who, by the way, is a bloody genius. And your sister and Ty are pulling out enough Christmas decorations to stock a department store."

"And we need a tree to put the decorations on. This was your idea, remember? You wanted something to keep everyone busy."

"Yes, to the keeping everyone busy part, but no to the decorating. That was Ty." He did an imitation of the other man clapping and saying *Oh my God*.

"You missed your calling. You should have been an actor."

He shuddered. "Not if my life depended on it." He responded to her raised eyebrows. "You have met my grandmother, haven't you? My father was an actor, too. As was my mother and my wife."

She blinked. "Your wife? I didn't realize you were married."

He shoved his hands in his jeans pockets and nodded. "It was a mistake. I was twenty-six and she was twenty-three. GG adored her. Something I should have thought about, but I was young and in love. We didn't have anything in common. She wanted a big, glamorous life, and I wanted a simple one. She hated that I worked for the Bureau. We lasted three years; six months of which were relatively happy. I came home one day to find her in bed with her leading man."

"I'm sorry. That's awful."

"It would have been worse if there were children involved." He took the gun from her hands. "And I wouldn't have met you."

She went up on her toes and kissed him. "Have I told you lately how happy I am that you're in my life?"

"Not today."

"Well, I am. So let's go get that tree, and then I'll show you just how happy you make me." She took her gun back, hooking the strap over her shoulder.

"Love, you do realize about six feet of snow has fallen since last night, don't you?"

"We're taking Easton's snowmobile, and I've got snowshoes. But don't worry, we're not going too deep into the back country."

"So why the gun?"

"Neighbors south of us saw a cougar three days ago."

"There's never a dull moment in Christmas, is there?"

"Not since you got here there isn't."

* * *

A wave of nostalgia washed over Cat as she took in the familiar wreaths, garland, and icicles hanging from the windows. Ty and Chloe had spent the entire day turning the house into a winter wonderland. It looked the same as it did every Christmas when their father had been alive. Their mother hadn't truly gotten back into the spirit of the holidays until two years earlier. Cat hadn't been home then, and last year Ethan and Skye's Christmas Eve wedding and their daughter's birth had taken precedence over decorating for the holidays. She glanced at Chloe, who handed Ty the last pillar candle. As he placed it on the mantel with Chloe looking on, Cat wondered if her sister felt the same. It was hard to tell. Chloe wasn't speaking to her and had avoided her all day.

Ty clapped his hands after he lit the candle, looking like he'd just been awarded a Daytime Emmy for set design. The candle's flickering flame joined that of the thirty others he'd placed throughout the room. "It looks beautiful, Ty," Cat said from where she sat between Grayson's legs on the bearskin rug in front of the fire.

Ty and Chloe had found the rug in the closet in the den. Deacon O'Connor, their father, had been an avid hunter, his animal trophies hidden away when Ethan married animal-activist Skye. They'd have to be sure to pack the rug away before her sister-in-law visited. Not that they were expecting her anytime soon. The snow hadn't let up, and the power hadn't come back on. They had a gas stove and an outdoor ice chest they'd transferred the food into, so it wasn't like they were going to starve.

And if they weren't currently under the same roof with her sister's would-be assassin, Cat would have been enjoying herself. Actually, she was more than enjoying herself with Grayson. Despite the stressful circumstances. She let herself relax against him, smiling up at him. He tweaked her hair and whispered in her ear, "Can we hurry this along? I'm tired and want to go to bed."

"It's nine o'clock."

"All that fresh air and tree cutting wore me out."

"Really? You had lots of energy when we were feeding the horses." She gave a teasing wiggle to remind him just how much energy he'd had in the barn.

"Careful, love."

"Single people here," Ty called out as he fiddled with the radio. "Stop flirting. You're making me jealous."

"Ty's right. It's nauseating and annoying." Her sister grabbed a blanket and curled up on a wingback chair. "When's Easton coming back with the milk? I want some hot cocoa."

Since they'd had no contact with the outside world,

Easton had used the milk as an excuse to check on Sam. With the weather conditions, Cat was more worried about the length of time he'd been gone than the milk.

"It's just as good with water, Chloe," Cat said.

"All right, fine. I'll have it with water." She looked at Cat, obviously expecting her to get up and make it. When she didn't, Chloe threw off her blanket and walked off in a huff.

"Good girl," Grayson said, patting her thigh.

He laughed when Cat called out, "I'll have one, too, Chloe. Thanks."

Ty finally got something other than static on the battery-operated radio, and Clay Aiken singing "Mary, Did You Know?" filled the room. Ty pressed his hands to his chest. "Oh, I love this song. It makes me cry every time I hear it." He started singing along with Clay.

George shook the ice cubes in his empty glass. "My wife loved that song, too," he said, slurring his words. "If it wasn't for—" He slammed the glass on the coffee table, muttering to himself as he lurched to his feet.

"Hey, there, why don't you sit and have another, mate? Decorate the tree, share—"

"Go to hell," George said, weaving his way toward the bedrooms.

"Don't mind him, Harry. He hasn't been the same since his wife left him," Molly said from where she sat curled under a blanket at the end of the couch.

"What's wrong with George?" Chloe asked as she returned to her chair with a steaming mug of cocoa.

"Oh, I don't know, Chloe. Maybe it's because, thanks to you, the man will probably be out of a job in the new year." Molly sneered at Chloe. "No, I don't buy that Cat demanded the change. None of us do. Everyone knows she's just a glorified gopher and not your manager." Molly made an apologetic face. "Sorry, Cat, nothing against you."

Cat shot her sister a disbelieving look, but didn't get a chance to say anything because Molly continued, "But I have a surprise for you, Chloe. Things aren't going to turn out as you planned. A little bird told me Tessa Hart won't be around much longer." Molly stood up. "I think I'll go to bed now and catch up on my beauty sleep because that same little bird told me Paula will finally get the on-air time she deserves." Molly patted Cat's shoulder as she walked by. "I hope good things happen for you, too. You deserve it after putting up with her."

Chloe watched Molly leave the room with her eyes wide, then turned to them. "Why aren't you doing something? She just threatened me!"

"You told them *I* was the one who demanded the changes?"

Chloe frowned and waved her hand as if it wasn't a big deal. "Of course I did. That's what a manager does. It wouldn't be right for the star of the show to demand changes in a script that benefits them. Their costars would hate them. But I had to do something. Our ratings were hemorrhaging. I had to stop the bleeding."

Cat didn't know what to say. She had signed on as manager, and some of what Chloe said made sense. Well, sense in her sister's mind at least.

Ty clapped his hands. "Okay, no fighting, girls. We've gone to all this work to make it a special night, so let's not let George and Molly ruin it. Time to decorate the tree."

He picked up a box of tissue-wrapped ornaments and placed it on the floor in front of the eight-foot blue spruce

Cat and Grayson had cut down and dragged home on the back of the snowmobile. Some of her anger at Chloe left Cat as she remembered her afternoon with Grayson. He gave her shoulders a comforting squeeze. "I'm going to check on Estelle and our guests, then I'll make you a hot cocoa. You want one, too, Ty?"

"Yes, please. Could you put some little marshmallows in it, too? Cat made me one earlier, and it was delish." He sat in front of the box and wiggled. "This is so exciting."

Chloe rolled her eyes. "You're acting like a kid at their first Christmas."

Ty ducked his head. "That's because it kind of is. The last Christmas my family celebrated I was five." He picked up an ornament, carefully unwrapping the tissue.

Cat frowned, then moved beside him, placing her hand over his. "How come?"

Chloe joined them, kneeling on the other side of Ty.

"My older brother was killed tobogganing a week before the holidays the next year. For the longest time, I thought Santa stopped coming because I asked for a Barbie doll." He gave a sad, little laugh. "Funny the things you come up with when you're a kid."

It wasn't funny at all; it was sad. Cat kissed his cheek and Chloe did the same. "I'm sorry about your brother, Ty," they both said.

"Oh, stop it now, you'll make me cry."

"Cat used to be afraid of Santa," Chloe said, in an attempt, Cat imagined, to lighten the mood. Her sister took an ornament out of the box.

"I was not. That was you. You slept with me every Christmas Eve."

It wasn't long before Ty was laughing, and so were Cat

and Chloe. They spent the next hour unwrapping the ornaments, telling Ty and Grayson the story behind each one. Every Christmas Eve, they were given an ornament that held a special meaning for them.

As Chloe laughingly told Ty and Grayson about the time Cat had caught their father putting the presents under the tree and jumped on his back because she thought he was a burglar, her sister's eyes met hers, and Cat knew, like her, Chloe was remembering the bond they'd once shared.

"Oh no," Ty said, as he unwrapped the second-to-last ornament, "it's broken." It was an ornament Chloe had given to Cat, a wreath in the shape of a heart with two bears holding hands and the words *Sisters Forever*.

Cat cleared her throat, but her voice came out husky with emotion. "It's okay. It was old."

Chloe looked away, then reached in the box and unwrapped the Christmas star. "Daddy used to say whoever got to put this on top of the tree, their wish would come true. We used to fight over it every year, remember, Kit Kat?"

Cat was afraid she wouldn't be able to get the words past her tight throat and simply nodded. Grayson, who was sitting beside her, pulled her close and kissed her cheek.

Chloe gave Ty a tremulous smile and handed him the star. "It's your turn this year."

Chapter Twenty-Three

Cat woke up immediately at the sound of her bedroom door opening. She hadn't let herself drift into a deep sleep in case Grayson needed her. He was on guard duty, waiting for Easton to return from town. A small shadow started toward her bed while a larger one filled her doorway. Cat twisted and flipped on the beside lamp.

"Sorry, love. She's upset, and I couldn't calm her down." Grayson reached behind him, tucking his gun in the back of his jeans.

"No, that's okay. Everything good?" she asked, wishing he was the one crawling into her bed and not her sniffling sister.

He nodded, giving her a tired smile. "I'll do another walk-through. Call if you need me."

"Thanks." He closed the door, and she turned to Chloe. "What's wrong?"

"I have to change. They said I have to change or I'm going to die a lonely old maid."

Her sister's cheeks were blotchy and tear-stained, and Cat felt a twinge of sympathy. She tucked the covers around Chloe's shoulders. "It's okay, you just had a bad dream."

"No, not a dream. *A Christmas Carol*," she sobbed, wrapping her arms around her waist and rocking.

Confused, she rubbed Chloe's shoulder. "A Christmas carol gave you a nightmare?"

"No, not a song, a book. *A Christmas Carol* by Charles Dickens."

"If it bothered you, why didn't you stop reading?"

"I wasn't reading." She sat up, thumping her chest. "It happened to me, Kit Kat. Just like Scrooge, the ghosts came to me."

Okay, now it was beginning to make sense. Not sense to a rational person, but to a person used to dealing with Chloe. "So you're saying the ghosts of Christmas past, present, and future visited you?"

Chloe fell back on the pillows. Cat ducked when she threw out her arm. "They came through my window. Anna, Easton's mom, was first. She showed me my past. All the times I was in the hospital, and when the kids teased me for being ugly and fat." Chloe covered her eyes, a tear running down her cheek.

Cat wiped the moisture from her sister's face. "You were never ugly and fat."

"I know what I looked like, Kit Kat, but...but that wasn't the worst. I had to watch what I did to Easton. What I did to you. It was horrible."

Easton's mother died of breast cancer more than ten

years ago. She'd been their mother's best friend. "It was just a nightmare. Mrs. McBride didn't really come to you in your—"

"Yes, she did, Kit Kat. She wasn't mean or mad at me though. She was kind and held my hand and kissed my cheek. S-She said that it wasn't too late. I could make things right." Chloe searched her face. "Do you think she meant Easton will forgive me? That I'm supposed to be with him?"

Cat had to handle this carefully. All she'd need was for her sister to think she and Easton were meant to be, that the angels had blessed their union. There was no doubt Easton blamed Chloe for their breakup, but really, the more Cat thought about it, he wasn't the type of guy to hang on to that kind of thing. The problem was he didn't like Chloe. He thought she was a spoiled brat. But Cat didn't know what to say that wouldn't make matters worse or hurt Chloe's feelings.

"Kit Kat?"

"Maybe you need to look at the big picture. What did the ghost from Christmas present say?"

"It was Daddy," her sister whispered, tears once again rolling down her cheeks.

Cat couldn't help herself. "How did he look?"

She gave her a watery smile. "Handsome, healthy." She leaned in and kissed Cat's cheek. "That's from Daddy. He wants you to know he's proud of you." She bit her lip. "He, ah, showed me how I've been treating you, how I've been treating everyone, but mostly you. I'm truly sorry. I'm not a very nice person."

"Did he tell you who was trying to kill you?"

Her brow pleated. "No, he didn't say anything about anyone trying to hurt me. That's kind of odd, don't you think? But he did say I would be given a chance to redeem myself, and I had to be ready. I couldn't let fear rule me anymore." She glanced at Cat from under her lashes, twisting the covers with her fingers. "Umm, you know how I said someone tried to strangle me?"

She gaped at her sister. "It was you. You faked the attack! Chloe, how could you?"

"I-I don't know what got into me. Well, I kind of do. Grayson told me you were together, and I sort of snapped. I thought he was my one, but he loves you. It was the same with Easton. And then I was listening to my audiobook, *Gone Girl*, and the idea popped into my head..."

"Do you know how crazy that sounds?"

"I know it does, but it's easy for you. Everyone loves you. They—"

Cat crossed her arms to stop herself from shaking her sister. "Don't, Chloe. Don't pull the self-pity crap on me. Mom and Dad doted on you. They spoiled you rotten."

"I know, Daddy told me the same thing. Maybe there's something really wrong with me, Kit Kat. Do you think I might be a narcissist or maybe a sociopath?"

"No, what you have is an overactive imagination. Stop looking for excuses. You know when you're in the wrong. You apologize, try to make things right, and in less than twenty-four hours, you go right back and do the same thing."

She nodded, biting her thumbnail. "That's what the ghost of Christmas future said. I think it was Ty's brother. He looked like him but without glasses. He didn't say much, but I think he might have a crush on me. So he was probably a little shy."

Oh, good Lord.

Chloe shuddered and wrapped her arms around herself

again. "It was awful, Kit Kat. Even more horrible than my past or present. He showed me this big house, but it was old and creepy and I lived there all by myself. I felt so alone and so cold." She touched her hair. "But my hair and face looked good, so I didn't get ugly and fat or anything like that."

Cat pulled the pillow out from under her and whacked Chloe with it. "You're doing it again. Who cares what you look like, Chloe?"

"That's easy for you to say. You were never ugly or fat."

"We're identical twins!"

"Well, you're not an actress." She held up her hands. "Okay, okay, I know what I have to do. I'll change. I'll become a better person. I promise. I'm going to be like Scrooge and give money to the poor, and buy them food and toys. I'll—"

"That's nice, and you should do it. But it's not about the money, Chloe. You have to think about the consequences before you open your mouth and act out. Don't be so self-absorbed. Be nice to the people you work with, to the people in town. Geez, you never even speak to Evelyn and Stella. They didn't think you knew who they are."

"I don't. Am I supposed to?"

Cat covered her face with her hands.

Chloe pulled them away with a serious look on her face. "I'm sincerely sorry for how I've treated you. I love you. I want us to be friends again. And..." She swallowed audibly. "...I'm very happy you found Grayson. He's your one. Michael wasn't. And if anyone deserves to find their one, it's you, Kit Kat." She hugged her, then lay back down. "Is it okay if I sleep with you? I don't think I can handle being visited by another ghost tonight."

"Sure."

"Thank you." She turned over and took all the covers with her.

Cat sighed and flipped off the light. "Night, Chloe."

"Night night, Kit Kat. Oh, and I know it was wrong how I broke up you and Easton, but he wasn't your one, either."

As long as Chloe didn't think he was hers, they'd be okay.

*   *   *

Cat woke up with a start the next morning in her empty bed. Ty stood framed in her doorway wearing Chloe's pink satin pajamas. Tears rolling down his face, he held a box in his hands. Cat sat up. "Ty, what's wrong?"

"My wish came true," he whispered. He walked to the bed and sat on the edge, turning the box to her. Growing up, the doll had been Chloe's prized possession. A limited edition signed Bob Mackie Gold Barbie. It had never been taken out of the box.

Cat smiled and rubbed his arm. "I'm glad you got your wish. She's beautiful."

"I didn't wish for a Barbie. I'm a thirty-year-old man. But she is gorgeous, isn't she?" He stroked the box. "My wish... What happened to your face? You have a red mark..."

She touched her cheek. "A red mark where?"

He looked past her and whimpered, pointing to her pillow.

Cat cast a nervous glance behind her. It was the *Sisters Forever* ornament, only it had been carefully glued back together. Her throat tightened as she leaned over and picked it up, holding the ornament to her chest. She worked to clear the emotion from her voice. "What was your wish?"

"That the Christmas star brings Chloe back to her home and family. Not literally, but here." He placed his hand over his heart. "She needs to remember where she comes from and what's important in life. That you're important to her. You try to hide it, but she's hurt you."

"You did it for me." She wrapped her arms around his neck. "You're a pretty amazing friend, you know that?"

He nodded, then gave her a wry smile. "Chloe's kind of grown on me, too."

Grayson walked into the room, his hair a sexy, rumpled mess, his face beard-stubbled. He had on a black T-shirt and black sleep pants, and his pale-blue eyes moved from Ty to her. "Everything okay in here?"

"Good. It's good." She nodded, turning her head to swipe at her face.

He sat beside her, taking the ornament from her hands. He smiled. "Your sister seems to have had an epiphany of sorts. She's out there making breakfast for Easton."

Oh God. "Is he being nice to her?"

"She talks, he grunts. But he doesn't look like he wants to strangle her, so given how he usually reacts, I'd say yes. He's being nice to her."

Ty looked up from his Barbie doll. "I'm so glad to hear he got back safe and sound. I was worried about him. He is safe and sound, isn't he?"

Grayson glanced at the box, and his mouth kicked up at the corner. "Yes, he's fine. He had to dig several cars out of the ditch."

"I should probably leave you two lovebirds alone and check on Chloe and the White Knight myself."

"Hang on a minute, Ty." Grayson turned to Cat and picked up her hand. "I'm heading into town with Easton.

Redding is well enough to be interrogated, and I want to talk to him and get your name cleared. Today. But if you're the least bit uncomfortable being left on your own, I want you to tell me. The roads are still pretty much impassable, and Gage and his deputies are working around the clock. Otherwise, I would—"

"She's not on her own. She has me, Estelle, Chloe, and... Molly or George. Both of them can't be in on it, can they?"

"Ty's right. We'll be fine. We'll all stay together." She frowned. Something felt off. She wasn't concerned about being left on her own, but she was a little surprised that Grayson was willing to leave her. He was a protective guy. Then again, she should probably be pleased he was confident in her abilities to look after things while he was gone. But... "Is there something you're not telling me?"

*   *   *

"So you think Cat believed you were heading into town to question Redding?" Easton asked as he parked the snowmobile on Main Street.

A few more minutes with her and she would have figured it out. It was difficult to hide anything from those perceptive green eyes. It's why Grayson had done his best to avoid her before they left. "Not entirely. She's smart. She couldn't put a finger on it, but she knew something was up." He took off the helmet and shoved his hands through his hair. "But damned if I was going to tell her that Turner was coming to town to push for her arrest. Has Chance gotten anywhere with Redding?"

"Last I heard, no. Do you want to head over to the hospital after you hand Turner's ass to him?"

That's exactly what Grayson planned to do. When

Easton had come into town yesterday, he hadn't only been checking on Redding. He could get cell service in town and wanted to see if he'd gotten any pings on his inquiries into Turner. He did. And now Grayson knew why Turner had gone above and beyond in his persecution of Cat. This was personal. Turner's brother-in-law had been a victim of Upton's Ponzi scheme. His brother-in-law and sister had lost their savings and were about to lose their home.

Once he was finished with Turner, not only would Cat be on the guy's most-wanted list, so would Grayson. If Redding didn't recant, Grayson had no doubt Turner would try to get him kicked out of the Bureau for fraternizing with a felon. He'd worry about that later. Proving Cat's innocence was his priority. "No, let's get this over with. I want to get back to the ranch ASAP."

They climbed over a snowbank to reach the sidewalk, wading through another foot of snow to get to the station doors. Turner, a tall, lanky man with his silver hair buzzed short, stood waiting for them. And if that didn't indicate how hot and heavy the man was to railroad Cat, nothing did. Given the road conditions, it would have taken him at least six hours to get here from Denver.

"Special Agent Alexander." He extended his hand.

Grayson ignored it. "Gage, mind if we use your office?"

"Be my guest."

Less than thirty minutes later, Turner slammed from the office and stormed out the doors. Grayson had laid out a concise and persuasive case in Cat's defense for both her involvement in the Ponzi scheme and Redding's charge that she'd hired him to kill her sister, which Turner had, as Grayson repeatedly pointed out, no jurisdiction over. Turner ignored him on all counts.

And that's when Grayson went over his head, pulling out his cell phone to call Turner's superior and leveling abuse of power and harassment charges against the man. His superior had been more than interested in hearing them. This wasn't the first time he'd had such complaints brought against Turner, something Grayson had been aware of thanks to Easton.

But Grayson didn't have a chance to savor winning this round with Turner because there was something else weighing on his mind. It had been gnawing at him ever since he'd laid out why Cat couldn't be behind the attempts on her sister's life. Other than when Chloe broke the heel on her shoe, which could have been accidental, each attempt on Chloe's life had actually put Cat in danger. She'd been pretending to be her sister when the railing broke and when the chandelier fell, and the boom had nearly taken her out, and not one of the bullets Redding had fired had ended up hitting the float. And the incident with the lights at the tree lighting had come back as inconclusive. The extension had shown signs of previous wear and tear. The only thing that kept throwing Grayson off was the latest attempt on Chloe's life. Unless Easton had been right and...

"That's one unhappy man," Easton said. "Is Turner going to give you problems?"

"Probably..." He rubbed his face, unable to get rid of the thought that the answer was right in front of him. Then it came to him, and his head jerked up. "It's Cat."

"What's Cat?"

He laid out each attempt to Gage and Easton. "Last night, Molly said she knew Chloe was behind the changes to the story line and not Cat. But all along, Chloe let them think that Cat, as her manager, was behind the requests." He repeated the letter to them verbatim. "Just as easily could be a threat against Cat as Chloe."

"First off, take the attempt on Chloe two days ago out of the equation. I'll guarantee she faked it. But—"

"She wouldn't do that, Easton," Gage protested.

"Yeah right, you don't know her like I do. And while your theory makes sense on one level, Grayson, here's where it falls apart for me. They're identical twins. You put hair and makeup on Cat, and there's no telling her apart from Chloe. Even her mother can't."

"I can."

"Yeah, but that's because...Hang on, what do you think you're doing?" Easton said when Grayson removed the keys from his pocket and headed for the door. "Where are you going?"

"To the ranch," Grayson said, trying to tamp down his panic as he raced to the snowmobile. "Try to get through to Cat on her cell phone and warn her she's in danger."

"She's well trained. She'll handle George and Molly if she has to," Easton said, pushing past his brother, who was already on his cell.

"I wouldn't worry if she knew she was the target. But she'll be trying to protect Chloe and won't protect herself." He was over the snowbank and on the snowmobile before Easton got down the station steps.

Chapter Twenty-Four

Cat looked up from filling a bucket with hay when the stable doors opened. Her sister, wearing the same jeans and thick cream sweater and hat as Cat had on, walked toward her. "I told you to stay locked in my room with Ty. And I don't swagger, so cut it out."

Chloe grinned and continued walking like a cowboy in an old western. "He fell asleep. They're all asleep. Besides, Molly and George would think I'm you anyway."

Cat sighed. "Not if they catch us in the same room together, they won't." She'd decided the best way to keep Chloe safe was to have her sister pretend to be her. Now that the storm system had cleared out and life was beginning to return to normal, Cat was afraid one of them would make their move here instead of back in LA. Maybe it would be better if they did. They still didn't have anything to go on. Right now their only hope was that

Grayson managed to break Sam. "Head back inside. I'll be finished up in a couple minutes."

Chloe crouched beside her. "I'm bored. I don't know how they can sleep away the entire day. I mean, I can understand why Estelle does . . . What's with the frown?"

"Ty hates to sleep. He's afraid he'll miss something."

"It was kind of weird. All of a sudden he said 'I'm exhausted' and fell back on the bed. I thought he was joking, and then he started to snore." Chloe's eyes widened. "You don't think he was drugged, do you?"

Yes, she did. But she didn't want to scare Chloe. Cat reached under the back of her sweater for the gun Grayson had left her. She froze at the sound of a male voice. "It should wear off in a couple of hours. Imagine his surprise when he wakes up to find his best friend dead."

"Don't react. You're me, remember?" Cat whispered, dropping her hand. Chloe wouldn't have a gun. She came slowly to her feet, pulling her sister with her. Together they turned to face George.

He caressed the rifle in his hand. He must have seen her with the gun yesterday and searched the den. It still didn't explain how he'd broken into the case. The glass was unbreakable. "I see you're wondering how I came to have this beauty in my possession. I hid in the den and watched you punch in the combination. It didn't work the first time, but I'm a very patient man." He came toward them. "But you've tried my patience long enough, Cat. Tessa my dear, come here. Your sister is done interfering in our lives."

It wasn't easy, but Cat locked down her emotions. She couldn't let him see the shock on her face upon realizing it was her he wanted dead and not her sister. Chloe's gaze shot from George to her. She tightened her grip on her sister's hand. She recognized the calculating look in Chloe's eyes, and it didn't bode well.

Chloe made a small, terrified sound in her throat, then jerked her hand free and ran to George. "Oh, Byron, I knew you'd save me. But why did you take so long? She nearly ruined everything."

Cat's heart skipped a panicked beat at the possibility her sister had been in on it all along. She immediately pushed the thought aside. They had their problems, but deep down she knew Chloe loved her.

"She's a cat. She has nine lives." George smirked, wrapping an arm around Chloe's shoulders while he held the gun on Cat.

What was her sister thinking? Cat couldn't get off a clear shot with Chloe pressed against him.

"You should have let me in on your plan. I could have helped." Her sister lightly slapped his chest. "All this time I've been terrified someone was trying to kill me, Byron."

"How do you know he wasn't trying to kill you, Chloe? He couldn't know it was me the day the railing broke or the day the chandelier fell."

"Of course I did. Your sister's graceful, you're a klutz. And I heard Ty call you Pussy when he was doing your hair. And you have a dimple when you smile."

"What about the day Chloe's heel broke? You weren't trying to kill me that day, were you?"

"I wasn't trying to kill her." The vein in his forehead throbbed. "I didn't like how she was behaving with Rand. I had to teach her a lesson." His features hardened and became menacing. "Just like my wife. Flirting with your fiancé at our party. Investing all our money behind my back."

Cat didn't understand what he was talking about until she remembered the time two years earlier that she and Michael had gone to visit Chloe in LA. Michael had loved the Hollywood scene. He'd wanted to go out every night, and now she knew why. He'd found more victims to prey on.

George continued. "Everything gone like that"—he snapped his fingers behind Chloe's back—"because of you and your thieving boyfriend. And you thought you got away with it, didn't you? But now you'll pay."

"My sister's a lot of things, Byron, but she's not a thief. She gave all her money to the victims' fund." Chloe lifted his arm from her shoulders and took his hand. "Let's leave now. You don't have to do this. We'll—"

Tilting his head, he stroked Chloe's cheek. "You're so naive, my dear. That was guilt money. It's how I knew what she'd done. And it hardly made up for what's been stolen from me. We're not going anywhere until she's out of our lives for good." He gave Cat a chilling smile. "Her life insurance will just about cover what she owes me. You will give it to me, won't you, Tessa darling?"

"Of course, but you don't need Cat's insurance money, Byron. I have more than enough for both of us."

"I know you do. But there's poetic justice in getting it from her, don't you think?" As he started to walk toward Cat, Chloe stayed behind. "Now let's get this over with, shall we? We don't have much time. In you go." He waved the gun at Blackheart's stall. "You didn't think I'd be stupid enough not to make it look like an accident, did you? I'm smarter than that pothead Sam. I should have known the idiot would get caught." He glanced back at Chloe. "I hope your writing is as identical to your sister's as your face is. We want the suicide note and her confession to look authentic."

Chloe lifted her assessing gaze to George and nodded, then glanced at Cat. Her sister was up to something. Cat prepared for Chloe to make her move.

"Good. Then all that's left for us to do is make sure Sam doesn't talk. We'll pay a visit to the hospital on our way out of town." George turned back to Cat and lifted the gun. "Move—"

Chloe ran and jumped on his back. George got out a startled "What—" at the same time Cat kicked the gun from his hands.

He lurched toward her before she'd lowered her foot and regained her balance, grabbing Cat by the neck.

"Get your hands off my sister!" Chloe shrieked, trying to pry his fingers from Cat's throat.

"Eyes. His eyes." Cat attempted to direct her sister, but because of George's stranglehold on her neck, the words were barely audible.

George bent at the waist, moving several steps back so Cat couldn't kick him. As stars sparked in her vision, she reached behind her for her gun. Chloe, as though realizing what she was trying to do, slid off George's back and ran behind Cat, taking the gun from her waistband. She pointed it at George and said in Cat's cop voice, "I said, get your hands off my sister."

Distracted by Chloe, his grip on Cat's neck loosened. She took advantage of his brief moment of inattention and quickly raised her right arm, twisting to the left, slamming it down across his arms. His hands dropped from her throat. She gave a hard, open-palm hit to his nose, then dropped him with a knee to the groin. He curled up in a ball, writhing in pain.

Cat bent over, hands to her thighs as she caught her breath. Chloe scooted past her, rolled George onto his stomach, and straddled him. She stuck the gun in the back of her jeans, grabbed his arms, and pulled them behind his back.

"Oh, God, I'm lying in...Let me up, let me up now!" He turned his head to squint through his red and running eyes. "How could you betray me like this, Tessa?"

"Shut it, George. You mess with my sister, you mess with me." She twisted to look at Cat with a huge smile on her face. "Sounded just like you, didn't I?"

The crazy woman was actually enjoying herself. "Yeah, you did." Cat shook her head with a raspy laugh. "I still can't believe you did that. For a minute there, I thought you were in on it with him."

"That's because I'm a fabulous actress." Her smile faded, and her eyes filled. "I redeemed myself just like Daddy said I would, Kit Kat. I wasn't afraid. I was mad... furious that"—she shoved George's face into the hay-strewn floor—"he was going to hurt you—"

"Cat!" Grayson ran into the barn with his gun drawn. The fear etched on his handsome face subsided when he saw George on the ground. A slow smile curved his lips as he crossed the stable. "Good job, Chloe." He patted her sister's shoulder and walked straight to Cat, pulling her into his arms. "Thank God." He pressed his ice-cold cheek to hers.

She pulled back and touched his face and his hair. "You're frozen."

His mouth flattened as his fingers gently feathered over her throat, and he raised glittering, ice-blue eyes. "He did this to you?"

"It's—"

"Cat." Easton tucked his gun in the back of his jeans and limped toward her sister. Gage and Chance followed behind him and asked, "Everyone okay?"

Cat and Grayson nodded, watching while Easton drew Chloe to her feet and his brothers hauled George off the ground, shouting, "Tessa, Tessa." They dragged him out the stable doors.

"Are you okay?" Easton asked Chloe. Lifting his hand to her face, he gently touched her cheek. "Cat, honey, answer me."

Chloe twisted a strand of hair in her fingers. "Um-hm," she murmured, leaning in with her face tipped up.

Cat couldn't believe her sister actually meant to kiss him. So much for turning over a new leaf. When would she ever learn. "Chloe," Cat said sharply.

Easton drew back, his gaze jerking from Chloe to Cat. "No way. There is no way this is Chloe."

Her sister crossed her arms. "Really? Why is Grayson holding Cat in his arms and not me, then?" She stamped her foot. "I mean, if that's me, Chloe, why is he holding me...Ugh, I'm confusing myself."

"He'd be holding Chloe because she probably fainted... You really are Cat?" he asked, looking from her to Grayson.

"No, I'm Chloe."

He looked down at her sister. "I'm not talking to you. I'm talking to her."

Chloe threw up her arms and stomped away, then pivoted, pulling the gun from the waistband of her jeans. She dangled it from the tip of her finger. "Maybe someone should take this."

"Jesus, it really is Chloe."

*   *   *

Cat stood with Grayson by the window. Sipping her eggnog while he talked on the phone, she looked at the colored lights from the tree reflected in the glass, the happy faces of the O'Connor and McBride families gathered in the great room. They'd started arriving an hour ago by snowmobile loaded down with food and holiday cheer.

Gage and Chance had taken Molly into town for questioning when they arrested George. She had been cleared of any involvement. Turns out George had left the magazine clipping in Molly's dressing room in the event suspicion fell on him. Despite that, Molly refused to leave her old friend and costar's side. She blamed Chloe for pushing him over the edge.

They'd also discovered how Sam had gotten Cat's gun. George had stolen it from her room the night of Estelle and Grayson's party. He'd asked for a tour of the house, which her mother had graciously provided.

It was finally over, Cat thought, turning to look at her family. Ty, along with Annie, Gage and Madison's oldest, swayed in front of the crackling fire singing "Believe" with Josh Groban on the karaoke machine. Her sister lay on the couch, looking like a movie star in a gold lamé wrap jacket and long black skirt, her hair and makeup perfect, since she had her own stylist in the house. Their mother stroked her sister's hair as Chloe told the story of how she'd saved Cat to an attentive audience. She was in her glory—Christmas's hero. Easton sat in the wingback chair, talking to Chance and Vivi, but every so often his gaze flicked to Chloe.

Grayson disconnected and shoved his phone in his jeans pocket. He smiled down at her. "I have a Christmas present for you."

She winced. "I don't have one for you. I haven't had a chance—"

He leaned in, whispering in her ear, "All I want for Christmas is you in my bed for twenty-four hours. No interruptions, no drama, no one trying to kill someone, just you and me together."

She flushed, and not from embarrassment. "Um-hm, I think that can be arranged. Maybe not for a couple of days though."

"Guess that'll have to do." He took her by the shoulders and turned her to face the room. "I think everyone's going to want to hear this. Whistle."

She laughed. "You want me to whistle?"

He grinned and took her glass of eggnog. "Yeah, it's hot."

She shrugged and put four fingers in her mouth and whistled. Everyone stopped mid-conversation. Ty pointed the microphone at her. "We're at the best part."

"Sorry, Grayson has an announcement." She looked up at him. "Floor's yours."

"I just got off the phone with the deputy director. Special Agent in Charge Turner has decided to take an early retirement. An official apology is being sent to Cat, and her file closed and expunged from the record. She'll also be hearing from her former captain with a job offer." He smiled down at her. "Merry Christmas, love."

The sound of cheering barely registered as she stared up at Grayson. She'd heard about his meeting with Turner, but she never expected anything like this. He'd given her her life back. She went up on her tiptoes and whispered, "You know how I said I'm falling in love with you? Well, I'm not falling anymore. I love you, Grayson Alexander. Without a doubt, you are the best thing that has ever happened to me." She lightly brushed her mouth over his.

He framed her face with his hands. "You know how you said you didn't have a present for me? Well, you just gave the most wonderful gift of all. I love you, Cat O'Connor." He kissed her, not a kiss that would embarrass her family and friends, but one that promised a future. Lifting his mouth from hers, he said, "What are the chances we're going to get some time alone anytime soon?"

"Slim to none. They're all sleeping over."

His eyes scanned the room. "All of them?"

"'Fraid so. But—"

"Kit Kat," her sister called, twisting to look back at her, "you can't take the job with the Denver PD. You live in LA with me. And Grayson does, too."

"Should we tell them?" he asked.

"Now's as good time as any, I guess. We can back each other up." She cleared her throat. "Chloe, I'm moving home. I'm taking a job with McBride Securities."

Chance and Easton high-fived each other, and Vivi released a resigned sigh, obviously realizing her husband would be shadowing her 24/7, whether she liked it or not.

Paul and her mother joined them by the tree. "That's the best Christmas present you could have given me, darling," her mother said as the rest of their family and friends clapped and cheered. Everyone except Ty and Chloe.

"But what about Grayson? Long-distance relationships—" Her sister began.

"Brace yourself," Grayson murmured, then raised his voice. "I've put in for a transfer. I'm moving to Colorado."

His grandmother stood up and stared at him. "But what about me? My arthritis acts up in cold weather."

"If you think it's bad in the winter, wait until spring. You should probably stay in California. Not you," Nell said to Grayson, "just your grandmother."

"I can't live alone," Estelle said.

Cat looked from her pouting sister to her pouting best friend, then to Estelle. "Ty's lease on his condo is up next month. Why don't the three of you move in together?" she suggested.

Grayson put his arm around her. "Well done, love."

While everyone joined in on that conversation, Nell walked toward them. At the determined look in the older woman's eyes, Cat said to Grayson out of the side of her mouth, "Brace yourself."

"So, when's the wedding?" Nell asked.

Well, that was even more embarrassing than Cat expected. "Uh, Nell, Grayson and I have only known each other for a month. Don't you think you're rushing things a bit?"

"No, I need a happy ending for your story."

Grayson raised an eyebrow at Cat. "We have a story?"

"You didn't tell him about our Christmas romance series?" She didn't wait for a response from Cat and went on at great length about the books. Half the room was turned their way, watching with amusement, especially Chance and Vivi. Paul appeared at their side, handing Grayson a glass of eggnog. "It's spiked. I have a feeling you'll need it."

At the end of her spiel, Nell said, "Yours is called *Snowbound at Christmas*, catchy title, eh? But you have to give me something for the ending. Skye and Ethan got married and had Evie. You're not pregnant, are you?"

Grayson choked on his eggnog.

Cat patted his back and scowled at Nell. "No, I'm not pregnant."

"Oh," Nell said with a disappointed look on her face. "How about secretly engaged?"

She wouldn't give up. And if Cat didn't put a stop to this now, she had a feeling Grayson would be running for the door. Cat felt a little bad for what she was about to do, but Vivi would understand...eventually. "Why don't you change it up a bit and end with your last couple's happy news?"

Nell frowned and turned her narrowed gaze on Vivi and Chance. "I haven't heard any happy news."

Vivi, as though she sensed the attention, looked up, her gaze moving from Nell to Cat. Her eyes widened, and she shook her head, giving Cat a don't-you-dare look. Which Cat ignored. "Don't say anything, but rumor has it they got married and are having..." Nell took off before Cat got the word *baby* out. Cat supposed she should have somehow relayed that to Vivi, because when Nell stood in front of the couple demanding a reason for the secrecy, Vivi said, "I'm not even three months along, Nell."

And that was it. Paul, Liz, and Nell started crying, Madison and Gage's daughters, Annie and Lily, jumped up and down. Ty was down with that and joined in. Basically, everyone went wild.

"That was well played." Grayson laughed, then waggled his eyebrows at her. "I doubt anyone would notice if we sneak away. Give me five minutes and meet me outside."

As Grayson made his way to the mudroom, Cat inched her way out of the room. She held her breath when her mother and Nell headed in her direction, but Easton called out to them. He caught Cat's eye and winked. Five minutes later, Cat, wearing her winter jacket and boots with a blanket in her hands, opened the mudroom door.

As she went to close it, she looked in at her family and friends. Paul had his arms around her mother's and Nell's shoulders, laughing at something his aunt said. Her sister, reclining on the couch with a radiant smile on her face, once again told the story about her heroic rescue of Cat, dramatically acting it out. Ty, with Cat's niece Evie in his arms, stood with Annie and Lily at the tree, pointing out the decorations. No doubt sharing the stories of the night before. She closed the door with a contented smile.

Above her, the Christmas star that had long ago guided the founding families to town shone brightly overhead, bathing the man sitting in the chair in a radiant light. Grayson turned his head and gave her a smile that made her heart flutter and her knees weak. She looked up at the star and whispered, "Merry Christmas, Dad."

About the Author

Debbie Mason is the *USA Today* bestselling author of the Christmas, Colorado, and Harmony Harbor series. Her books have been praised for their "likable characters, clever dialogue and juicy plots" (RTBookReviews.com). When she isn't writing or reading, Debbie enjoys spending time with her very own real-life hero, their three wonderful children and son-in-law, and their two adorable grandbabies in Ottawa, Canada.

You can learn more at:
AuthorDebbieMason.com
Twitter @AuthorDebMason
Facebook.com/DebbieMasonBooks
Instagram @AuthorDebMason

Evangeline Christmas will do anything to save her year-round holiday store, including issuing real-estate developer Caine Elliott a bargain: fulfill three wishes on the Angel Tree featured in her shop and she'll stop protesting his plans to turn her charming little town into a tourist trap. Caine accepts the challenge thinking there's no way he can lose. But working alongside Evangeline to grant the town's wishes has him seeing Harmony Harbor—and Evangeline—in a whole new light. Can the magic of Christmas bring this unlikely couple the happy ending they deserve?

A preview of *Christmas in Harmony Harbor* follows.

Chapter One

A power outage on Black Friday was the last thing Evangeline Christmas needed. As the owner of Holiday House, a year-round Christmas store located in the town of Harmony Harbor, Massachusetts, Evie had been planning for this day for months.

She'd scrimped and she'd saved and she'd begged and she'd borrowed (from her tight-fisted mother), pouring every nickel and dime into making this the biggest kickoff to the Christmas season yet. She'd spent more on advertising for this weekend than she had for the past year's holidays combined.

She wasn't alone. Her fellow shop owners along Main Street were also pulling out all the stops to get customers through their doors and turning over their credit cards once they had them there. Although Evie more than anyone needed those customers today. Her entire future hung in the balance. She wasn't being a drama queen or a Negative Nellie.

Evie was a thirty-year-old woman who typically saw her glass as half-full rather than half-empty. But after the week she'd had, her optimistic spirit was flagging. Now, standing in the dark an hour before customers should be clamoring to get into her store, that glass was bone-dry.

If only she could pick up the phone and call her dad. He'd had a way of making everything better. She could practically hear him in her head. *There's always tomorrow, Snugglebug.*

"I wish that were true, Daddy," she murmured, her fear of the dark causing her heart to beat against her rib cage as she blindly edged her way past the display tables to the sales counter with only the light on her cell phone to guide her. She caught movement near the front window and whipped around to confront the shadow in the corner.

Show no fear. *Show no fear,* she repeated in her head with more force, as if that would vanquish the nauseated roll in her stomach. She pictured herself in combat boots instead of the Naughty and Nice knitted booties she wore and with a fierce, don't-mess-with-me expression on her face. She held up her cell phone. "You better get out of here. You've got two minutes before the police arrive."

Hoping to blind her would-be assailant, she aimed the light where she guessed his eyes would be. It hit him dead-on, right in his painted black eyes that didn't blink. A small, mortified groan escaped from her. She had nothing to fear from the blow-up Santa Claus.

She wished her fears for Holiday House's future were also in her head, but they weren't. Three days before, her circumstances had become as dire as George Bailey's in *It's a Wonderful Life.* Just like poor old George and the savings and loan, she had a conniving schemer trying to bring her down—billionaire developer Caine Elliot.

His glass-and-steel office tower would not only destroy the seafaring charm of Main Street, but the national discount chains destined to be housed in the tower's street level would put the future of Harmony Harbor's mom-and-pop shops at risk.

With some help from Harmony Harbor's Business Association and some really good friends, Evie had managed to stall the development of the three empty lots beside hers for more than a year. But this past Tuesday, she'd learned Holiday House was in imminent danger.

Harmony Harbor's town council would vote on Monday whether or not to take her land to accommodate the parking spaces required by a long-forgotten bylaw for a development the size of the office tower. A bylaw she herself had brought to the town council's attention in a last-ditch effort to quash the development.

"And look how that worked out for you," she said as she tried first the landline and then the credit-debit machine on the counter, neither of which worked.

Turn your frown upside down and sit a spell, Snugglebug. Let those endorphins do their work. You'll have your answer in no time.

Despite feeling like the dark cloud hanging over her was about to burst and bury her under a mountain of debt, Evie couldn't help but smile at her dad's favorite refrain. Taking his advice, she lowered herself onto the stool behind the counter, once again wishing he was a phone call away. He'd know what to do. He always had.

If wishes were horses... The cell phone's light glinted off the tarnished gold cash register. It was almost as old as

Holiday House. At least she'd be able to ring sales through and accept cash, she thought, giving the antique register a grateful pat and her dad a silent thank-you.

She glanced over her shoulder at the three generations of her father's family looking at her from the framed photos on the wall. Each of them had successfully run the store before her. She wondered what they would have done had they found themselves in her position.

"They wouldn't have been in your position. The three stores beside you wouldn't have burned down, leaving the lots ripe for development. And Caine Elliot wouldn't have been born." The reminder helped, she thought, getting up from the stool on a wave of determination. It wasn't entirely her fault she was days away from losing a business that had been in the Christmas family for a century.

Chewing the peppermint-flavored ChapStick off her bottom lip, she moved the light on her cell phone to the stairs leading to the second level. A redbrick three-story with classic wood beams and plaster interior, Holiday House had been the family home before her great-great-grandparents had turned the front rooms on the main floor into a Christmas store. The wooden Christmas ornaments her great-great-grandfather made had been the biggest draw back then.

Last year Evie had taken up residence in the attic, converting three of the second-floor bedrooms into showrooms for the other popular holidays. If she roped off the stairs and found a way to light up the main floor, at least customers could shop in relative safety.

She bent to open the cupboard under the sales counter, moved aside two boxes of bags, and found a flashlight. A lone flashlight and cell phone wouldn't do the trick, but the fieldstone fireplace across the room would help...Candles too. Lots of them. She'd have time to make more to fill the orders, especially if...No, she wouldn't lose hope. She couldn't.

All she had to do was walk into Monday's town council meeting with a sack full of this weekend's sales receipts and the testimonials she hoped to wrangle from customers to prove that Holiday House was an integral part of the community, a much-loved piece of their history that they couldn't allow Caine Elliot to destroy for his modern-day eyesore.

She forced her lips into another smile in hopes the action would release a bunch of stress-reducing endorphins. Though there probably weren't enough endorphins in all of Harmony Harbor to reduce her level of stress. It was Caine Elliot's fault.

Almost a year ago to the day, she'd picked up the phone and a velvet-smooth deep voice had come over the line. As annoying as it was to admit now, she'd initially been seduced by his dreamy Irish accent. She'd even begun to fantasize about the man behind the voice. A lovely, mildly erotic fantasy that had been rudely interrupted as soon as Caine Elliot got the social niceties out of the way.

She didn't care about his statistics and facts, his company's success, or his many business degrees. No matter that he presented his development as the best thing to happen to Harmony Harbor since the advent of electric lights, she knew exactly what would happen to the small town she loved if no one stood up to him.

At the time of that first call from the Ogre of Wicklow Developments, Evie had been running Holiday House for only two months. But she had a long history with the small town. Every year, she and her dad would leave her mom and the sweltering heat of New York to stay with Evie's great-aunt Noelle and help out at Holiday House for the entire month of August.

They'd visit in the fall and winter too, but it was the month-long summer stays that Evie treasured most as they readied the store for the holiday season. Some of her best memories had taken place in Holiday House.

She'd felt safest here, happiest here, and no way was she letting some hotshot developer steal that from her or anyone else, which she'd told him that day. And he'd told her that she was allowing her emotions to color her decision and that sentimentality had no place in business. The call had devolved after that as emotions got heated. Her emotions at least. As far as she could tell, Caine Elliot didn't have any. The man was coolly unflappable and arrogant. Their conversations over the last year had only served to validate her initial opinion of the man.

"Okay, enough. Time to get this show on the road." Her voice sounded odd, higher-pitched than usual. She kept talking to herself anyway. She needed the distraction as she made her way around the tables and out of the shop, heading for the storage room and boxes of candles. "Only an hour until the doors open and all those Christmas-loving customers pile..." She trailed off as the darkness swallowed her whole.

Her *It's okay. You're okay. There's no one here but you and Santa Claus* was interrupted by a rap on glass from the front of the store and her friend Mackenzie's voice calling to her through the door. Evie ran from the back hall into the main room, almost knocking over a display table. Relieved to hear dull thuds and not the sound of shattering glass as several items fell to the wood-planked floor, she held on to the edge of the pedestal table until it stopped wobbling. Once it had, she rubbed what felt like a bruised thigh and limped her way to the front of the store. Thanks to her trembling fingers and sweaty palms, it took longer than it should to unlock the three dead bolts and open the door. Evie smiled as she stepped aside to let Mackenzie in, hiding her hands in the pockets of her knitted green-and-red sweaterdress.

"Are you all right?" Mackenzie asked, looking around the shop with a frown while closing the door behind her. Gorgeous, with long caramel-colored hair, the owner of Truly Scrumptious handed Evie a bakery box.

"Other than the power being out, I'm fine, and these gingerbread cookies smell amazing. They're still warm," she said, praying Mackenzie didn't notice the box shaking in her hands. "Isn't your power off too?"

"No." Mackenzie glanced out the window. "It looks like everyone has power but you. The streetlights are still on."

Something Evie had failed to notice. Clearly nerves had messed with her powers of observation. Of course they had. She'd thought Santa was about to run across the store and attack her.

"Right. I..." She trailed off as the consequences of Holiday House being the only business without power hit her. What if Tuesday's payment to the electric company had bounced? Could she have forgotten to make it after learning Holiday House might very well be bulldozed into the ground to create a parking lot? She checked her banking app for a notice or payment receipt.

"Evie, are you sure you're all—"

"My payment went through."

"Oh, okay, that's good," Mackenzie said in a halting tone that seemed to indicate Evie's smile appeared more manic than relieved. "You probably just have to change a couple of fuses."

And there went her profound relief, right out the front door. The fuse box was in the basement. A basement that hadn't been updated since the early 1900s and looked like it could be a stand-in for the basement in *The Evil Dead*. The closest Evie had come to going down there since she'd taken over the store was opening the basement door for the furnace repairman.

At the thought of descending the wooden stairs into the dark, unfinished cave-like space with only the flashlight to guide her, she cleared the ball of terror from her throat. "You know, I think I'll leave the lights off. The customers will feel like they've been transported back in time. I'll light the fire, put candles all around. I even have an oil lamp I can use. I'll put it over here." She gestured to a table that held a collection of Fitz and Floyd tea sets and Christmas dinnerware. Behind the table sat an artificial fir tree decorated in antique ornaments of red and gold. "I'll set out your cookies on one of the platters. Did you bring me more business cards?"

Not only was Evie showcasing Mackenzie's gingerbread cookies, but each of her tables displayed items from the shops on Main Street. The other stores were doing the same for her. Mackenzie had two of her Fitz and Floyd Christmas cookie jars on display at the bakery.

"I do, and I need more cookie jars. I sold yours yesterday." She pulled an envelope from her jacket pocket, handing it to Evie.

"You didn't buy them, did you?"

Less than an hour after Evie had been informed about

Monday's vote, her friends had begun arriving at the store, declaring they absolutely had to have whatever their eyes landed upon. Their gazes had landed on a lot, but Evie was more grateful for their friendship than the sales. She didn't want them buying her merchandise just to help her out. She had a special connection with nearly every piece in the store, and she wanted her customers to feel the same.

"I bought one and my sister bought the other one, but we love them. Honest. Give me the singing Christmas trees to display today. I promise I won't buy them."

Evie understood why. Listening to "Rockin' Around the Christmas Tree" every time someone opened the lid on the plastic tree got on her nerves, and she'd celebrate the holiday year-round if she could. Which she supposed she already did.

"All right." She moved the cell phone light around the room. "Now I just have to remember where I put them."

A muffled *ping* came from Mackenzie's pocket, and she pulled out her cell phone. "It's Julia. She's opening Books and Beans early and needs her cupcakes. Drop the cookie jars off whenever you get a chance," Mackenzie said as she walked toward the door. She turned back, digging around in her pocket. "I almost forgot. We've been collecting signatures for Monday's meeting. So far we have a hundred names on our petition to save Holiday House." She handed the papers to Evie. "I'm sure we'll get double that this weekend."

"I don't know what to say."

"Don't say anything. This is what friends do for friends." Mackenzie hugged her. "I've gotta go. Let me know if you need more cookies."

"I will, and thanks, Mackenzie. Thanks for everything.

I don't know what I would have done this year without all of you in my corner."

"It's us who are grateful to you, Evie. You're the one who's led the fight against Wicklow Developments from the beginning. You've done all the heavy lifting, and it was for our benefit as much as yours. Now it's our turn to fight for you and Holiday House. And we've got a secret weapon. Rumor has it that Theia Gallagher is like a sister to the CEO of Wicklow Developments, and *he* can't refuse her anything. We've got this, girlfriend." Mackenzie gave Evie a fist bump. "Have fun this weekend and forget about Monday."

Surprisingly, it was easy. With so much to do in such a short amount of time, her mind was kept occupied. And while hauling the candles from the pitch-black storage room took longer than it should have, she'd gotten the job done. It was better than making the terrifying descent into the basement of horrors. Eventually she'd have to ask someone to help her with that. She could play the helpless-little-woman-who-didn't-know-how-to-change-fuses card, which she really hated to do. But if it meant she saved face while at the same time saving herself a trip into her own personal nightmare...

She took one last look around the room, from the candles that flickered on every available flat surface to the flames dancing in the fireplace. Despite the three decorated Christmas trees not being lit up, the room was not only well and safely lit, but the ambience was as warm and as inviting as she had hoped. She just needed one more thing to complete the welcoming ambience. As she went to pull up the holiday playlist on her phone, *The Grinch*'s theme song, her mother's ringtone, shattered Holiday House's happy vibe—and Evie's.

She was tempted to hit Decline—her morning had been difficult enough—but instead she did what her dad would expect her to. "Happy Thanksgiving, Mom!"

"You're a day late."

"Well, I know, but remember I told you I'd be busy getting everything ready for the Thanksgiving dinner at the community center yesterday. I did text though."

"Texts don't count; nor does a video of dancing turkeys."

Her dad would have loved it. "I'm sorry. I should have called. Did you have a nice time at Auntie Linda's?"

"Of course not. How could I? Her grandchildren were there. They're spoiled and have no manners."

Her cousin's children were adorable and well behaved. It was just that her mother subscribed to the adage that *children should be seen and not heard.* Evie wondered if she should text an apology to her aunt and cousin. It used to be her dad's job.

"But that's not why I called. I received a registered letter from Wicklow Developments regarding the offer they made to buy Holiday House last month."

Evie's heart banged against her rib cage. "I don't know why they sent it to you. It must have been a mistake."

"I have a fairly good idea why they sent it to me, young lady. They've obviously learned that I own shares in Holiday House and wanted to be sure I was apprised of the situation. The situation in which the majority shareholder doesn't have a shred of business sense. You're just like your father. Too soft and sentimental. Honestly, I don't know what possessed me to loan you the money. Now, as soon as I hang up, you are going to call Wicklow Developments and accept their offer."

"Mom, you don't understand. They don't want to buy Holiday House. They want to bulldoze it into the ground." And that offer would no longer be on the table since they had a ninety-five percent chance of getting their wish without paying a penny, which wasn't something she would share with her mother.

"So let them. You're barely eking out a living. Your last quarter—"

Evie hummed *The Grinch* theme song in her head. Her mother wasn't shy about sharing her opinion on Evie's and Holiday House's shortcomings and did so on a regular basis. Neither of them measured up to her mother's exacting expectations.

Evie knew it was her own fault for hiring her mom to do her books, but the thing was, if anyone could teach her how to manage inventory, cash flow, and pricing, it was her mother. Lenore Johnson (she'd refused to give up her maiden name) was a highly regarded accountant who'd won New York's Outstanding CPA in Industry Award three years in a row.

But more than business acumen and advice, Evie had hoped Holiday House would give them something to bond over. Because of course glass-half-full Evie had been positive that she could turn around the family business. And make her mother proud, she thought with a sigh.

"Mom, Holiday House has been in the Christmas family for more than a century. Daddy would want me to do this. You know he would."

"Of course he would. He was up for any lamebrain scheme you came up with. Remember when the two of you got it into your heads that you'd make a fortune selling candles for the holidays? There's still a box of them in the spare bedroom. Or what about the time you two took up knitting Christmas stockings? Noelle sold them for less than it cost for the wool."

Evie looked around the shop, wondering if her mom had a spy cam installed. "I was twelve, Mom."

"Your father was old enough to know better than to encourage you like he did. It's time you admit defeat and rejoin the real world. How you could up and leave New York and your job at the hospital to run Holiday House, I'll never know. You have a doctorate in psychology, Evangeline. You were making a decent living. You had benefits and a 401K, and now what do you have? Nothing but—"

At the mention of her old job, Evie headed straight for the front door, unlocked it, opened it, and reached under the Santa attached to the outside of the door to flip his battery to On. Then she began opening and closing the door with Santa *ho, ho, ho*-ing as she did so. "Sorry, Mom. It's getting busy. I've gotta go. I'll call you later." As soon as she disconnected, Evie looked at Santa. "I love you. I really do."

"Probably a good thing, considering you own a Christmas store," said a smooth-as-silk male voice.

A tiny shiver of awareness danced inside her. Some women had a thing for handsome faces; she seemed to have one for sexy baritones. She turned slowly as she worked to smooth the reaction to his voice from her face. Some people wore their emotions on their sleeve; she apparently wore hers on her face. At least that's what her friends told her.

Whoa. His voice had nothing on his face. Which, if she was reading the slight uptick of his sensuous lips that were half-hidden by his beard correctly, meant he knew exactly what she was thinking. Unless she'd said *Whoa* out loud instead of in her head. She snorted at herself. The stress must be getting to her. She wasn't a fan of men with beards. Except he kind of had her revaluating that opinion.

She had a feeling that, with one look from those incredible blue eyes and that sexy half smile of his, he'd have her reevaluating her opinion on just about everything: like not dating a man until he had a psych evaluation (given by someone other than herself), not sleeping with a man until she'd dated him for at least three months, or like chocolate was better than sex.

Okay, so maybe not everything.

Not that it would matter because he was out of her league. And no doubt, with the length of time she'd been staring at him, she'd now embarrassed herself not once but twice. Possibly three times if she'd said *Whoa* out loud. She needed to say something, some witty remark to redeem herself.

"Ha ha, yeah, I love my men with beards... White beards, I mean, and jolly. Jolly with big bellies." What was wrong with her? She should have simply smiled and walked back inside the store. Wait a minute. When had she walked outside?

"Brr, chilly out, isn't it?" She wrapped her arms around her waist and pretended she hadn't responded to the siren call of his voice and face and had instead come outside to check her window display. "Okay, everything looks good from here." She tapped the glass. "I'd better get back inside. Nice, ah..." It had been a one-sided conversation, and she couldn't say *looking at you*, even though it was true. "Have a good day."

The corner of his mouth twitched as he walked around her to hold open the door. She glanced at the Red Sox ball cap he wore with a gray knitted scarf, black leather bomber jacket, and jeans. He wore the hat rather low and the scarf rather high, almost like a disguise...

"Um, thanks." Her heart bumped against her ribs when he followed her inside. He hadn't seemed as intimidating outside as in. Maybe because being this close to him she noticed how big he was compared to her. He had to be at least six foot four to her five foot three.

"Sorry. I didn't realize you wanted to come inside. Are you looking for anything in particular?" Nerves caused her voice to come out a little high and a little breathy.

"Yeah, you."

Copyright © 2019 by Debbie Mazzuca

Fall in love with these charming contemporary romances!

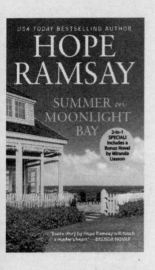

SUMMER ON MOONLIGHT BAY
by Hope Ramsay

Veterinarian Noah Cuthbert had no intention of ever moving back to the small town of Magnolia Harbor. But when his sister calls with the opportunity to run the local animal clinic as well as give her a break from caring for their ailing mom, he packs his bags and heads home. But once he meets the clinic's beautiful new manager, he questions whether his summer plans might become more permanent. Includes a bonus novel by Miranda Liasson!

WISH YOU WERE MINE
by Tara Sivec

When Everett Southerland left town five years ago, Cameron James thought it was the worst day of her life. She was wrong: It was the day he came back and told her the truth about his feelings that devastated her. Now she's having a hard time believing him, until he proves to her how much he cares. But with so many secrets between them, will they ever find the future that was always destined to be theirs?

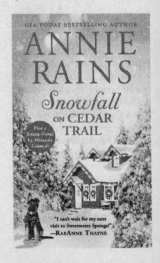

IT STARTED WITH CHRISTMAS
by Jenny Hale

Holly McAdams loves spending the holidays at her family's cozy cabin, but she soon discovers that the gorgeous and wealthy Joseph Barnes has been renting the cabin, and it looks like he'll be staying for the holidays. Throw in Holly's charming ex, and she's got the recipe for one complicated Christmas. With unexpected guests and secrets aplenty, will Holly be able to find herself and the love she's always dreamed of this Christmas?

CHRISTMAS IN HARMONY HARBOR
by Debbie Mason

Evangeline Christmas will do anything to save her year-round Christmas store, Holiday House, including facing off against high-powered real-estate developer Caine Elliot, who's using his money and influence to push through his competing property next door. When her last desperate attempt to stop him fails, she gambles everything on a proposition she prays the handsome, blue-eyed player can't refuse. Includes a bonus novella!

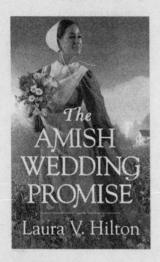

THE AMISH WEDDING PROMISE
by Laura V. Hilton

After a storm crashes through town, Grace Lantz is forced to postpone her wedding. All hands are needed for cleanup, but Grace doesn't know where to start—should she console her special needs sister or find her missing groom? Sparks fly when the handsome Zeke Bontrager comes to aid the community and offers to help the overwhelmed Grace in any way he can. But when her groom is found, Grace must decide if the wedding will go on…or if she'll take a chance on Zeke.

MERMAID INN
by Jenny Holiday

When Eve Abbott inherits her aunt's inn, she remembers the heartbreaking last summer she spent there, and she has no interest in returning. Unfortunately, Eve must run the inn for two years before she can sell. Town sheriff Sawyer Collins can't deny all the old feelings that come rushing back when he sees Eve. Getting her out of Matchmaker Bay when they were younger was something he did for her own good. But losing her again? He doesn't think he can survive that twice. Includes a bonus novella by Alison Bliss!

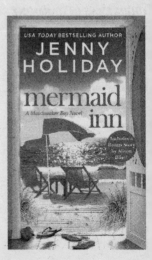